"Castille takes the MC genre ... nt my very own Sinner's Tribe Motorcycle Club bad boy!"
—Julie Ann Walker, *New York Times* bestselling author

"A sexy and dangerous ride! If you like your bad boys bad and your heroines kicking butt, *Rough Justice* will rev your engine. A great start to a new series!"
—Roni Loren, *New York Times*
bestselling author of *Nothing Between Us*

"Raw, rugged and romantic, *Rough Justice* is so gorgeously written you'll feel the vibration of the motorcycle engines in the pit of your stomach, smell the leather and fall in love with this story!"
—Eden Bradley, *New York Times*
bestselling author of *Dangerously Bound*

Praise for
USA Today and *New York Times* **bestselling author**
SARAH CASTILLE
and her sizzling-hot romances . . .

"Castille's debut is steamy."   —*Publishers Weekly*

"Hot, hot, hot."   —*Nocturne Romance Reads*

"Smart, sharp, sizzling and deliciously sexy . . . a knockout."
—Alison Kent, bestselling author of *Unbreakable*

★ SINNER'S STEEL ★

Sinner's Tribe Motorcycle Club #3

SARAH CASTILLE

St. Martin's Paperbacks

This is a work of fiction. All of the characters, organizations, and events portrayed in this novel are either products of the author's imagination or are used fictitiously.

SINNER'S STEEL

Copyright © 2015 by Sarah Castille.

All rights reserved.

For information address St. Martin's Press, 175 Fifth Avenue, New York, NY 10010.

ISBN: 978-1-250-05662-7

Printed in the United States of America

St. Martin's Paperbacks edition / October 2015

St. Martin's Paperbacks are published by St. Martin's Press, 175 Fifth Avenue, New York, NY 10010.

10 9 8 7 6 5 4 3 2

To my precious Little One, for all the things you do to make me smile.

★ ACKNOWLEDGMENTS ★

To Monique, Alex, and the team at St. Martin's Press for the magnitude of what you do, and to my agent, Laura Bradford, who never gives up hope that I will learn American spelling. To my fabulous Street Team, Sarah's Sassy Readers, for all your enthusiasm and support, and to Danielle Gorman for keeping me organized. To Danielle Barclay and Mandy Lawler for your boundless energy and creative ideas. And, finally, to my own little tribe for their patience, love, support and blueberry and cucumber kebabs.

★ ONE ★

Nine Years Ago

"Zane. Stop. Please."

Evie's cry rang out in the forest, the distress in her voice spearing Zane's chest. He ground to a halt, just a few feet short of Stanton Creek, sucking the warm Montana summer air into his lungs. He would do anything for her, even if it meant having his heart broken all over again.

She caught her breath as she came up behind him, her steps barely audible in the soft grass. "What's wrong? Why did you leave?"

For a moment, he couldn't speak. How could he explain the emotions he'd kept bottled up inside for the last nine years, the hopes and dreams that shattered when he saw her in Jagger's arms, the desperate need that would never be fulfilled? He wanted them to be happy, but he couldn't fight the sense of jealousy he felt toward his best friend, and the utter despair at losing Evie before he had a chance to tell her how he felt.

"I'm losing you both." Slowly, he turned to face her.

"You aren't losing me, Zane. You'll never lose me."

Her pale green dress fluttered in the breeze, clinging to her sweet curves. Evie rarely wore dresses, preferring clothes that didn't hamper her ability to run and climb, jump creeks and walk fences. His Evie had a wild streak. But when she'd walked into the graduation party tonight looking like an angel, his breath caught in his throat. So beautiful he ached inside. He'd been desperate to give her the present he had slaved over for the last three months. A good-bye present. A don't-forget-me present. A tiny glimpse into his heart.

If only he hadn't waited.

She stepped out from under a willow tree, its thin leaves already fading to bronze as summer came to a close. The evening sun caught the golden highlights in her long red hair as it spilled over her shoulders. In the nine years he'd known her, he'd only seen it down a few times. Ponytails were more her style. He wanted to run his hands through those silken waves, follow them down the gentle curve of her back, smooth his hands over her perfect ass . . .

Jagger's ass now. Jagger's hair to touch. Jagger's girl.

A black hole opened in his chest. Gritting his teeth, he looked away. "I saw you and Jagger together. I'm happy for you. Really—"

"Zane." She took another step forward and he backed up to the creek, his foot skirting the gravel edge. He couldn't be near her simply because he didn't know what he would do if she came too close.

"There's nothing between me and Jagger. We're friends like always. It was a friendly kiss."

"Didn't look friendly to me."

A pained expression crossed her face." And I put him straight. I love him like a brother. But someone else has my heart."

Hope flared in his chest and he immediately stamped it out. Who was he to hope? How dare he hope! He was nothing and came from nothing. No family, save for a deadbeat drug-dealing father. No money. No future. No friends except for Evie and Jagger, and by next week, they would both be gone—Evie to college and Jagger to the army. And yet his lips still formed the question. "Who?"

"You, silly." She closed the distance between them

until she stood only a few inches away. His hands shook with the need to touch her; his body ached with longing. Nineteen years old and he still wanted the girl he'd met when he was ten.

"It's always been you," she said softly. "Ever since the day we first met. But I never thought I'd have to wait until I was seventeen before I could tell you."

She wrapped her arms around his neck and kissed him. *So soft. So sweet.*

His world shifted, darkness becoming light, despair turning to desire. Although he had dreamed of this moment, wanted her with an intensity that took his breath away, he reigned it all in and brushed his lips over hers, returning her kiss with a gentleness that belied the torrent of emotions flooding through his body.

She sighed into his mouth, and he slid his hands around her, struggling with the need to crush her against him, make them one instead of two. Sensation overwhelmed him: the minty taste of her lips, her scent of jasmine and the warm summer breeze, the softness of her body. His knees trembled and he pulled the present from his pocket, now less of a gesture and more of a distraction to give him a chance to regain some semblance of control.

"Is this for me?" She stroked a finger over the pink tissue paper, now crumpled and torn.

"It's stupid. I'm sure what Jagger got you—"

"Jagger got me Devastation Planet Three," she said. "He has his PlayStation all set up and ready for us to kick some alien butt tonight. So unless you got me the same thing, I'll love it. And even if it is, I'll love it, because it came from you."

She tore off the paper and stared at the photograph in the handmade frame. Jagger's dad had taken the picture of him, Evie, and Jagger on the couch one afternoon as they were celebrating the successful completion of yet another video game. Although both he and Jagger had placed an arm around Evie, sitting between them, she leaned into Zane, her body tucked against him as if that was where she belonged.

Zane had hoped on that picture, dreamed on that picture; it was his most treasured possession. And when he'd made the frame after work, carved it with their names, lacquered and polished it until it shone, he prayed she would understand the message.

"It's beautiful, Zane. I love it. It'll be the first thing I put in my room at college." A tear rolled down her cheek, and Zane caught it on his finger, wishing he could keep it forever—keep her forever.

I love you. The words stuck in his throat, held back by fear, a profound lack of self-worth, and a lifetime of rejection.

Gently, he drew her down to the forest floor. He didn't mean for things to go as far as they did, but he couldn't deny the emotion that spilled from his chest.

And he lost his heart under the setting sun on the last day of summer in Stanton.

★ TWO ★

If it ain't broke, don't fix it.
—SINNER'S TRIBE MOTORCYCLE REPAIR MANUAL

"Axle's gotta die."

Zane "Tracker" Colton drew his weapon from beneath his cut, the leather vest worn by all outlaw bikers, in response to the words uttered from the shadows. His eyes fixed on the lean, dark-haired man across the street, the object of a hunt that had taken far too long and covered too many miles. Zane preferred silence in the moment before an attack—time to reflect and consider the ramifications of his actions—but Jagger had always been a yapper, and as president of the Conundrum Chapter of the Sinner's Tribe Motorcycle Club (MC), Jagger had the prerogative to yap even if his vice president disagreed.

"You got nothin' to say?" Jagger dismounted his motorcycle and motioned for their biker brothers to do the same. "How long have we been chasing him? How many times did he slip through our fingers? You could show a little excitement that our MC will finally be avenged."

"One year. Three escapes. And yeah, I'm fucking thrilled we're finally gonna off the bastard who hurt your girl," Zane replied. "But I keep it inside."

Once a senior patch member of the Sinner's Tribe MC, Axle had betrayed the club and threatened to kill Jagger's old lady, the biker equivalent of a civilian wife. Even after the Sinners had forcibly removed Axle's Sinner's Tribe tattoo and left him for dead, Axle not only lived to tell the tale, but joined the Black Jacks, the Sinners' biggest rival for outlaw biker dominance in the state of Montana.

"You keep everything inside," Jagger said. "One day it's all gonna become too much and you'll explode. Man like you needs an outlet."

Man like you needs to mind his own business.

If they'd been alone, Zane would have said the words that burned on the tip of his tongue. Friends since they were five years old, he and Jagger were brothers in all but name. But Jagger was president of one of the most powerful outlaw MCs in the state, and any public display of disrespect could erode his power base if it wasn't immediately addressed. And right now, before a hit, the last thing Zane needed was a broken nose.

"Gimme thirty seconds with Axle and I'll dance a fucking jig." Zane nodded toward Big Bill's Custom Motorcycles, Paint, and Artwork shop, still brightly lit and open for business, although the sun had almost set. "He's inside now. Ready to move?"

Jagger signaled to the four Sinner brothers who had accompanied them on their road trip. Axle had too much information on the Sinners to be allowed to run free, especially now that he'd patched over to the Jacks.

Hunting him down hadn't been easy, but Zane, a.k.a. Tracker, hadn't earned his road name by letting weasels like Axle get away. They had followed him all over the state, ending up almost where they started, only one mile outside the border of the town of Conundrum, the base for the Sinner's Tribe.

Zane crossed the street and took up a position to the left of the front door. Jagger joined him on the right. T-Rex, a junior patch member of the MC, blond and built like a linebacker, ran to cover the back door, and the remaining three Sinners took up guard positions in the near-empty parking lot.

"There's a camera above the till and four civilians inside." Gunner, the club's sergeant-at-arms, peered through the window. As the tallest member of the MC, all brawn and bulk, he had the strength and level head to handle the job of keeping order in the club. "Two ladies . . . one very, very hot redhead and a tiny blonde with more piercings than I got girls begging for my attention," he murmured. "There's also a geeky guy with glasses, and a big older dude who I'm guessing is Big Bill."

Damn. Zane hoped the girl wasn't too hot. He had a weakness for redheads, and right now, he couldn't afford any distractions. Not that he would do anything about it. He'd tried getting it on with a couple of redheads and every encounter ended in disaster. His mind would fill with visions of Evie—the girl he had loved and lost. And then he would remember their last night together and his gut-wrenching despair when her father, the town sheriff, found them together. And yet that pain was nothing compared to what came after.

He gave himself a mental shake. Memories of Evie were a distraction he couldn't afford. Especially now, at the culmination of their hunt.

"Fuck." Jagger lowered his weapon. "Too many witnesses. We'll have to wait until he's outside."

"We don't have time." Zane pointed to the sea of headlights coming down the mountain pass. "Black Jacks. Same number of bikes we saw at the bar in Columbus last night. We need to get in and out before they arrive."

"You and I'll go in, grab him, and pull him outside," Jagger said. "Gunner can deal with the civilians. T-Rex and the brothers can keep the Jacks distracted if they get here before we're done. Keep your face clear of the camera."

Jagger pulled a ball cap from inside his cut and tugged

it low over his face. Zane followed suit, although with his dark hair just brushing his shoulders and his skin deeply tanned, he was more readily identifiable than his clean-cut friends. Sure, the cops would know from the cuts they wore that Axle had been offed by the Sinners—the Sinner patch, a skull with wings and stars, was emblazoned across the back of every cut. But if the authorities couldn't make a positive ID, they'd be less inclined to come banging on the Sinner clubhouse door, especially now that the Sinners had a friend inside the Conundrum sheriff's office.

Jagger pushed open the glass door and Zane followed him inside, skirting the rows of shiny new motorcycles dominating the shop floor and staying out of the direct line of the camera.

"Nobody move." Zane raised his gun to Axle's back and then caught the gaze of the redhead behind the counter.

In that moment, his thoughts crystallized and shattered. All but one.

Evie.

Except for a new softness in her face, and a rounding of her curves, she looked exactly as she had the night he left Stanton. From her long, thick, red-gold hair, to her perfectly proportioned oval face, and the full sensuous lips he had dreamed about kissing night after night. Her delicate nose turned up slightly at the end, accentuating her softly angled cheekbones, and her lush body was meant to fill a man's palms. Her eyes, now wide with fear and confusion, sparkled with the same emerald green. Her beauty hit him like a fist to the gut, stealing his breath and rendering him incapable of speech.

And unable to pull the trigger.

Unfortunately, Jagger appeared to be having the same reaction. Evie had been his friend, too. The three school friends had bonded over broken families, childhood disasters, and teenage woes until the night Jagger held a good-bye party and Zane ran away.

"Evie." Jagger spoke first, recovering fast as yappers always did, using the nickname he and Zane had given her when they first met on the school playground.

She frowned, little creases forming between her brows. "My name is Evangeline."

Jagger touched his cap as if to remove it, and Zane hissed a warning. "Camera."

Her gaze snapped to him and Zane pulled his hat lower as nine years' worth of longing turned into nine years of pain. After fleeing their hometown of Stanton, Montana, wanted for a murder he didn't commit, he had gone back for Evie—albeit three years later—only to find her with a child and another man: Mark, the two-bit loser who had panted after her in high school. As he watched her with her new family in the school playground, where he'd first fallen in love, bit by bit and day by day, his heart hardened, and he promised himself he would never think of her again.

A promise he had yet to keep.

"It's me." Jagger turned his back to the camera at the till and lifted the visor of his cap.

A tumult of emotions crossed Evie's face, from shock to disbelief, and then her hand flew to her mouth.

"Oh my God. I thought you died in service. I heard about the grenade and the shrapnel—"

"Takes more than a little shrapnel in the heart to kill me." He glanced over at Zane, no doubt puzzled by the fact Zane hadn't spoken up. But Zane simply wasn't ready for this. He didn't deal well with change or surprises. His life had been utterly out of control until he joined the Sinners. Now, control held him together. Control over his world. Control over his life. Control over his emotions. And right now, those emotions were threatening to overwhelm him and distract him from the task at hand.

Zane raised his gun, only to discover that Axle had taken advantage of the distraction to sneak through a sliding metal door at the back of the store.

"Fuck. He's getting away." Zane ran, slamming the door aside as he shouted a warning to T-Rex out back. He chased Axle through a large workshop filled with half-painted motorcycle fairings and gas tanks on stands, partially dismantled bikes, and empty bike lifts. The shop smelled of grease, paint, turpentine and the distinctive scent of fear.

The door at the far end of the workshop thudded closed and Zane's feet pounded on the concrete floor.

Damn.

"You okay, brother?" He knelt beside T-Rex and felt for a pulse. T-Rex groaned and Zane whipped out his phone just as Jagger opened the door behind him.

Jagger caught sight of T-Rex and let loose a volley of curses. "How bad?"

"No bullet or knife wounds," Zane replied. "I think he just took a hard knock to the head. I'll call Shooter and tell him to bring a cage to take him to the clubhouse. Doc Hegel will look after him."

Their new prospect, Shooter, a wannabe Sinner, who had almost finished his pledge year, had already proved to be one of the MC's best drivers and marksmen, albeit a bit of a speed demon with an overly happy trigger finger. As a prospect, he handled all the driving. A full patch brother only rode in an enclosed vehicle if he had a family, and since Zane had just been voted "least likely to ever settle down" there was little chance he'd ever be "caged."

"Where's Axle?" Jagger asked.

"Forest." Zane texted Shooter, and then gestured to the trees behind the shop. "We'll need flashlights. If he makes it to the road, he might hitch a lift and get away."

"This is my damn fault." Jagger scraped a hand through

his hair. "But . . . Evie. Can you believe it? After all these years?"

No, Zane couldn't believe it. Nor could he accept it. Evie was part of a past he had locked away, a pain he couldn't handle. Part of him wished tonight had never happened. And yet . . .

Evie.

His heart squeezed in his chest, an unfamiliar feeling for a man whose heart had stopped beating the day he discovered love was a one-way street.

With T-Rex under the care of the junior patch, and Gunner and the rest of the brothers tasked with calming the employees and sending them home, Jagger and Zane took over the search, crashing their way through the underbrush, their guns primed and ready on the slim chance that Axle hadn't already made it to the road.

"Why didn't you let her know it was you?" Jagger asked, his voice barely audible over the cracking branches underfoot.

"It's complicated." After meeting on the elementary school playground all those years ago, Jagger, Zane, and Evie had stuck together, leaning on each other for support and comfort, sharing good times and bad, but mostly playing video games after school on Jagger's couch. As they grew into adolescence, Evie's once-friendly touch became sweet torture for Zane. But he never even hinted about his feelings. The bond he had with Jagger and Evie was too precious, their friendship too important, to throw away on a teenage fantasy. Even after fantasy had become real, he'd kept it from Jagger, afraid if he spoke the words out loud, the memory would disappear.

"Why do I get the feeling, there's something you're not telling me?" Jagger raised his voice and gestured to a bush in front of them.

"There's a lot I don't tell you. Get over it." He carefully made his way around the bush, his finger on the trigger of the gun.

"I got over your reserved nature when we were ten and met Evie and our entire playground conversation, which until then had consisted of grunts and one-word answers, evolved into naming the guys we were going to beat up after school because they'd hurt or scared her in some way."

"Those were good days." Zane signaled that he was in position, and shone his flashlight on the bush. Twigs cracked and leaves rustled in the warm summer breeze. He aimed his gun. And then a fox shot between his legs and took off into the night.

"Fuck." Zane's adrenaline surged and he slid his finger off the trigger. "Can't you tell the difference between a man and a fox?"

"It's dark. I heard a noise."

"I almost shot off your damn head." Zane tucked his weapon away. "We're not gonna find him in the dark. Not without more men. I say we regroup at the shop and keep a watch on the road."

"Agreed." Jagger lowered his weapon. "But his bike is forfeit. We'll get it repainted, and give it to Hacker. I promised I'd help him out with a bike after we patched him into the club. He's still riding that ancient Electra Glide his dad left him. They do painting here. I'll get Evie to give us a deal."

"You're gonna ask a bunch of civilians to paint a stolen bike?" Zane didn't want any ties with Evie's shop. He didn't want a reason to come back. Hell, he didn't even want a reason to remember this night.

"It's not stolen. It's ours." Jagger laughed. "And it's not like Axle's gonna go to the cops and report it missing."

They walked the rest of the distance to the shop in silence. What the hell was Evie doing here so far from home? Had she and Mark moved to Conundrum? If she'd been his girl, no fucking way would he have allowed her to work in such a deserted location at night. Or in a motorcycle shop which, no doubt, would attract some of the worst elements of society.

Kinda like him.

"You want to talk to her about the detailing?" Jagger pulled open the back door to the shop.

"I think we should stay the hell away from her," Zane replied. "Let her lead her nice civilian life." He followed Jagger inside. Did Evie work in the shop or in the store? Had she gone through with her plan to get a Fine Arts degree in college? If so, what the hell was she doing here? And why the fuck did he care?

"I figured that out when you didn't say hello. And if there's something you need to tell me, now would be a good time. Otherwise I'm gonna come back tomorrow, have a talk with her about the bike and catch up on her life. You should tag along. After all, you knew her as well as me."

Better. Intimately. And he was pretty damn sure Jagger didn't appreciate all the little things that made her Evie: from the soft lilt of her laughter, to her penchant for tight jeans, kick-ass cowboy boots and fringed leather jackets; her risk-taking wild streak that had made his heart pound, to the compassion, that had drawn him in when they were young.

Jagger probably hadn't noticed that she cried over books and romantic movies, preferred nachos to cake, and never passed an elderly person without smiling and saying hello. His Evie had a big heart. But he'd figured that one out when, at eight years old, she held a wet paper towel over his eye after his father had beaten him one of many terrible nights.

Too bad she had no fucking loyalty and no damn faith.

"I'm pretty sure we won't find Axle tonight, so I'll be busy tracking tomorrow," Zane said. "You go catch up with her. Just . . . don't mention me."

Jagger looked back over his shoulder. "For a man with a string of blood patches on his cut, you're sounding like a pussy. It's Evie, dammit. You're acting like you're afraid of her."

"I'm not afraid of Evie." But he *was* afraid of himself, and what he might do if he saw her again.

★ THREE ★

*If you jump into a repair, without planning it through,
you will break something. Guaranteed.*
—SINNER'S TRIBE MOTORCYCLE REPAIR MANUAL

"Where are the biker hotties today?" Connie Vandenberg, store clerk and Evie's best friend, tugged down the neck of her black Big Bill's Custom Motorcycles T-shirt, exposing a few extra inches of her modest cleavage. Gene, one of Bill's junior mechanics, a thin, lanky man with thick glasses and a perpetual frown, dropped the box of riding gloves he'd just brought out from the stockroom and stared. Which was entirely the point. Connie had hit a dry spell and since Gene was the only unattached man in the store, she'd decided he should be the one to assuage her thirst.

"We already spent an hour talking about your biker love last night when I was supposed to be asleep." Evie stashed her purse in the secure drawer under the till and tucked her phone in her pocket.

"Sleep? Who could sleep after that tribute to testosterone walked in the door last night?"

"You're forgetting they had guns and clearly intended to shoot Axle in the back." Evie still couldn't believe Jagger, one of her two best childhood friends, had become an outlaw biker. What had happened to the boy who had been so proud to join the army, and fight for what was right? And why the hell wasn't he dead? Not that she wanted him to be dead, but she'd heard from old friends in Stanton that shrapnel from an RPG had lodged in his heart while he was on tour in Afghanistan and he died in a hospital in London. Why did no one know he was still alive?

"At least Axle had time to give you Vipe's message. Your new boyfriend doesn't seem the type who would cope well with being stood up, although if that was an issue he should think about joining the twenty-first century and buying a phone." Connie tied her store apron around her narrow waist. She was pixie pretty, slim and petite with blond hair cropped short in the back and long in the front and wide bluish-gray eyes, she could have passed for a teenager if not for her loud, slightly obnoxious, firecracker personality.

"His name is Viper, not Vipe."

"Well, he's not a relaxed, chilled out kinda guy," Connie continued. "I thought he'd found out Bill was skimming off the weapons shipments he's been running through the store and Axle was here to make sure it didn't happen again. Permanent like."

Evie flipped through the post, checking for sale flyers. Her custom paint business was doing so well, Bill had given her carte blanche to order new supplies. "Three dates doesn't make Viper my boyfriend. And they were very chaste dates considering he's the president of a biker gang. We went to a couple of bars, watched a game, went out for dinner, had a few goodnight-at-the-door kisses. I haven't even had a chance to find out if he's a badass in bed."

"Ah yes." Connie snorted a laugh. "The gentleman bad boy biker. I believe that's called a contradiction in terms."

"More like the biker who realized the dull civilian single mom wasn't cut out for the excitement of biker life." Evie had figured he wasn't interested in her after their last date when he dropped her at home without even the usual goodnight kiss. Served her right for trying to spice up her love life with a badass biker. She knew better, but her wild streak had reared its head when Bill introduced them. Although Viper was much older than her, there was something about him—a confidence, an aura of power he projected the moment he walked into the shop, or maybe it was the darkness she sensed inside him—that reminded her of Zane. And even though she'd gotten over Zane and moved on with her life—as much as a person could do with a broken heart—she thought about him over the years, especially since she saw his face in miniature every day.

"Three dates plus how many times did he come here to the shop?" Connie didn't wait for Evie's answer. "First to do that deal with Bill. And then for detail work. Both legit. But after you painted his fender, why all the visits? Touch-ups on a perfect paint job? Discussions about his tank? A burning need to buy a pair of summer gloves? He came back for you. And Axle coming here to set up a third date proves it."

Connie poked her in the ribs and Evie wiggled away. She hated being tickled. Her mother had always tried to tickle her when she was drunk, forgetting, in her alcohol-fueled delusions, that Evie wasn't a child anymore. She'd never really had the chance to be a child. Her mother had been totally incapable of looking after herself, much less Evie, once she hit the bottle. With her father always out on patrol, Evie had taken on the role of cook, housekeeper, and 911-caller when her mother passed out or fell down the stairs. She had only ever felt free, truly free, during her stolen moments with Zane.

"I don't know if I should go out with him again," Evie said. "I have a nice, comfortable, normal life. I work. I chauffeur Ty and his friends to school and activities. Occasionally, I let you drag me out to a club or send me on a blind date where I meet comfortable, normal guys."

"Ah . . . " Connie raised an eyebrow. "What about Roy the Rock Star? He wasn't normal. Fucking you behind the drum kit during a rehearsal is hot, but not normal. Or what about Don the Dom? Kinky sex clubs don't really rate on the normal scale. Sometimes you let your inner wild child out. Nothing wrong with that. Only problem was, Vipe didn't give it to you the way you thought he would. *He* acted normal. Big disappointment. Give the guy another chance. He's all kinda badness. He's probably afraid he'll scare you off."

Maybe Connie was right. She couldn't deny the delicious thrill of being wanted by someone who radiated such power. It was the same kind of feeling that had drawn her to Zane, dark and brooding, two grades above her in school, with a reputation that kept even the teachers away.

She'd watched him for the better part of a year, the ferocity with which he defended Jagger, his total unconcern with being popular on the playground, and the bruises on his face that came and went, until one day his pain drew her in. After she'd tended his wounds, he became her protector, giving her the sense of safety and security she didn't get at home. And then he'd abandoned her. Just like her parents.

Connie sighed and leaned over the counter, elbows on Evie's papers, her chin in her hands. "Of course, now that Viper has put us in danger and exposed us to the scourge of the biker world, who happen to be tall, ripped, and devastatingly gorgeous, I'm softening toward him. When do I get my introduction to your old friend?"

"They're *outlaw* bikers," Evie protested. "Jagger had a one percenter patch on his cut. He's not the boy I knew growing up. He went from fighting for his country to flouting the law, all in the space of nine years." Although Jagger had come from a broken home—his mother had walked out on him and his dad when Jagger was seven years old—he was the most straight-up person she'd ever known. Zane, on the other hand, had been the risk taker, darkly dangerous and as wild as her. He was the friend most willing to break the rules, the only person who had managed to see the side she kept so carefully hidden.

"If you're trying to put me off," Connie said, "you're doing a bad job. Especially since you have your own bad-boy biker panting after your ass. Maybe we can double date. But if you're not happy with me going out with your friend, I'll take that strong, silent dude who came in with him, or their friend, Gunner, who sent us home. I'm desperate. Not fussy." She left the till and went to help Gene stock the shelves, mouthing over her shoulder, *As you can see.*

Evie unlocked the front door and turned the sign to OPEN. During the four years she'd been working with Bill, she'd made a name for herself as one of Montana's top custom motorcycle painters. But she would never have made it without Bill's help and support, and she was eternally grateful that he'd taken a chance on a fledgling artist, giving her the opportunity to get away from Stanton and a marriage that should never have happened in the first place.

"If Viper finds out about Bill's scam, he'll probably be back with his entire MC," Connie whispered when Evie brought in the last box from the shipment they received that morning, leaving Gene free to return to the mechanic shop out back. "Imagine. Dozens of hard-riding outlaw bikers camped outside our door. It would be Christmas in July."

Evie placed the box on the stack beside the rack of motorcycle jackets. "More like a slaughter. Bikers don't like witnesses when they do something bad."

"They can witness me doing something bad." Connie raised her voice. "Ain't that right, Gene? You like a bad girl, don't you?"

Gene reddened and turned his attention to the sliding doors that separated Evie's paint shop and the garage from the store. Bill had a senior mechanic and three juniors working out back. Evie did the detail work, and Connie took care of sales out front. Bill handled the illicit gun running, and although his employees knew about it, no one was involved, which turned out to be a good thing when they discovered he was skimming off the top.

"You know what I'm talking about, Gene," Connie teased. "Friday night. You and me and a bottle of . . ."

Evie gave her a nudge. "Leave him alone. He might sue us for sexual harassment."

"Sexual harassment is your hot biker friend walking in the door and me not getting an introduction." She gestured over Evie's shoulder. "Look who just came to visit."

"Jagger!" Evie greeted him with an outstretched hand, and was promptly swept up in his arms.

"Can't tell you how nice it is to see you again. Too bad it wasn't under better circumstances." His deep rumble caught her off guard. He was a man now, not a boy, and the evidence wasn't just in the breadth of his chest or the lines on his face, but also in the shadows in his eyes. Maybe the life of an outlaw biker wasn't all it was cut out to be.

"Is this a social visit or are you here to kill someone again?"

Jagger raised an admonishing eyebrow, and she swallowed when her eyes fell on the president patch on his cut. He had always been the leader of their threesome, so she wasn't surprised to see that he now led the Sinner's Tribe, and he wore the mantle well. Not many people could say as much with just the lift of a brow. "I came to find out what the hell Axle was doing here, deal with his bike, and visit with you. No shooting today."

"Excellent." Connie cleared her throat. "Today isn't really a good day to die. I have . . . overdue library books."

Evie cringed on Connie's behalf. "Um . . . this is Connie. Short for Constance." She made the obligatory introduction and Jagger nodded.

"Pleasure."

"All mine." Connie's cheeks brightened. "Maybe we should all go for a coffee at the restaurant down the road, and get to know each other. Gene can man the till while we're gone. Well, not really 'man' the till, 'cause he's not really a manly type. More like a boy, since he can't legally buy alcohol until next year, and he can't rent a car—"

"Connie—"

"Although he doesn't look like a boy with his head all shaved and those piercings in his ear, which some of the girls think are hot, but not me because I don't like the competition. Unless, of course, you have piercings and then I might change my mind."

Evie raised her voice. "Connie."

"You're a beautiful girl, but I got an old lady." Jagger flashed the grin that had sent no less than half the senior girls in school into a frenzy. Okay. So some things hadn't changed.

"Old lady?" Connie frowned. "You look kinda young to have an old lady."

"He's twenty-eight and an old lady is the biker equivalent of a wife." Evie buried a tiny sliver of disappointment. Aside from Zane, Jagger was the only other man she'd ever really cared about. Mark, her ex, had been a port in a storm that had turned out to be a sinkhole. After her mother died, and she'd been left alone with her twelve-month old son, Ty, the void in her life had begged to be filled. Although she didn't love Mark, and had told him as much, he'd had a crush on her since high school and wanted to give marriage and fatherhood a try. She should have known a Vegas wedding after two weeks of dating was a recipe for disaster. The thrill had lasted only until the first time she caught him with a bottle in one hand and a woman in the other.

"How about we talk about that bike out there that needs a new paint job?" Jagger gestured to the Harley Softail in the parking lot, visible through the store window.

"I thought that was Axle's bike."

"It's now a Sinner bike by forfeit," Jagger said with a straight face. "And it needs that Black Jack patch on the fender covered with a Sinner patch."

Connie licked her lips. "You're just a whole lotta nasty, aren't you? Got any friends who don't have old ladies?"

"One hundred or so."

"Well, be sure to tell them that Evie is the best custom painter in Conundrum, probably the entire state, and while they're here getting some new artwork, they just might want to browse the store and see what's on offer. Like me."

Oh, God. Connie could lay it on thick, and she was going all out this morning. But then she'd said last night that she thought outlaw bikers were more exciting than the everyday bikers who frequented the shop. Not that Connie had led a sheltered life. Her facial piercings, tattoos and short, perky bob hinted at her rock star roots—her dad was the guitarist in a famous heavy metal band and her mother was the band manager. She'd spent her childhood on the road, and she was always chasing the same kind of adrenaline rush that had eluded Evie ever since Zane ran away.

"You painted all those tins in the shop out back?" Jagger's eyes sparkled. He had always encouraged her artist talent, whether it was drawing pictures in the mud beside the creek that ran through Stanton, or sketching portraits of her friends.

"Never made it to college so, yeah, my artwork is now splashed on the gas tanks and fenders of Conundrum's bikers. But I draw the line on stolen bikes." Especially since the bike in question belonged to a member of Viper's MC.

Jagger's jaw tightened almost imperceptibly, and his voice dropped to a low, commanding tone. "I need it covered before I move it." He folded his arms and glared, a look all the more frightening for the weapon holstered under his leather vest. "The Evie I knew would have jumped at the chance to take a bit of a risk."

Evie startled at his sudden change of demeanor. So this was the new Jagger. Did he really think he could boss her around, and drag her into his criminal world? Well, she knew the old Jagger and the old Jagger wouldn't make her do something she didn't want to do. She just hoped that part of him was still here.

"This Evie isn't interested in doing anything illegal,"

she countered. "Like handling stolen property. I have a child at home and no one to look out for him if his mother lands her ass in jail. And since I have a strong feeling you aren't going to pull that gun on me and make me do your bidding, you're welcome to come and catch up in my shop while I work."

She would have to steer the conversation clear of her relationship with Viper—if that was what it was. Somehow she didn't think either of the two outlaw biker presidents would be happy she knew the other. And as for risks, she'd taken one big risk in her life and it had led to both her greatest heartbreak and her greatest joy.

Jagger's annoyance was evident in the firm press of his lips and the tightening of his shoulders, gestures she knew very well. She suspected few people ever disobeyed him now that he was president of an outlaw MC, and the fact that she had made him capitulate gave her no small amount of pleasure.

"I'll just stay out here," Connie called after them. "Alone. Stocking the shelves. Just in case any of Jagger's friends stop by."

Evie bit her lip to suppress a grin. She looked back over her shoulder as she led Jagger to the shop. "I'll send Gene out to help you."

Bill's mechanics worked in the front half of the garage Bill had built when he first purchased the shop. Bike parts, rags, lifts and jacks were scattered over the wide, concrete space. Evie waved to the grease-smudged mechanics as she skirted around a few bikes to get to her paint shop in the back, stopping to tell Gene he was needed in the store.

"Connie actually likes Gene," she said to Jagger. "But in a brotherly love kinda way."

"Like you, me, and Zane."

"Yeah. Kinda like that." She headed for the cupboard to gather her supplies. Bill had spared no expense fitting out the back end of the garage for her custom paintwork. He'd cut large windows on both sides and a skylight in the ceiling to fill the space with natural light. Long wooden benches ran along each wall, holding paints, supplies, her portfolio, and an assortment of fenders and gas tanks at various stages of design. She'd set up a few stands in the center to hold the tins while she worked, along with stools for any clients who wanted to watch.

"Amazing work." Jagger pointed to three finished fenders waiting for pick-up. "I don't know why I haven't heard about you before. I thought I knew all the good detailers in Conundrum."

"I've only been here a few years," Evie said with a shrug. "If you have anything not stolen, I'd be happy to do a piece for you."

"How 'bout my new bike outside?" He gave her a cheeky grin. "Someone defaced it with a Black Jack patch, but really I want it to have this." Jagger spun around to show her the Sinner's Tribe patch on the back of his cut, the top and bottom rockers proclaiming the name of his club and the Conundrum chapter.

"I hear outlaw bikers are very particular about their patches, especially if someone paints over them."

He lifted an eyebrow. "You afraid of the Jacks?"

I'm dating a Jack. The words almost slipped out, but she bit her tongue. "I don't like to piss off my customers. It's bad for business."

"Is that why Axle was here? Is he a customer?" He dropped the question almost casually as he examined a charcoal drawing she had tacked to the back wall, but the tension in his shoulders suggested it was anything but casual.

"No. It was personal."

"I remember this." Jagger pointed to the charcoal variation of the photograph Zane had given her the night he disappeared. "We'd just finished Grand Theft Auto and Zane had the highest score. Did you do the drawing?"

"Yeah. I still have the picture, but I wanted something

larger." Evie tilted her head to the side, considering. "We didn't come out quite right in charcoal, though."

"Zane looks exactly the same now, except for—" He cut himself off with an irritated grunt.

"You've seen him?"

Guilt flickered across his face, but it was so fleeting she thought she might have imagined it. "Yes."

Her cheeks heated and she turned away, wanting and not wanting to know what had happened to Zane. She grabbed a soft cloth and rubbed it vigorously over the fairing she intended to paint that afternoon.

"Does he live around here?" She tried to sound nonchalant but the question came out sounding almost desperate.

"Yes."

Puzzled by his abrupt, monosyllabic answers, she looked up, but Jagger had turned back to the drawing. She had the original picture in a frame beside her bed—the frame Zane had made for her—and she often wondered if she could ever be that girl again. Happy. Content. Secure in the knowledge that nothing and no one would ever hurt her while she had Zane and Jagger by her side.

"So . . . what does he do now?"

Silence.

"Jagger?" She gave the fairing a vicious rub, hating herself for wanting to know about the man who had broken her heart.

"Not sure what he's doing right now." He shifted his weight and the hair on the back of Evie's neck prickled. Jagger had never been good at deception. Even when they'd played video games, he would send his characters headlong into danger, often winning simply through his brute force attacks. Zane, on the other hand, excelled at games that involved risk, stealth, and strategy. Evie was the one who took chances, or tried the crazy moves that no one thought would work. Together, they made the perfect team.

Stan, the senior mechanic, revved an engine near the door, and the familiar scents of paint and turpentine were overshadowed by gasoline fumes. When the noise dimmed to the usual clatter and bang, they chatted about their hometown and old school friends and her failed marriage to Mark.

"I was sorry to hear about your dad." Jagger's face softened. "He was a good man. A good sheriff. I know you two were close."

Emotion welled up in Evie's throat. Not a day went by that she didn't mourn the loss of her father or wonder what had happened the night he caught Zane and her together by Stanton Creek. She'd waited all night for Zane to come and tell her what happened, to let her know he was okay. Instead, her father's deputy showed up at her door to tell her that her dad and Zane's father had been found dead outside Zane's father's trailer. Zane was missing. Suspected of murder. She never saw him again.

"My mom died, too," she said softly. "She couldn't handle life without him and her alcoholism became worse. She drank herself to death two years after the funeral."

"Ah, Evie." A pained expression crossed his face. "I wish I'd been there for you. I can't imagine how hard it must have been for you to go through that alone."

Not totally alone. Ty had given her a reason to go on. But she didn't mention Ty for fear that Jagger would want to meet him, and once he did, he would know, without a doubt, the identity of Ty's father.

"You had a good excuse." She forced a smile and changed the subject. "So how did you come back from the dead?"

While she prepared the bike for painting, Jagger told her about his brief stint in the army, the shrapnel that had lodged in his heart, his miraculous recovery and honorable discharge, his new life as a biker, and the love of his life, Arianne.

"Evangeline. You have a client." Connie's voice echoed

through the speaker system. Usually she piped in music depending on her mood, her tastes ranging from death metal to Buddy Holly, and the occasional polka.

"I'll let you get to work." Jagger took one last look at the picture before turning to Evie. "The boys will be round with a cage to pick up the bike, and I'll be sending a few brothers to watch the shop in case Axle comes back since I get the feeling if he comes in you're not gonna call."

"Ratting on customers is bad for business."

Jagger gave her a considered look. "Are you gonna warn him we're around if he shows?"

She supposed that would be the right thing to do if Axle came with another message. Viper had stopped carrying a phone after the Bureau of Alcohol, Tobacco, Firearms and Explosives (ATF) took a sudden interest in the biker war in Montana and set up camp in the Conundrum sheriff's office. But she didn't want to get on Jagger's bad side either. "Also bad for business. I'm hoping to paint a few Sinner tins in the near future."

"You don't want to get involved with Axle or the Black Jacks," he said. "They aren't friendly guys."

"And you are?" She pointed to the one percent patch on his cut that marked him as the one percent of bikers who didn't follow civilian law.

"We're nice outlaws." His face softened again, and her tension eased.

"Isn't that a contradiction in terms?" She was glad Connie wasn't around to hear Evie steal her phrase.

"Aren't you?" He gestured around the shop. "This is the last place I ever would have expected to see my sweet, innocent sheriff's daughter who played video games, painted landscapes, and thought the world was really a beautiful place."

"It was a beautiful place," she said. "Now it's just real."

★ FOUR ★

*Don't mess around unless you know
what you're doing.*
—SINNER'S TRIBE MOTORCYCLE REPAIR MANUAL

Zane watched Big Bill's Custom Motorcycle shop all afternoon.

From his vantage point on the picnic table outside the diner across the street, he could see everyone who went into or came out of the building. And what he couldn't see—Evie and her shop out back—he imagined. And then he would picture Mark and their son, and his stomach would twist in a knot. But this time there was nowhere to run. Conundrum was his town; the Sinners' town.

The shop closed at 6 P.M. and the mechanics and salesclerk left together. He hated them simply because they knew Evie and because they made her smile when she locked the door behind them.

How long had it been since he'd seen that smile?

When she didn't follow them out, he crossed the road, and walked around the building to the back of the shop. Jagger had spent the morning with her, and whatever she'd told him made his best friend unusually distant and frustratingly uncommunicative. But he had grunted his approval when Zane offered to take first watch on the shop in case Axle returned.

Although tempted to look in the window, he didn't want

to scare her, so he leaned against a storage shed across from the back door. Should he wait or should he go in? What would he say? Did he really want to see her?

What the hell was he doing here?

He pushed away from the wall, intending to return to his bike when the shop door opened.

Evie.

Although he was prepared this time, he couldn't stop the rush of blood pounding through his veins when she stepped onto the gravel, a piece of fairing in her hand. She wore tight jeans that clung to the swell of her hips, and a T-shirt, cut low enough to expose the crescents of her breasts. Her ponytail swayed gently as she held the fairing up to catch the light. More beautiful now than she had been as a girl. His words died in his throat. All but one.

"Evie."

She froze, her head snapping to the side. And then her eyes widened. Recognition dawned. With a gasp, she dropped the fairing and staggered back. "Zane."

He had imagined this moment every night for the last nine years: the words he wanted to say; the emotions he'd kept bottled up inside—anger, despair, loneliness, and a pathetic longing that just wouldn't go away. In the fantasy, he lambasted her for not waiting for him, accused her of betraying him, let loose a stream of shouts and curses about her inconstancy, and after unburdening his heart, he walked away.

But he did none of those things. Instead, he concentrated on fighting back the desire to take Evie into his arms and hold her, the way he'd held her the last time they were together. Although his need for redress was strong, stronger still were the feelings he'd had for her since he was ten years old.

"I thought it was you," she said softly. "Last night, when you spoke . . . your voice, and the way you were standing . . . but when you didn't say anything—"

"You look good. Older." Fuck. Not the right thing to say to a woman, but his tongue wasn't working the way it should. She was beautiful and sexy, with a confidence she hadn't had as a girl. But he hadn't expected any less. She had always taken his breath away.

"Well, it has been nine years. People change," she said bitterly. "Although it seems you haven't, except for the whole biker thing. Still the silent, brooding type skulking in the shadows. I mean, who doesn't say hello when you're standing in front of someone you haven't seen for nine years?"

"Had a job to do."

"So did Jagger and yet he managed to say hello."

Damn. This wasn't going well. He cocked his head to the side and forced a smile, as if her anger hadn't touched him where it hurt the most. "Hello, Evie."

A smile ghosted her lips, and her voice lost its edge. "Hello, Zane. I go by Evangeline now."

Encouraged by her gentle tone, he took one step, then another, until he stood only a foot away, close enough to see her eyes glisten. "Why? You hated that name."

Desperate to touch her, connect, assure himself she was real, he cupped her jaw and stroked his thumb over her cheek. So soft. So utterly perfect. Did her hair still feel like silk? Did she still wear jasmine perfume? Without thinking, he leaned down, his lips brushing over the curve of her ear as he inhaled her scent and then . . .

She slapped him.

His head snapped to the side under the force of her blow and the pain shook him out of the haze that had brought him to her side. He grabbed her hand and slammed it up over her head against the metal door, an instinctive reaction and one born of years of hard living. Evie's eyes widened, and then she scowled.

"You have no right to touch me. After you left, after I lost everyone I cared about, I had to start over." Her jaw tightened and she lifted her chin, her eyes both defiant and challenging. "I married Mark Dubois after I gave up hoping you would ever come back. He always knew me as Evangeline."

He threw down his own gauntlet, one that he had carried for years. "I saw you together," he spat out. "And your boy." He drew in a ragged breath. "Because I *did* come back, Evie. Just like I promised. You didn't wait." He leaned in toward her, resting his forearm against the door beside her head, her wrist still in his grip. Intimidating? Yes, given his size relative to hers and the fierce emotion that made his body shake. But she wasn't scared. Fear made Evie tremble and she wasn't trembling now.

"I waited three long years for you." Her eyes blazed with fury despite the fact he was holding her against the wall, caging her with his body, more than capable of breaking the fine bones of her wrist with only the slightest squeeze of his hand. But his Evie had never been a coward.

"Everyone said you killed my dad, but I didn't believe them," she continued. "I said you weren't a killer. I said the Zane I knew would never do anything like that. You would never hurt me that way. So I waited for you. I thought you'd come back for me. Explain. But you never did." Her voice tightened with emotion. "How hard would it have been to call or text? How long did you expect me to wait? But that's not what it was about, was it? You got what you wanted from me and moved on. You hurt me, Zane. You made me realize I didn't know you at all."

He would have waited for her forever, but he wasn't about to tell her that. Not when she was clearly lying to him. "You already had a kid when I came back," he growled. "So don't pretend you waited. He was walking for fuck sake. How long was it? One month? Two? Were you seeing him before I left?"

Bile rose in his throat at the thought of her and Mark together. A rising star on the football team, Mark had been sidelined after he was arrested for drunk driving. Zane had

warned him away from Evie shortly after he was released
on bail. She'd suffered enough with an alcoholic parent.
She didn't need to be dumped back in the cycle again. His
Evie deserved better.

Better than Zane.

"No." All the anger and passion drained out of her and
she sagged against the wall, his hand on her wrist seem-
ing to be the only thing that held her up. Evie? Backing
down from a fight? Emotion welled up in his chest, an
unfamiliar, uncomfortable sensation. He didn't do emotion. He didn't do feelings. He'd locked up that side of
himself long ago when he became a Sinner and channeled
all his energy into the club.

"Evie?"

"Let me go." Her words were barely a whisper and his
anger faded beneath a wave of concern when she tilted her
face to look up at him, her eyes pleading. Maybe if he
kissed her, the emotions would go away. He would know
that there was nothing left between them. He would feel it
in his bones. He might even taste Mark on her lips. Then
he would finally be able to move on.

Still holding her hand against the door, he gently traced
the bow of her mouth with his thumb. As a teenager, he'd
dreamed about her ripe, sensual mouth, and when he'd finally kissed her that night by the creek, her lips were
softer and sweeter than he had ever imagined.

Her lips parted and she pressed her free hand against
his chest, then bunched his shirt in her fist, as if undecided
whether she wanted to pull him forward or push him away.
Zane took advantage of her indecision to lean closer. She
smelled of jasmine and the warm summer nights when
they lay in the grass and looked up at the stars. The world
faded beneath the pounding of his heart and the raging desire to taste her again.

"Zane. Please . . . "

But he was already moving, his head dipping down, his

body unable to resist the pull of yearning . . . And then she stiffened and shoved him away.

"Behind you! It's Axle. He's got a gun!"

"Leave her alone, Sinner," Axle shouted. "She's not yours to take."

Fucking Axle.

"It's okay, Axle," Evie said. "He's a friend."

What the fuck?

Axle's bitter laughter rang out around them. "Not to me, and definitely not to Viper."

"Don't move until I turn around." Zane slid his free hand beneath his cut. "Then get the hell out of here. That your car parked out front?"

Her eyes darted over his shoulder, and then she nodded. "But what about you?"

"I'll be cleaning up the mess." His hand closed over the weapon holstered at his side, and he loosened his grip on her wrist. "Ready?"

"Ready. But . . . you can't kill him, Zane. He's not here to . . . You're not a . . . " She choked on the last word, and he knew right then why she hadn't waited for him. She thought what all of Stanton thought. Zane was nothing. He'd come from nothing. Worthless. No good. And a killer.

Her lack of trust was a sledgehammer to his gut, and the heat between them gave way to a chill that froze his heart.

"Go. I don't know what the hell is going on with you and the Jacks, but Axle betrayed the Sinners and killed one of my brothers. His life is forfeit and we've been after him a long time."

He spun and fired, covering her escape around the side of the building, but Axle had anticipated his move. He dove behind the shed and returned fire. Unprotected, with nowhere to take cover, Zane pulled the trigger again and again, dodging Axle's return fire. Bullets pinged off the concrete beside him as he reached for the door. Finally, he felt the smooth surface of the handle beneath his palm. Wrenching the door open, he stepped inside and leaned against the wall to catch his breath.

"You're going down, Zane!" Axle shouted. "I know you were the one who held the torch that burned off my tat, and you were the one who fucking shot me in the leg up at Whitefish last year. You don't know whose girl you're messing with."

Zane peered out from behind the wall and pumped bullets at the shed. Dammit. Axle had more lives than one hundred frickin' cats. They'd kicked him out of the club, beaten him, taken his bike, burned off his tat, wounded him in a gunfight, and hunted him relentlessly for over a year all to avenge the disrespect he had done to the Sinners. And he just came back, again and again, first as a thieving contractor, then as a member of the Jacks, and now . . .

Now he had some kind of mark on Evie.

Mark. If not for the bullets flying at his head, he might have pondered the irony. Instead, he shoved a new magazine in his gun. He couldn't get rid of Mark, but he sure as hell could get rid of Axle.

"So . . . when is your date with old Vipe?" Connie leaned against her car, a red Pontiac G6 convertible that she had financed to the hilt. She'd promised Ty a ride home from summer camp in style and that didn't mean chugging through Conundrum in Evie's beat-up Ford Focus.

Evie waved to one of the mums waiting in the school parking lot for the camp bus. "Don't call him Vipe. His name is Viper."

"That can't be his real name. His momma didn't pick him up from the cradle all bundled in a blue teddy bear blankie and say, 'He's so cute. Let's name him Viper.'"

Evie's cheeks heated and she twirled a strand of hair around her fingers. "It never came up. Bill brought him around to the shop and introduced him as Viper, said he wanted some detail work and that was it. He never told me any other name and after our second date, I was too embarrassed to ask."

Still, she couldn't deny her attraction to the president of the Black Jacks. Tall, with a barrel chest, two full sleeves of tats, and a cut worn and heavy with patches, Viper screamed danger with every stride of his long legs. Although he was almost twenty years older than her, hardened by life on the street, and striking rather than handsome with his long black hair fading to gray, and a broad scarred face, weathered and worn, he dominated every room with the force of his presence alone. And when he focused all that power on her, Evangeline Monroe, single mom and custom painter, he was difficult to resist.

"So you call him Viper? How's that gonna go down in the sack? Give it to me hard, *Viper*? Lick me there, *Viper*? Although snakes do have forked tongues . . ." Connie pushed up her enormous sunglasses, blinking as her eyes adjusted to the bright sunshine glaring off the asphalt. "Come to think of it, Viper does have a bit of a badass ring to it."

"I don't know if it will get that far," Evie said, blushing. "I'm not sure where things are going with him anymore."

A grin split Connie's face. " 'Cause of the ex of sex? Mr. Deep, Dark, and Delicious? You gonna get back together?" Connie knew all about Evie's recent encounter with Zane and their past together. She was the sister Evie always wished she had, although with a bigger mouth and a sharper tongue.

"No. Definitely not." Evie sipped her second iced coffee of the day. She needed at least three cups of caffeine to keep going; four if she didn't get a good night's sleep, which was basically every night for the last four nights since she'd seen Zane.

Alone in the darkness with nothing to occupy her thoughts, the emotions she'd bottled up over the years, the hopes and dreams that had shattered when she realized he wasn't coming back, came spilling out. Every night she tossed and turned. And she thought about him.

She slid her hand into her purse, her finger stroking over the edge of the picture frame Zane had given her all those years ago. On impulse, she'd grabbed it this morning and put it in her purse, with half a mind to talk to Ty about the man in the picture who so closely resembled him.

Damn Zane looked good. No. Not good. Breathtaking. Older, yes, but age had just made him sexier His tall, lean frame was now filled out with solid muscle; his face hard and weathered; and his jaw rugged and rough with a five o'clock shadow. Only his eyes hadn't changed, and his dark, piercing gaze still sent a delicious shiver through her body.

But who did he think he was, showing up after all those years and thinking they'd pick up where they left off? That slap should have showed him she wasn't the same girl he left behind—the girl who waited by her window all night after her dad sent him away, and for another three years because her heart couldn't believe what all of Stanton believed to be true.

She tucked the picture away and zipped up her purse. Eight years ago she laughed and ran, climbed trees and took risks simply because she knew Zane would be there to catch her. Now she had her life together, and she knew better than to trust a handsome face.

Which was one of the reasons she'd agreed to go out with Viper. No chance of losing her heart to a man who looked so fierce and feral it was hard to believe he was as articulate, entertaining, and well-mannered as he had been with her—albeit, his sexual restraint was somewhat disappointing.

"What about Ty?" Connie asked. Connie and Ty were very close and she had already expressed her concern that Zane might not want to have anything to do with his son.

"I'm not sure yet. I need to give it some thought." Her hand hovered over her purse again. "He has a right to know about his son, and I need to know the truth of what happened that night. But I don't want Ty to get hurt if Zane's not interested in being part of his life. Zane didn't come looking for me. If he hadn't been chasing Axle, he would have been content to spend his life not knowing or caring where I was."

"Well, you probably don't have to worry about it." Connie ran her fingers through her hair. She'd added blue and red streaks after Ty's favorite superhero character as a welcome home-from-camp surprise. "Sounds like you slapped some sense into him and now that he's got Axle, he has no reason to come back." She paused and frowned. "What's Vipe gonna think about man getting shot by your ex at your shop? What if he thinks you're involved?"

"I'm not. And I'm definitely not interested in getting it on with a man who would shoot someone in cold blood."

"'Cause Vipe's such a saint, is that right?"

"You're very irritating." Evie huffed. "Did I ever tell you that? And I haven't seen any evidence that Viper is a bloodthirsty killer. He's a biker is all."

Connie laughed. "I call 'em as I see 'em, and right now I see you still got feelings for Zane 'cause it's only eleven o'clock and you're on your second coffee of the day, which means you can't sleep. Not only that, you're already having second thoughts about the first guy who's caught your interest since I've known you. Not that I'm in Vipe's corner, but so far he's treated you good and you were all excited when Axle showed up to set up the next date."

"Maybe he's too old for me." Evie lowered her voice when she spotted one of Ty's friend's moms headed in their direction.

"Didn't seem to bother you until you laid eyes on the same version—intense outlaw biker, leather cut, kick-ass bike—but twenty years younger." Connie mused. "I sense a little age discrimination going on. Lookit those fifty-plus movie stars getting hitched to women twenty or thirty years younger. You don't hear those women whining that their man is too old."

"That's true. But when I think of Viper in bed as compared to . . . oh, I don't know . . . maybe Zane, there really is no contest." She glanced at Connie, blushed. "Of course I've never slept with Viper and only once with Zane, and that was in a forest on some scratchy leaves and cold grass with rocks digging into my ass, so it's not really a fair comparison—more of a thought comparison—but, my God, you should see the pipes on Zane now, and that chest . . ."

"I'm not wearing pink to your wedding," Connie said. "I have a closet full of pink frothy bridesmaid dresses. I want something slick and chic. Maybe black leather if you're getting hitched to a biker."

The school bus door opened and the crowd surged forward taking Connie and Evie with them. "Nice to see you're already getting me married off," Evie braced herself against the stampede. "If the day ever comes, I won't want a wedding. So no need to worry that I'll deck you out in flamingo pink." She waved when Ty appeared at the top of the stairs.

"You are SO a wedding girl," Connie said. "Some people are meant to shack up and live in sin. Like me. People like you, however, who hide a fundamentally conservative nature behind a streak of wild, are meant to wear tulle, dance to "At Last" by Etta James, and have a happily ever after."

"You've got it backward." Evie gave in to the tide and let the crowd push her forward. "It's the wild in me that's gone into hiding. When Zane and I were in high school, we'd do all sorts of crazy things—climb trees, walk fences, drag race . . . stuff like that. One Saturday night we got up on the church roof, watched the stars, smoked a joint, and talked until dawn. Then we rang the church bell and just got away before my dad and his deputy showed up. Jagger used to have fits when we told him what we did, although I think secretly he was jealous. He was just too responsible to join us." She hesitated, bit her lip. "I always felt the most like me when I was with Zane, like I could do anything and he would be there to catch me. I still miss that feeling."

She made it to the front of the crowd just as Ty came down the steps. "And, by the way," she said over her shoulder. "If I was going to have a wedding, my first song would be Radiohead's, 'True Love Waits.'"

Connie laughed. "I'm definitely wearing leather."

"Hey, bud. How was summer camp?" Evie squeezed Ty in a hug as soon as he stepped off the bus. He had grown over the last two weeks. She didn't remember his head coming up to her shoulder, or his dark hair brushing his collar, but he was thinner, and deeply tanned. Had they not given him enough to eat?

"Great." He returned the hug and then just stood in the circle of her arms, still young enough not to be embarrassed by her affection like some of the older kids were. Her Ty was quietly affectionate, grounding himself in stillness. Just like his dad. She suspected he would never be one of the kids who pushed their parents away. After what they had been through in Stanton, they were very close.

"Hi, Tiger." Connie ruffled his hair. "Check out my streaks. Who does that remind you of?"

Ty pulled out of Evie's embrace and frowned. "Superman?"

"No."

"Fourth of July?"

"No again." Connie gave an indignant sniff. "One more wrong answer and you're back on the bus for another two weeks of starvation."

"Is Connie joking?" Ty looked to Evie for confirmation and she laughed. He was always so serious and intense, and Connie, with her sharp wit, took full advantage.

"Connie's always joking," she said, taking his bag. "That's why I don't pay attention to anything she says."

"I heard that, and now I'm only talking to Ty. Not you." Connie put an arm around Ty's shoulders and led him to her car. Evie followed behind, warm in the knowledge her son was home.

He was like Zane in so many ways, and now that she knew Zane lived in Conundrum, how could she not tell Ty he was here? Over the years, she'd shared as much of the truth as she thought Ty could handle: his father left before he was born, and although she tried to find him, she'd been unsuccessful. She had been careful to make sure he understood Zane's absence wasn't a rejection. There was no point in sharing her bitterness or turning him against a father he didn't know. Maybe because she'd always hoped one day she would find Zane again.

Well, now she had found him, but things hadn't gone as she imagined they would. Her anger at his abrupt departure had paled beneath her outrage when he told he had come back and left again when he'd seen her with Mark. All those years missed with his son, and he had the audacity to be angry with her. With so much hurt and so many secrets between them, she couldn't imagine they would ever find their way back together, but she didn't want to stand in the way of a relationship between Ty and his father.

If that's what Zane wanted.

"Should we go out to lunch to celebrate?" She gave Ty's hair a tug from behind. He had been fair until he turned four, then his hair had darkened and he'd taken to wearing it long—too long for a mother's taste. But now, having seen Zane, the resemblance was unmistakable. No one could doubt he was Zane's son.

"Can we get pizza? Camp food was crap, except for campfire nights."

"Don't swear, Ty. You know I don't like that language." At least not from him. But at Bill's shop, swearing was a way of life, and she'd long since stopped trying to get the mechanics to curb their language.

"You swear," he said. "All the time. You say 'damn' when things don't go well."

"And I put a quarter in the swear jar every time." Good thing he had never heard her when she hung out with Zane and Jagger. They'd given her an entirely new vocabulary of swearwords that had taken a long time to shake after she became a mother and adopted a more conservative outlook—one that apparently made Connie think she was wedding material.

And yet sometimes the rebel in her broke free—the rebel Zane had fed with his own kind of wild.

What would Zane think about her dating Viper? Or would he even care?

★ FIVE ★

Before you start, get comfortable with your tools.
You never know what you will need, and when.
—SINNER'S TRIBE MOTORCYCLE REPAIR MANUAL

Zane knew Jagger would find him.

No way would his best friend let this one slide. But he was grateful Jagger had, at least, given him a few days to get himself together after seeing Evie. Too bad he'd used that time to fall apart instead.

"I heard this has become your new home." Jagger pulled out a chair at Zane's table and waved his hand vaguely at the room in front of him, encompassing the full expanse of Rider's Bar. The Sinners owned several legitimate businesses in Conundrum, including bars, strip clubs, nightclubs, trucking companies, and shops, all convenient for laundering money, hiding shipments of stolen goods, and turning over a profit for the club. Some members worked on the legitimate side. Others, like Zane, Jagger, and most of the Sinner executive board, handled the sale and supply of illegal arms.

"What of it?" He raised his voice over Foghat's "Slow Ride." One thing about Rider's Bar, they always played good tunes. Too bad they couldn't do something about the smell. Usually, Zane didn't notice the thick yeasty scent of beer overlying the more pungent aroma of cigarette smoke, but tonight his belly roiled with every whiff.

"How many have you had, brother?" Jagger settled himself in the chair and pushed aside the collection of bottles Zane had asked Sherry to leave behind. Once a house mama at the Sinner's Tribe clubhouse, Sherry had been thrown out of the MC after Axle used their relationship to steal guns from the club. At the urging of the executive board, and because Sherry had been physically coerced, Jagger had partially forgiven her betrayal and agreed to let her work at Rider's Bar. Sherry had accepted her dismissal with good grace, but everyone knew she was just putting in time, hoping Jagger would let her back into the club.

"Sherry's counting. Not me." He stared at the sea of bottles, unable to meet Jagger's gaze. This was not a conversation he wanted to have, and especially when he couldn't think straight. Jagger had a way of cutting through the bullshit and right now the bullshit was the only thing keeping his heart from spilling out of his chest.

"She says you're not fit to ride."

"Sherry doesn't know dick all about me."

"Apparently, neither do I." Jagger leaned back in his chair, folded his arms behind his head. "All these years, you've been going on about the woman who betrayed you and ripped out your heart, and you never told me it was Evie."

"She tell you that?"

"Nope. But you just did." Any other man would have smirked, but Jagger wasn't the smirking type. He just laid it on the line.

"Didn't matter." Zane drained his bottle and shoved it across the table as the bitter taste of beer lingered on his tongue. Usually he went for the harder stuff, whiskey or rye, bourbon if Cade, the club treasurer was pouring, but when Sherry had come to take his order, he'd asked for beer—Corona—the kind he'd dropped on the kitchen floor of Jagger's house after he saw Evie in his best friend's arms.

"I'd say from the bottle count on the table it matters a hell of a lot."

"Fuck off, Jag. I'm not in the mood." Zane lifted a new bottle and Jagger grabbed his wrist.

"Fair warning. We had an executive board meeting scheduled for this afternoon. When you didn't show up, I postponed the meeting and sent Shooter to hunt you down. The meeting is being reconvened right here at your table. You got ten minutes to sober the fuck up and do your job, so you might want to reach for the water I told Sherry to bring you instead of that bottle."

They locked gazes, and tension hung in the air between them. "Get your fucking hand off me."

Jagger released his wrist, and Zane tipped the bottle into his mouth. The vile taste of warm beer spread across his tongue. But damned if he would let Jagger tell him what to do.

"Wrong choice, brother."

Zane snorted. "My life has just been one wrong choice after another. At least I'm consistent."

"What happened between you and Evie that night of the party when you two ran off and left me playing vids on my own?" Jagger cut to the chase; he wasn't a man who had time to waste. As president of the MC, he had over one hundred men depending on him, a multitude of businesses to run, and politics to handle. Although the executive board helped spread the load, in the end, he was the man in charge. And he loved it. Zane had never been interested in leadership, but he did enjoy his position as vice president and Jagger's right-hand man. Power from the shadows. That was him.

"You mean the part before her dad tried to kill me and I became a wanted man? Nothin'." He took another swig from the bottle and thudded it on the table. If Jagger kept this up, he'd be forced to leave and he didn't know if he'd be able to stand, much less walk a straight line through the bar.

"Does it have something to do with Mark?"

"Jag." He barked the name, cutting Jagger off. He

couldn't talk about Evie and the thought of her married to that no-good piece of slime made his stomach twist. Anyone who spent their study breaks getting drunk under the bleachers wasn't good enough for Evie. In his eyes, no one had been good enough for her, and he'd made sure every guy in Stanton High School knew the score.

Lucky for Jag, the executive board made a timely arrival. Sparky and Gunner pulled up some extra tables. T-Rex and Tank, the junior patch members-at-large, brought chairs. Dax followed them in with Cade and Shaggy on his heels.

After Sherry served their drinks, Jagger gave the floor to Cade for the treasurer's report. Tall, blond, and nicknamed "Thor" by the sweet butts for his resemblance to an actor who played the character in the movies, Cade had enjoyed the fringe benefits of being a biker—a new woman in his bed every night—until he met Arianne's best friend, Dawn. Now the club's notorious manwhore had an old lady, two adopted daughters, and a baby on the way. Zane had taken up the mantle of "Brother Least Likely Ever to Get Hitched" that Cade had passed down to him, and he expected to keep it until the day he died.

Cade reported that the war with the Jacks had drained their finances, and although the Sinners had some robust long-term holdings, they needed short-term gains to pay salaries and keep their businesses afloat—gains that were usually financed through the arms deals that the Jacks now sought to take over.

Dax, the club torturer, and father of five boys, offered to hire out his services to other MCs to bring in some extra cash. Lean and dark, relished his victim's screams. Not many of the brothers could stomach Dax's "work," but Zane didn't have a problem watching Dax use his psychology background to inveigle information from those who had been deemed a danger to the club. And when the psychology failed, and the tools came out, well, Zane had screamed louder the night after he got his mother's name tattooed on his arm, and his dad cut it off with a rusty blade.

The whiskey went down smooth, with only the slightest burn, and for the first time since he'd seen Evie in Big Bill's shop, Zane felt a flicker of warmth in his chest. He slumped back in his chair and prayed the meeting would be over soon so he could go back to the clubhouse and crash.

After turning down Dax's offer, and similar suggestions from board members, Jagger turned the focus of the meeting back to the Black Jacks and their ambition to become the dominant outlaw MC, not just in the state, but nationwide. Instead of a full-on assault, the Jacks had infiltrated Sinner support clubs, turning members into puppet Jacks, willing to do their dirty work in exchange for the promise of being allowed to set up their own chapters. The Jacks had undercut some of the Sinners' more lucrative arms contracts by using locals to run guns and evade detection.

Fed up with being on the defensive, Jagger and the national Sinner's Tribe president had come up with a plan to plant an informant inside the Black Jack clubhouse who could feed them information, allowing them to gain the upper hand. National would be fielding candidates, but did the board have anyone in mind?

"I'll do it." T-Rex, now sporting a massive bruise on his forehead from Axle's blow, jumped up when Jagger threw the question to the table. Easygoing and good-natured, T-Rex was well-liked and respected by the club members, but he didn't have the edge that their rat would need to stand up to Viper, president of the Jacks.

"Needs to be someone connected to the club," Jagger said. "But not in an obvious way. We have to assume they know who we are, so we're looking for people who owe the club a favor. They gotta be smart and savvy otherwise Viper will sniff them out. We all know what happens to rats."

"Same thing that shoulda happened to Axle, but the bastard got away," Zane mumbled.

"Hard to believe he got away from you," Gunner said. "You're the fourth best shot in the club."

"Fourth?" Tank, a dark-haired, slightly stockier version of T-Rex, scratched his head.

Gunner glanced over at Jagger and smirked. "Me, then Arianne, then Jagger, then Zane, then Cade."

Cade bristled. "Girls don't count."

"And even if they did," Jagger's lips quirked at the corners. "Arianne can't outshoot me."

"That's not what she says." Gunner turned his attention back to Zane. "So now you're bumped up to third. Makes it even harder to understand how Axle got away."

"I had him trapped behind Big Bill's shop and I ran out of ammo." Zane didn't see any need to mention Evie, or the fact he'd let Axle go to ensure she got away safely. Nor did he feel a need to mention the fact that Evie and Axle knew each other in what seemed to be more than a business-related way. Not until he understood what the fuck was going on.

"You ran out of ammo?" Gunner's incredulous look would have been almost comical if not for the fact he sounded really pissed off, and pissing off the MC's sergeant-at-arms was never a good idea. At six feet five inches tall, and heavy with muscle, his bald head tatted and his fists like clubs, Gunner could beat any man in a fight without breaking a sweat. Although Zane was vice president, Gunner was in charge of order in the club, and Zane was pretty sure letting a Black Jack go was a serious breach of the rules.

"I ran out of ammo. You got a problem with that?" Obviously Gunner did have a problem because he was now out of his chair and eating up the distance between them with easy strides of his long legs.

"What were you carrying?"

"Full-size Springfield XD." Too late Zane realized his

mistake—a mistake he would never have made if he'd been sober. Gunner came by his road name because he knew everything about weapons, and he would know exactly how much ammo Zane's weapon held.

"The magazine holds thirteen. You missed thirteen shots?"

"Maybe I emptied it out earlier when I used your bike for target practice." Zane pushed his chair away from the table. If Gunner wanted a fight, he'd get a fight. Something to liven up an otherwise dull meeting, and take Zane's mind off the woman who had dominated his thoughts all week.

"Stand down." Jagger shoved Zane back in his chair. "Gunner, take a seat. I'm not paying to have this bar re-done again. The Jacks did enough damage the night they came here after Arianne."

"Fucking Jacks," Zane mumbled. And they were. Fucking. Jacks. They'd shot up Rider's Bar in retribution for the Sinners blowing up their ice house, and only Arianne's timely intervention and skill with a weapon had saved the bar from being totally destroyed.

"Fucking Axle," Gunner said as he settled back in his chair.

"He's like a cockroach." Cade drained his glass. "No matter what we do, he keeps coming back. We can't catch him. We can't kill him—"

Gunner cut him off with a snort. "He's been at Big Bill's shop twice in the last few days. There's something there he wants which means he's gonna be back. This time, I'll be there waiting for him. I don't mind keeping watch, especially if that cute little detailer is around. Man, she's got the sweetest little ass, and those jugs . . ."

Zane pushed himself up so fast his chair fell backwards. He didn't want any of the Sinners around Evie. Although she was married, he knew his brothers, and some of them weren't deterred by things like wedding rings or kids.

"Christ. Not again. Get a fucking grip." Jagger held out an arm, blocking Zane's path to a stunned Gunner.

"She's an old friend." Jagger raised his voice over Ted Nugent's "Cat Scratch Fever," now blasting through the speakers. "Zane and I both knew her growing up. So no disrespect."

Gunner held up his hands in a placating gesture. "No disrespect intended, brothers."

Still primed and ready for a fight, Zane turned and pounded his fist into the wall, leaving a dent beside the many other dents from the many other bikers who came to the bar to drown their sorrows and vent their rage during a war that had seen far too many causalities.

"I agree with Gun." Jagger folded his hands on the table as if Zane wasn't about to explode beside him. "We need someone posted inside Big Bill's shop during work hours and someone outside when it's closed over the next few days. It's our best shot at catching Axle. Evie said he was there for personal reasons. I'll give her a call to see if she'll give me any more information, but she's reluctant to talk because both the Jacks and the Sinners are potential clients for her."

Zane opened his mouth to ask Jagger to handle the surveillance personally, and closed it again when he remembered the kiss that had started it all, and the night he'd discovered that there was pain worse than the abuse he had suffered at the hands of his father. Although nine years had passed, and Jagger had found the other half of his soul with Arianne, Zane didn't think his heart could go through that kind of pain again.

"I'll do it." Zane settled back in his chair. "Shooter can stay outside and I'll take the inside watch."

"You sure? I need someone to check out the local support clubs for puppet Jacks." Jagger lifted an eyebrow, giving Zane an out if he wanted it.

"Yeah. Although maybe not first thing in the morning, 'cause I don't think I'm gonna be able to get out of bed."

Jagger clapped him on the back. "Shooter will take you back to the clubhouse. He's waiting outside with the bikes.

I couldn't let him come in because last time he almost shot the place up when he saw some dude at the bar wearing a TV show cut."

"That boy's got a serious gun problem," Zane said. "He carries more weapons on him than Cade had notches on his belt before hooking up with Dawn. Sometimes I wonder how he stands upright."

"Well then it's a good thing he'll be your second." Gunner raised a challenging eyebrow. "No risk that boy's gonna run out of ammo."

"Fuck you." Zane steadied himself with the back of the chair. Holy Hell. He couldn't remember the last time he'd been this drunk. Usually he stopped at one drink, sometimes two, because he didn't want to impair his ability to ride. Well, he'd kicked that record under the table tonight.

"Easy, brother." Jagger steadied him with a firm hand. "You need a good night's sleep."

"Haven't had a good night's sleep in nine fucking years," he mumbled, half to himself. "I doubt I'm gonna start tonight."

"We've got a big problem." Connie sipped her coffee, leaving a bright pink lipstick stain on her chipped white mug. The small kitchen in Evie's rental bungalow was barely big enough to hold a table and two chairs, but with with a wall of white lacquer cabinets, green accents and a black-and-white tiled floor, it was cozy and eclectic. And it was hers. Sort of.

Small droplets of water slid down Connie's hair and splashed on the shiny green table. Two days of rain and no sign of a break in the clouds. Evie had sent Ty down the road to have a playdate with a friend to get him off the gaming console, although she suspected that was exactly what he would be doing when he got there.

"I guessed that from your unexpected visit in a downpour on our Sunday off." Evie poured herself a second cup of coffee then lifted the aerosol container of whipped cream beside her and squirted it over the top. She had been awake all night trying to figure out how to introduce Zane and Ty without taking the risk Zane might not want to be involved. She didn't want Ty to get hurt, and if Zane wasn't interested in being a parent, it would be better to feel him out first before making the introductions so she could prepare Ty in advance, or even not tell him at all.

"That looks good in a bad sort of way." Connie shook her head when Evie offered her the container. "But whipped cream on black coffee? Why don't you just add cream and sugar like normal people? It's not hot chocolate. It's not dessert. It's not a latte. Hell, it's not even a man's—"

"Don't go there." Evie added a last dollop of whipped cream and then licked it off the top.

"Do you let Ty see you do that? What kind of mother are you?" Connie stirred her coffee, her attempt at righteous indignation totally lost in her accompanying snort of laughter.

"The kind who's addicted to whipped cream, and when no one is looking, sprays it into her son's mouth to his utter delight." She licked her lips and grinned. "Plus, this is more efficient. Why add cream and sugar when they come already mixed together? And this is real cream. No chemicals. I only buy the best. I've turned Bill to the dark side, too. There's a can of whipped cream in his office fridge."

Connie's smile faded. "Bill is gone. That's what I wanted to tell you."

"I guessed that when he didn't show up at work all week."

"No. I mean gone as in disappeared. I haven't seen him since the night Axle came in one door and Bill slipped out the other. I went by his place, and when I looked in the window, I saw food spoiling on the counter. I think the Black Jacks got him."

Evie's hand tightened on her mug and her mouth went dry. "Maybe he just ran after seeing Axle at the shop. He might have figured Axle had a message for him that he didn't want to hear."

"You think they found out about the skim?" Connie dabbed at the water drop on the table. "I never understood why he would take the risk of stealing from the Jacks, especially after introducing you to Viper. Is the store doing that bad?"

"We've been in the black for the last year, although we're not making a huge profit," Evie said.

Bill had sold half his interest in the business to Evie after he got involved with the Jacks. His gun running took him out of the state for weeks at a time and he needed someone reliable to look after the shop and the employees. Evie had to do a lot of soul searching before she parted with her cash, but after her accountant gave the deal a thumbs up, the opportunity to double her earnings as a part-owner of the business and to secure a better future for Ty had been impossible to turn down.

"Maybe he just panicked," she suggested.

"That's what I'm feeling now." Connie's face paled. "What if they got him? What if the Jacks tortured him to find out where the guns are?" Her voice wavered. "What if your Black Jack boyfriend shows up for your date and tells you he just made a fresh kill? Or worse . . . what if Bill's pulled a runner and they come after us looking for the guns?"

"Then we'll tell them where the guns are." She had no doubt the Black Jacks were involved in illegal activities, but Viper rarely mentioned his club around her, never brought her to the clubhouse, never talked business, and except for Axle, had never introduced her to his biker brothers. He had a wide variety of interests, however, and when they were together, they talked about everything from politics to entertainment and from sports to art.

She laughed, trying to put Connie at ease. "I'll make

sure Viper knows that torturing my friends is a deal breaker, and he'll have to find another civilian to date. And if it makes you feel safer, you can stay here. I have my own personal Sinner's Tribe biker guards so you can be sure the Jacks won't be coming around."

"I noticed them standing on the street on my way in." Connie licked her lips and grinned. "Cute, but in a menacing kind of way."

They left the kitchen to check out the bikers, now huddled together under a tree as the rain streamed around them. Evie recognized the blond from the night Axle had paid his first visit to Bill's shop, but not his dark-haired partner.

"I texted Jagger," she said. "Apparently Axle escaped from Zane so now Jagger has his boys watching my house and the shop in case Axle shows up again. I told him none of the Jacks know where I live, and Axle won't be coming around again, but he insisted. They really want the poor guy bad. I'm afraid to think what they might do to him."

"You know exactly what they're going to do. Zane was trying to kill him." Connie's lips quivered at the corners and she shot Evie a sideways glance. "They're looking kind of wet. And cold. The hot, dark one shivered when I walked by earlier. It would be terrible if they died of pneumonia right there on the street. And they look so young . . . early to mid-twenties . . . same as us. I don't know if I could live with myself, knowing I was the cause of their deaths."

Evie tipped her head back and groaned. "You're as bad as Ty when he's trying to guilt me into buying him something he doesn't need."

"Please, Evie." Connie gave her a soulful look. "Can't they come inside?"

"Okay." Evie sighed. "They can sit on the porch, but you're responsible for them."

"I'll just give them food and water and clean up their mess. And I won't ask to keep them." Connie pulled open the door. "You can have the blond, but leave the dark-haired one for me."

Evie leaned out and waved the bikers over to the house. Yeah, the blond guy was cute, but she wasn't looking for a man. She hadn't had a serious relationship since Mark, and Viper was just . . . an interesting distraction. Especially now that she'd seen Zane. She brought her fingers to her cheek, remembering the heat of his breath, and how she had almost let him kiss her.

Zane.

The intense connection and chemistry that had first drawn them together hadn't changed. But she had. She was finally in control of her life. No longer at the mercy of her mother's emotional abuse, or longing for a father who was rarely home, she had embraced normal to the extent she knew what normal was. She made her own choices, cleaned up her own messes, and occasionally let her wild side out to play. And that most definitely wasn't going to be with the man who had left her alone and pregnant, wishing on a promise he didn't keep.

She let Connie fuss over the bikers while she called to check up on Ty and chatted with him about his game. By the time she made it outside, Connie had everything ready: coffee, sandwiches, and cookies. She introduced Evie to the bikers, dark-haired Tank and his companion, T-Rex.

"Much obliged for the snack." Tank stood to make room as Evie joined them on the porch.

"Thank Connie, not me. She's the one who felt sorry for you standing out in the rain."

Tank leaned back and stretched out his long legs, the patio chair creaking beneath his weight as they chatted about the town and the club. He was a bear of a man, but all muscle and no flab, with a cheeky smile and a dry sense of humor. She could see why Connie was practically drooling over him. T-Rex had a similar build to Tank, but without the bulk. He was fun and easygoing and she was surprised to hear he didn't have a girlfriend. Connie gave her a nudge when T-Rex made the big reveal, but he was too nice, even though he was an outlaw, and Evie had never been attracted to the "nice" guys.

Still, she'd never thought outlaw bikers could be such fun, and when Connie switched their coffee for beer, and the conversation turned flirtatious, she felt the stress of the last two days sliding away. Between the jokes and the laughter, they all turned a blind eye to the fact the rain had stopped and the sun had come out. And when T-Rex put a hand on Evie's knee as he leaned over to get another beer, she wondered if she'd been too hasty dismissing the nice guys. Maybe that's what she needed in her life. Someone relaxed and even-tempered, without a hint of Zane's dark, brooding, passionate depths, or Viper's feral power.

And just as Zane's face flickered through her mind, there he was. How he had managed to drive down her street and climb the steps without any of them noticing was beyond her, save as a testament to just how much fun they'd been having.

"Jesus fucking Christ," he snapped by way of greeting. "What the hell is going on?"

★ SIX ★

Think before you act. If you do impulsive,
stupid things, you will break parts.
—SINNER'S TRIBE MOTORCYCLE REPAIR MANUAL

Evie gently removed T-Rex's hand from her leg and stood to greet her guests. But Zane clearly wasn't interested in hellos. His gaze locked on T-Rex and his lips peeled back in a snarl.

"What the fuck are you doing touching her?"

Zane's companion, a young, slightly crazed-looking biker with a thin, angular face and a dark, pointed goatee joined him on the porch, and pulled a gun from his cut.

"You want me to take someone out?" He waved the gun vaguely over their small group and Connie screamed.

"Dammit, Shooter. Put that away. We're in a residential area and if someone calls the fucking cops, I'm not bailing you out." Zane slapped Shooter's wrist and the aptly-named Shooter tucked the gun away with a mumbled apology.

T-Rex and Tank scrambled to their feet. T-Rex hung his head like a kid who'd just been called to the principal's office, and Tank followed suit.

"It was . . . uh . . . rainin'," Tank said. "And the ladies offered us a snack and a chance to dry off."

Zane's lips pressed into a thin, tight line. Evie knew that look, just as she knew the throb of the pulse in his neck.

She'd seen that look back in their school days when he found out someone had hurt her, or worse, asked her out. Alarmed by his anger, Evie took a step toward him.

"Don't." He raised his hand and she froze, stunned by his command and his authoritative tone. So unlike the Zane she remembered. Like Jagger, he radiated power, but without Jagger's softer edge.

"How the fuck can you watch the street if you're gabbing with a coupla chicks?" Zane's hands curled into fists. "Shooter and I drove around the block, parked our bikes out front, walked right onto the porch, and you two idiots didn't even bat an eye."

"Sorry, man." T-Rex held up his hands palm forward in a placating gesture. Evie gave him credit for remaining cool in a crisis. Zane had been frightening in his anger as a teenager, but now that he was a man, his intensity had ratcheted up to a whole new level.

"Sorry doesn't cut it if someone gets killed." Zane's voice rose to a shout.

Worried that the confrontation would escalate out of control, Evie covered his hand with her own, startling when a zing of white lightning shot straight to her core.

"It's okay," she said softly. "We're okay. No one came down the street except you."

Zane jerked his hand away so fast, Evie lost her balance. Reacting quickly, T-Rex grabbed her arm to steady her. Zane lost control. He grabbed T-Rex by the collar and yanked him forward, dislodging his hand from Evie's arm.

"Get your fucking hands off her."

Evie opened her mouth to ask what the hell was going on, but closed it again after a warning cough from Tank. Following his lead, she thanked them for watching out for her and moved to the side to let them pass.

"Why aren't you at the shop?" Zane turned his anger on her, and Connie discreetly ushered Shooter down the steps.

"It's Sunday." She struggled to keep her voice calm and

even. "We usually have the day off and Bill runs the store alone, although he seems to have disappeared so it's closed today." She tilted her head to the side. "Why? Did you need something?"

"Yeah." His voice softened, and their eyes met. Caught in the intensity of his gaze, Evie was drawn back to the first time she realized her feelings for him went beyond friendship. After school one warm spring afternoon they'd climbed their favorite tree to check out a robin's nest. As always, Zane went down first. But that time, when he wrapped his hands around her waist to help her, something changed. Warmed by the press of his hands on her body, she stared into his dark eyes, and knew deep in her soul she was exactly where she was meant to be. In that moment, the world shifted irrevocably between them, and when he let her go, she felt instantly bereft.

After that afternoon, she'd made up excuses to touch him—brushing her thigh against his leg when they sat on Jagger's couch, a hand on his arm when she lost her balance, a gentle stroke on his hair to remove an imaginary leaf—and every time she felt the rush, a curious sizzle that went straight to her core. But except for that brief moment when he'd held her, his eyes soft, his breath warm on her cheek, he never treated her as anything more than a friend.

Until the night he ran away.

"What are you looking for?" She looked down, letting her hair cover her face so he couldn't see the flush in her cheeks. "I have a few hours free this afternoon, and since Bill isn't there, I don't mind going in to help you out. Ty . . . my son . . . is with a friend."

"Paint."

God, this was as bad as getting Ty to tell her about his day at school. "Do you need to buy paint or are you looking for artwork?"

"Art. Yours."

Evie fought back a smile. Zane had always reverted to monosyllabic answers in emotionally stressful situations, and she had a feeling his stress wasn't because of T-Rex and Tank shirking their duties. "You want to see my portfolio and some samples or do you have something in mind?" She sidestepped around him, heading for the door so she could grab her purse. Her body brushed against his and just that tiny touch—the feel of his hard chest against her breasts, the scent of his leather cut—sent her pulse skyrocketing, and she stumbled.

Zane put out a hand to steady her, then yanked her against him, holding her fast with an arm around her waist. "You were always touching me, Evie," he murmured. "Drove me outta my fucking mind. You playing games with me now?"

Her chest expanded and she sucked in some badly needed air. This wasn't Zane the teenager, who fumbled with her clothes beside the creek, his hands shaking as he touched her bare skin. This was Zane the man, confident, self-assured and strong, with a dominance that made her knees weak and a body that made her mouth water.

Dangerous. Maybe even a killer.

No. She pushed the thought away. Even after she gave up hope of seeing him again, she never believed he was responsible for her father's death.

"We should go." She pulled away, at least she thought she did, but his hand stayed firm on her lower back. "I'll show you my portfolio."

"Saw it when I stopped by the shop on my way here. You got real talent. Always did."

"You broke into the shop?" The warmth of his hand seeped through her body making it difficult to keep her spine stiff and her indignation firm.

A half grin spread across his face, and his shoulders relaxed. "Thought maybe you were unconscious inside since the hours on the door said the shop was open on Sunday."

"And you didn't think to call Tank or T-Rex who were parked outside my house?"

"I'm a man of action, sweetheart." He nuzzled the side of her face, the rasp of his breath in her ear so damn erotic she wanted nothing more than to drag him into her house and do something insanely stupid.

"I hope you didn't rampage through the shop during your break-in. It's partly my business, too."

He jerked back and his smile faded. "You think I'm gonna steal from you?"

She cringed at his sharp tone, but better to have him annoyed than sexy and seductive. "You are an outlaw biker. Isn't that what you do? Mayhem, theft, arson . . . the more illegal the better?"

"We do what we gotta do to live the way we want to live."

Evie pulled away, putting some much-needed space between them. "The way I want to live includes having a way to pay the rent, and that's not going down if anything happens to the shop. Plus, Axle won't be back. I told Jagger, but he didn't believe me. He was just delivering a message from someone." She turned to the door, cringing at the reveal she hadn't intended to make, but before she could step inside, Zane clamped a hand on her shoulder.

"Who?"

Her heart pounded a warning, but she couldn't outright lie, and the question suggested he already knew the answer. "Viper."

Zane hissed in a breath. "What was the message?"

She twisted a lock of hair around her finger, and looked back at him over her shoulder. "It's . . . sort of . . . personal. We're . . . um . . . friends."

His gaze locked on her finger and his eyes narrowed. Damn. He knew her anxiety tell as well as she knew his. "Viper doesn't have friends."

"Maybe you don't know him that well."

He released her and took a step back. "Maybe I don't know you."

* * *

Zane flicked the throttle on his Harley and the bike surged forward, forcing Evie to tighten her grip around his waist.

He could do this.

The distance between Evie's house and Bill's shop couldn't be more than twenty miles. And look. He'd already made it to the highway. If she would just stop wiggling on the seat behind him . . . and if she didn't hold him quite so tight with her breasts pressed up against her back . . . and if her fingers weren't dangling over the bulge in his jeans, which was getting more pronounced the closer she pressed her body against his . . . then he might actually make it to Big Bill's shop without either crashing the bike or spilling in his pants like a teenage boy.

He couldn't remember feeling lust like this since the night he'd left Stanton. Sure he'd had women. The sweet butts were always warm and willing, and if he wanted to keep things discreet, the Sinners owned several strip clubs in town. But he rarely felt the need to take advantage of the opportunities the cut provided. And when he did, every woman morphed into Evie. She had been burned onto his brain for eighteen years, ruining him for other women forever.

And now her soft, sexy body was pressed up against him, her thighs brushing his thighs, her hips firm against his ass, and her damn fingers resting on his fly.

His groin tightened and he swerved the bike.

Fuck. Concentrate. But it was so damn hard.

He wondered what Mark would think about his wife riding on the back of Zane's bike, holding on to him, legs parted, cheeks flushed from the wind. If she'd been his, there would be no way he would allow her on the back of any man's bike. Hell, he wouldn't let her near another man. Look how he reacted to her, despite the stain of her betrayal still tainting his heart.

By the time they reached the shop, his cock was rock hard and his body thrummed with need. Shooter pulled up beside them and Zane prayed for Evie to dismount quickly so he would have time to get himself together and calm the fuck down so she wouldn't see the evidence of his desire.

He wanted her. She'd hurt him and he wanted her. She was with another man and he wanted her. She'd slapped him and damned if seeing Evie come into her own hadn't made him want her more. And back there on the porch, when she'd brushed her breasts against his chest, the way she'd touched him when they were young, telling him with her body what she couldn't say out loud, he'd almost taken her.

"Gotta talk to Shooter," he said after she slid neatly off his bike. "I'll meet you inside."

"I'll go check out the damage." She gave him a wink and then walked to the door, making his groin tighten all over again at the sight of her beautiful ass perfectly outlined in dark denim.

After the door closed behind her, he briefed Shooter on surveillance techniques, which basically meant finding somewhere to stand where you aren't visible and don't fall asleep. He sent Shooter to the picnic table across the street, and then walked around his bike and tried to get his fucking lust in check. He considered the various bike parts, how they fit together and how easily they came apart, and how hard it had been to replace his stock exhaust with a longer, harder, thicker pipe, and how he had to fight with Sparky to get an upswept ball-end megaphone muffler.

When he realized the direction his thoughts were leading, he gave up the fight, made a careful self-adjustment, and headed into the store.

Rows of motorcycles gleamed under the overhead lights. Bill had a lot of stock for a small shop, mostly new models, but a few bobsters, and some custom pieces. The walls held parts and supplies, racks of leathers, helmets, and boots. Although half the stock was used, the scent of new leather and fresh paint permeated the air.

He found Evie in the garage spraying primer on a gas tank perched on an A-frame stand. She had stripped down to a skintight tank top and tied her hair back in a messy ponytail. Loose strands framed her beautiful face. Damn she was hot, standing in that gritty shop, surrounded in motorcycle parts, and with a spray gun in her hand . . .

Christ. Was everything going to make him think about sex?

"Thought I'd get a head start on my work for tomorrow while I was waiting. My portfolio is over there if you need to look at it under more legitimate circumstances, or if you've brought a design, just leave it on the bench and I'll take a look."

Zane walked along the wall beside the benches filled with paint supplies and airbrush guns. He had already checked the place out, trying to find clues about her life from the personal items in her workspace: a handbook from Conundrum College; a parenting magazine; a coffee cup from a restaurant in Stanton; a motorcycle magazine; and the charcoal drawing of him, Jagger, and Evie on the wall—a rendition of the picture he had given her. Even now, seeing it again, a lump welled up in his throat—not just because of the memory, but because she'd kept it, and made it larger than life.

"Find anything in the portfolio?" She came up beside him, and he couldn't stop from brushing one of the loose strands of hair back from her face. The sharp scent of primer took the edge off his desire, and he was finally able to untangle his tongue.

"No. But your work is exceptional." She'd always been artistic, which was why he had been so unsure of the gift he'd made for her graduation. Although he knew her as well as one person could know another, he'd worried it wasn't good enough . . . that he wasn't worthy. Just like her father had said as he beat Zane by Stanton Creek after finding him with Evie.

"You're nothing and you come from nothing. You've got

nothing to offer my daughter. No future. No skills. Hell, you couldn't even finish school. All you got is a trailer full of drugs, an addict for a father, and shit for brains."

Perversely, he'd been happy for Evie, thinking at least her father cared, despite the fact that he spent very little time with her. But then Zane said the words that started the whole devastating chain of events. Angry words. Four words he wished he could take back the moment they dropped from his lips.

I know about you.

Zane had known that Evie's father was on the take for years. Once a month, Sheriff Monroe showed up at his dad's trailer to pick up a few kilos of coke and then transport them across state lines in his cruiser. And it wasn't just drugs. He had his hands in the underground arms trade, too, not to mention all the nights he spent in the massage parlors in Stanton's red light district.

But Zane had never told Evie about her dad's extracurricular activities. Not because he felt any loyalty to his old man, and not because he was scared of Sheriff Monroe. But because Evie adored her father. She thought he was a hero. An honorable man. She forgave him all the nights he left her alone with her alcoholic mother because she thought he was out protecting Stanton's citizens and saving the day. Zane couldn't take that away from her, couldn't bear to hurt her by shattering the illusion.

It was only the night Sheriff Monroe showed up at his trailer with a gun, that Zane realized his mistake. A man without honor or compassion wouldn't understand that Zane would keep the secret from his daughter. Desperation drove a man who was afraid.

"Thanks." She put down the spray gun. "I never made it to college, and I sort of fell into custom painting when one of my friends asked if I could paint something on her husband's motorcycle as a surprise for his birthday. He recommended me to his friends and it sort of spiraled from there. I never thought about it as a career until I went to a motorcycle show in Helena with a couple of my pieces and met Bill. He offered me a job in Conundrum, and . . ." She bit her lip, hesitating. "It was the right time for me to leave Stanton."

"Ever think about setting up on your own?" Zane leaned against the table, all thoughts of a paint job disappearing when she pulled out her elastic and rubbed a hand through her hair.

So beautiful. He wanted to run his fingers through those red-gold strands, feel that silky softness in his palm. And then he wanted to twist her hair in his fist and hold her head still so he could ravish her mouth, or better yet, her body. She had curves that could bring a man to his knees.

Her cheeks flushed and she looked down as if she knew what he was thinking. "Um . . . no. I'm comfortable where I am. This setup gives me a good source of customers. Plus, now that I'm a part owner, it's my shop, too." Pride shone in her eyes and Zane smiled. She had never been one to hide her emotions.

"So what do you think happened to Bill?" He gripped the tabletop behind him to keep from walking toward her and enacting his fantasy right here, right now. What the hell could he talk about that would keep his desire at bay?

Her smile faded. "I'm not sure. Connie and I thought maybe the Jacks scared him away. He was—" She cut herself off with a grimace. "Never mind."

Zane filed that one away for later. Only way the Jacks would scare a man away from his business was if he'd done something to piss them off. Was he paying them protection money or had he got something going on the side? Damn stupid if he did, and even more stupid if he had put Evie in danger. The minute Bill showed up again, Zane would be taking him out for a little talk about keeping Evie safe.

"You got a bike?" He was scrambling now, trying to avoid the real reason he'd brought her here, and it wasn't for paint.

"No. Can't afford it. One day though. Maybe when I make it big I'll buy myself a present. Mark has a Harley Fat Boy, which is a pretty sweet ride."

Ah. Mark. Now that effectively killed his desire. Zane released the table and folded his arms. "What does he do?" Middle manager? Sportscaster? Or was he still a coach after all these years?

A pained expression crossed her face. "I wouldn't know."

"You don't know what your husband does?"

"Ex-husband. I left him a few years ago to move out here."

"You're not married?" His voice cracked and he drew in a ragged breath. She wasn't married. His Evie was . . . free. "What about his boy? Doesn't he come to see him?"

Her voice tightened. "No."

Their eyes met and the air crackled between them, as if her last word fanned the flames that had been smoldering since that moment on the porch when all he wanted was to drown in her arms.

"What kind of father doesn't want to see his son?" For all that Zane hated his father, and for all the abuse he had taken, when Zane needed him most—the one and only time in his life—his father had been there for him.

Evie tilted her head to the side and stared at him, considering. Then she twisted her hair around her finger. Around and around and around. Zane remembered that little quirk—something she always did when she was anxious.

"A stepfather," she said, finally.

"He's not Mark's boy?"

A gunshot cracked the silence, and then another. Zane's heart pounded and he slid his hand into his cut, closing his fingers around his gun. "Stay here until I come back for you. Hide." He ran back into the store and spotted Shooter just outside the front door, firing his gun into the trees.

"Who is it?" He shouted from the cover of the doorway. "You see Axle? One of the Jacks?"

"Squirrel." Shooter yelled. "Red tail. Tricky little bugger but I got him trapped in that bush."

"Jesus fucking Christ." Zane ran over to Shooter and grabbed his wrist. "Put the weapon down." He unleashed all his tension in a volley of curses directed at Shooter, his mental state, his mother, and his dubious parentage. "This is a surveillance mission. That means you don't draw attention to yourself. You don't shoot things. Gunfire has a nasty tendency to rile up civilians and then they call the cops. And right now the ATF are camped out in the sheriff's office. You want to explain to the fucking ATF why you're shooting squirrels on private property?"

"He was on your bike, gnawing on your seat."

"Gimme that gun." Zane grabbed the weapon and fired three shots into the bush. "Take that, you goddamn fucking bastard," he hollered. "You wanna eat my leather? Now you're gonna be eatin' crow."

"You missed."

Zane handed him the gun. "You got a new job now, prospect. Clean my seat, fix the leather, then bring me that fucking squirrel's hide."

"Yes, sir."

Adrenaline pounded through his veins as he returned to the store, whether from the shoot-out or finding out Evie had split with Mark he didn't know, but damned if he could get himself under control. He took a few deep breaths as he crossed through into the shop, clenching and unclenching his fist by his side.

"Evie?"

"Here." Her voice was faint. "Can I come out now?"

He followed her voice to a storage closet at the far end of the shop and found her reaching for something on the top shelf.

"I figured I'd tidy up while I was in here and I saw a

box of paint I'd forgotten about. Could you get it down for me?" Half in the shadows of the small, musty room, she looked back over her shoulder. "I'm not quite tall enough."

Zane walked up behind her and grabbed the box. His body brushed up against her, his hips against her ass, his chest to her back, his chin brushing over her floral-scented hair.

Walk away. Walk away. Walk the hell away.

He slid his free hand around her waist and pulled her against his body. So perfect. So right.

"Zane." Her voice came out in a choked whisper.

"You're not with Mark?" He leaned down and pressed his lips to her ear, inhaling her scent of jasmine as the adrenaline streamed through his veins, straight down to his groin.

"No."

His hand splayed over her stomach, pulling her close, and he nuzzled the hair away from her neck. "You got a man, Evie?"

"No." Her voice wavered. "But . . . I kinda . . ."

He shoved the box onto a lower shelf and reached around to catch her jaw in his hand, pulling her head back against his shoulder, exposing her neck to the heated slide of his lips. Somewhere, in the foggy recesses of his mind, he knew he was being too rough, but he was barely in control and rough was as gentle as he could be. "So no one's gonna shoot me between the eyes if I do this?" With his thumb he gently stroked the underside of her breast.

Evie sucked in a sharp breath, trembled. "No."

His hand slid higher, tracing over her ribs until he held the full weight of her breast in his palm. "You gonna stop me from touching you, sweetheart?" He feathered kisses along the column of her neck, praying she didn't deny him because he was already so far gone he didn't know if he would be able to stop.

"Zane." She shuddered, her nipples peaking beneath her thin cotton tank top. He circled one taut nipple with his thumb and she groaned and wiggled her ass against his erection, nestled tight in the crack of her cheeks.

"Stop me, Evie," he whispered. "Because I can't stop myself."

She melted against him with a sigh, her body softening. For the briefest of moments he soared, higher and higher, soaking in her light, her warmth, her essence . . .

He should have known what would happen if he flew too close to the sun.

"I can't do this." Evie pulled away, her cheeks burning with a flush of heat. She knew Zane, the dark, passionate, slightly awkward high-school senior who made her stomach flutter when he smiled; the boy with a good heart who'd been dealt a bad hand in life; her protector and one-time friend. But this man . . . this biker—broad and heavily muscled, tatted and pierced, ruthless and dominant, who walked and talked with confidence and swagger, and so easily manipulated her body, awakening long dormant passion and desire—was a stranger to her.

A stranger who made her body respond with a single touch. A stranger who ignited a blazing hot chemistry that made her feel alive. A stranger who had disappeared when her father's body was still warm on the ground.

Zane released a tortured breath and turned her to face him. "Things didn't go right between us when we met the other day. We had things we needed to say, and we didn't get to say them." His corded throat tightened when he swallowed. "Ask me, Evie."

Emotion welled up in her chest, pushing the words to the tip of her tongue. Although she knew the question was a betrayal in itself, she needed to hear the truth. For Ty. And for her own peace of mind. "Did you kill my dad?"

"No, sweetheart. It wasn't me."

Her breath left her in a rush, her knees giving way. If not for his arms around her, she would have fallen to the ground.

"In my heart I knew, but I needed to hear it," she whispered.

"And I needed to say it." He brushed a rough finger over her cheek. "After I saw you again, and we had words, I thought we were done. I thought I wouldn't be able to get over the fact you didn't wait for me. But I couldn't stop thinking about you. When I was at your place, and T-Rex had his hands on you . . ." He drew in a ragged breath. "We're not done, Evie. I don't expect you to forgive me for leaving the way I did, and maybe one day I will understand why you didn't wait and forgive you, too, but I will never be done with you." He cupped her face between his hands and kissed her.

At first, his lips were soft, hesitant, as if he thought she might slap him again, but when a low moan escaped her lips, he deepened the kiss, pulling her closer as he ravaged her mouth. Evie wrapped her arms around him and molded her body against his as she met every desperate stroke of his tongue with one of her own. His grip tightened and when she tried to pull away, gasping for breath, he nipped her bottom lip, demanding more.

Shocked by the intensity of her reaction, she wrenched herself away, the rapid rise and fall of her chest matching his, but when she took a step back, he followed, one hand curled behind her neck, the other gentle on her hip as he pressed his lips to her temple. "I got shit to do tonight, but I need to see you again. I'll swing by your place tomorrow night."

Her blood chilled, and not just because she wasn't ready for him to meet Ty. "You can't. I . . . I have plans."

"Cancel them."

God, those two words, demanding and confident, laced with expectation and desire, did strange things to her stomach. If it had been anyone else she had agreed to meet for dinner, she would have done as he asked. But she had no way of contacting Viper other than making a trip to

his clubhouse, which she wasn't prepared to do, and as
Connie said, he wasn't the kind of man to blow off in such
a casual manner. Plus, she needed some distance. Kissing
Zane had never been in the program.

"I can't."

"Then I'll find you." He didn't wait for a response. Instead he reached over her for the paint box, then took her
hand and led her out of the closet, as if he could keep her
from running with only his touch.

It would be so easy to give in, pick up where they left
off, introduce him to Ty and play happy families, if outlaw bikers had happy families. He seemed so sure of
himself and what he wanted, but he had broken her heart,
and it had taken her far too long to get over him. Giving
him a second chance wasn't just stupid, it was dangerous,
especially since he hadn't changed. Deep, dark, and emotionally intense, he still took what he wanted with a total
disregard for rules and authority. As a boy, he did what he
had to do to survive, but as a man, he had made lawless-
ness a way of life.

Not the kind of life she wanted . . . for her or for Ty.

"I don't want to rush into anything. We're not the same
people anymore." She gestured to the door, although the
last thing she wanted was another ride on his motorcycle,
with the motor vibrating between her legs and his hard
body tucked up against her breasts. "I don't know Zane the
biker, just like you don't know Evie the mom and painter.
It's like meeting someone new, but with all our past bag-
gage tacked on. I've moved on and I'm just not looking for
anything or anyone. I have a nice, normal, quiet life now.
I'm happy as I am."

He studied her, as if he could see into her soul and pluck
out the lies. "Don't tell me you didn't feel something, because I know you did. After all the time we spent together,
I know what it means when you bite your lip, and when
your cheeks flush pink. I could feel your heart pounding

in your chest, same as mine. And yeah, I don't want to re-member the past either, and especially not the day I saw you with Mark and your son. But that doesn't mean there's nothing between us, Evie."

"Evangeline."

"You'll always be Evie to me." He shoved the door aside and let her pass before yanking it closed. "Doesn't matter how many times you tell me, I can't call you something else, especially after I had to listen to nine years of you moanin' about how much you hated that name."

Zane checked out the parking lot while she locked up, and then they joined Shooter at the bikes. But before she could climb on the seat, Zane put out a warning hand.

"Prospect. What instructions did I just give you?"

"Um . . . you wanted your seat cleaned and repaired and the offending rodent . . ." He glanced quickly at Evie and then back to Zane. "Managed."

"So why are there teeth marks on my seat?" Zane gestured to the leather saddle and Evie squinted. Although the light was low, the seat looked perfect to her.

"Um . . . well . . . his teeth were pretty sharp and I didn't know how to repair the leather. I cleaned and polished it, though."

Zane folded his arms. "My girl's not ridin' on rodent marks. How's she gonna get home?"

His girl? Hadn't he been paying attention when she told him she wasn't looking for anyone? And what about Viper? Although the more time she spent with Zane, the less interest she had in pursuing that relationship.

Shooter shifted his weight and grimaced. "Taxi?"

Poor Shooter received a cuff to the head. Evie cringed on his behalf. She knew from biker books and television shows that prospects were given the worst jobs and the least respect during the time they were pledging to the club, but she hadn't expected Zane to be quite so harsh.

"You want me to take her on my bike?" Shooter asked.

Alarmed at the way Zane's hands curled into fists, Evie

slid onto the pillion seat of his vivid black, Harley Night Rod Special. "This girl's ass isn't so precious that it can't withstand a few teeth marks. Let's ride."

Zane turned his anger and outrage on her. "I'm teaching the prospect a lesson."

"And I have a son waiting for me to pick him up."

He glared at Shooter as he mounted his bike. "Clubhouse. One hour. And you better be standing on the drive with a repair kit in one hand and a squirrel pelt in the other. Fucking rodent disrespected my girl."

Again with the "his girl." But his insistence on protecting her even from hungry squirrels made her feel warm and tingly inside.

"Hold on tight, sweetheart." He started his engine and the deep rumble vibrated through her body.

Oh, she'd hold on tight. But would she be able to let go?

★ SEVEN ★

*There is no substitute for good information
and a helping hand.*
—SINNER'S TRIBE MOTORCYCLE REPAIR MANUAL

Zane hated the morgue.

And not because of the smell. He could handle the cloying scent of antiseptic. Even the underlying odor of death and decomposition. But what got to him was the sadness. There was never anything good waiting for the people who went through the heavy silver door leading from the waiting room to the identification area. And he would know. He'd been in the morgue too many times to identify the bodies of his brothers who had become collateral damage in the war against the Black Jacks.

This time, however, he and Jagger didn't know if the body the police had found in an alley in the center of town was one of their own.

"You sure you guys want to see this? Like I said on the phone, he's unrecognizable. Forensics is doing the ID through his teeth." Deputy Sheriff Doug Benson led them into the low, brick building. Once an upright law enforcement officer, he had been brought down after a misguided attempt to save Cade's old lady, Dawn—then Benson's friend and love interest—from the biker world. Benson was now on the Sinner payroll, providing information and tips and the occasional assistance in exchange for keeping his body intact.

"If he's one of ours, he deserves our respect."

"Your call." Benson pushed open the door to the waiting room. "One of the ambulance attendants . . . young guy . . . threw up when he saw him. Cause of death was . . . well, let's just say he suffered multiple stab wounds on top of his multiple stab wounds. The patch was cut off his jacket and his tat was burned off his skin so we weren't sure if he was a Sinner or a Jack."

Benson cut himself off when they reached the waiting room. Four people sat on metal folding chairs in the stark, white room, faces pale and drawn as they waited to be called. No one ever cried in the waiting room; the tears always came after . . . when hope was gone and the world became a darker place. He'd been there. Not just after losing a brother, but after seeing Evie with Mark.

But now she was free. She might fight their attraction, but the chemistry was still there. He had felt her tremble against him, heard her sigh when he kissed her . . . So why had she pushed him away? If anyone had a right to be wary, it was him. After all, he had gone back for her. Just like he promised.

He would find out tonight. If she wasn't home, he would find her. Although he had decided to go by his real name in the MC—executive board members were given the choice of using their road name or first name—he had come by his road name, Tracker, for his uncanny ability to find anyone, anywhere. Evie wouldn't stay off his radar for long.

"Zane? You coming?" Benson ran a hand through his dark hair, and Zane followed the deputy's lanky body, clothed in regulation police blue, into the chiller.

The large sterile room, a mix of white cabinets and steel counters, examination tables and fluorescent lights, smelled strongly of disinfectant, but even the sharp scent could not mask the sickly sweet stench of death.

The pathologist, a thin, nervous dude with a receding hairline, who had been on the Sinner payroll for years, wasted no time. He pulled open one of the steel drawers that lined the east wall. "You know him?"

Zane startled at the body, covered in a thin white sheet. Unrecognizable didn't even begin to describe the swollen, battered face, but the arms and hands were remarkably unscathed, save for the long, thin scar on his right hand between two fingers. Familiar. "Turn him over."

Jagger glanced up from the other side of the body. "You see something?"

The pathologist rolled the body to the side and Zane pointed to the scarring on the man's left shoulder. "Isn't that where we burned off Axle's tat? And isn't that scar on his hand from the night you put your knife through his fingers?"

"Fuck." Jagger leaned closer to take a look. "You're right. It is Axle. And lookit the "J" carved into his chest. He must have pissed Viper off. Damn. He owed us for what he did to Arianne and the club. I promised her I'd be the one to pull the trigger."

"Hello." Benson waved from the corner. "Law enforcement officer here. Let's not have any threats or admissions in front of a witness that I might be forced to report."

"You open your mouth and it will be you in this ice box," Zane said evenly. "And you won't look so pretty. How's that for a threat?"

"As far as threats go, it has a certain deterrent factor that I can't ignore," Benson said dryly. "What do you want me to do with the body?"

"He was a Sinner and he died a Jack. He's dead to us. Do whatever the fuck you want." Jagger grabbed the pathologist's clipboard and scrawled a name on it. "That's his real name. Don't know if he's got any family, but if so, you can tell them he still owes us a debt."

"That's hardly fair—"

Jagger cut Benson off with a scowl. "When we choose this life, we choose it for our families, too. If he wasn't prepared to take that risk, he never should have joined the club."

Zane handed an envelope to the pathologist on their way out. Small payments to the local businesses smoothed the way for the Sinners to get things done quickly and quietly. Benson would get his envelope at the end of the month since he was now on a permanent Sinner retainer.

Shooter and Gunner were waiting curbside beside the bikes. Zane insisted on a security detail for Jagger whenever he left the clubhouse, but pride meant Jagger would accept their presence only on the pretense they were there to watch the bikes. Zane briefed them about Axle while Jagger called Arianne. Axle had threatened her life on more than one occasion and Jagger had promised her justice. Now, he owed her an apology.

Zane caught the reflection of sun in a mirror as he waited for Jagger to finish his call. The skin on the back of his neck prickled. What the hell? It was probably just a reflection from the vehicle behind the Jeep parked across the street, but the angle was wrong, and with the war on, they couldn't be too careful. Especially not with the Sinner president out in the open and only three brothers to guard him. He'd tried to dissuade Jagger from coming out to the morgue, but Jagger wasn't the type of man to sit still when there were things to be done.

"Gun. Shooter. Stay with Jagger. I'm just gonna check something out."

"Get back, sir!" Shooter whipped his weapon from beneath his cut and slammed Jagger in the chest with his arm in an attempt to push him back from what he clearly assumed was an unseen threat to the president's life.

"Christ, Shooter. I'm on the fucking phone." Jagger shoved his arm away.

Damn overzealous prospect was in for one hell of a

beating when they got back to the clubhouse. No one touched the president, and especially not a prospect who hadn't even earned the right to wear a Sinner patch.

Zane crossed the street to the fading cacophony of curses and Gunner's sharp admonishments. He kept to the grassy verge of the sidewalk, and beneath the trees along the edge of the park that fronted the morgue. He made his way past the Jeep, and stopped when he saw a biker between two parked cars, peering out into the street, his Black Jack patch on display.

Son of a bitch. Zane withdrew his weapon and bit back a growl. Conundrum was Sinner turf. Black Jacks were not just unwelcome, but risked death if they chose to cross the border. He aimed his weapon, a Sig Sauer P226, just as the biker leaned back in his seat, giving Zane a clear view of the top rocker on his cut, "Property of Viper."

Well damn. Not a he, but a she. Viper's old lady. Had she come to see the body or was she watching the Sinners? Not that it mattered. Aside from Viper himself, or one of the Black Jack executive board members, there was no greater prize.

With his weapon aimed and ready, he came up behind her bike, then veered slightly to the side. He tensed, then lunged, wrapping one arm around her throat while he pressed the gun to her head.

"Don't move, princess."

She stiffened, pressing her head against his chest to relieve the pressure on her throat. When she looked up, her soft brown eyes pleading, Zane's stomach twisted. She was younger than he thought, early twenties if he had to guess, and pretty, if you liked long, platinum blonde hair and a truckload of makeup. Young for Viper, who had to be in his late forties, too young to be taken prisoner, but he'd made his decision and damned if he would go back on it.

"Off the bike. Nice and slow. Hands out front where I can see them."

She complied with his instructions, her body shaking,

but she didn't put up a fight and minutes later he had her in front of Jagger.

Jagger looked down at the prisoner, bemused. "What's this?"

"Present from Viper. Looks like he sent us his old lady." Zane released her throat, but kept his gun to her head while Gun called the clubhouse for transport.

"Welcome to Conundrum, love." Jagger grinned.

Her face paled when she saw Jagger's "president" patch, but damned if she stood her ground. "I was on my way to see my sister in Hardin. Took a wrong turn. Didn't mean to wind up here."

"But you did and it would be bad manners if we didn't offer you some hospitality, Sinner style." Zane led her into the alley beside the morgue to wait for the cage. Gunner patted her down. As expected, she was armed—two guns, three knives, and a throwing star—Viper's old lady was no shrinking violet and she knew better than to scream for the police..

"So . . . " Zane stared at the patch on her cut. "Doreen. You're Viper's old lady." A statement, not a question, and not something she could deny since she wore Viper's patch on her back.

"What if I am?" She looked up at him and glared. "You think you can use me as bait? Do you really think Viper is the kind of man to care about a fuck toy?"

"He gave you his patch. Makes you more than his fuck toy."

"You don't know shit about me or Viper." Doreen morphed from helpless young woman into hard biker bitch in a heartbeat. "Just do what you're going to do. I'm tired of yapping with you morons."

Jagger grabbed a fistful of her hair and yanked her head back. "Respect, love. You're in Sinner territory now. I'm not inclined to hurt a woman, but Zane here—"

"Yeah, I know about him." She cut Jagger off and turned to face Zane. "You're the one who shot Axle in the leg up in Whitefish. And I know you're after Viper's girl. Axle saw you together before he . . ." She choked up and looked away, a strange reaction given she was Viper's old lady.

"The cut says *you're* Viper's girl." Jagger's lips twisted in a smile. "Or has he started a harem?"

"I'm payment for Axle's debts. So whatever you think you're going to get outta holding me, it's not going to happen. He won't give a damn. And the only man who did is lying in that morgue."

Zane and Jagger shared a glance, and Zane frowned. "You were Axle's old lady?"

"Went to pay my respects to my old man and you damn Sinners snatched me." Tears welled up in her eyes. "Viper will kill me if he finds out I came here. So if you take me, do me a favor and kill me. Don't leave me to his mercy."

Zane's mind whirled as he tried to put the pieces together. Was she talking about Evie? Was Viper the reason Evie couldn't see him tonight? Or was Doreen talking about one of the other women he'd seen over the past week? Damned if he could keep track. "What girl are you talking about? I got lots of girls."

"I'm sure you do, looking the way you look," Doreen said. "But that information will cost you. I want to see Axle before they take him away. I want to say goodbye."

Jesus Christ. The bitch had balls of steel. "Not gonna happen."

"Then I guess you gotta call up all the girls you've been with and ask them if they've got the hots for Viper. Or you could just wait for Viper to take you out, 'cause he knows you touched her, and he doesn't like anyone messing with his property."

His property? But how could Evie be with Viper? He was the antithesis of everything Evie stood for—a normal, comfortable civilian life. It made no sense. She had her son and a job and a life in Conundrum. From what he could see, she was happy. No way would Evie go out with an outlaw biker. Or was she still after the adrenaline rush she'd used to fill the emptiness in her life?

"Well then he'll be happy to pay to see your pretty face again." Zane folded his arms and leaned against the brick wall. The alley had the same sickly sweet disinfectant scent of the morgue, and his nose wrinkled. Death definitely had a smell. "How about you give us some more information about this woman I have that Viper wants, and I'll give you my word you'll make it through this alive?"

"Viper gave me his word, too." Her bottom lip trembled, belying her bravado. "He said he'd let me go after Axle died. Instead I got this cut and the pleasure of being chained to his bed."

Zane smoothed his face, hiding his surprise. An old lady cut was akin to a civilian wedding ring, a sign of commitment, not bondage. "I've never broken my word."

She studied him intently and then she smirked. "The redhead from Big Bill's shop. Only reason I came to Conundrum today is because Viper is away tonight. He's meeting her at a bar in Red River, since he can't come into town."

He didn't need to look at Jagger. They'd been through this drill before. Protecting Evie. It was what they had always done. "Jag, you got Evie's number?"

"I'm on it." Jagger bashed the screen on his phone, waited. "No answer."

"I'll head out to Red River." He walked down the alley, his heart thudding in his chest. Evie and Viper. Christ. And he'd thought Mark was no good for her.

"Gun can take over here. I'll go check Evie's house." Jagger hesitated, called out. "Zane . . . she might not be happy to see us."

Zane kept walking. "She never was, but we saved her anyway."

★ EIGHT ★

Things are going to go wrong when you're dealing with complex machinery. Don't give up. Just do a better job each time you try.
—SINNER'S TRIBE MOTORCYCLE REPAIR MANUAL

"Well, look at you." Connie looked over her shoulder from her seat on Evie's couch and put down her video game controller. Beside her, Ty groaned.

"You're dead. Now I have to reset."

Evie grimaced at Connie's slow perusal of her date-night outfit, a sleeveless black sheath dress that buttoned up the back, knee-high boots, a silver chain belt, and chunky silver earrings. The neckline of the dress dipped low, but not too low, showing only a hint of cleavage.

"Nice with a naughty twist," Connie concluded. "Old Vipe's gonna have a heart attack when he sees you. But then that's the problem with dating an old man."

"He's in his mid-forties. That's not old. He was in his late teens when his daughter, Arianne, was born. Same age as I was when I had Ty." She straightened a pile of magazines on the glass table behind the couch. She and Ty had chosen glass and beige leather when they decorated the living room to brighten up the small space. Ty had picked out a few shaggy beige cushions and a matching area rug that were a nightmare to clean, but he said they reminded him of the sheep from his favorite video game, and she didn't have the heart to refuse.

"Maybe he's after you because he's having a midlife crisis." Connie picked up her controller, turning her focus to the screen. "Although what do bikers do when they have a midlife crisis? They already have the young girls, fast cars, and hot bikes. Maybe they buy a minivan and waist-high jeans, slip on some socks and sandals, get an office job, and start mowing the lawn."

"You're dead again, Connie." Ty fist pumped the air. "You want to start again or play something else?"

Connie stood and ruffled his hair. "How about a board game? You know about those things? From the prehistoric age? They don't have a controller and no one dies a painful death, especially me. Just good, clean, old fashioned fun."

"I think I've got one of those."

"Now who's sounding old?" Evie laughed as Ty raced to his room.

"Wish I was coming along on your date," Connie said wistfully. "My dry spell is getting drier every day and I'm guessing Vipe's not gonna show without his mouthwatering biker posse to keep him safe. Maybe I could have some Black Jack fun. Although Tank was kinda cute. And he gave me his number."

"I might end it with him tonight," Evie said, fiddling with the links in her belt. "That's why I picked this dress. I thought maybe he'd change his mind about me. I like him, but the whole shooting thing outside the shop scared me. And Zane . . . I mean it's over between us, but if he's going to be part of Ty's life, things could get complicated since they're from rival clubs. I just don't know what to do."

"If you were going for the matronly look, you haven't succeeded. You'd look hot wearing a burlap sack." Connie lifted an over-tweezed eyebrow. "And do you really think a man like Viper hasn't already figured out what you've got going under that dress? Or that he isn't interested when he sends one of his men to set up a date? If you don't want to see him anymore, you'll need to tell him flat out, otherwise I don't think he'll be turned off by the way your boobs are busting out all over the place."

Evie glanced over at the hallway leading to Ty's room and lowered her voice. "They aren't busting out."

"Honey, if I flipped a coin at your chest, it would definitely get stuck between your girls. With me, on the other hand, that baby would sail right through my nonexistent cleavage, bounce off the floor, and come up and hit me in the chin."

"Now I think I'm too dressed up." Evie sighed. "I've never been to the Riverside Bar. What if it's a rough, dress-down kind of place?"

Connie put a hand on her hip and sashayed toward the door. "I think you should work it. If you decide you want him, he'll be drooling all over the floor. If you don't want him, he'll never forget you. Either way, you'll leave an impression. Although, I have to say, the couple of times he came into the shop, he didn't strike me as a man who took 'I don't want to see you any more' for an answer. And since you're not interested in getting involved with Zane again, he's your best option for getting a little biker down 'n dirty."

And wasn't that part of the reason Evie had agreed to see him the first time? After years of dealing with Mark's insecurities, there was something utterly compelling about a man who dripped power and confidence. She had been flattered by his attention, intrigued by his charm, and slightly awed by the fact he had so many men to do his bidding.

A tiny part of her had thrilled at having captured his interest, and there was no danger of getting caught in the trap of thinking her relationship with Viper was anything more than a fling. Viper was a statement to herself that she'd gotten over the emotional abandonment issues that had driven her to seek safety and security with Mark despite knowing he was wrong for her. She could look after herself, face the world on her own terms. And what better way to prove it than to play with the biggest baddest biker in town?

But that was before Zane returned. He was everything that had attracted her to Viper, but without the ruthless edge. Where Jagger and Viper wore their power for all to see, Zane commanded respect without the show. She'd seen how his biker brothers deferred to him, and how even Jagger looked to him for advice. Not that she wanted to get involved with Zane. Even though she now knew he'd returned to Stanton, he was three years too late, and he wasn't there when she needed him. But more than that, he had broken her heart.

In his own way, Zane was as dangerous as Viper, and his very presence cast Viper in a new light.

"It's not like we're in a real relationship." She pulled out the elastic from her ponytail and ran her fingers through her hair. "We don't text or talk to each other every day. We haven't slept together . . . just kissed." Perfectly adequate kisses, considering the scratchy beard, the rough lips, and the fact he always seemed amused when he backed away.

"Then he'll be all over you tonight." Connie smirked. "Biker presidents aren't known for their restraint. He probably didn't know how to handle a civilian at first. Better bring some condoms 'cause I'll bet he'll be wanting more than a kiss tonight."

Viper's kiss. So unlike Zane's kiss.

Oh, God. That kiss. Fueled by desire, filled with passion, Zane's kiss had been deliciously hard and hungry. He had taken everything she had to give and demanded more. After her shower this morning, Evie had inspected the bruises he left on her skin, remembering how it felt to be held tight, totally and utterly claimed, if only for a moment. The spark was still there between them, but now, when her heart had finally healed and she had moved on with her life, he wasn't the right guy for her. She couldn't control a man like Zane. Or maybe the problem was that she couldn't control herself around him.

So maybe she was better with second best.

A loud knock on the front door startled her and she peered out the window into the twilight, spotting the motorcycle parked on the street only seconds before Jagger shouted from outside.

"Evie. It's Jagger. Gotta talk to you."

She pulled open the door and he brushed past her, stalking into the house before she could speak.

"You with Viper, Evie? Is it true?" His gaze traveled down her body, taking in her outfit, and he scowled. "That where you're going tonight? You're meeting the fucking president of the fucking Black Jacks?"

Evie closed the door, taking a minute to compose herself before she whirled around. "Not that it's any of your damn business, but yes."

"Jesus Christ." He scrubbed his hand over his face. "All those bastards we saved you from in high school, and you've still going for the most dangerous fucking scum of the earth. Except Viper's not just dangerous. He's lethal. He'll fucking chew you up and spit you out if he doesn't kill you first."

"Don't patronize me, Jagger." She folded her arms and leaned against the door, her cheeks heating in anger, only vaguely aware of Connie in the hallway behind her. "I'm a grown woman now and I'm perfectly capable of looking after myself. I know who Viper is and he's never been anything but kind to me."

"Kind?" Jagger's lips curled in disgust. "Kind is not in Viper's vocabulary. Zane's gonna go out of his fucking mind when he finds out that Black Jack bitch wasn't lying." He pulled out his phone but before he could type out his text, his eyes widened, and his mouth dropped open in a manner unbecoming an outlaw biker president. "Holy. Fucking. Shit."

Evie didn't need to turn around to know the reason for his outburst, and it was too late to undo what had been done. Damn. She wasn't ready for this. The timing was off. She hadn't prepared or even thought about what to say. And really, Zane should have been the first to know.

"Hell, Evie. Tell me he isn't—"

"He is." She held out her hand to her son. "Ty. This is mom's friend, Jagger. And Jagger, this is Ty."

"Jesus Christ." Jagger ran a hand through his hair. "He looks just like him."

"He swears," Ty said with delight. "Just like a real biker." He ran to the kitchen and returned with the glass jar Evie had designated as their swear jar to curb the bad language Ty was learning at school. "You owe four quarters. Or does Jesus Christ count as two swears?"

"Ty!"

"I was just saying what he said."

"Hey, Ty. How about we go find that board game so mom and her friend can talk." Connie took the jar from Ty and led him down the hallway to the bedroom.

Jagger let out a long breath and then sat heavily on the couch, taking up the bulk of the space with the vast spread of his long legs. "Zane doesn't know, does he?"

"He left Stanton before I even knew I was pregnant." Evie sagged against the wall. "He told me he would come for me. And when I found out about the baby, I tried to find him. I didn't believe he killed my dad like everyone said. I waited, kept trying to find him, but after a while I lost faith. He's still wanted by the police, Jagger. There's a warrant out for his arrest."

Jagger leaned forward on the couch, dropping his hands between his legs. "I know about the warrant. He told me about it when he joined the club because he was worried it would come back on the MC. He had changed his last name, got fake ID, grew his hair. I didn't give a damn. I know Zane and I didn't need the details. Neither did the brothers. The club protects him now."

Evie sighed and twisted a loose strand of hair around her finger. "No wonder I couldn't find him. I tried everything, even got child services involved on the basis he wasn't paying child support just because I thought they'd have more resources to track him down. Then my mom died and I was so alone. I had to sell the house to cover the debts. I was struggling, and I had to accept that Zane wasn't coming back. Then I bumped into Mark."

She didn't tell him the rest—Mark's insecurities and controlling behavior, the drinking, the affairs, the money problems, and the night she finally had enough—not just because she knew it would anger Jagger, but because she was embarrassed that she'd stayed so long.

Jagger shifted on the couch. "You have to tell him, Evie."

Her mouth opened then closed again. Yes, she had to tell him, and if Ty got hurt, she would help him through it and they would move on. But now that she'd spent more time with Zane, she wondered if that was really a concern. He'd been outraged at the thought Mark hadn't been there for his son . . .

"Evie." Jagger's deep voice echoed in the small space.

"Yes, of course. I just . . . I want it to be right. I've been worried Zane wouldn't want to be involved and I don't want Ty to get hurt."

"You think he wouldn't want to be involved? That's his son." Jagger stood and paced the room. "All these years he's been talking about a woman who betrayed him, a woman who broke his heart—although he never said it in so many words. I never imagined it was you. I never even thought you and he . . . I thought we were all just friends."

"We were. At least until that one night when Zane and I suddenly realized we were more." She bit her lip, her forehead creasing in worry. "Do you think he'll want to be a part of Ty's life? I mean, you guys don't really live a family-friendly lifestyle."

"Do you really need to ask that question?" Jagger's

voice thickened. "Despite the shit he went through at home, he was always there for us. He even dragged me out of bed one night to rescue you from that heavy metal guitar player who lured you to his trailer . . . Derek. Zane called him Derek the Dick."

Evie's stomach tightened at the memory. Derek had been wild and exciting, irreverent and cool. All the girls in high school wanted the talented frontman and he picked her. She hadn't even stopped to think what might happen in that trailer after the concert when Derek invited her to join him and the rest of the band. But, of course, Zane had known and he came to her rescue.

"Zane flew across the ocean using a fake passport to save me," Jagger continued. "Even though he was wanted by the police. I was dying in a fucking hospital bed and he came to give me a kick in the ass so I would get on with my life. He's had my back since the day we met. There is no man I trust more than Zane. No man more loyal. And once he finds out about Ty, nothing will tear him away."

"I don't know if I want Ty involved in your life, Jagger. It's dangerous."

Jagger pulled out his phone. "It's too late to make that choice. He is involved because Zane is involved. You know my views, but I won't push you. Do I tell Zane you're safe and arrange to meet him at the clubhouse, or do I tell him to come here?"

"Mom?" Ty appeared in the hallway. "Can I play my game again?"

Evie smiled at Ty, the spitting image of his father, and let out a ragged breath. "Tell him to come. I'll get Ty ready."

Hope was his friend once more.

Zane pulled up in front of Evie's house and nodded to Shooter and Tank, keeping watch as he'd instructed while their president was inside. He'd been at the far edge of town when he got Jagger's message that Evie was safe at home.

He dismounted his bike, wondering what he was going to say. This wasn't high school. He couldn't grab Viper in the locker room and threaten to dismember him if he went near Evie again. He couldn't stop Evie from seeing him if that's what she wanted to do. Hell, he didn't really know her any more. He didn't know if she still preferred running outdoors to spending time in the gym. He had no idea if she still liked her pizza with anchovies and olives, or if she liked pizza at all. What did she do when she wasn't at work? How did she look after her boy alone? How often did Mark show up to see him? Why the hell *had* she married Mark, and what the fuck was she doing with Viper?

The door opened before he could knock, and Jagger blocked his way. "Brother . . ." He hesitated, his face a curious mix of sympathy and pain. "I'm not goin' anywhere. I'll be right outside. You need me, I'm here. You need to ride, we'll ride." He gestured behind him and Connie slipped past, giving Zane a wan smile.

"Hey, there, biker boy. You got a surprise waiting inside for you."

Zane's skin prickled as Jagger followed her onto the porch. "What the fuck is going on?"

When nobody answered, he entered the house, slamming the door behind him. "Evie?"

"Is that him, mom?"

His gaze fell on the young boy in front of Evie. He looked to be about seven or eight years old, his dark hair long enough to cover part of his face. Evie had her hands on his thin shoulders and he was staring at Zane, his dark eyes curious.

"Ty, this is Zane. He's your . . . dad." She looked up and swallowed. "Zane. This is your son . . . Ty."

His.

Son.

The words hit him in the gut like a goddamned sledgehammer, knocking the air from his lungs.

"He's eight years old," she said in a rush, as if he might not believe her. "His birthday is in June."

But he had no doubt Evie was telling the truth. He could see the similarities, from Ty's dark eyes to his lightly tanned skin, and from his overlong brown hair to the sharp planes and angles of the boy's face.

That night—the one perfect night in his life—had produced this perfect child.

He opened his mouth, but words failed him. Caught in a maelstrom of emotion, he fought an internal battle against his instinct to walk out the door, jump on his bike, and ride until he ran out of road. He needed time to come to terms with what he'd just heard. Who he was looking at now.

He had a son.

With Evie.

And he'd left them.

Regret stabbed him in the gut, a pain so sharp he dropped to his knees. Not only had he left them, but when he'd returned and saw her with Mark . . . saw his son . . . he'd jumped to a conclusion that had cost him another five years. Jesus H. Christ. To think another man had looked after his boy, and all it would have taken was a word. A step.

Faith.

"Why isn't he talking to me?" Ty's voice wavered and he looked back at Evie. "Doesn't he like me? Doesn't he want to be my dad?"

Did he want to be a dad? It would be so easy to turn and run, just like he'd done in Stanton. He could leave all this behind—leave them behind—return to the club. Hell, half the Sinner brothers had kids they didn't see. He could get back to doing what he'd done before.

Searching. Hiding in the shadows. Longing.

"He . . ." Her voice wavered with uncertainty. "He's just so happy to see you, he doesn't know what to say."

"Hey." Zane had no other words. What did a man say to the son he never knew he had?

Ty studied him in silence and then tilted his head to the side? "Are you my real dad?"

"Seems like."

No wonder Evie never made it to college to pursue her dream of getting a Fine Arts degree. Alone, with a baby to look after, her parents dead, waiting for him to return . . .

He bowed under the crushing weight of guilt at having doubted her all these years. How long had he expected her to wait for him? She'd been alone.

So goddamned alone.

"So you're a biker?" Ty asked.

"Yeah."

"A real biker? Like, is that your job or do you just ride for fun?"

Zane sucked in his lips, considering. He'd never thought about the club in those terms, but he'd always known it was where he was meant to be. "It's my life."

"Cool. Can I ride your bike?"

"A biker doesn't let—" *Fuck it.* This was his son. And his son wanted to sit on his bike. "Yeah, you can sit on my bike."

"What kind of bike do you have? I love motorcycles. I have a whole collection. I'll show you." Ty ran off before Zane could answer his question, returning only moments later with an ice cream pail filled with toy bikes. He placed them one at a time on the coffee table and Zane bent down to help while Evie perched on the arm of the couch, watching them.

"You got a lot of foreign bikes here." Zane grimaced as Ty pulled out a miniature Kawasaki Ninja ZX-10R. A real biker only rides American. Harleys."

"I have Harleys." Ty fished around in the pail. "I have a silver V-Rod, and a black Springer Heritage, and a red Electra Ultra Glide, and I've got the whole Series 28 and 31 Harley Davidson collections, and for my birthday, mom got me the Sons of Anarchy collection, except it only has three bikes in it, not six like the others."

"You got a Night Rod Special? That's what I ride."

Ty shook his head. "Will you buy me one?"

"Ty!" Evie shot him an admonishing glance. "We don't ask people for presents. It's not polite."

"I'm not people," Zane snapped, surprising even himself at the vehemence in his tone. "I'm his dad. I'm buying him a bike. I'll take him to the toy store and we'll buy all the goddam bikes they got."

He knew he'd spoken too abruptly when Evie startled. But fuck it. He'd missed out on eight years of his son's life. Eight years of buying him toys and all the shit Zane had wanted growing up but could never have. Eight years of being a dad.

"Why did you leave us?" Ty's voice broke his train of thought, and Zane's mouth went dry.

Ah. The kicker. But how could he tell his son he'd left because he thought Evie's father was right about him? He wasn't worthy. He was nothing and had come from nothing. He knew the cops wouldn't believe the truth, and he'd been afraid—so afraid—Evie wouldn't believe him either. But more than that, he left to spare Evie the heartbreak of discovering her father wasn't the hero she thought he was.

"I didn't know about you. If I had, I never would have left."

Ty brushed his hair back. "But you left Mom."

Damn. This was worse than an interrogation with Dax. "Hardest thing I ever did in my life." Biggest regret he ever had.

"Where's your bike?"

Zane stared at his son, his mind trying to keep up with the abrupt change of track. Here he'd exposed his soul, spoken a truth he had never admitted to anyone, and Ty brushed it off to ask about his bike.

His son. The words rolled around in his mind, fresh and new, words he had never even contemplated being able to say. He'd never considered a future with children because he had never considered a future with any woman except Evie.

"It's outside. You want to see it?"

Ty looked back at Evie and she shook her head. "I have to get going and Connie's going to put you to bed. Maybe another time."

"Zane says it's okay." His bottom lip trembled and Zane felt no small amount of pride in the fact his son was already pitting his parents against each other. Did he know eight missed years led to a whole lot of guilt and guilt would buy him pretty much anything he wanted from his old man?

Although the burden of those eight years could have been one week lighter if Evie had told him when they first met again. Or had she not intended to tell him and Jagger forced her hand? He fought back a flare of resentment. Now was not the time.

"Your mom said no, and she's the person who looks after you." Zane pushed himself to his feet. "That means you gotta do what she says."

"But you're my dad. You have to look after me, too. What do you say?"

Hell. Were all eight-year-olds that smart? He didn't know. Hell, he knew nothing about kids and he wasn't leading a family kind of life. He was a bachelor through and through. So how the hell was he supposed to handle this? Pay the occasional visit? Show up on the weekend and take the boy to a game? He had no frame of reference, no skills, no one to guide him or tell him what to do.

"I say you gotta listen to your mother."

Ty spun around and pushed past Evie, spilling his motorcycles on the floor. "I thought you were cool, but you're just the same as Mom." He stormed into his bedroom and slammed the door.

"He just needs some time," Evie said softly. "He doesn't deal well with change and this is a lot to handle."

"I get it." More than got it. If he hadn't developed self-restraint over the years, he'd be slamming the door behind him, jumping on his bike and riding until he'd had time to process everything and clear his head. But, of course, he didn't have that luxury. Not with Evie and his son to protect.

"Why didn't you tell me when we first met?" His words came out sharper than he intended, but he couldn't hide the emotion that burned in his chest.

Evie hugged herself and leaned against the wall. "I just . . . I didn't know if you'd want him and I didn't want him to get hurt and I wasn't sure about involving him in your biker life. I was going to talk to you about him first, and then I wanted it to be perfect, a meeting in a neutral space—"

"There is no perfect." He cut her off, his hands curling into fists. "You should have told me right away. I lost even more time—"

"Don't take out your guilt on me," she snapped. "You're the one who left. You're the one who decided to drop off the face of the earth. You're the one who came back and assumed Ty was Mark's son."

Zane turned and smashed his fist into the wall, making the cheap bungalow shake. "And you were the one who jumped into bed with the first man who crossed your path." He regretted the words the moment they dropped from his lips and tried to soften the blow. "I get that you were alone, but I have never broken a promise. I came back, Evie." His voice caught as his emotion spilled over. "Fuck. I came back."

And then she was pressed up against him, holding him tight, soothing his pain just as she had done the day they met. "I know you did."

They stood in silence and he buried his face in her hair, breathing in the familiar floral scent, wishing he could turn back the clock and live his life all over again.

"What are you going to do?" she murmured against his chest. "Do you want to . . . are you going to be around for him?"

"He's my boy." Why would she ask that question? Did she honestly think he would walk away again? Did she think he'd leave his son without a father?

"I got lots of money," he continued. "Anything you need—"

Evie pulled away, frowning. "I don't want your money. We do okay."

"You don't do okay." Overwhelmed by his feelings, and unable to get it together, he raised his voice and struggled against a tidal wave of guilt. "Living near a trailer park at the edge of town and driving a shit vehicle that's about to fall apart is not okay. Working in a shop that's almost all guys, with bikers coming in and out all the time, and a boss who goes missing when the Jacks show up—which should be a warning to you—is not okay." Everything he'd held inside since the moment he saw Ty erupted in a burst of concerned anger. "I want my boy to have what you had—a nice house with a big yard in some leafy suburb where everyone is decent—"

"Like my mother?" Her face tightened. "You know that's all an illusion. Good people and bad people are everywhere, Zane. It doesn't matter whether there are nice cars in the driveways, or trees on the street. Sometimes the worst people can be found in the nicest homes."

"And worse people can be found in the worst homes," he responded. "And the fucking scum-of-the-earth, cocksucking murderous bastards of the world can be found in Red River where you are definitely not going tonight. You and Viper. That's over." His body shook as he drowned in a maelstrom of fear, anger and regret. "I'll buy you and Ty a house somewhere nice where you can meet nice people. And I'll buy you a decent car. Something safe. And Ty can have all the toy motorcycles he wants."

She twisted her hair around her finger and glared. "And then what? You're going to go back to your biker life? How does that work? Gunfight in the morning; baseball in the afternoon? Lock Evie up in the kitchen so she doesn't date men you don't like?"

"I gotta figure it out." He didn't know what else to say, or what to do, his emotions still trying to play catch-up with his mind. He couldn't think beyond the next hour, much less the future.

"Figure this out." She poked him in the chest. "You can't just walk into our lives and change everything you don't like. Ty goes to school in this neighborhood. He has friends here. You want to buy him hundreds of toy motorcycles, but where will he put them? What kind of values does that teach him? I totally understand you want to make up for lost time. And I want you to spend time with him. But we need to talk about what's best for him, and how we go about making this work. And part of that is you not telling me how to live my life. I'm going out tonight. With Viper. And there's nothing you can do about it."

Like fuck there wasn't.

If that's how she wanted to play it, he'd let her go.

But no way in hell was she going alone.

★ NINE ★

Don't sweat it if you break something.
You can always get another part.
—SINNER'S TRIBE MOTORCYCLE REPAIR MANUAL

Evie pulled open the heavy wooden door to the Riverside Bar and stepped inside, the warm air instantly thawing the chill from her skin. Too bad it couldn't thaw her all the way through. How could she be here after what happened with Zane? She felt too raw, as if her deepest secrets had been exposed to the light.

And yet, how could she not be here? Zane had to understand that being part of Ty's life didn't mean he was part of her life. And there was no better way to drive that message home than to go through with her date as planned.

Still, her enthusiasm for meeting up with Viper had diminished over the course of the drive. Did she really want to keep seeing Viper when all she'd been able to think about over the last week was Zane? Especially since he was the rival of a member club.

She smoothed down her dress, wished she'd worn her jeans. Riverside was so not a dress-up bar. If she'd walked in any other night, she would have turned around and walked right out. Rough didn't begin to describe the customers—mostly bikers, a few skinheads, shifty looking guys in shiny suit jackets—Zane would have a fit if he saw her here. He'd probably throw her over his shoulder and stalk out the door.

A smile teased the corner of her lips. Now wouldn't that be hot in a totally primal kind of way.

The bar was bigger than it appeared from the outside, with a small stage in the far corner, and a sea of tables between the front door and the bar. Warm air, scented with yeast and the distinct tang of chicken wings, engulfed her as she made her way through the crowd looking for Viper.

"Nice to see you again, kitten." He came up behind her, his voice a warm rumble in her ear. "You look lovely as always." Viper's warm hand slid around her middle and he pulled her into his chest, his lips brushing over her ear. "Good enough to eat."

"I didn't see you hiding in the shadows." She looked back over her shoulder and Viper laughed.

"I live in the shadows. No one ever sees me coming." He led her to a table in the back corner, guarded by four of the scariest bikers she'd ever seen. Clearly none of them had ever used a razor or had a haircut, judging from their full beards and long ponytails. But then who was going to complain given their height, the breadth of their shoulders, and their massively muscled chests and arms.

And yet, for all that Viper didn't have their bulk, he was no less imposing. His arms were thick with ropey muscles and covered in colorful tattoos. His cut, worn and heavy with patches sat on broad shoulders and covered a barrel chest. He had trimmed his salt-and-pepper beard since she had last seen him, and tied his long hair in a ponytail. His broad face, weathered and scarred, was distinguished, rather than handsome, and he wore six rings on his fingers, the largest, a snake's head with ruby eyes.

"My bodyguards." Viper answered her silent question as he pulled out Evie's chair.

"I think just one of them could take out everyone in the bar," she whispered. "Much less four."

"Actually there are six." Viper winked as he sat beside her.

Evie toyed with the handle of her purse. "I didn't know you were being threatened. You've never brought them before."

"Circumstances have changed." He covered her hand, drew it away from her purse, and slipped something into her palm.

"What's this?" Evie stared at the key fob in her hand.

"You can't ride around in that piece of junk you call a vehicle." He slid his hand into her purse and fumbled around.

"Hey . . ."

"Your vehicle isn't safe." Viper pulled out her keys and tossed them to the nearest bodyguard who caught them neatly with one hand. "I bought you something new and worthy of a woman associated with the Black Jacks."

"You bought me a car?" She stared at him in shock.

"Not just a car. A Mazda MX5."

"I can't accept this. I want my keys back." She offered the key back to him, but he shook his head.

"It's a gift. You can't return it. But you can thank me for it." He dropped his hand to her thigh under the table and Evie sucked in a sharp breath. Viper had never been sexually aggressive before, and his sudden change in demeanor disconcerted her even more than the flippant way he dismissed her protest.

"Vip—"

"You can start with a kiss."

"Here?" She looked around the crowded bar, her gaze flicking to the band only ten feet away, now warming up with a few guitar riffs.

"Here. Now." He slid his hand beneath her hair to cup her neck, pulling her forward. "I want a taste of those sweet lips, kitten. Show me your gratitude." His hand slid higher on her thigh, pushing up her dress. Uncertain whether the pounding in her heart was from arousal or fear, she tried to pull away, but Viper tightened his grip.

"One kiss. Is that so much to ask? Or have you been teasing me all this time?"

Teasing? She'd been annoyed he only wanted a kiss. So what had changed? Why did the thought of that bristly beard brushing against her skin set her teeth on edge? Or maybe she was just overthinking. Only one way to find out.

"Okay. Just one kiss. I'm not that comfortable with public displays of affection."

"That's not what I heard."

Before she could ask what he meant, he pulled her toward him and sealed his mouth over hers. A shudder ran through Evie's body, and she tried not to wrinkle her nose as his beard rasped over her skin. Cold, hard lips forced her mouth open, and when he thrust his thick tongue past her teeth, she almost gagged at his milky taste. When he finally pulled away, she was almost overwhelmed with the desire to brush her teeth.

"Damn you've got a soft little mouth." He rubbed his thumb over her bottom lip, making her think of a school visit to a local farm where the farmer had pried back a horse's lips to show off its teeth.

The first few notes of the band's "The Edge of Darkness" cover, drowned out the chatter of the crowd. Viper sent one of his bodyguards for drinks, then hooked his boot around the front leg of her chair and dragged her closer, throwing an arm around her shoulders. "Good cover band. They always start off with Iron Maiden." He gave her a wink and a self-satisfied smile. "After they're done we can pick up where we left off."

Her eyes flicked to the door and a shiver licked up her spine. This wasn't the Viper she knew, charming, teasing, and flirtatious. Tonight, he exuded a subtle, threatening sense of power that rattled her more than she cared to admit. She felt no excitement at the prospect of picking up where they let off, no thrill of desire. Instead, for the first time since she met Viper, she felt an uncomfortable sense of wariness.

The band played. Evie sipped her cooler. Viper downed his whiskey in one gulp, then peppered her with questions about the shop and her work. He asked for her opinion on the sexual escapades of her favorite radio show host, and lamented the governor's latest stance on crime. Although his body language appeared relaxed, and his conversation witty and entertaining, she sensed anger simmering beneath his skin, and lust, barely contained.

"Call your babysitter," he said, after the band announced a short break. "Tell her you won't be home tonight."

Evie's blood chilled. She'd been careful not to mention Ty, not wanting to share too much of her life until she knew where the relationship was going, to protect him if things went wrong. "How do you know I have a babysitter?"

"I know everything about you, Evangeline." He slid his hand up her thigh, his long, thick fingers brushing along the edge of her panties. "Except one, and I'm going to find out just how tight and wet your pussy is tonight."

Evie sucked in a breath and stood so abruptly, his hand slid away. "I need to use the restroom."

"Rob will go with you." He gestured to the biggest and scariest of the bikers and Evie swallowed past the lump in her throat.

"I don't need an escort. I can find the restroom on my own."

"I'm sure you can." Viper's cool, shrewd gaze chilled her to the bone. "But someone needs to protect you from the Sinners. I understand they've been following you around."

Run. Run. Run. But where would she go? Viper had taken her keys. Controlling. Just like Mark. Although Viper's need for control was clearly not the result of insecurity. Still, it had taken her years to break free and she had promised herself she would never again get into a situation where a man would control her life. Straightening her shoulders, she said, "They were looking for Axle."

"They found him this morning." His dark eyes bored into hers, challenging. "At the morgue."

She didn't take the bait, swallowed the question on the tip of her tongue simply because she didn't want to know the answer. "I'm sorry to hear that you lost one of your men. It was nice of you to come out tonight when you must be in mourning."

Viper stood, annoyance flickering across his face at the hint of sarcasm in her tone. He slid an arm around her waist and pulled her close. "Don't you think this game has gone on long enough, kitten?"

"What game?"

"The game where you pretend to be innocent and I pretend to be civilized." He leaned down and nuzzled her neck, the scrape of his beard on her sensitive skin sending a shiver down her spine.

She tried to pull away, but he slid one hand over her ass and squeezed her cheek, grinding her hips against the bulge in his jeans. "I've been patient. I've played the civilian game, and I have to admit it was entertaining. But we both know where this is heading, and now that the Sinners are sniffing around you, I can't wait any more to stake my claim."

Evie bristled, fear warring with indignation. "I'm not a piece of land."

"But you are a piece of pussy." He fisted her hair and yanked her head back, his lips, wet and cold, sliming a trail across her cheek.

Evie raised her hand to slap him. Lightning fast, Viper grabbed her wrist, twisted it, and wrenched her arm up behind her.

"Jesus Fuck," he growled under his breath. "Why did you have to do that? I can't tolerate disrespect, especially in front of my men."

"What's wrong with you?" Anger surged within her. "Why are you acting like this?"

"Did you think I wouldn't find out about you and the Sinner VP?" Viper tightened his grip, forcing her up on her toes. "I don't want to hurt you kitten, but I had you first, and I am not a sharing kind of man."

"Let go." She struggled to hide her fear, taking deep breaths to keep her voice even. "You're hurting me."

"If you want to play around with a Sinner, and disrespect me in front of my men, you gotta pay the price. What's a little pain, kitten, when I'm going to give you a whole lot of pleasure?"

His heated words were followed by the scrape of chairs and the pounding of feet. As the people seated around them moved to the far end of the bar, the bouncers approached, only to come up against a solid wall of Black Jack muscle.

"I'm not playing games with you," Evie gritted out. "I'm not with Zane. I grew up with him. I hadn't seen him for nine years until the night Axle came to bring your message. What Axle saw . . . I didn't want that."

Viper loosened his hold on her hair, and gripped her jaw, forcing her to meet his stony gaze. "You grew up with him?"

"In Stanton. But we lost touch after high school. I didn't even know he was in Conundrum."

His dark eyes bored into her as if searching for the truth. But she had nothing to hide. Well, except for Zane's relationship to Ty. Still, she met his cold, hard stare full-on, although she trembled inside. Zane had been angry about Ty, but she knew in her heart he would never hurt her. She couldn't say the same about Viper.

"You know why I like you, Evangeline?" His voice lost its edge, becoming smooth and sickly sweet like her mother's bourbon.

"No."

"Because you're honest and you can't lie for shit." He released her arm, one hand snaking up her back to her hair, the other firm around her waist. "You aren't like the deceitful, conniving bitches I got at my club. You aren't jaded from living an outlaw life where every day is a struggle to survive. I believe you."

Her body sagged with relief. "Then let me go because you're scaring me."

Viper laughed and tugged her head back. "You wouldn't be out with me if you didn't like it a little rough. You know how many women I've asked out? The key word there is asked?"

She shook her head, and he ran his thumb over her lips, parting them with gentle pressure.

"None. I don't ask when it comes to women. When I want a woman to suck my dick, I push her to her knees. When I want to fuck her pussy, I spread her legs. The women in my club will do whatever I tell them to do because I own them. But Black Jack women are hard women and they're always wantin' something, and that makes 'em cold. You're warm. You're soft. You're sweet. You're real. You don't want anything. Me being president of the Jacks doesn't mean shit to you. Never had that before. Not willing to give it up."

He leaned down and brushed his lips over her neck. "The fact I did nothing other than twist your arm after you tried to slap me says it all." He bit down on the delicate skin between her neck and her shoulder blade, drawing it between his teeth. Evie gasped as a curious mix of pleasure and pain surged within her.

"What are you doing?"

"Thought I'd leave my mark." Something sharp and feral flashed in his eyes, and then he kissed her, his lips firm and hard. Possessive. "Just in case your Sinner trash doesn't get the message."

"Zane? Why would he—?" Her voice caught as Viper

turned her around, sliding one arm around her waist and pulling her into his chest in a gesture she didn't understand until her gaze lifted to the door.

Zane.

"Because he wants what I have." Viper nuzzled her neck and Zane's dark eyes hardened.

"Looks like you have to make a choice, kitten," he said softly. "Choose wisely."

★ TEN ★

*Repairing a bike is a long, arduous process.
You will require patience, skill, and the
proper tools. But mostly patience.*
—SINNER'S TRIBE MOTORCYCLE REPAIR MANUAL

"I'm gonna kill him."

"Hold back, brother." Jagger put out an arm to stop Zane from drawing his weapon in the middle of the crowded bar. "She came here by choice. Nobody forced her."

"Fuck, Jag. She just tried to slap him. You saw what he did to her." He shook off Jagger's arm and slid his hand into his cut.

"And then she kissed him," Jagger said, his voice cold. "She's not screaming for help, brother. Not like when we saved her from Derek the Dick."

"You're the one being a dick." He had never spoken to Jagger that way before, and if they hadn't been alone, he wouldn't have dared. But goddamnit. This was Evie. Their Evie. No. *His* Evie. The mother of his son. And she was in danger.

"Maybe you suddenly got tired of living." Jagger's hand tightened on Zane's arm. "Friend or not, you don't speak to your president that way, and your president is saying we're not taking Viper out tonight. Too many witnesses. And Benson texted to warn me the cops are on their way. Despite the disrespect, I've gotten used to having you around. You still got a warrant on your head. I don't want to see you spending the rest of your life in jail."

Zane's blood pounded in his ears so loud he could barely hear. Of all the men Evie could have chosen . . . Or maybe it wasn't a choice. Maybe Viper had forced her to go out with him. Maybe he was blackmailing her, or worse, threatening her life. There would be no other reason why she would want to be with that evil cockfucking piece of bastard slime who had to be twice her age.

As if he knew what Zane was thinking, Viper locked gazes with Zane over Evie's head and brushed his lips over her ear. It was a challenge Zane couldn't ignore.

"This is worse than the night with Derek the Dick." He closed his hand around the smooth, cool steel of his weapon. He had never understood Evie's interest in Derek, a high school dropout who fronted a heavy metal band in town. But when she'd blown him and Jagger off to go on a band road trip with Derek and his pals, he hadn't hesitated to hunt Jagger down and convince him to go after them. They'd almost been too late, and it was the first time in his life he realized he could cross a line not many would cross. Only Evie's intervention had saved Derek's life, but he spent three months in the hospital and never played guitar again.

"You think she knows he's using her as a shield?"

Viper stroked his thumb along the underside of Evie's breast, and Zane slid the gun from its holster.

"She looks mighty pissed off," Jagger said. "But I'm not sure if that's 'cause we've caught them together or because he's feeling her up in front of us."

Tables emptied around them as the bar owner and his bouncers encouraged people to make use of the back exit so they didn't get caught in the middle of a biker showdown. The band scurried off the stage. Over in the far corner, a few civilians, most likely off-duty law enforcement from their posture, fatigues, and disregard for the danger of the situation, watched with interest as Viper's body-guards fell into position behind him.

"How many brothers we got outside?"

"Five," Jagger said. "And Tank didn't see any other Jacks outside, so we're evenly matched. Your choice, brother. If you want to fight, we got your back, but put the gun away."

"You aren't fighting in my bar." A short, stocky man in a Riverside Bar T-shirt strode into the center of the bar as Zane tucked his gun into his holster. "I've already called the cops. Last time we had bikers here, I was shut down for three months. You want to have a shoot-out, take it outside."

"Not here to fight," Viper said. "Just here enjoying the music with *my girl*."

Mine. In that moment the choice became no choice. Zane couldn't stand by and watch Evie be manhandled by any man, much less Viper. He closed the distance between them in three quick strides and ripped Viper's hand away.

Although braced for the intervention of Viper's body-guards, he wasn't prepared when the biggest and ugliest brute lifted him as if he weighed nothing and tossed him across the bar.

"Fuck." Jagger yanked open the door and yelled for Sinners who had accompanied them to the Riverside Bar. "We got a fight."

"Evie. Come." Zane pushed himself to his feet, keeping some distance between him and the monolith in front of him as he held out one hand and drew his weapon with the other.

If he thought she'd throw herself sobbing into his arms with gratitude like she'd done when he saved her from Derek, her livid expression quickly dissuaded him of that notion.

"I've got this, Zane. Thanks. This isn't high school. I don't need you running to my rescue."

"You gotta respect a woman with her own mind, Sinner. She wants to be with me." Viper nuzzled her neck. "Let's go, kitten. Your new chariot awaits."

"I'm not going with you either." She twisted out of Viper's grasp. "I'm not a damn chew toy to be fought over. Give me my keys. I'm going home."

Zane saw the flash of a blade, felt the slight disturbance in the air. Adrenaline surged through his body and he mentally kicked himself for not seeing the danger. While Viper kept him distracted, he'd left Jagger unprotected and at the mercy of the bodyguards who had taken the advantage of the cleared-out bar. Viper had baited a trap and Zane had fallen right in.

With a shout of warning, he flung himself to the side. The blade sliced through the sleeve of his shirt, cutting his arm, before it deflected and hit the wall only inches from where Jagger stood.

Jagger drew his weapon just as the door slammed open and Sinners poured into the bar. T-Rex fired a warning shot at the ceiling, covering Jagger while Gunner and Sparky pulled him to safety, despite his growled protests. The club was nothing without their president, and for all Jagger wanted to have his back, Zane would do anything to protect him.

"Zane!" Evie ran toward him, her face twisted in anguish. She threw her arms around his waist, her momentum carrying him back toward the door.

Zane put one arm around her and caught Viper's hard gaze.

Mine. He mouthed the word at Viper, clenching his fist against Evie's back in triumph.

Viper's mouth tightened and he met Zane's silent challenge with a derisive snort. Then his bodyguards closed in around him, and Zane pulled Evie away.

Evie handed Zane a beer and sat beside him on her front steps. Moonlight glinted off the chrome on his bike, parked in her driveway where her car should have been. She pulled the key fob Viper had given her from her pocket, and ran her thumb over the smooth, black surface. On their third date, Viper had asked her about her dream car, and they'd had a fun evening checking out pictures of luxury vehicles on her phone. She'd never thought he would buy the Mazda for her, nor had she ever considered that he'd take her car.

Damn Viper and his stupid gift. She wanted her car, rusty and worn as it was. She'd bought it with the last of her savings from Stanton the morning after Mark pushed her down the stairs in a drunken rage. Only quick thinking and years of daredevil stunts with Zane had saved her, and she managed to grab the railing on her way down. Although Mark was horrified at what he'd done, Evie had finally had enough. She'd put up with his insecurities, affairs, and controlling behavior to give Ty a family and to fill the hole in her life that had consumed her after losing everyone she cared about. But the price had become too high.

"What's that?" Zane gestured to the key fob.

"Viper gave me a vehicle—a Mazda MX5—and he took the keys to my car. He said it wasn't safe. The Mazda is still in the parking lot at Riverside Bar. I didn't want it, or I wouldn't have taken the ride home with you."

"Hate saying this, but he's right. Your vehicle wasn't safe."

"Do you seriously think I would drive Ty around in an unsafe vehicle?" she snapped. "It might not look like much but I had it all checked out. Bill's mechanics said it was running fine."

Zane sipped his beer. "So . . . you and Viper?"

"I've been on a few dates with him, although he's never acted like he did tonight. Obviously. Because if he'd twisted my arm and pulled my hair on our first date, I wouldn't have gone out with him again. Although he said what he did was all for show." She twisted her lips to the side, considering. "If I tried to slap Jagger in front of his men, what would he do?"

Zane choked on his beer, wiped his mouth. "Pretty much the same thing Viper did. A one percenter president can't let any disrespect slide. Makes him look weak, and a weak president is a dead president."

Did that excuse Viper's behavior? If she'd understood biker culture, she wouldn't have made that mistake. And except for that one incident, he had been nothing but charming and kind. Although his jealousy had frightened her. Was that the real Viper behind the mask? The man who had so crudely called her a piece of pussy and wanted to take her to bed just so Zane couldn't have her?

"What about you?" She tucked the key fob away and opened the first aid kit she'd brought from the house. Although the cut on Zane's arm wasn't deep, there was still the risk of infection, and she suspected he wouldn't be running to the hospital with a knife wound on his arm.

"I could never hurt you, Evie." His hesitated, as if he had more to say. "In any way."

She dabbed antiseptic on his wound, remembering how many times she'd treated his injuries over the years. From school fights to reckless stunts, she had always been there to pick up the pieces. And he had done the same for her. They'd missed so many years together because they were too afraid to destroy their friendship, and yet, in the end, they destroyed it anyway.

"Then why did you leave me?" Her voice tightened as nine years of heartache bubbled over. "What happened that night?"

Zane covered her hand with his, drawing it away from his arm, threading his fingers through hers. "Your dad warned me away from you down by the creek after he sent you home. He said I wasn't good enough for you. Later that night, he came to the trailer. He . . . saw . . . all the drugs and cash. There was a fight. He shot my dad. I ran at him, knocked him down. He dropped the gun. My dad grabbed it and shot him. I didn't think anyone would believe I wasn't involved. Maybe shot them both. Everyone in the trailer park knew how my dad beat me; they heard us shouting at each other every night. And I figured your dad had told people I'd been with you and everyone would think I'd decided to get him out of the way. The town would need a scapegoat and I was an easy target."

Evie's skin prickled with awareness. He wasn't telling her everything. Even after all these years, she knew he was holding back, whether it was the way he stumbled over his words or how he stared out into the darkness, or from the set of his jaw. There was more to the story than he was letting on.

"The police thought my dad went to arrest your dad for drug dealing," Evie said. "They figured there was a fight, my dad shot yours in self-defense, and then you picked up the gun and shot my dad in revenge for killing your dad. Your prints were on the gun. Your footprints were all over the scene. Witnesses had placed you there . . ." She pressed her lips together, fighting back a wave of anger. "They didn't want to go to the expense of doing an autopsy or getting forensic reports. They just issued a warrant for your arrest."

"Figured as much." He squeezed her hand. "Small town. Saving money. Taking the easy way out."

"Why didn't you come to me?" She leaned her head against his shoulder, closed her eyes against the images of her father dying alone, tried to come to terms with what really happened that night. "I was waiting for you. I waited all night."

"I was worried you wouldn't believe me either." He said the words so quietly, she almost didn't hear them.

She supposed she could understand his concern. Her father had ripped Zane off her, thrown him to the ground, shouted harsh, cruel, horrible things. Then he stood over him and ordered her to go home. He said he and Zane were going to have a talk, but she would never be allowed to see him again. At first she refused to leave, but Zane begged her to go. Promised he'd see her later. Seventeen years old, innocent, trusting, unsure of herself in the world, she'd made the biggest mistake of her life and did as he asked.

"I would have believed you."

With a sigh, Zane released her hand. He walked down the steps and into the small copse of trees bordering her property, as much lost in his thoughts as he was in shadows.

"Zane?" Puzzled, she followed him, stopping only a few feet away when she spotted him leaning against a tree trunk, worrying the corner of the label on his beer bottle, the gesture so achingly familiar it twisted her stomach in a knot.

"At first, I meant to come back for you," he said, his gaze focused on the trailer park across the field. "I was going to come at night in disguise. But as I got farther away from Stanton, I began thinking it might be best if I stayed away. I mean, you were going away to college. You were going to meet guys who were smart and had things in common with you. And who was I? No skills. No future. A warrant on my head. Like your dad told me, I had nothing to offer you."

"I loved you." She choked back a sob as the words she'd held back for nine years spilled out. "I never thought for a moment you were responsible. I had faith in you, but you didn't have the same faith in me. You broke my heart."

Zane rubbed his forearm across his face, then pitched his bottle over the fence and into the field. "I fucked up. Big time. I'll spend the rest of my life regretting it. Hell, I regretted leaving the moment I drove away and I've regretted it every day since."

Part of her wanted to go to him, wrap her arms around him and tell it him it was okay. It had felt so right when he kissed her. Like coming home. Maybe they could pick up where they left off. Erase the past. But the other part of her knew she couldn't erase the pain of losing him, of losing hope and faith and love. She couldn't erase the soul-destroying marriage to Mark or the years of hardship of raising Ty alone. They had changed. She wasn't Evie anymore. She was Evangeline. And Zane wasn't Zane. He was a Sinner, an outlaw, and he lived in a different world.

"I'd better go," she said. "I have to be at work early, and I have a babysitter coming over to look after Ty."

"Maybe I should come over . . ."

Evie shook her head. "Let's take it slow with you and Ty. One thing you two have in common is that neither of you is good with change."

"What about you and me?"

Her mouth went dry, and her stomach churned. "There isn't a you and me outside of Ty. I have my life, Zane and you have yours. We don't have anything in common anymore."

"And you and Viper do?" His voice dropped to a growl, so fierce and low the tree frogs stopped croaking, silencing the night. "How'd you wind up with that piece of shit?"

"He came to the shop for some detailing. I didn't know much about the Jacks so I thought he was just another biker. He was charming, intelligent . . . probably the most interesting guy I'd met since coming to Conundrum. When he came back a third time for a touch-up on his fender, he asked me out. Bill told me who he was and said I should be careful."

"Probably made you want him more," he said quietly.

"Maybe it did. Maybe I wanted to prove to myself I could handle a man like him—the way I couldn't handle Mark—and that I didn't need anyone to save me. I made a decision to take control of my life when things went wrong with Mark. I realized I'd spent too much time chasing a dream of finding someone to look after me when really I needed to look after myself. But that's not all it was. I liked him, and I was flattered by his attention. I enjoy his company. I'm not ashamed of that." She turned back to the house and Zane grabbed her arm, spinning her back to face him.

"You're done with him. I don't give a fucking damn how you feel about him, or what you've got going on. He's a vicious, ruthless, coldhearted bastard. I know you got that wild in you, and maybe that's why you're with him, but he's dangerous and I won't let him near you or my son."

Evie shook him off, anger warring with confusion, her emotions battling against her aching want for the only man she'd ever loved. "Maybe the reason I was with him is because he reminded me of you."

Wrong thing to say. Eyes glittering, he lunged for her, clasping her wrist in his warm palm, pulling her to him. "Then be with me."

"I can't." Her throat tightened and she had to force the words out. "What we had is broken and it can't be fixed. I can't do this with you again. I just couldn't bear to be with you and have you disappear again. And I've moved on. I don't need you that way anymore."

He wrapped his arms around her, buried his face in her neck. "What we had is still there. I can feel it and I know you feel it, too."

His warmth seeped into her skin, his arms strong around her. Yes, their chemistry was still there. She could feel it pulsing through her veins, an arousal so fierce she could feel it in her fingers and toes.

"Kiss me." Zane's voice was hoarse, tight. "Kiss me and tell me you don't feel what I feel. Kiss me and tell me you want him and not me."

Unable to pull herself away, her mind clouded with desire, she acquiesced to his demand. Twining her fingers through his hair, she pulled him down and kissed him. Zane groaned and squeezed her so tight, she could feel the press of his buckle against her stomach. His tongue tangled with hers and he took over, returning her kiss with an intensity that left her breathless and made her knees tremble. She ached for him, wanted nothing more than to strip off his clothes and drown in the heat of his body.

"I wanna see you, my sweet Evie. I wanna bare your body, lick every inch of you, feel your skin against mine. I wanna be inside you so deep you forget everything but me."

Evie took a quick glance to each side to make sure they weren't in view of the neighbors, but with the trees around them, and a field to the back, they were well hidden in the shadows. And although she knew she should refuse him, walk away, and hold firm to her resolve, she licked his taste from her lips and whispered, "Yes."

He slid down the straps of her dress, undid the catch of her bra, dragging it over her arms, baring her breasts to his heated gaze. "Ah, God," he whispered. So fucking beautiful." He cupped her left breast in his palm, kneading it gently as he ravaged her mouth with sensual kisses. White-hot heat sizzled down to her core and she moaned.

"I remember that sound," he murmured. "I remember everything about that night in the forest, the softness of your skin, your breath on my cheek, your hard little nipples, the slickness of your pussy. I remember what it feels like to be inside you. That night ruined me for other women, Evie. I've only ever wanted you."

He held her arms behind her, pinning her wrists with one hand while he kissed her breasts, sucked gently on her nipples, tasting, devouring her. She tugged against his grip, wanting to touch him, slide her hands over his broad chest, work her fingers through his hair, and caress those broad shoulders. But he held her fast, and the restraint aroused her, made her more wanton, more desperate to have him inside her.

"Are you wet for me, sweetheart?" He slid one hand up her thigh under her dress. Far from the shame and disgust she'd felt when Viper had done the same, passion suffused her. Sweet desire. And when he shoved aside her panties, slid his finger through her wet folds, she almost came right then.

"Tell me, Evie." His voice dropped to a husky growl,

and he thrust one finger deep inside her. "Tell me you want me."

"I want you," she whispered, trembling at the exquisite intrusion. "It was always you."

A dog barked. A man shouted. She heard the low rumble of a quad in the field and suddenly the fog in her brain lifted. She was a mom. Ty was sleeping inside. Her neighbors were sleeping only fifty feet away. She'd just ditched the man she'd been dating for the last four weeks. What was she doing only hours later in her backyard with the man who had broken her heart? A man who had walked away and would no doubt leave her again. A biker. Living the biker life.

Steeling herself, she forced herself to meet his gaze. "But when I gave up hoping you would ever come back, I let you go. I'm sorry, Zane. I'm not ready to open that door again."

He released her so abruptly she almost lost her balance, but if she'd thought to push him away, she was gravely mistaken.

"Whatever it takes for you to trust me, I'll do." He wrapped his hand around her neck and leaned down to kiss her cheek. "If you want me to go slow, I'll go slow. If you need gentle, I'll be gentle. I will do what it takes, however long it takes. But I won't let anyone else have you. You are mine, Evie. You've been mine since you were eight years old. And now that I've found you again, I'm not gonna let you go."

★ ELEVEN ★

*Sometimes the most difficult problems can be
easily fixed with teamwork.*
—SINNER'S TRIBE MOTORCYCLE REPAIR MANUAL

Zane usually enjoyed watching Dax work—especially
during the first half hour of a torture session. Not because
he was into blood and pain—he wasn't—but because Dax
could get even the most hardened of men to talk without
laying a hand on them. No wonder the CIA, FBI, and every
covert organization in the U.S. had offered Dax a job after
he completed his PhD thesis on psychological terror at
Yale.

And he turned them all down for a piece of tail.

Zane couldn't understand it. Sure, Dax's old lady, Sandy,
was attractive in a honey-blond goddess kind of way. And
she had to be good in bed since they had five kids—or
maybe he was Catholic, although who ever heard of a
Catholic Sinner?—but still it seemed a lot to give up for
good sex and a career as an outlaw biker, especially since
torture was in his blood. Why else would he have joined
the Sinners with the stipulation that he be given free rein
to practice his craft?

"Haven't had a woman under my knife for a long time,"
Dax said as they descended the stairs to the clubhouse
basement. "I'm surprised Jagger allowed it."

"No harm." Zane skirted around the pool table and

grabbed a set of keys from the wet bar in the corner. The vast, poured concrete basement served as a games room and wet bar, as well as housing three cells for prisoners and interrogations. "Terror only. That's why I'm here."

Better here than driving the roads around Evie's house looking for Jacks. Or in his room thinking about her. He'd told her Viper was the kind of man who took what he wanted—as if it were a bad thing. But hell, he was that kind of man, too.

And he wanted Evie.

He had lied to himself last night just as much as he had lied to Jagger after Viper left the bar under a truce born solely by the fact they were evenly matched in both men and arms, and neither club wanted to attract the attention of the ATF. Yes, he wanted to rebuild his friendship with Evie, make up for all that had transpired. But friendship wasn't enough, just as it hadn't been enough when they were young, and damned if Viper would get in the way.

"You're here because you're a secret sadist." Dax laughed and lowered the duffel bag he'd been carrying on his shoulder. "You have a fascination for extremes— extreme pain, extreme emotion, extreme desire. You like to see how far a person can be pushed. What you don't seem to realize is that, really, you're pushing yourself."

Dax was always direct. And when it came to analyzing people, he hit too close for comfort. One of the reasons Zane kept his sexual liaisons discreet was because he didn't think his brothers would understand his need to dominate in a way he couldn't as VP. He needed the kind of control he hadn't had over his life. Whether it was because of his abusive father or the girl he loved but couldn't have, he didn't know, but Dax had the unique ability to pin him down, and although he knew himself well, he had no desire to have his inner motivations brutally exposed.

"Save the psychoanalysis for Doreen." Unable to hold Dax's searching gaze, Zane turned and unlocked the door. "You're gonna need it. Never met a woman like her before.

If you so much as loosen the ropes on her wrists and ankles, she'll throw herself at you and claw out your eyes. Piston is in the medical suite right now with Doc Hegel because he was taken in by her tears. But make no mistake . . ."

"I never do." Dax pushed open the door and they stepped into the bare, cinder block room, lit only by a single bulb on a wire hanging from the ceiling.

"I see Mr. Tall, Dark, and Brooding brought a little friend to play." Doreen swung her bound legs over the side of the camp bed Jagger had provided for the comfort of their female prisoner. "Who's gonna be first, or are you gonna both do me at once?"

Dax turned slightly to the side as he removed the tools of his trade from his duffel bag, holding each one up as if to assess it under the light. Zane had watched this performance before. Some prisoners caved when Dax pulled out the blade saw, for others the nutcracker was enough. He suspected the nutcracker wouldn't frighten Doreen, although she had bigger balls than many of the prisoners who had warmed that very bed.

Dax carefully placed his tools on the table—whips, knives, cuffs, gags, a squeaky toy . . . If he hadn't known Dax was a torturer, Zane would have thought the guy had a kink. Maybe he did, although Sandy didn't strike him as the submissive type. And with five kids, when would they find time to play? That was one benefit of remaining unattached. No kids to tie him down or interfere with his lifestyle. No lives to ruin because of his total lack of a role model for being a dad.

"How did it go last night?" Zane leaned against the wall, paying no attention to the prisoner on the bed. After the Jacks had left Riverside Bar the other night, the Sinners launched a revenge attack, setting fire to one of the restaurants the Jacks were known to frequent. He could have asked any of the brothers about the outcome of the restaurant hit, but the conversation worked well into the game he and Dax played to unsettle their victims, an easy banter that took the focus off the prisoner and onto the collection of torture toys.

"Good." Dax placed a pair of forceps on the table. "The restaurant burned down in a matter of minutes. Too bad for Mario. But then he shoulda thought about what might happen if he let too many Jacks into his establishment."

"You burned down Lucky Mario's?" Doreen's baby blues widened. "That was Viper's favorite restaurant. He's gonna hit you so damned hard, you'll be over at his clubhouse on your knees begging for mercy."

Dax pulled out a whip and flicked his wrist, the crack echoing in the small space. "Someone's gonna be begging for mercy, and it isn't us."

"You can't hurt me," she said quickly. "Zane gave me his word. And I got a kid. He needs me."

"If I know Zane, and I do, he probably gave you his word that you won't be harmed. But there's a world of difference between hurt and harm."

Wasn't that the truth. His old man knew the difference. Zane's father was always careful to hit Zane where the bruises couldn't be seen. But the emotional abuse, the constant accusations that his mother died because of him, that he was worthless and no good and a burden on his dad, caused irreparable harm. If not for Evie and Jagger, Zane doubted he would have made it through school without some serious psychological damage, or landing his ass in jail.

Dax studied Doreen, his lips twisting to the side. Then he put away the whip and pulled a pair of scissors from the bag, holding them up to the light. "That hair's gonna get in the way. Maybe I'll give her a pixie cut, shaved up both sides with a piece in the middle for holding on to." His phone buzzed in his pocket and he dug it out and frowned. "Damn. Timmy's back in the principal's office. That's the problem with having five boys. I gotta spend half my day gettin' them outta trouble. Excuse me love, I'll be right back."

Zane straddled the only chair in the cell and faced Doreen, resting his elbows on the metal back. "So who's looking after your kid?" He'd never thought about the people their prisoners left behind, and especially not kids, but now that he had one of his own, he wondered how it all worked in the context of his world. What would happen to Ty if Viper snatched Evie and threw her in his dungeon? What kind of boy was he? Would he curl up in his room and cry? Would he dial 911? Would he go to a friend's house?

Would he call his dad?

His fingers tightened on the chair. Fuck. What the fuck was he doing here when Viper was still roaming the streets? He'd arranged for two brothers to watch their house, but he should be there looking after his own damn family instead of trying to take care of this one.

"Like I'm going to tell you." Confident now that Dax was out of the room, Doreen shuffled back on the bed and leaned against the wall, her gaze focused on the table where Dax had left his equipment.

"I got a kid, too." The unfamiliar words slipped off his tongue. "Just wanted to make sure yours wasn't alone." He glanced up at the camera, hoped the mic was off. He'd never live it down if the brothers heard him showing concern for a prisoner. Hell, they'd be shocked he showed concern for anyone. He had a reputation as a loner, an "ice man," and he liked to keep it that way.

Doreen exhaled a long breath. "He's with my mom in another town. Viper sends all the kids away. He doesn't want the women he's fucking to be distracted. It's hard to blow a man when your kid is whining for juice, especially because no one bothers with closed doors in the Black Jack clubhouse. MC women don't get a choice of where they get fucked."

She gave him a sly look, her eyes slightly narrowed and a smirk on her lips. "Just like your redhead from the shop. She's got no choice either. Viper wants her bad. Never seen him want a woman the way he wants her."

"She's with me."

"And I was with Axle. Look what happened to him."

Zane forced his muscles to relax, feigning disinterest. "Viper killed him to get you?"

Doreen opened her mouth and then closed it again, her eyes flicking back to the table. "It's a long story and not one I'm wantin' to share unless you're gonna let me outta here. But I think it's pretty damn obvious that Viper doesn't let anyone or anything stand in the way of what he wants."

"Neither do I."

"So why are you here talking to me? He's probably on his way to get your redhead right now."

Evie dusted the tank of the Honda CB600F Hornet. Her client loved the matte black but needed a touch-up on the paint. The factory had put the clear coat over the decals and when he pulled them off the marks were visible. Even worse, the aftermarket front end's color was off from the rest of the bike. Not a big job. She had a stock of color match paint and there weren't many dents to fill. Maybe three hours and then she could get back to the work she enjoyed best, the custom designs, creative artwork that reflected the owner with a little bit of her soul thrown in.

Stan and Gene were working on a Kawasaki Ninja in the corner, badly damaged after the owner had skidded in the rain and dropped his bike under a stopped SUV. The fenders were dented beyond repair and there was substantial mechanical damage—almost a write-off, but not enough for the bike's insurers who were footing the bill. Insurance claims made up the bulk of the mechanics' work, taking them away from the custom builds that had first drawn them to Bill's shop.

"Morning, all." As if on cue, Bill walked into the shop through the back door, all relaxed like he hadn't just up and disappeared a week ago. "Can anyone tell me why the back entrance is covered in bullet holes?"

Big Bill, so named because he was six feet five inches

tall and maybe half as wide, with long, dark shaggy hair and a thick beard to match. He had inherited the shop from his old man, and although he loved bikes, he wasn't a businessman. After running the shop into the red in its first three months of operation, he'd hired the best staff he could find and let them run the shop for him.

"How about you tell us first where you were?" Evie folded her arms across her chest. She'd been happy to partner with Bill when he first approached her, but now she was pretty much running the show on her own and his unreliability was becoming an issue.

"Tables in Helena were calling, darlin'. I was feeling lucky."

Unfortunately, Bill had a gambling habit and had fallen into gun running for the Jacks as a way to earn money to feed his addiction. But when the Sinners took over the arms trade in Montana, and his work started drying up, he started skimming off the shipments and selling weapons on the side. Only Evie and Connie knew where he kept his stash, and only then because they'd just happened to be driving past the Conundrum cemetery one Saturday evening, and spotted Bill's Harley Fat Boy with Evie's custom paint on the fender. His daddy was still helping him out, he said, when they called out to him from the fence, even from the grave.

"Jacks and Sinners had a shoot-out the day after Axle came to the shop, and you slipped out the side door and left us alone." Evie mounted the tank on one of the stands Bill had bought for her work after he realized she was bringing in more clients than the mechanics and the sales departments together. He'd also splurged for some high-end paint guns and a supply of paints from most of the well-known dealerships.

Bill had the good grace to look sheepish. "Sorry about that, but I didn't want to take the risk he had a message for me, too." He looked back over his shoulder, as if he were expecting someone to be there. "Got a little antsy when I saw a coupla Jacks buzzing around my house the other week, but things seem to have cooled off. I heard Axle bit the bullet so at least we won't be seeing him around here anymore. Jacks left him with their initials carved into his chest."

So Viper hadn't been lying. "Do you know who . . . ?"

"Word on the street is he pissed off Viper." Bill waggled a finger at her. "I hope you finally got the message not to get involved with him, or it will be you lying in the county morgue."

"Thanks for the concern, but I'm done with outlaw bikers. I had my wake-up call last night." Evie didn't know where she stood with Zane, but she did know that a man who would hurt her once would do it again. And Viper . . . Well, no question that relationship was over.

"I had a wake-up call, too," Bill said. "That's why I'm here. I'm gonna tie up a few loose ends and then I'm taking some of those guns up to Great Falls. Got a Canadian buyer who can get them across the border. You'll be in charge."

"I think I'll start off giving myself a raise." Evie gave him a half smile. "Since I'll be doing twice as much work."

Bill laughed, the sound echoing off the walls. "You already do all the work. That's how I can be as relaxed as I am. I know the shop will be in good hands."

"Why are you still skimming, Bill?" She followed him to the door. "If Viper really killed one of his own men, imagine what he's going to do to you. Is it really worth the risk?"

"Got nothing much in my life except the thrill of living on the edge." Bill traced one of the worry lines on her forehead. "It's a gamble, darlin'. Just like at the tables. Maybe I'll win. Maybe I'll lose, but at least I've enjoyed the game."

The rumble of motorcycle engines reverberated around the building, and Bill paused, half in and half out of the shop. "Anyone expecting a client or six?"

"Two Man Crew are coming in today for a tune-up."

Stan called out. "I think they said they were bringing in five bikes."

"Must be them." Bill let out a relieved breath. "For a minute there I thought it was the Jacks. I'll be in my office. Back in five to say goodbye."

After he left, Evie headed to the paint rack for some matte black Honda paint. She tested the paint against the fender and waited for it to dry. Ten minutes passed. Then twenty. Something nagged at the back of her mind, and she felt a growing sense of unease. She checked her client book to see who was next on the list and made a few calls for pickups. After half an hour, she left her work and went to talk to Stan.

"Did Two Man Crew show up?"

"Not yet. They're probably out front talking to Bill and Connie. They always buy new gear when they come in."

"They've been out there a long time," Evie said. "I'll go check on them."

She tidied her equipment away and then pushed open the shop door, her nose wrinkling as the familiar scents of paint and gasoline, morphed into the sharp, tangy odor of . . . blood.

A moan broke the stillness. The sound of rapid, panting breaths, the crack of flesh on bone. Bill. Shirtless and on his knees in front of the helmet display, his hands and feet tied, blood trickling down his chest. Black Jacks scattered around the shop. Connie. Near the rack of leather jackets. A Black Jack with his arm around her waist. One hand over her mouth.

Viper. Holding a knife in the air.

Everyone turned away from her, watching the show.

"Please." Bill groaned. "I don't know nothing about missing weapons. I swear it."

Viper sliced the knife across Bill's shoulder, leaving a thick red trail down to his heart. Bill shrieked, the pain in his voice stabbing through Evie's chest. Without thinking, she ran for the cash register where Bill kept his shotgun.

"Morning, kitten. I was just coming in to see you." Viper turned, wiped the sweat from his brow with bloody fingers, leaving a smear across his forehead. His dark, soulless eyes froze her mid-step. He sheathed his knife and stretched out his hand, gesturing her forward as Bill keened to the side.

"Please stop. Don't hurt him anymore." She saw no point asking why he was beating on Bill, or even pretending she didn't know. Time was of the essence, the shotgun was in reach, and she had no interest in games.

Viper mocked a sympathetic look. "I'm afraid we have to hurt him. Then we have to kill him. He tried to cheat us and steal our weapons. No one disrespects the Jacks. I thought you got that message last night."

Oh, she got the message. Loud and clear. He didn't need the veiled threats to remind her that she'd made the biggest mistake of her life the night she agreed to that first date. She reached under the counter and felt around for the gun.

"Come give me a kiss, Evangeline." He cupped his groin and made a lewd gesture with his hips. "Nothing gets a man off more than a good beating. And there's no point looking for the weapon. Your friend already tried that, and you can see the result."

Evie glanced over at Connie, spotted the bruise on her cheek, tears rolling down her face, her Big Bill's shirt torn at the neck. Nausea roiled in her belly and she gripped the counter to hold herself up. "I know where the weapons are. If you let him go, I'll take you there."

"I gave you an order; I expect you to obey." Viper snapped his fingers and pointed at the floor beside him, a thin smile gracing the merciless slash of his mouth. "Now. Or I'll kill him in front of you."

So this was the side he had hidden from her beneath a veneer of civility. His cold, dark, malevolent gaze sent a chill through her body, but not as much as the implacable resolve on his face. Bill was going to die unless she saved him. And yet, without a gun, what could she do?

She trailed her hand along the shelf under the counter as she walked, her fingers brushing papers, pens, and, finally, the packing knife Connie used to open boxes. She closed her hand around the wooden handle, and slid it under her sleeve, the five-inch serrated blade pressing against her wrist. It was nothing compared to the blade Viper carried, and she doubted she would be able to do much damage, but maybe she could cause enough of a distraction to call for help.

"Please." She begged when she reached him. "Don't do this."

"There's a good kitten." Viper put an arm around her waist and pulled her against him. Evie bent as far back as she could, trying not to touch his shirt, even as the acrid scents of blood, sweat, and leather assailed her nostrils. But Viper tightened his grip and pulled her closer, grinding his erection into her stomach. Evie fought back the bile that rose in her throat. God, the violence turned him on.

"After I'm done here, I'm going to take you back to the clubhouse and I'm gonna fuck you the way I wanted to fuck you when I first saw you out in your shop." Viper threaded his hand through her hair and yanked her head back. "I wanna hear my name on your lips when you scream, kitten. And then I wanna hear you scream just for fun."

"I thought you wanted me because I was different from the others." Evie wondered how much of this was posturing and how much was real. She couldn't reconcile the beast of a man who held her now with the charming biker who had wined and dined her over the past four weeks.

"But you're not," he said. "You made the wrong choice last night when you got on that Sinner's bike. I did warn you, sweet Evangeline. Now I'm gonna have to beat that sweet outta you, which is the last thing I wanted to do. You'll wind up as hard and rough as an old lady, and I already got one of those."

"You have an old lady?" She looked at him aghast and laughter erupted from Viper's chest.

"Yeah, I got an old lady. And a clubhouse full of sweet butts to soothe the ache from playing games with you. Did you think you were the only one? Or that you could get me all wound up and then walk away? Man like me has needs, kitten. Booze, drugs, women, sex, and goddamn justice for what the Sinners did."

Evie swallowed past the lump in her throat. "I told you last night . . . I'm not with them."

He pulled her hair so hard she feared he would rip it from her scalp. "That why you jumped on that Sinner's bike last night, Evangeline? After I laid my claim, and made it clear that you belonged to me, you invited him over for a quick fuck anyway? You think I wouldn't be watching? I'd say that's cheating, but to be fair, I hadn't fucked you yet so maybe you didn't understand. I'll be taking care of that problem right after I take care of your boss." He took her mouth in a bruising kiss, his teeth scraping over the tender skin of her lips, his tongue ravaging her mouth until she fought for breath.

"That damn pussy you've been keeping under lock and key better be as sweet as your fucking mouth." He held her against him and drew a weapon from beneath his cut. "Now stay right here while I teach Bill what happens when you fuck with Jacks."

She turned her head, gasping. "I'll come with you if you let Bill go."

"Only place Bill is going is to ground," he growled. "And you're going with me because I say. There is no negotiating."

"No!" Heart pounding, she slid the knife from her sleeve and plunged it into his shoulder.

"Fucking bitch." Viper shoved her away and ripped out the knife. His face contorted in a snarl and then he tossed the knife to the side and stalked toward her. Evie scrambled to her feet, but before she could run, he was on her, his hand around her throat, his body coming at her like a freight train. He slammed her up against the wall so hard, her vision blurred and then he pressed his lips to her ear, keeping his voice so low only she could hear. "Why the fuck did you do that? Why? I thought you learned your lesson last night. Nothing you do is gonna change the fact that Bill's a dead man. And now I gotta punish you and I gotta do it in front of my men or I lose face 'cause I got stabbed by a fucking bitch. I didn't want this, Evangeline. I wanted you the way you were when I met you. Sweet, soft, and untainted. Now I gotta break you, and when I do, what I wanted from you is gonna be fucking gone."

Sweat trickled down her breasts and she heard Connie sob. He seemed totally unaffected by the stab wound, although blood seeped through his shirt. With a disgusted snort, he released her neck and then shoved her forward until she was only a few feet away from Bill.

"I'm sorry," she whispered when Bill looked up at her, his eyes glazed over with pain. "I tried."

"S'okay." His voice cracked. "Sometimes you win. Sometimes you lose. Take care of my store, love. Look after yourself."

The crack of the gunshot came so close she caught her breath, stiffened. Bill slumped to the ground and Evie screamed, her knees shaking so hard, she would have fallen if Viper hadn't grabbed her with his free hand.

"Love that sound," he murmured.

She didn't know if he was referring to the gun or her scream, but either way she wanted his filthy, murdering hands off her. She twisted in his grasp, only to find herself facedown on the counter, her hands pinned behind her back.

"Your turn for punishment, kitten." Viper leaned over her, pressing her hips into the counter with the weight of his body. "What's it gonna be? My dick or my belt. Either way, you'll be getting both by the end of the night, but the boys here need to see what happens when you disrespect your man."

"Go to hell."

"You might want to do as the lady asks." T-Rex stepped through the door to the shop with a semiautomatic rifle in each hand. "Get away from her. She's Sinner property."

A flicker of annoyance crossed Viper's face. He pulled Evie up and held her in front of him like a shield. "This doesn't involve you, pup. And put those guns away before you shoot off your fucking dick. She's my property. I marked her and right now I'm gonna fuck her. You want in on the action, stand in line."

"Let her go." T-Rex leveled his weapons and Evie squeezed her eyes shut. She had no idea if T-Rex was a good enough shot to hit Viper and miss her, but she hadn't missed the brief flicker of indecision in his face, and she suspected Viper hadn't missed it either.

"You know what I'm gonna do with her after I'm done here?" Viper taunted. "I'm gonna take her back to the club-house, chain her to my bed, and fuck her till she's all used up. Then I'll give her to my boys to play with. There's noth-ing they like better than sweet, used civilian pussy."

"She's got a kid. Take me instead."

"No!" Evie stared at him in horror. "Don't. Please. I can take care of myself."

"Shut it, girl." Viper clamped a hand over Evie's mouth. "You got a name, junior patch?"

"T-Rex." The guns wavered in his hands and Evie's heart sank. He couldn't pull the trigger, couldn't cross the line that Zane had clearly managed to cross. And Viper knew it.

"T-Rex." Viper chuckled. "I like it, although you don't look like a T-Rex to me. Well, T-Rex, why the hell would I want a junior patch with more balls than brains?"

"We got your old lady."

"Hmmm. And you think they'll trade her for you?"

Oh, God. Viper was actually considering the trade. She clawed at Viper's hand, trying to get her mouth free to warn T-Rex not to deal with Viper, to run while he still had the chance.

Please don't sacrifice yourself for me.

"What do you think, kitten?" Viper's breath in her ear sent a chill down her spine. "Can you wait another day for my dick? 'Course by then I'll have been fucking hard for you for so long, I won't be able to go slow and gentle. We'll have to skip the foreplay and get straight to the tears and screaming."

Evie shook her head, but Viper caught her earlobe between his teeth and bit, stilling her. "I'll bet if I took my hand off your mouth," he murmured against her ear, "you'd beg me to fuck you to save him. But this will be so much more fun. I get a Sinner to play with in my dungeon, and then I get to hunt you down all over again and make a sinner of you, too. Nothing is more exciting than the chase." He released her and pushed her away so hard, she stumbled toward Connie.

"Today's your lucky day, T-Rex. You got a deal."

"No. I don't want this. I don't agree." Evie moved to intercept T-Rex, and Viper yanked her back by the hair.

"Bitches don't deal. Now shut the fuck up and appreciate what young T-Rex has done for you. Gotta respect a man who will sacrifice his life to save a woman who doesn't even belong to him."

One of the Jacks took T-Rex's weapons and two more grabbed his arms.

"T-Rex!" Evie lunged toward forward as they dragged him through the store. "I'll call Jagger. He'll get you back. I'll make him do the trade."

"There won't be any trade." Viper tucked his weapon into his holster. "I don't give a damn about the old lady. If the bitch is stupid enough to get herself caught, then I've got no place for her in my club. Jagger can do whatever he wants with her."

"But . . . that was the deal."

"The deal was him for you," Viper said. "What I do with him is my business. And the deal was for today. Nothing was agreed about tomorrow when I'm coming for you. He bought you a day, kitten. Better enjoy it."

He brushed past her and jerked his chin at the remaining Jacks. "Burn the shop down."

"No!" She stared at him aghast. "Please. It's all I have to make a living."

"After tomorrow, you won't need a job." Viper licked his lips and the darkness in his eyes made her skin crawl.

"You'll be making a living pleasuring me."

★ TWELVE ★

When repairing a bike, always expect the unexpected. This goes for life, too.
—SINNER'S TRIBE MOTORCYCLE REPAIR MANUAL

Zane saw the smoke before he saw the flames, a great pillar of black rising up into the clear blue sky. Already pushing one hundred miles an hour, he accelerated his bike down the highway and prayed they weren't too late. Jagger matched his speed, and in the distance he could hear the rumble of the Sinner bikes behind them.

Thank fuck for T-Rex. He had been the first to volunteer when Zane had put out a call for brothers to watch Evie's house last night, and he must have followed her to the shop. How else would he have been able to send that warning text?

Viper and 6 Jacks at Big Bill's. Evie in danger.

Within minutes, Zane had rounded up every brother in the clubhouse and then he hit the road at full throttle. He could only hope T-Rex hadn't done anything rash. The junior patch had courage beyond his years but often his sense of honor and duty were misguided in the context of the biker world. More than once he'd questioned T-Rex's decision to follow the outlaw life.

The world became a blur as he raced toward the burning shop. Was this Viper's payback for the restaurant, or something else? The Sinners had no ties to Big Bill's business except through Evie.

A wave of heat hit him as they pulled into the parking lot. The fire was well and truly out of control, no doubt accelerated by the gasoline in the bikes, and the various paints and lubricants in Evie's shop. Sirens wailed in the distance, and Zane's heart thrummed in his chest. Evie's car was at the far end of the parking lot alongside T-Rex's bike, safe from the flames. But where were they?

"Evie!" He parked his bike and ran toward the burning building.

"T-Rex!" Jagger headed to the back of the garage at a safe distance from the flames.

Zane took a step forward with every intention of running inside, but the flames surged as he approached and part of the roof caved in, crashing into the building.

"Evie." Over and over again, he called her name, until his voice was hoarse and his face singed with soot. Jagger emerged from the opposite side of the building, just as the rest of the Sinners pulled into the parking lot.

"I didn't see anyone, and the fire is spreading into the trees," he said. "Too hot to get in. Maybe she left with Connie."

"What about T-Rex?" Zane scrubbed his hands over his face. "He would never go anywhere without his bike."

Two fire engines pulled up across the street and Zane ran over to the driver. "You got a spare suit? I worked for the fire department in Sioux Falls. There may be people inside. I'll go take a look."

"No extra suits, and even if we did, we couldn't let you go in." The fireman gave him a sympathetic look. "Legal issues, first of all, and it's too far gone. You wouldn't make it."

"Gimme a fucking suit." Zane grabbed the firefighter by the throat and pushed him against the engine. "I'm not giving up. I'm gonna go in."

Strong hands clamped around his shoulders and Gunner and Cade pulled him away from the firefighter.

"C'mon man," Sparky said. "Let him do his job. If he says they wouldn't have made it . . ."

"Fuck." Zane fought their hold. "It's my choice. I'm willing to take the risk."

"But I'm not." Jagger came up behind him. "I almost lost you once. I'm not losing you again. She was my friend, too, Zane, and T-Rex is our brother, but even I can see there's no chance."

As if on cue, the rest of the roof fell in, the building imploding in a burst of flame. The police arrived and cordoned off the area, forcing the Sinners back and across the street.

"I'm sorry, man." The firefighter Zane had assaulted ushered him back from the raging inferno. "There's nothing we can do."

Noooooooooooooooo.

Pain suffused Zane's body, filling his lungs until he thought he would drown in anguish. Blind with panic, he stumbled across the street, feeling for his bike, his only port in the storm of regret and longing that swept through his soul. He slid onto the seat, clutched the handlebars, doubled over, and let himself go. If he could do it all again, he would tell her what really happened that night he left. He would tell her his feelings had never changed, not even when he'd seen her with Mark. He'd tell her that he'd never had a serious relationship because every woman reminded him of her—every face, every laugh, every smile. And if she was with someone else, he would win her back. Or die trying.

Maybe it wasn't too late. Maybe he was giving up too soon. He'd made that mistake back in Stanton. He wouldn't make it again.

He shot up in his seat, saw Jagger standing beside him. "I'm here, brother. Whatever you need."

Zane drew in a ragged breath, forced himself to get it together. "Gonna drive around town in case we missed something. Maybe they found another way out, or they're sitting at the restaurant down the road havin' a coffee."

"They think they found a body—"

Zane cut Jagger off with an abrupt shake of his head. "It wasn't her. Or T-Rex."

"Neither of them are answering their phones, brother. When has T-Rex ever failed to answer a call from the club?"

Zane's hands tightened around the handlebars. "What does Viper gain by killing them? He wants Evie. And they're not gonna kill T-Rex for no reason because they know we'll retaliate and take one of their own. There's gotta be another answer."

"Never thought of you as an optimistic man." Jagger flicked the kickstand on his bike. "But I'll follow you to hell and back. Just like you did for me."

"I'm a desperate man," he said.

"Well then let's ride, desperado, and find your girl."

Evie slumped against the passenger door of Connie's vehicle, physically and emotionally drained. How did Zane do this for a living? One week of bikers and her life had been turned upside down. In the last hour, she'd been threatened with sexual assault and physical violence, witnessed the murder of the man who had been like a father to her, owned and lost a business, and poor T-Rex . . . She groaned and scrubbed her hand over her face.

"They'll kill him, Connie. And all because of me."

Connie reached over and squeezed her hand. "You can't think like that. Jagger will find a way to get him back. You heard what T-Rex said. The Sinners have Viper's old lady. It's all about posturing. They'll do the trade—"

"He doesn't want her."

"I'm sure he was just saying that to make himself seem tough." Connie took a sharp right and Evie fell against the window, hitting her shoulder so hard she winced. Viper hadn't even flinched when she stabbed him. He wasn't human. Or maybe he'd been stabbed so many times he didn't feel it anymore.

"Of course he wants her," Connie continued. "Look what he's gone through because he wants you, and you're not even in his club. She's his old lady."

"He won't want me now that I stabbed him," she said, following Connie's line of thought. "That was probably a deal killer." *And a T-Rex killer.* "Oh, God." Her stomach twisted in a knot so fierce she doubled over. "I'm not worth it, Connie. I'm not worth his life."

"Don't talk like that." Connie's voice rose in pitch. "You are worth it. And Ty needs his mother. Viper was right about one thing. You have to respect the sacrifice T-Rex made. You need to take Ty and get out of town before the day is up. Look after your son and let the Sinners look after their brother."

"I need to call Jagger and tell him what happened." She fished around for her purse and froze. "My purse . . . It was in the shop. And my phone was in it."

"Then it's gone." Connie dug her phone from her pocket. "I have Tank's number in there. You can give him a call and he can give a message to Jagger . . . and Zane." Her voice softened. "I think he'll want to know you're okay." She pulled up at a red light and handed Evie her phone. "His name is under "T" for Tank, although his real name is James. He likes Tank, though. Says it fits him better."

"Why do you have Tank's number?"

"He's hot. He's cute. He's a biker. And he spent last night in my bed." She bit back a grin.

"You and Tank? Why didn't you tell me?"

Connie shrugged. "You were a little preoccupied running away from the man you've been lusting after for the last nine years, while being chased by the biggest baddest biker in town."

"Not anymore." Evie called Tank and he promised to get a message to Jagger and Zane to call as soon as they could.

"I think you're right. I need to get out of town," Evie

said. "Ty's at home. His best friend's older sister, Moira, is babysitting today. We'll have to pack, pick up some supplies, rent a car . . ."

"I don't think you should be making any public appearances." Connie hit the gas and accelerated through the intersection. "If you haven't already noticed, Vipe's not one of the good guys. He'll probably show up and say that in his world, one day means one hour." Her chin wavered and Evie mentally chastised herself for forgetting how Connie often hid behind false bravado. No doubt she was shaken, too.

"You don't need to be involved. This is about me and Viper and the Sinners. Turn the car around and I'll call a cab to take me home."

"If I didn't have to have two hands on the wheel, I'd give you a slap." Connie lifted one hand and gave Evie a soft thud above the ear. "Oh look. I can drive with one hand and slap you around with the other. I'm your friend. That means when the chips are down, I don't run away. Plus, my life was gettin' kinda dull and I was hoping something like this might happen: murder, arson, assault, my best friend being fought over by two outlaw bikers, me meeting the biker of my dreams, Bill getting . . ." She choked on her words, wiped a tear from her cheek.

"Connie . . ."

"Shush." She drew in a ragged breath, forced a smile. "I'm thinking about what to wear when Tank takes me for a ride through the mountains. Do you think they make red leather biker trousers?"

"No."

"I'll get my grandma to whip me up a pair. She'll be overjoyed to see me since I haven't visited her in six months. By the way, did I mention I'm taking you and Ty to stay with my grandma in Joliet? You'll love her, but she's got a sewing addiction. So bring an extra suitcase 'cause you won't need to buy clothes for you or Ty for the next few years."

* * *

Evie hit the ground running when they arrived at her house. She paid Moira and sent her home, then tugged the suitcases out from under the bed and threw in her clothes and supplies. Connie raced to Ty's room and filled a bag with toys and clothes.

"What's going on?" Ty stood in the doorway, his forehead creased in confusion.

"We're going on a little holiday." Evie tore a dress off its hanger. "Connie has invited us to spend some time with her grandmother in Joliet. She says there are lots of kids there to play with."

"What about your work?"

Evie paused, not wanting to lie, but not wanting to worry him either. "I'm taking some time off."

Before he could answer, the front door banged open. "Evie. Thank fuck." Jagger stalked across the room and pulled her into a warm hug. "When I got Tank's message . . . Christ. We thought you'd been bur—"

"I'm okay," she said quickly, mindful of Ty in the hallway behind her.

"Jacks are on the move." Jagger heaved in a breath. "Shooter spotted three of them heading this way."

"No." Evie took a step back. "Viper said I had a day. He was going to . . ." She stumbled over her words. "Take me, and then T-Rex offered himself in my place. He thought Viper would trade to get his old lady back."

"Well from the looks of it, he's coming for you now," Jagger said. "Zane stopped at the clubhouse to pick up a cage. He'll be here any minute to take you and Ty to our safe house. I'll make sure Connie gets home. Shooter and Tank are gonna try to intercept them and Cade is coming with some brothers."

She stuffed clothes in her suitcase, glanced down the hall to make sure Ty was out of earshot. "I don't want this, Jagger." Her voice wavered. "I don't want to be part of this world. And I don't understand why Viper is doing this. I ended it with him last night. Doesn't he realize if he wants me, hurting me and my friends and forcing me to go with him is entirely the wrong thing to do?"

"You're thinking about him like he's a normal man, a civilian." Jagger pulled the curtains on her windows. "He might want you, but it's in his nature to be cruel and violent. He might have been able to hide it, even enjoy playing the game, but there was only one way the game was going to end, and it was with you in his bed even if he had to hurt you to get you there. He's a man who takes what he wants, and from the moment you caught his interest, he was never going to leave you alone."

"Everything was fine until you and Zane showed up at the shop. Before that, he was a different man." She zipped the case closed and grabbed her coat.

Jagger gave her a tight smile. "When we showed up, we just added politics to the mix. He wants you even more now because a Sinner wants you. And I wouldn't put it past him to use you as a pawn in the bigger game. The Sinners and the Jacks have been warring over dominance in the state for years. He might not want to use you, but he will. He might not want to hurt you or break you, but he won't be able to stop himself. He is who he is, Evie. He loved his daughter, Arianne, but he was prepared to kill her when he found out she was with me."

"You think he would kill me?" She stared at him aghast.

"I think he would break you," Jagger said. "And if he does, death would be a mercy."

★ THIRTEEN ★

*Just getting your repair started can be the
hardest part of the whole job.*
—SINNER'S TRIBE MOTORCYCLE REPAIR MANUAL

"Evie!" Zane bolted from the Sinner SUV and crossed the lawn to Evie. Ripping the suitcase from her hand, he wrapped his arms around her and held her tight. Relief flooded him, becoming a shuddery ache as she melted into his body. She was okay. His Evie was alive. Even when he'd received the text from Tank, he hadn't believed it. He had to see her for himself. Hold her. Assure himself it wasn't all a dream.

"Zane, I can't breathe." She pushed gently at his shoulders and he loosened his hold, but he couldn't let her go.

"It's okay," she whispered. "I'm okay."

He tried to release her. But no. His arms weren't cooperating. He wanted her here against his chest, feeling her heartbeat forever.

"Baby, you've got to let me go."

Baby. She'd started using that term of endearment her last year of high school, when Zane would meet her after work, dirty from a day hauling lumber and framing buildings, when he looked nothing like a baby and more like the kind of man who shouldn't be spending time with a girl like her. But he loved the term of endearment. Loved that it was only for him.

With a sigh he released her. Still unable to speak, he lifted Ty in his arms, and grabbed Evie's hand, half dragging, half pulling her to the vehicle parked outside her house. The boy weighed almost nothing, and he wondered if Evie had been feeding him right. How much were eight-year-old boys supposed to weigh? Maybe he would ask Dax. With five boys under his belt, Dax would know everything about raising a son. Less, though, about relationship troubles he and Sandy had been happily married since they graduated from high school.

"Keys." Evie held out her hand after Zane unlocked the door to one of the club's black SUVs.

Zane settled Ty in the back seat, finally finding his voice. "I drive when there's a woman in the car. That's how it is."

"I drive when my son is in the car. And that's how it is." She put her hands on her hips and glared. Zane fought back the urge to just lift her and deposit her in the front seat. This wasn't the time for feminist bullshit. They were in danger and it was his job to protect them.

"You can fight me all you want," he said. "But I'm in control of any vehicle I ride in, especially when I got you and Ty to look after."

"So, it's a macho thing?" She released a sigh. "Would you really feel that much less of a man if I drove?"

"Yes."

"Fine." She yanked open the passenger door. "Far be it from me to dent your masculine pride, since it is one of your more attractive qualities."

Zane straightened his back, puffed out his chest and fought back the urge to fist pump. His woman appreciated his protective nature, the essence of his maleness. And she was letting him drive.

After Evie and Ty were securely buckled in, Zane slid into the vehicle and hit reverse. The tires squealed as he kicked the vehicle into drive and accelerated down the road.

"Slow down," Evie protested. "This is a school zone and no one is behind us. There's no need for excessive speed when there's a child in the vehicle."

"This isn't excessive speed. I'm just wanting to drive faster than that kid on his tricycle." He gestured out the window. "Maybe we should stop and ask him for a tow."

Evie's cheeks reddened. "Sarcasm doesn't become you."

"Neither does your bullshit. You always loved speed."

She'd also loved drag races, occasionally cutting class, and dating guys who set Zane's teeth on edge—the fringe elements of high school who had their own bands, spent time in juvenile detention, or rode motorcycles to school. Jagger had figured it was a case of opposites attract, but Zane had a different view. Evie was one of them. She just couldn't admit it.

"This is like the movies." Ty bounced in his seat. "I can't even read the street signs we're going so fast."

Zane glanced up in the rearview mirror and spotted four bikes at the end of the road. Black Jacks. "Son of a bitch. How the fuck did they get here so fast? And where are the goddamned Sinners?"

"Language," Evie warned.

"I'll swear all I want when we got fucking Black Jacks on our tail," he growled. "And I already squared it away with Ty. I put fifty bucks in his swear jar as advance payment."

"Zane says we'll be able to afford to take the fucking space shuttle to the fucking moon now that he's around." Ty rattled his swear jaw and Evie turned and glared.

"Ty. You are now down two quarters, and if I ever hear that kind of language again—"

"I'm just saying what Zane said." Ty caught Zane's glance in the rearview mirror and smiled. Well, damn. His son was no fool. But he'd have to be more careful or he'd get them both in trouble.

Pulling his gaze away, Ty peered out the back window. "Why are those bikers chasing us?"

"'Cause they want something they can't have." Zane cranked the wheel to the left and the vehicle dipped as they took a sharp corner. Evie sucked in a breath and Ty gave an excited shout.

"Mom, you should drive like this. Zane is awesome."

"He's dangerous, darling. Make sure you have your seat belt on." Evie gripped the door handle and muttered under her breath. "No point saving us if you're planning to kill us en route."

Although he didn't have to do it, Zane took another sharp left and then a right. Evie and Ty jerked from side to side in the vehicle, and he bit back a laugh when her muttering turned to soft curses only he could hear. But his good humor faded when he glanced up in the rearview mirror and saw the Jacks gaining on them. Where the hell were Shooter and Tank? Or his brothers? It shouldn't have taken them this long to find the Jacks.

"We can't outrun them in this damn cage. We need a place to hide so I can call the boys and get them off our back."

"How about that car wash?" Ty pointed to the gas station ahead. "The doors close when you go inside. Mom doesn't like it, but I think it's cool."

"Good idea." The boy was smart. Musta got that from his mom. There were no good genes in the Colton family.

Zane turned into the car wash and jammed his credit card into the payment slot, praying they had enough time before the Jacks caught them. The heavy metal door lifted with a groan and he drove inside, counting off the seconds until the door closed again.

"How long we got? I paid for the Special. Never been in a car wash before. We detail our bikes by hand."

"Probably about five minutes." Evie loosened her seat belt as water sprayed over the vehicle. "Do you think it will be enough?"

"Should be. They'll go past and assume we're ahead. We can double back and then head out to Sparky's place." He pulled out his phone and typed a text. "I'll tell Tank what's going on. See if he can head them off so we have a clear run to the safe house."

When Ty removed his seat belt and turned to watch the sprayers, Evie leaned over to Zane. "You don't have to stay with us when we get there. I know you want to go looking for T-Rex. If you leave me a weapon, we'll be fine. And tomorrow I'll call Connie. She was going to take us to her grandmother's place."

"You won't call anyone." He tucked the phone away. "And you won't leave the safe house until I've got the situation under control. Then I'll send you outta town."

"It's my situation to control." Her voice rose in pitch. "This is all about me."

"It may have just been about you, but you and Ty are Sinners now so the Sinners will protect you." Well, not totally true. Sinner protection usually only extended to family, old ladies, sweet butts and house mamas. They'd be stretched thin if they had to look out for girlfriends and hook-ups, too. But Evie was . . . Evie. And he'd been incredibly relieved when Jagger gave the order to protect her. If he hadn't, Zane would have done the unthinkable, and turned in his cut.

"I can't just hide and wait for things to happen." Evie twisted her hair around her finger. "The shop was half mine, and I'll have to deal with the fire, the insurance, and the employees who need work to pay their bills. You can't just send us away. Ty needs to see you."

"Fuck, Evie." Zane slammed a fist on the dashboard as soap slid down the windshield. "We're not playing games here. You're in danger. Your life at the shop is gone. I can't protect you if you're running around."

"Don't shout at Mom." Ty leaned over the seat, his face now pale and drawn. "And don't hurt her." Without warning, he climbed over the seat and curled into Evie's lap, his arms around her as if he was protecting her, while seeking her comfort at the same time. "No one is allowed to hurt her again."

Again? Zane stilled, his momentary anger forgotten. "Who hurt your mother?"

"Mark." Ty's voice was muffled by Evie's shirt. "Mark shouted and broke things and once he pushed her down the stairs and she almost died. I saw it."

"He pushed you?" Zane's world narrowed to one single purpose, and it had nothing to do with Viper or the Jacks. Nothing mattered save for the fact that someone had hurt his Evie and was still walking the streets.

"Just forget about it." Evie hugged Ty, stroking the back of his head with her hand. "He was drunk and it only happened once. We left the next day. That part of my life is done. It was years ago."

"Fucking cowardly piece of shit. He still in Stanton?" Zane sucked in a breath of soap-scented air and almost choked on the humidity.

"You're going to run through that fifty dollars pretty damn quick," Evie snapped, cringing at her hypocrisy. "And yes, he's in Stanton, which is why we left. He and I are done. I divorced him and started a new life. It's over."

Zane gripped the steering wheel so hard, his knuckles turned white. "Once we got this situation fixed, I'll be heading up to Stanton. Pay him a visit."

"No, you won't."

"The fuck I will."

Ty tightened his grip around Evie and his body trembled. Zane bit back the next words he'd intended to say. Damn. He'd scared the boy, and from what he'd just seen, Ty had been scared enough. He and Jagger had definitely pegged Mark right. And the situation screamed for justice. Sinner style.

"Maybe we should go to Hawaii instead of the moon,"

Evie said, stroking Ty's head. "At the rate Zane's going, it should only take a few days."

"How 'bout I just pay for the vacation and then swear all I like?"

Evie's lips quivered with repressed laughter. Ty turned his head and met Zane's gaze. Then his face broke into a smile.

That was the moment Zane knew.

He was home. And nothing would take him away.

The noise woke him. A soft murmur that he couldn't identify as a threat, but which made him uneasy just the same.

Zane pulled his weapon from under the cushion and sat up on the couch, trying to pinpoint the sound. The safe house, an open plan apartment above Sparky's garage, afforded little space to hide, which left the bedroom, the small office they'd fixed up for Ty, or the bathroom, as the source of the noise.

Not bothering with his shirt, he made his way through the sparsely furnished apartment. Bathroom clear. Ty sleeping soundly on the camp bed they'd set up beside the desk. Kitchen empty. He paused outside Evie's room and heard the sound again. Then he pushed open the door.

He'd never seen Evie cry. Through high school breakups, verbal and emotional abuse from her alcoholic mother, and the longing for her absent father, she'd always held fast. But now, she sat on the cold, wood floor, her back against the wall, the phone pressed to her ear, and tears streaking her cheeks. Her eyes widened when she saw him and she murmured into the phone. "I've got company. Have to go."

He wanted to know who was on the phone, and whether that person had said something that made her cry, and if so, who he was and where he lived. And why was she on the phone with someone else when Zane was sleeping just outside her door?

She needed comfort. He could provide. Weapon holstered, he crossed the room and pulled her to standing, his gaze taking in the T-shirt that barely skimmed her lips. He wrapped his arms around her and hugged her to him, enfolding her in his warmth. No words. Just silence. He had always loved silence.

After a few moments, she relaxed against him, her arms circling his waist, her cheek pressed against his chest. She had taken out her ponytail and her hair fanned over her shoulders, the gold highlights shimmering under the soft glow of the bedside lamp. So beautiful. So fragile. His Evie.

"It's been a rough day," she whispered. "Viper . . . She choked on the name. "I lost Bill, and the shop, and T-Rex. We're on the run, and you . . . you want to send us away. What about Ty?"

"I'm not about to walk away from my responsibilities."

Her breath left her in a rush. "I don't want him to be just a responsibility. You're his dad. I want him to have a relationship with you."

"Like I had with my old man?" He couldn't hide the bitterness in his voice. "Some kids are better off without their parents."

"I just thought . . ." She tried to pull away and he held her closer, the slight movement of her body sending shock waves to his groin.

"I'm not leaving you or Ty." At least not while Viper was out there. But after he dealt with Viper, what then? How did he integrate a son into his life? And Evie. How could he win her back? How could he ask her to forgive him when he couldn't forgive himself?

"I guess I don't know you that well after all." But the desire that burned in her green eyes said otherwise, and when she met his gaze, her little pink tongue flicking out to wet her lips, he couldn't deny his hunger.

"Then get to know me again." His hand cupped her jaw

with infinite care. Drawing her close, he dropped his head and claimed her mouth in a long, sensuous kiss.

"Yes." Evie moaned into his mouth, the sound reverberating through his body, firing his blood, decimating the last of his restraint. He groaned, shoved her against the wall, and her lips apart for the soft slide his tongue. She tasted of coffee and cream, and something sweet.

Hard kiss. Demanding kiss. Desperate kiss. A kiss that turned her inside out, and told her the man he had become was not the boy she once loved.

He was more.

His hand snaked around her, pulling her against his hard body until her breasts pressed tight against his chest and she could feel every thud of his heart. There were no more gentle caresses, no fumbling with clothing, no whispered endearments. His free hand dove beneath her nightshirt, determined, demanding. He wanted her as she wanted him. Hard. Fast. Now.

"Panties off." He yanked and her panties came away with a soft sigh.

She was wet, so wet she wondered if she could come just by pressing her thighs together, but before she could put the theory to the test, Zane thrust a thick thigh between her legs.

"Open for me, beautiful girl."

Her legs parted, and the rough fabric of his jeans grated over her sensitive skin sending ripples of pleasure straight to her core.

Evie slid her arms around his neck and opened to him, needing his touch, the total release of surrender to wash away her fear and tension. She drew him in and kissed him with all the hunger she had buried away the day he left, as if she could assuage a never-ending thirst with the cool touch of his lips.

She felt his low, deep growl of approval in every cell of

her body as he slid his cool hands under her shirt to cup her naked breasts, kneading them gently, his thumbs flicking over her nipples until they peaked. Evie had never been with a man as forceful and dominant as Zane, never been handled so roughly. He was how she had imagined Viper would be, but ten times hotter, controlled, but not violent, and terrifying only because he made her want more.

"Look at me." He dragged in a harsh breath, then swept his tongue inside her mouth, touching, tasting, claiming every inch, showing her what he meant to do to her body. She sank beneath the ferocity of his need, her eyes lifting to his, drowning in the depths of a chocolate sea.

"I need you," he gritted out. "Now. Here. I need to know you're real. I need to know you're safe and you're mine. I can't promise to be gentle. Not this first time."

"I don't want gentle." She threaded her hands through his silky hair, then fisted it and pulled him down to her mouth, nipping his bottom lip to let him know she could take whatever he wanted to give.

"Christ, sweetheart," he groaned. "You're not ready for all that I've become. Don't push me too far, or I won't be able to hold back." He drew her hand down to the bulge in his jeans and pressed her palm against his erection. "Touch me."

She hesitated, still uncertain around this new Zane, so confident and commanding. Although she was tempted to go where he led, uncover the dark secret he struggled to hide, she wasn't ready to open herself up, to trust. Not when she still had questions about the night he left Stanton. Not when he might leave again. But for now, she wanted to lose herself in him, forget about the day and give in to the yearning she had lived with for the last nine years.

Hand trembling, she undid his belt and opened his jeans, releasing his cock from its restraint. Zane groaned, and jerked his hips, thrusting into her palm. Nine years ago he had been a teenager. Now he was all man. His chest was broad and thick with muscle, tattooed with the Sinner's Tribe logo and scarred by what looked to be a blade; his cock huge and hot, lay heavy in her hand. The boy had touched her with a sweet hunger, gentle and hesitant, awed and forgiving. The man in front of her knew exactly what he wanted, and how he wanted it. He was utterly confident and in control, raw and primal, a tsunami of heat and desire. And the thought of unleashing that power, having all that hunger and intensity focused on her . . .

Zane drew Evie's shirt over her head, tossed it on the floor, then drew her nipple between his lips, rolling it with his tongue. The cool air on her skin coupled with his hot, wet mouth sent a shiver of need straight to her core and she moaned and arched her back, offering him more.

"That's right, sweetheart. Give it to me." He released her nipple and turned his attention to her other breast, his hand on her hip grinding the curve of her sex against his thigh.

Her body heated, flamed, and she rocked against him, needing more than the tease of denim against her clit. She tightened her grip on his shaft, and worked him as hard as she dared, sliding her hand from balls to tip in a steady rhythm until he gave out a tortured groan.

"Harder."

Harder? She'd never held a man harder than she held him now. "I don't want to hurt you."

"I like the edge. The line between pleasure and pain." He nipped her nipple sending a sizzle of electricity straight to her clit.

"Do you feel it?"

A shiver ran down her spine. Feel it? One more bite like that and she'd come just from the pressure of his thigh on her clit. "Yes." The word escaped her lips in a moan, a plea for more, although she didn't know what more there could be than an arousal so fierce she would give anything to come right now.

Zane pulled a condom from his back pocket, and tore it open with his teeth. Evie moved back as he sheathed himself, wondering how different life would be if they'd taken that precaution before. But then she wouldn't have Ty or the memories of that beautiful night.

And then his hands were on her hips and he was lifting her, bracing her between his broad chest and the wall, until his cock pressed against her entrance, a delicious, tantalizing pleasure.

"Don't stop." She wrapped her legs around his narrow hips, trembling as he lowered her inch by inch over his shaft, giving her time to accommodate to his size. Her sex throbbed as he slid deeper and deeper until he was fully seated in her core, as close as two people could be, as close as they had been the last time they were together, except then she had given herself completely to him, body and soul.

"Fuck." He grabbed her hips and they moved together, Evie bracing her forearms on his shoulders, trying to match his steady rhythm with her own. Unlike their first time together, their joining wasn't slow or tender. There was no exploration, no kisses, no hesitation. It was hard, desperate, animal fucking, and she was totally on board.

Her orgasm built, climbing higher and higher, flaming her blood until sweat trickled between her breasts. Close. But not close enough.

"Zane," she panted her breaths. "I need—"

"I got you, sweetheart." He reached between them to stroke her clit. One touch was all she needed. One touch and she had to bite her lip to hold back the scream as she climaxed, riding his long, deep thrusts as wave after wave of pleasure spiraled out to her fingers and toes.

Zane drew out her orgasm, driving his cock deeper as her sex rippled around him. Finally, he stiffened and groaned, his shaft becoming impossibly hard before he climaxed, the throb of his orgasm sending tiny aftershocks through her pussy.

Evie collapsed against him, resting her forehead on his shoulder as she caught her breath. It felt too good to be with him like this, too right. Dangerous.

"You're real after all," he murmured, stroking a warm hand down her back.

"Apparently so." She wiggled to let him know she wanted down and he eased out of her and lowered her to the floor. Now that her physical hunger had been sated, Evie didn't know what came next or what she should do now. She crossed her arms over her chest, feeling inexplicably shy as he tugged on his jeans.

Seemingly unaware of her sudden withdrawal, he brushed a kiss over her cheek and left to dispose of the condom.

Evie grabbed her nightshirt and tugged it on, then settled on the bed with her tablet, the blanket over her legs, her back up against the headboard, giving her the distance she needed to process all that had happened.

Zane paused in the doorway, and frowned, his beautiful body making her want him all over again. Damn he was fine. Those cut indents on either side of his abs made her want to rip off his jeans and follow that V down to its peak. But that's all she wanted. Hearts weren't made to break more than once.

"What are you doing?"

"Trying to sort out funeral arrangements and insurance. Getting in touch with Bill's staff. Catching up with some friends." She feigned a laugh. "Getting out a few posts to let people know I won't be around because I'm being hunted down by a psychotic outlaw biker." She cringed inwardly at her very obvious and cold attempt to brush him off so soon after they'd been intimate, but he needed to get the message: they had dealt with the sexual tension between them and now it was time to move on.

"It's not a joke, Evie. Viper is a real threat."

"If I thought it was a joke, I wouldn't have uprooted my life and come here."

When he didn't move, she tried again, clutching the tablet like a life preserver. "I'll be up for a while. You'd best hit the couch and get some sleep." She dropped her gaze and stared at the blank screen on her lap. There. She couldn't be more blunt than that, but if she'd hurt him, she couldn't tell from the low, even timbre of his voice.

"Come here, sweetheart."

She looked up, saw nothing but concern and understanding on his handsome face. Still she, pressed her lips together and stared at the screen.

"Zane. Really I—"

"Come to me, Evie." His voice carried a hint of command, although his expression was gentle.

She put down the tablet and went to him, not because of his command, but because she was already lonely behind the walls she had so quickly put up after their intimate encounter. And because, even after all these years, Zane knew when she was afraid and hurting, knew when she needed him most.

Zane circled her with his arms and drew her into his warmth. With a sigh, Evie slid her arms around his waist and pressed her cheek against his chest, listening to the steady beat of his heart.

"I've got you," he whispered.

His words melted her just enough that the tension drained from her body, the walls falling down as quickly as she'd put them up. Myriad emotions assailed her, and she clung to him, drawing from his strength.

"I tried to save him." Her words stuck in her throat. "There was so much blood. And then I stabbed Viper. He was so angry. He tried to . . ." She choked on her words.

Zane's arms tightened around her, holding her firm, protecting her from the memories, whispering soft words as she shuddered against him.

"Breathe, sweetheart. Let it go."

A tear slid down the side of her face and she took comfort in his arms. Not just because she felt so safe with him, but because she could feel him, remind herself he was real, and not just memory.

"If it wasn't for T-Rex, Ty would be alone."

"He'll never be alone." He brushed his knuckles over her cheek. "Neither will you. I'll keep you and Ty safe, Evie. And the Sinners will always have your back."

His hand was cool on her skin, his body warm against her. She didn't know how long he held her, but she knew he would never let go until she asked.

"Thank you." She tilted her head back, met his gaze as she brought her hand up and swept the long dark strands of hair from his face. So handsome. So perfect. She ran her fingers over the hard planes and angles of his cheekbones, trailing them slowly over his jaw, rough with a five o'clock shadow.

"Pleasure."

She leaned towards him and brushed her lips against his. He responded with a gentle kiss, tracing her lips with his tongue then dipping into her mouth.

"Goodnight, sweetheart."

She waited until his footsteps faded away and then fell back on the bed. How the hell was she going to keep this up? It was everything she could do not to run after him and tell him she'd changed her mind. He'd just shown her that the Zane she had loved—the sensitive, caring Zane who knew her better than she knew herself—was still there, hiding beneath the leather cut and the cool exterior. Part of her wanted to cuddle up to him in her bed with his strong arms wrapped around her, and feed that longing to feel safe and secure, but the other part wasn't prepared to give up control in any other part of her life. If she let her guard down, if their connection felt too good, she would just be setting herself up for more pain when he disappointed her again. And although she felt a deep connection to Zane that went beyond the child they shared, she had lost her trust and faith in relationships.

Intimacy and connection only lead to pain. And she'd had enough pain to last a lifetime.

★ FOURTEEN ★

Try and try again. Don't think you're stupid if it doesn't go right the first time. Even experts make mistakes.
—SINNER'S TRIBE MOTORCYCLE REPAIR MANUAL

Someone was watching him.

Zane slid his hand under the cushion and grabbed his weapon. He had only just fallen asleep after tossing and turning all night on the couch, wondering what the hell had gone wrong with Evie, or whether, in fact, it had gone right.

Did he really want to get involved? He'd been on his own so long he couldn't imagine integrating not just a woman, but a kid into his life. And what kind of life did he have to offer? If he'd thought himself unworthy of Evie back in Stanton, he certainly hadn't improved the situation by becoming an outlaw biker. Wasn't it better to have dealt with the sexual tension between them so they could both move on? The answer came in a heartbeat. There was no other woman for him. He'd been searching for her since the day he left Stanton, and now that he'd found her, he wouldn't let her go.

But first, there was a threat to deal with, and Evie and Ty were under his protection.

In one smooth motion, he rolled off the couch and onto his feet, his weapon pointed in the direction of the shallow breaths that had awoken him. It took him a moment to register the face in front of him, a mini mirror image of his own.

"Don't shoot me." Ty covered his face with his arms. "I didn't mean to wake you up."

Christ. Talk about the wrong way to start the day. He placed the weapon in its holster across his chest, and fell back on the couch, drawing in a calming breath as adrenaline surged through his body. "Sorry about that. Not used to people sneaking up on me. You got quiet feet, but loud breathing."

"Is that good?" Ty lowered his arms, his thin wrists protruding from his Batman pajamas. *Good choice.* Batman had always been Zane's favorite superhero. Dark, secretive, isolated, not given to overt displays of emotion. But the whole Robin thing . . . he didn't need that lame-ass sidekick.

"You want to keep your presence hidden, you got to breathe through your nose, quiet like. Become one with the room. Even then, people can sense when they aren't alone, so standing in plain view isn't the best plan."

"I wasn't trying to hide. I was just seeing if you were awake." Ty's eyes drifted to the gun. "Is that real? Can I hold it?"

"Yeah it's real. Can't protect you if I got a play gun." He pulled the gun from its holster and removed the magazine, then handed it to Ty.

"Who are you protecting us from?" Ty pointed the gun at Zane and pulled the trigger. Sweat beaded on Zane's brow, and he silently congratulated himself for having the foresight to remove the magazine as opposed to just putting on the safety, even as he fought the urge to dive behind the couch, an instinctive response after what seemed a lifetime of gunfights with the Jacks.

"Bad guys." He gently pushed Ty's hand down so the gun pointed at the floor. "This isn't a toy. You point a gun at a man, you gotta be prepared to kill him." His pulse slowed and he wiped his brow. Lesson number one. Kids didn't have a lot of common sense. Or maybe his son wanted to scare him to death. So far he was two for two this morning.

"Aren't you a bad guy? I thought all bikers were bad. I see them on the news 'cause they blow up buildings and set fires and hurt people." Ty handed the gun back to Zane, then spun around and walked around the room, holding his fingers in the form of a make-believe gun. He aimed at the vase on the kitchen table, then the window, then Evie's bedroom door. "Pow. Pow. Pow."

"Sometimes people hurt you and you gotta teach them a lesson so they don't do it again." Zane shifted on the couch. Did Ty need to learn those lessons yet? Wasn't he too young?

"Pow." Ty pressed his fingers to the back of Zane's head.

"Jesus Christ." Zane leaped off the couch, heart thudding in his chest. "You gotta learn to be careful with weapons. Even pretend ones."

Ty's face fell, and his bottom lip quivered. "Sorry."

Fuck. Five minutes and he'd already screwed this up. He handed his gun back to Ty. "Here. I'll show you how to handle it properly."

For the next half hour, he showed Ty how to hold and carry a gun and load the magazine. He told him about the safety and how to aim at a target. He explained about recoil and how someone without much strength would have to brace against the backward thrust after a shot. Ty caught on pretty fast, considering he was only eight years old. When he held the gun perfectly balanced, his stance relaxed and his arms braced for an imaginary recoil, Zane felt a sting of pride. His son was no pansy. He'd get him out to a shooting range and—

"What's going on? Ty! Put down that gun."

Maybe not.

By the time Zane reached the clubhouse, the executive board was in session. Shooter and two senior patch members

were at the safehouse keeping watch. Zane had checked
all the locks and run a perimeter around Sparky's shop
before he left to make sure there were no Jacks hanging
around. Evie had been more bemused than angry to find
Ty learning to use a gun, and after Zane cooked them breakfast she seemed to forgive him. Still, there was an undeni-
able tension in the air, and he wondered if she regretted
what they'd done last night.

He hadn't intended for things to go as far as they did,
and although he had relished the feeling of being intimate
with her again, it was the time after, when she'd come to
him for comfort, that told him what he wanted to know.
She needed him. And even though he'd fucked up, she
trusted him with her body, and maybe even with a little of
her heart.

Jagger gave him a curt nod and brought him up to speed.
Tank and two of the junior patch had been out all night,
hunting down leads on T-Rex. Their sources suggested
Viper had an underground dungeon at his clubhouse, but
because no one had ever left it alive, they didn't have any
details.

As expected, Viper refused to trade Doreen for T-Rex.
Undeterred, Jagger had tabled a motion to defy National,
the Sinners' mother chapter, and go ahead with a raid on
the Jacks' clubhouse, not just to rescue T-Rex but to put
down the Jacks for good.

"All in favor." Jagger lifted his hand and all the board
members followed suit without hesitation.

"We need someone inside now," Gunner said. "We can't
wait for National's approval. I know Cade's been working
up local Black Jack suppliers, trying to find someone who
owes us a favor—"

Cade shook his head. "No luck so far. A favor isn't
worth the risk of being caught by the Jacks."

"What about Mario?" Zane rocked back in his chair. He
hated board meetings. They were the worst part of his role
as VP. Give him his bike and the open road and he was a

happy man, but sitting around the table, taking hours to make a decision he and Jagger could have made in three seconds, grated on him something fierce. Gunner shared his view. Always on the move, the club's sergeant-at-arms could rarely sit through an entire meeting, and he was already on his feet, pacing the room as he spoke.

"We burned down his restaurant," Gunner said. "He won't be taking any risks for us."

Zane would have killed to pace the room with him, but as VP he was forced to maintain decorum. "I had some of the junior patch check him out when we first talked about getting someone inside. The only reason the Jacks took over his restaurant, aside from the fact he's a good cook, is 'cause he owed them fifty large that he gambled away. Even though the restaurant is gone, the Jacks won't wipe out the debt. They still think he owes them."

Gunner nodded, following Zane's train of thought. "What if he offers his services as a personal chef to Viper? Once we get the intel we need from him, we give him the cash, he pays them off and we help him disappear."

"That's a huge risk and a lot of cash," Cade said. "I mean, what if he cooks up a bad meal and Viper decides to off him 'cause he doesn't like shrimp?"

"You ever have a bad meal at Mario's?" Gunner licked his lips. "He's a genius. The things he can do with salmon are fucking sinful."

"Christ. We're not interested in hearing about your kink," Sparky said, his nose wrinkling in mock disgust.

Zane bit back a smile. "Maybe Mario shoulda thought about the risk when he borrowed fifty grand from the Jacks." Just like he should have thought about the risk of what he'd done with Evie last night. But she was as much an addiction for him as gambling clearly was for Mario, and one taste wasn't enough.

Jagger drummed his fingers on the boardroom table, once a fancy dining table, now carved with the Sinner logo and stained with coffee rings. "Without the restaurant to pay off the debt, he's out of options. He knows the Jacks will be coming to him for the money, and with all the connections they have now there's nowhere he can run. I like the plan. Everyone vote." All hands went up and Cade and Tank offered to pay Mario a discreet visit that afternoon.

"Don't forget the party tonight," Jagger said after he officially ended the meeting. "We're having it at Sparky's shop instead of Rider's Bar because it's more secure."

"It's not right," Tank grumbled. "We shouldn't be partying when T-Rex is being held prisoner."

"I hear you, brother." Jagger clapped him on the shoulder. "But this is the best way to get everyone fired up about the rescue mission, and to make sure we're all still thinking about T-Rex. This party is about him. We're gonna toast him and pledge to do what it takes to bring him back. But we're going to need that Sinner bond to be as damned strong as it can be before we go in. I've made one last offer to Viper. If he turns it down and we have to raid the Black Jack clubhouse to get him out, I can't promise all of us will come back without a few scratches."

After the meeting broke up, Zane headed down to the basement with Dax to interrogate Doreen. Assuming T-Rex was in the Black Jack clubhouse, they needed more information before launching a full-on assault, and Doreen was the key to getting T-Rex out alive.

"These are the moments I live for," Dax said as they descended the stairs to the basement. "Torture sessions and the time I spend with my family."

"You're one sick fuck." And yet, last night with Evie . . . this morning with Ty . . . he wouldn't trade those moments for the world. But Evie kept trying to push him away. Should he respect her wishes and back off? What the fuck did he know about being a dad? Or being in a relationship when his loyalty was to the club? Christ, it was all fucked up. Good thing he was with a brother who specialized in this very thing.

"So, I got this friend . . ."

"You don't have friends." Dax laughed as they stepped out into the games room. "You have brothers. And brothers look out for each other. Jagger already told me what went down 'cause he was worried about you, and he didn't want anyone getting hurt." He paused at the bottom of the stairs. "So, to recap, you found your long lost girl who turns out to be Viper's girl. You decided to steal her away, but you don't know if you want her or she wants you. You got a son you didn't know about, and the whole shebang scares the shit out of you 'cause who the hell can prepare themselves to be a dad when they don't even know it's coming?"

Zane bristled. "I'm not scared."

"Then you're not human." Dax ran his hand through his dark hair, slicked back to show off his widow's, peak. "I was scared shitless the first time Sandy got pregnant, and I had nine months to prepare and the love of my life to catch me when I fell. And boy did I fall. First month, I took every job Jagger had on offer just to get away. But Sandy set me straight. One night I came home and she dumped Jett in my arms and told me it was her turn for a month off. Then she walked out the door. I didn't know she was just stayin' next door with her friend. But hell, by the end of the night, Jett was still breathing, and I was feeling pretty damn good about myself. Sandy came back the next day and I told Jagger I'd be slowing things down for a while."

"He's not a baby." Zane leaned against the worn pool table that had seen one too many games. His gaze flicked to the wet bar in the corner. If he didn't need his wits about him to interrogate Doreen, he would be over there pouring himself a shot of the good stuff. "He's eight. I missed . . ." His throat tightened. "All that."

Dax's face softened. "Yeah, you did. And the way Jag tells it, that's another burden you have to bear. Who we are as teenagers isn't who we are as men. We don't have the maturity or even a sense of responsibility under our belts. They say the male brain doesn't fully develop until we hit twenty-five, and I'd say that's about right. Women on the other hand are born mature. That's why they can so easily fuck us over. They've got years of practice before we come into our own."

"Evie . . ." Zane toed the concrete floor with his boot. When they'd first done the reno of the new clubhouse, they'd put down industrial carpet, but after a few parties, a couple of orgies, and a few fistfights, they'd decided to rip it up and go back to the basics. "She had a hard time growing up. And in the end, everyone abandoned her, including me and Jag. She doesn't trust me. She thinks I'm gonna leave her again."

"Are you?"

"I don't know," he answered honestly. "I keep thinking maybe she's better off without me. I'm not a family man. Didn't have any role models for how that kind of thing works. She was doing okay before I came along, and she doesn't want to be involved in our life. But then there's Ty. I'm not about to abandon my son. I wanna do right by them. I just don't know what right is."

Dax lifted the key from the hook beside the door. "You've got to figure that one out. When people are abandoned, they wind up with a need to feel safe and secure, but they can't trust anyone because the people who were supposed to love them let them down. So they push everyone away. If you want her, you need to make her feel secure. She won't feel that way if it looks like you got one foot out the door."

Well, hell. Here he'd been thinking only about Evie, but Dax could have been talking about him. He'd never thought about being abandoned as a kid. His life was the way it was, with a mom gone and a dad who didn't give a shit about anything but drugs. He'd never really seen the parallel between Evie's alcoholic mother and his druggie father, but it was right there, staring him in the face. They'd bonded over a loss they hadn't realized was a loss at all. They'd found safety and security in each other's arms.

Dax paused, one hand on the door. "Not that I like intruding on people's lives—okay, actually I do—but, there's something else."

"She's gotta forgive me."

"No. You have to forgive yourself."

"Viper doesn't want me back, does he? That's why you're here." Doreen folded her arms and leaned against the wall. She had taken off her cut and tied her hair up in a ponytail, bringing the dark circles under her blue eyes, and her pale skin into sharp relief. But as with all old ladies, appearances could be deceiving, and so far she'd shown herself to be vicious, cunning and resourceful, all of which meant Zane had to stay alert.

"He has one our brothers," he said. "We offered him a trade, and he turned us down. He said if you were stupid enough to get caught, he'd kill you himself if you showed up at his club." Zane didn't pull his punches. She needed to know she was alive now only by the grace of the Sinners.

"I'm not as stupid as he thinks," she muttered, half to herself, but Zane didn't miss the pain that flickered across her face.

He pulled up the chair across from her bed and rested his elbows on his knees, studying her body language—legs stretched out on the floor, ankles crossed, leaning back on her hands. Certainly not the language of fear.

"So are you going to kill me? Torture me for information? You want to know what they've done with your brother, don't you?"

Dax unloaded his duffel bag on the table by the door. "If you're willing to cooperate, we'll let you go. If not, we'll get the information we need in whatever way we have to do it."

"Let me go?" She moved as if to stand and Zane

motioned her back on the bed. He had no desire to get physical with her, but if she tried anything stupid, he would have no choice.

With a sigh, she pushed back and leaned against the wall, legs bent up, her arms resting casually on her knees as if they were just hanging out having a chat, instead of in a dungeon with a torture expert who was ready and willing to ply his trade. "You've tainted me. If he sees me on the street he'll think I did a deal with you to get free, which would make me a traitor. Only way I can go back to Viper is if I bring him something useful to prove my loyalty. You wanna tell me your secrets? Maybe give me a crate of weapons to buy back his love?"

"Torture and death it is then." Dax clapped his hands together. "And Zane thought this wouldn't be fun."

Doreen shrank back the tiniest bit. "What about a door number three? Like I give you something and you give me something that doesn't end up with Viper hunting me down and slitting my throat?"

"What do you want aside from freedom?" Zane met her gaze, challenging, defiant. He liked her. Not in a sexual way, although she was an attractive woman, but because she'd been through hell and didn't break. Kinda like his Evie, but with rougher edges and a harder heart.

"Protection."

"You're a prisoner," Zane said. "Can't get more protection than that."

"Not for me. For my kid. I don't want Viper to get him. I want someone to look after him if I don't make it. He's with my mom, but she's only interested in booze and drugs and her place isn't exactly kid friendly." She pulled her bottom lip between her teeth, a hesitant, slightly apprehensive gesture that was at odds with what they'd seen of her so far.

"Why would he care about Axle's kid?" Dax voiced the question that was on the tip of Zane's tongue.

Her eyes widened and she quickly looked down,

worrying a thread on the rough wool blanket covering the bed. "Viper has no boundaries. I wouldn't put it past him to grab my kid just to make sure I don't talk to you."

Zane ran a hand through his hair. Something else was going on here, more than just an old lady who'd been unwillingly taken to pay her old man's debt, but he couldn't put his finger on it. "We'll take it to the executive board, but you have to give us something as a show of good faith. You do that and Dax will write down your mom's address before we leave and we'll check it out to make sure it's not a trap."

"He'll be in the torture chamber," she said quietly. "Under the clubhouse."

Zane's head jerked up. "So there is a torture chamber?"

"That's where he puts all his prisoners. Looks like a medieval dungeon and the stuff that he's got in there . . ." Doreen shivered, giving authenticity to her words even before her lips curled in disgust. "He likes to hear them scream. He likes their pain. Sometimes he keeps them in there for days or weeks. I heard he has another dungeon at his house, but I've never heard of anyone being taken there."

"Sadist." Dax said. "Like that's a surprise."

Doreen's voice dropped to a whisper. "Never wanted to leave the Jacks as much as the first time I was sent down there to clean up. Axle was no saint but he wasn't twisted like Viper. Torture turns Viper on. Even the hardest old ladies didn't want to go to his bed after he'd been down there."

Zane's jaw clenched. "How do we get in?"

"The main door to the dungeon is outside the clubhouse. The yard is fenced off with electric wire and there are guards on the gate, as well as guards patrolling the grounds. And dogs." She drew in a ragged breath. "Viper has the only key and he keeps it in his office."

"Don't need a key when we have explosives," Zane said.

"Someone will need to get close enough to plant them. That's not gonna be easy." Doreen twisted her hands in her lap. "A couple of other clubs have tried. The guys who made it past the fence never made it out again. It's a suicide mission for whoever you send."

"That'll be me," Zane said.

T-Rex had sacrificed himself for Evie. Zane owed him a debt. And if he had to repay it with his life, he would die a happy man. He had held Evie in his arms one last time. He had a son to carry on his name.

What more could a man want?

★ FIFTEEN ★

*Don't get distracted while doing your repair.
You have one goal, and one goal only.
Make it run and make it run good.*
—SINNER'S TRIBE MOTORCYCLE REPAIR MANUAL

Perfect woman for Jagger, Evie thought as she shook Arianne's hand. In the fifteen minutes she and Ty had been in Sparky's shop, Arianne had barked orders at a couple of bikers, thrown a wrench at Sparky, and tuned up a V-Rod Muscle to the thudding beat of Saxon's "Motorcycle Man." A little heavy for midday, but no one complained when Arianne hooked her phone up to the speaker system and blasted the tunes.

Evie tried not to stare, but it was hard to look away from the contrast of Arianne's beauty—long, thick brown hair, startling green eyes, sharply-defined features—and the baggy gray coveralls she wore for her work as a journeyman mechanic in Sparky's shop. Evie had always wondered what kind of woman could put up with Jagger's forceful personality, but now she knew. Formidable in her own right, Arianne was his perfect match.

"So you're Zane's new girlfriend." Arianne gave her a frank, appraising look and gestured her over to the worn brown couch in the corner. Tucked away in the corner of an industrial estate, the corrugated metal warehouse had been converted into a spacious, brightly lit garage, complete with neatly filled tool racks, comfortable furniture, and work bays for five bikes.

"I have to say I never thought I'd see him with a woman," Arianne continued. "He's a dark horse, our Zane. When I first came to the club, he thought I was a Black Jack spy sent to seduce Jagger and take down the Sinners, and he did everything he could to get rid of me."

"I'm surprised he's still alive."

Arianne's eyes widened and she grinned. "Jagger likes him so I let it slide."

"We're not really together," Evie said quickly. "We were friends growing up, and then we lost touch." So they'd had sex. It hardly counted for a relationship, although she knew a lot more about Zane than she did about most of the men she had dated. But that was Zane before. Not Zane now.

"Friends who have a son together." Arianne nodded at Ty who was watching attentively as Sparky changed a tire.

"Yeah. I don't know how that's going to work out. I mean, with the whole biker thing . . ."

"Lots of the club members have kids," Arianne said. "They just keep their home life separate from their biker life, except for Sunday rides and club parties when the old ladies show up and cause trouble. You'll get a taste of that at the party tonight."

"Don't scare her off." Sparky, the Sinner road chief, and serious a contender for Tall, Dark, and Handsome Man of the Year, with his thick, brown hair and piercing blue eyes, wiped his hands on an old rag. "At least not until she's given us the down and dirty about Jagger and Zane."

"That kind of information is only shared among old ladies." Arianne smirked. "So unless you want to hang with Sandy, Dawn, Evie, me and a bunch of old ladies tonight, you're out of luck." She put her feet up on the coffee table, and her brow creased. "Evie's also going to tell us what she was doing with Viper when Zane was riding around available for the taking, 'cause I'm guessing she's a few years younger than me and given that Viper's my dad, that's kinda . . . not something I really want to think about."

Evie's cheeks heated and she drew in a deep breath, inhaling the familiar scents of grease and paint. "I didn't—"

"And I'm outta here." Sparky tossed the rag on a tool bench affixed to the wall. "Gotta get back to man stuff: fixing engines, tuning bikes, using tools—"

"What I was just doing," Arianne interjected.

Sparky flipped her the bird. "Ty. Bud. C'mon over here and I'll show you my manly socket wrenches."

"You don't have to tell me anything," Arianne said after Sparky had taken Ty to the furthest corner of the garage. "I just found it hard to believe when Jagger told me. I never saw any kindness in Viper. He was a cold, hard, cruel father, and a vicious, ruthless bastard who twisted my brother, and killed my mother because he thought she was having an affair."

Evie's mouth opened and closed again. She was at a complete loss for words. Had everything between Her and Viper been an act? Every word? Every conversation? His gentle kisses and soft words? As with Derek and Mark, had she failed to see the monster behind the man? Was she making the same mistake with Zane? How could she ever trust herself?

"I'm sorry." Arianne grimaced. "I shouldn't have said that. You obviously saw a side of him no one else has seen. Maybe he was different with you. There were times when he was caring with my mother. Obviously. Or she would never have stuck it out."

Was that it? Or had she been wearing blinders all her life, shutting out what she didn't want to see in her dogged pursuit of a dream that never was going to come true? "Maybe she stayed because of you," Evie said. "I stayed in a bad marriage for Ty. That's why I'm done with relationships."

Arianne lifted an admonishing eyebrow. "Better tell that to Zane. He came down here and laid down the law.

It was the usual possessive, protective, territorial biker thing: you're his, blah, blah, blah; he'll kill anyone who touches you, blah, blah, blah; no one who wants to keep his balls can look at you, blah, blah, blah; don't even breathe the same air . . . you get the drill."

"He said that?"

"He said it with a difference." Arianne's smile faded. "Because he's Zane. He doesn't talk much, but when he says something, he means it."

Sparky's shop shook with the hard beat of metal music, the thud of the bass carrying up the stairs where Evie had just put Ty to bed before changing for the party. She had only packed one fancy outfit in her suitcase, a Scandinavian-style black dress in a crepe fabric with unique cut outs on the sides and front, and a wide bandeau strip across her breasts. Not really her style, but Connie had convinced her to buy it one Saturday afternoon by feigning a collapse in the store dressing room when she tried it on.

Zane met her in the hallway at the foot of the stairs. He'd been out all day at the clubhouse dealing with the situation with T-Rex. Evie's gaze skittered from the tips of his heavy, dust-covered biker boots, to his low-riding jeans, snug in all the right places, and then over his muscle-hugging T-shirt to his tanned, frowning face. Memories of what they'd done last night sent a wave of heat through her body and her cheeks flushed.

"You're showing a lot of skin." His frown became a scowl as his gaze swept over her body. "Do you know what it does to a man when he gets a glimpse of something he's not supposed to see?"

"Does that mean you like it?"

Zane splayed his hand under the back panel of the dress, his fingers skimming the edge of her panties as he pulled her against him. "It means I only got two hands, and there's a lot of brothers who won't be able to take their eyes off you since you're showing more skin than dress." He pulled his hand from beneath her dress, and slapped her ass. "Go change."

Evie cried out in surprise. The slap was more of a sting than true pain, but the responding throb in her sex shocked her, made her wonder what would happen if he slapped her again. But the sudden thrill quickly turned to indignation.

"Seriously?" Evie glared at him, her mouth agape. "You're ordering me to go and change my clothes? I've seen some of the clothes the old ladies are wearing. I look like a nun compared to them."

"You got a habit upstairs, I'll be a happy man."

"I'm not changing, Zane." She leaned against the wall, folded her arms over her chest. "Even if we were together, which we're not, I wouldn't let you tell me what to wear. I went through that with Mark. He was insecure right from the start because he never felt he could measure up to you and Jagger. When he lost his job, he started drinking again and that just made it worse. And when we had to rely on my income, he couldn't deal with it. He started following me around, trying to cut me off from my friends, checking my phone, and showing up at work. He threw out some of my clothes, called me a slut . . ."

"Jesus Christ. Once we get T-Rex, I'm fucking going after him." Zane leaned one elbow beside her and traced the cutout on the left side of her dress with his free hand, his finger warm against her skin. "What if I ask real nice?"

Evie bit back a smile at his sudden change in demeanor. "Jagger saw my dress. He didn't have a problem."

"Because you aren't his." He slid his hand beneath the front panel of her dress, his finger dipping down to her mound, sending a sizzle of erotic sensation straight to her clit. "You're mine."

Flustered by his possessiveness given that she'd pretty much booted him out of her room last night, she had no idea what to say. And when he pulled her in close and lowered his face until their noses were almost touching, she wanted nothing more than to run her tongue over his lips and forget about speech all together.

"You showing something that belongs to me makes it my problem," he murmured.

"I don't belong to you, Zane."

"Last night." He feathered kisses along her jaw, following her jugular to the hollow at the base of her throat. "Says you do." His hands slid down to her ass and his fingers dug into her cheeks. "Way I feel now, thinking of the brothers lookin' at you, touching you, and you showing off what you shared with me last night, says you do."

Desire pulsed through her, a deep throb that intensified with every second. "It was just sex."

"You and me, sweetheart . . . it's never *just* anything."

"C'mon you two. Jagger's about to give a speech." Sparky's voice pulled Evie out of the moment and she clasped Zane's hand.

"Looks like I win by default," Evie said. "I wouldn't want to disrespect Jagger by missing his speech."

He stared at her for a long moment, and then he dropped her hand and slid his arm around her waist. "It's gonna be a long fucking night."

They made their way into the shop, now emptied of bikes and filled with bikers. Zane introduced her to Cade, the club treasurer, a blond, blue-eyed, drop-dead gorgeous biker with a cheeky smile, and his old lady, Dawn, who could have passed for his sister. After chatting with them and meeting a few more bikers, she spotted Tank sipping a beer at the far edge of the garage and excused herself to join him.

"You're looking kinda down." Relieved to be away from the crowd, she eased herself up on the bench beside him, her feet dangling off the floor.

"Missing T-Rex."

Evie wasn't surprised. In the short time she'd been around the Sinners, Tank and T-Rex were always together.

"Yeah, I was surprised the Sinners were having a party when T-Rex was still . . . with Viper."

He shrugged. "It's Jagger's way of boosting morale before the big raid. We're goin' in to get him, and he says not all of us are gonna come out in one piece."

Evie caught her breath. "Jagger's sending you on a suicide mission?"

"We gotta get T-Rex. We don't leave brothers behind. And while we're there, we're gonna take down the Jacks. They're outta control. One-percenters like us don't got many rules, but we got some and the Jacks are breaking them all. No one is safe—old ladies, kids, even civilians."

"Is everyone going on the raid?"

Tank gave her a sympathetic look. "Every brother who can ride. Even the family men. We're all in or we're all dead, the way things are going now. Zane's on point. That means he's going in first, taking the biggest risk. He says it's 'cause he owes T-Rex a debt and if someone's gotta die—"

"No one is dying on my watch." Jagger came up behind Evie and rested his hand on her shoulder. "And this isn't going be some haphazard raid. Everything will be planned with military precision. Nothing will be left to chance."

"Except we don't know if T-Rex is alive or dead." Tank's voice wavered. "Or even if he's in the Black Jack clubhouse."

"We got some good intel on that this afternoon, brother." Jagger made a fist and bumped knuckles with Tank. "We all care about T-Rex and we're gonna bring him back. But maybe I'll save all that for my speech. I'm going to get an update from Shaggy, and then we'll toast T-Rex."

Sparky and Shooter waved them over to the makeshift bar after Jagger left, and soon had Evie laughing about how the club picked biker road names from events that happened when each biker was a prospect. Road Kill, Rubber, Sweet Cheeks, and Hard On had suffered the most from the Sinners' collective sense of humor. Executive board members were allowed to use first names when they were elected and Jagger, Zane, Dax, and Cade had taken that option.

"What's Zane's road name?" She hadn't even thought to ask, just as she hadn't thought to ask Viper's real name. Evie made a mental note to ask Arianne, not that she planned to see Viper again, but she still couldn't understand why she had seen a different side of the man, one that no one else had seen, and why that man had disappeared the night she met him at Riverside Bar.

"Tracker. 'Cause he can hunt down anything or anyone that's gone missing." Gunner, a giant of a man and well-suited to his role as club enforcer, shoved four Tequila Slammers across the bar, and Evie grimaced. Nothing went to her head faster than the fizzy combination of tequila and soda. Exactly what she needed tonight.

They did two slammers each and then Tank raised his third glass.

"Here's to T-Rex." Tank covered the drink with his hand, slammed it on the counter, then shot it back with one gulp. Beside him, Sparky did the same, and then Shooter followed suit.

Evie covered her glass, but before she could slam the drink on the counter, a warm, broad hand covered hers, and Zane came up behind her. "I think you've had enough."

Oh did he now? Evie pressed her lips together and glanced over at Tank with his wide eyes and vigorously shaking head. How utterly humiliating. As if she didn't know how much she could drink.

"Okay." She looked back over her shoulder and forced a smile for the dark, glowering man behind her, arm tensed for the moment he removed his hand.

Zane grunted his approval and slid his hand up her arm to her shoulder, his touch sending a sensual prickle over her skin. "Maybe we should—"

Slam. She banged the glass on the counter, waited two

seconds until it fizzed, and then shot it back. If she'd learned anything during her marriage to Mark, it was how to set boundaries. Although Mark was controlling, he was at heart an insecure man. Zane, on the other hand, was utterly dominant and if she didn't draw her line in the sand now, he would walk all over her when it came to decisions about Ty. "Thanks, Gunner. I'll have another."

She turned and met Zane's gaze, lifting her chin the tiniest bit just to let him know his dark scowl didn't affect her, but deep inside, fear curled in her belly. Not because she was afraid of him—for all the darkness in him, and the fear and respect he engendered in his brothers, he was still her Zane—but because she didn't know if she'd pushed him too far. Was this the moment he would walk away?

Silence. No one moved. No one spoke. Clearly she had crossed some hidden line.

Braced for his reaction, Evie expected a growl or even a shout, perhaps even the sight of his back as he walked away. So when he grabbed her hair, yanked her head back, and sealed his lips over hers in a fierce, possessive kiss, she gave in without a fight, her arms twining around his neck as he ravaged her mouth.

"Well . . . that was . . . unexpected," she said when he gave her a moment to catch her breath. "Maybe I should have another drink."

He drew her to the side of the bar, away from the curious stares of his brothers. His hands slid over her bare skin, exposed by the cutouts in the dress, and then he yanked her against him and pressed his lips to her ear. "Don't push me, sweetheart."

"I already pushed you."

"And I'm still here," he said quietly, giving her the reassurance she needed, although she had no idea how he understood her so well.

"Maybe we can be friends again." She pressed herself against him, breathing in his scent of leather and liquor, and the faintest hint of smoke. He snorted a laugh. "Friends don't fuck like we did last night."

Crude. But true. In fact, she'd never had a boyfriend who'd made her come the way Zane had last night. And he was right; it wasn't just sex. They had a connection. Whether it was from their shared past, their child, or something deeper, she didn't know.

He kissed the rise of her breasts above the thin strip of fabric, his hands encircling her waist, fingers trailing up and down the small of her back. "And they don't fuck the way I'm gonna fuck you now."

"Maybe I don't want to fuck in the middle of Sparky's garage while the Sinners party around us."

Just saying the word *fuck* sent a naughty thrill through her body. And the thought of *fucking* Zane right here, right now made her mouth water. How long had it been since she'd taken a risk? How many years since she'd felt that rush of adrenaline she'd shared only with Zane?

"I can smell sex on you, Evie," he murmured as he licked along the shell of her ear. "If I slid my hand into your panties, I'd find you wet and ready for me."

His dirty talk made her pussy wet, her nipples hard, and sent desire through her like a crashing wave. Her hips swayed, grinding ever so lightly against his rigid shaft, and she gripped his forearm when he slid one hand beneath the front panel of her dress, and into her panties, his fingers resting just above her clit. The world faded away, the bikers laughing and talking around them, the music pulsating through her body, the clink of glasses as Gunner poured drinks. There was just her and Zane and an ache only he could take away.

"That makes you hot." With his free hand he caressed her thigh, just at the hem of her dress, lifting it slowly, exposing her creamy skin to his ardent caress.

"Yes," she whispered. There was no point denying the potent chemistry between them. Plain and simple, Zane made her burn.

"I make you hot." Passion and raw hunger blazed in his eyes, and something darker, deeper, something that curled warm in her belly, spreading out to her fingers and toes.

"Scorching." She rocked against him.

"Tell me you want me." His hand snaked up her back, fisted her hair. She gasped at the sharp pain, felt a rush of heat between her legs.

"I want you, Zane." And she did. She wanted this, the thrill, the risk, the rush.

She wanted him.

Fuck she was sexy, with her lush lips, pink and glistening, wanting him to fill her sweet mouth. She labored her breaths, teasing him with the view of her breasts rising and falling, taut nipples just waiting to be pinched. The act of claiming her, knowing his brothers were watching, curious about the first woman Zane had ever brought to a club function was unexpectedly, inexplicably erotic and he'd never gotten so hard so fast in his life.

Consumed with desire, he released her and led her out of the shop and into the hallway leading outside. With a low growl, he shoved her up against the wall between the stairwell and the washroom, then yanked her dress up over her hips.

"Zane!"

Heedless of her cry, he pushed her silky panties aside and pressed a finger into her wet heat, angling his body to keep that particular intimacy hidden from anyone who might be watching.

"You're so fucking wet."

"And you're so fucking sexy." She rocked her hips against his finger.

Christ, was there anything hotter than his woman needing him? Zane's blood pooled in his groin. He would give her what she wanted and more. When he'd first arrived at the shop this evening, he'd been off-kilter, still thrown by her withdrawal the night before and the mess he'd made of the morning with Ty. But now, with Evie willing and responsive to his touch, he felt grounded. In control.

"He removed his finger and replaced it with two, parting her thighs with a gentle nudge of his knee.

"Oh, God." Her nails dug into his forearm as he thrust his fingers deep into her wetness. "Is this what happens at all the Sinner parties?"

"I wouldn't know. Usually I take watch." He rubbed his fingers along her sensitive inner walls, and her pussy tightened around him.

"They must have been . . . surprised . . . to see you . . . tonight." She stammered, breathless, close to climax, her body trembling.

"More like shock." He slowed his thrusts, teasing her with light, shallow strokes, taking her down so he could send her higher, make her scream. "Never brought a woman to the club either, so they got a double dose."

Her head fell back against the wall and she moaned. "I feel flattered."

"What else do you feel, sweetheart?" He added a third finger and thrust in so deep her breath caught in her throat.

"I feel like I need to come."

"Soon. But not here." He withdrew his fingers, wiping her wetness along her inner thigh so she would have something to remember as they made their way upstairs. "I don't want to share any more of you than you've already shared with my brothers."

"Yo! Zane." A highly inebriated Tank stumbled toward them as Zane steered Evie toward the stairwell, his mind focused on getting her naked and upstairs as quickly as possible.

"Not now, brother."

"Where's Connie tonight?" Oblivious to Zane's scowl, Tank leaned against the wall and took a swig from the beer bottle in his hand.

Blushing, Evie reached out to steady him. "She's with her grandmother in in Joilet."

Tank leaned closer, slurring his words. "She's one hot chick."

"Back off." Zane shoved Tank in the chest. "Maintain a perimeter."

"Hey, brother. We were just having a conversation." Tank jerked away from Zane's touch and the beer in his hand splashed over Evie's dress.

"Jesus. Fuck." Without thinking, Zane hauled back and punched Tank in the face. Control around Evie, it seemed, was fleeting.

Evie gasped as Tank staggered back and into the shop, Zane following him. People scattered. Someone chanted "Fight! Fight!" and a space cleared around them. Unlike civilian parties, fights were expected and, in fact, encouraged at biker events.

Tank recovered quickly and launched himself at Zane, who stepped neatly to the side, sending Tank sailing in the crowd. Sparky and Gunner lifted Tank and pushed him back into the ring. He spun around and scowled. "I didn't mean any offense, fuck-wit."

"Offense taken." Zane hit him again, landing a punch in Tank's stomach. Tank retaliated with a quick thrust kick, followed by a sequence of punches that had Zane reeling.

"Zane. Please. Stop. He didn't mean it," Evie shouted. But now that his tension had found an outlet, Zane wasn't interested in stopping until Tank was on the ground.

Of course, Tank was so named for a reason and he absorbed blow after blow, until Zane's wrists ached from the effort of trying to knock him down.

In a last-ditch attempt to end the fight, Tank ran at Zane, picking up speed as he crossed the floor to the cheers of the drunken crowd. He plowed into Zane, carrying him back with his shoulder and straight into the wall.

Jesus. Fuck. He was so not going to lose this fight with Evie and the brothers watching.

"Stand down." Jagger pushed his way through the crowd, but Zane was already in motion.

Fuck Jagger and the rules. Fuck Tank for making him lose control. Just. Fuck. He pounded his fist into Tank's sternum, grunting his satisfaction when Tank dropped to his knees.

"I said stand down, brother." Jagger got in his face, shielding Tank with his body. But Zane was too wound up to stand down. Vulnerable, raw and exposed, his control already stretched thin by his decision to bare his personal life to his brothers, he hauled back, ready to punch Jagger, although the repercussions would be severe. But before he could let loose, Evie grabbed his hand.

"It's okay, baby. I'm okay. But you won't be if you throw that punch. Even I know there's no going back if you hit Jagger." She kept her voice low as he allowed her to back him away from Jagger, away from Tank and the fight he didn't want, away from the shop and into the hallway.

"And if you get hurt," she continued, "or Jagger kicks you out, then we won't get to finish our evening the way I want." She slid one hand down his chest to his belt and then tugged his hips toward her. "You know what I want?"

Already peaked, Zane's primal instinct took over and he grabbed her hands and slammed them up over her head, thrusting his thigh between her parted legs. "You want to be fucked."

Her eyes dilated and she licked her lush lips. "No."

No? Had he read her wrong?

Evie took a breath, arching toward him, her breasts straining against the wet fabric of her dress. "I want to be fucked by you."

★ SIXTEEN ★

*When you're ready for your first test run, turn on
the gas, put on the choke, and kick.*
—SINNER'S TRIBE MOTORCYCLE REPAIR MANUAL

Zane pulled Evie against his body, and claimed her mouth
in a brutal kiss. She tensed at first, wary of his loss of control, but then she met his passion with her own, lips clash-
ing with his, driven by the same deep desires.

Dark, delicious Zane. She moaned, letting him know
she wasn't afraid of the fierceness of his kiss, loved the way
he mastered her mouth. She couldn't remember ever being with a man who made her feel such passion, who made
her feel alive. Well, maybe she did. Except back then he'd
been a boy.

"Take me upstairs," she whispered, melting against
him, as he released her hands.

"Go, Evie." He pulled away, a pained expression on his
face. "Not after the fight . . . I'm not safe, not in control . . . "

"I don't want to run from you." She teased him with a
tiny nip on his bottom lip, and he growled and slanted his
mouth over hers, his kiss hard and aggressive as he re-
claimed her lips, leaving no doubt that he wanted her just
as much as she wanted him.

"Fuck." He pulled away and slammed a fist on the wall
beside her. "I lost it out there. You in that dress showing
so much skin, drinking, the brothers looking at you like

they wanted to fucking eat you up, then Tank just blew off the lid . . ." He pressed his body against hers. "That doesn't happen to me. I am always in control."

"Except when you open yourself up. You let them see the real you, Zane. You shared something about yourself. There's nothing wrong with that." Evie ground her hips against the bulge in his jeans, her pulse pounding as Zane unraveled in the darkness. He had never shared his feelings except that one night they were together, never bared himself the way she did when things went wrong, and now that he had shown himself to his brothers, to her, he clearly couldn't handle it. Emotions couldn't be controlled and Zane was always in control.

"Take me," she whispered. "Take what you need from me."

"You don't understand." He groaned. "There's a side of me . . . I'll hurt you." He released her and pushed her toward the stairs. "Go upstairs and lock the door."

A shiver ran up her spine. "You want me to run from you?"

His entire body shuddered, like he was fighting something that grew larger by the second. "Evie." His voice dropped to a warning growl. "Run."

She made a split second decision and then kicked off her shoes and took off, a grin splitting her face. Her bare feet pounded on the concrete hallway and she hit the door to the parking lot at full tilt. He wanted her to run, so she'd run. But not in the way he expected. Because she understood—the loss of control to passion, emotion so intense it overwhelmed, the instinct of a predator to chase its prey.

As she surged forward, she felt the rush of adrenaline she hadn't felt in years, the freedom of baring herself to the night.

"Evie. Come back."

She crossed the parking lot and ran into the small field

behind the shop, praying there wasn't anything sharp in the grass. Warehouses dotted the commercial area around her; giant, corrugated metal structures surrounded in barbed wire. Spotlights, streetlights, and the bright moon gave her a clear view of the soft grass underfoot. She veered over to a small thicket of trees, hoping to find more cover. Although she worked out a few times a week, the thrill of fear coursing through her body ratcheted her pulse up to a level that would have made her kickboxing teacher proud.

Chase me.

And he did. The door slammed open, clanging against the metal wall, and she heard him call her name, this time with a growl of determination that sent a delicious shiver up her spine. This was her game now. She was in control. If she wanted him to catch her, she could slow down her pace. If she wanted him to chase her, she could pick up speed. If she wanted to hide, she could head for the dense underbrush ahead. He was hers to command. Zane, VP of the Sinner's Tribe. Dark warrior. First love. The man who had stolen her heart.

Chase me. Chase me. Chase me.

Her heart pounded furiously with each footfall, her speed hampered by her tender feet and the fabric of her dress. She heard him call, nearer now, his voice echoing in the stillness, but now that she was going she couldn't stop. Not until he caught her. And God, she wanted him to catch her. But first he had to prove himself worthy of his reward.

Evie laughed as she ran, drawing in breaths of air scented with pine and a hint of diesel. She couldn't remember the last time she'd felt such a rush, fear and excitement mixed into a heady cocktail that made her heart race and her sex throb.

Exhilarating. Had Zane felt like this the night she chased him through the forest? Had he run in anticipation of being caught, as she did now, or had he run in fear? Had he succumbed to her desires simply because she brought him down?

The crack of a tree branch behind her made her kick up her pace, every step a delicious thrill that made her heart flail against her ribs, her body tense in anticipation of the moment he caught her.

"Jesus. Fuck. Evie." With a grunt, he lunged, his shoe just brushing the back of her heel. Finally, blissfully, his hand closed around her neck. She tensed for the impact, but he pulled her against him and rolled, taking her to the ground in the cradle of his arms. She almost came at the surge of adrenaline that accompanied her capture, her legs shaking so violently, she was grateful when he rolled again, positioning her on all fours in the cool grass, covering her with his body.

"Need you."

Evie looked over her shoulder. His eyes glittered in the semi-darkness, his face masked by shadows.

"Yes."

Zane shoved her dress roughly over her hips, then tore her panties away with an animalistic growl. "Now. Can't wait."

Evie's body flared to life, seized by a lust unlike anything she'd felt before. Zane reached around and cupped her breast, his thumb rubbing over her nipple until it peaked beneath her bra.

"More," she rasped. "Take off my dress."

"Like the dress. Naughty dress. So fucking hot it drives me outta my mind. Wanna fuck you in this dress, but I won't be gentle."

She wished she could see his face, although the torment in his voice told her what she needed to know. "If I wanted gentle, we wouldn't be here."

He groaned and kicked her legs apart with his thigh, sending a shock wave of pleasure through her belly. His big body pressed hard against hers, and Evie trembled in anticipation, her ragged breaths the only sound in the still of the night.

"Mine." He swept her hair aside and pressed his lips against her nape, his teeth scraping over her skin. Sweat broke out at the base of her spine and spasms contracted her inner muscles. The men she'd been with since Zane had been nice, kind, but dull in the bedroom. Mark, in particular, had been appalled at her suggestions for spicing things up, and she'd resigned herself to the most traditional positions, taking her own pleasure in private to fantasies of rough men and even rougher sex.

"Harder." She rocked back against him, grinding her ass into his huge erection.

He hissed out a breath. "I came to the shop tonight thinking last night shouldn't have happened, that we had too much hurt between us. Then I saw you and I couldn't think anymore. I don't know how we got to be here, but if you don't want this, tell me now."

"I want this. I want you."

He nipped her shoulder, his body covering hers, keeping her warm despite the chill of the night air. A bird fluttered above them and the pine boughs swayed in a silent breeze, scenting the night with a fragrance both fresh and sensual. Primal.

Evie spread her knees wider, inviting. This was how it should be. In the forest, the way they had first come together. But rough instead of gentle; hard instead of sweet. They weren't the same people anymore, no longer innocent in any sense of the word. She wanted Zane the way he truly was; she wanted the side he had kept in the shadows, the way he was now. All man. All biker. All beast.

"Ah, sweetheart," his breath whispered over her skin, sent a shiver down her spine. "You do that, and I can't get you ready for me."

"I am ready for you." If she were any wetter she'd be dripping on the grass. "Touch me."

He palmed her cleft, sliding his fingers through her folds. With a groan, he pushed one finger inside and her body clenched around him.

"So hot. So wet."

She heard the rattle of the chain on his belt, the soft slide of leather and the harsh rasp of a zipper. Unable to hold back, she looked over her shoulder and watched as he released his shaft, huge and heavy, the tip gleaming wet in the moonlight. She wanted to take him in her mouth, as far he could go, wrap her hand around his straining length, and suck him until he lost control.

"Evie . . ." His warning growl sent a bolt of lust straight to her clit. God, she wanted to tease him, torment him, make him punish her again like he had with that slap. Her pussy clenched and she wiggled her ass. How could she make him slap her again?

"You wanna be spanked, sweetheart?" He dug a condom from his pocket, tore it open, and sheathed himself. "You want me to punish you for running away?" He smacked her cheek so hard she caught her breath. The burn spread across her skin turning into pure, delicious sensation by the time it reached her clit, and she bit back a low groan.

"Yes, she does," he murmured to himself. "She's a fucking naughty girl, but that's all she's gonna get." He thrust a thick thigh between her legs, opening her for him. Evie ground her sex against the delicious friction of his denim.

In her entire life she'd never felt as wanton as she did now, uninhibited, free. After Mark, she'd resigned herself to casual relationships, keeping her encounters brief and focused on only one thing. No risk of relying on a man to look after her. No risk of staying too long when she needed to walk away. But it was different with Zane. She'd been down that road with him before, knew where it led. There was a comfort in inevitability, and if she had doubts along the way, if occasionally he broke through the walls around her heart, she could shore them up with the memories of the nights she'd sat up waiting for him to come back, and the sunrises that crushed her hopes for yet another day.

"Gonna fuck you, sweet Evie." His voice dropped to a husky rasp. "Gonna bury myself so deep you're gonna feel empty every time I pull away. I wanna hear you scream. I want you to come for me."

"Lotta talking," she said, her voice thick with desire. "Not a lot of doing."

His hands tightened on her ass and he entered her with one hard powerful thrust. She could feel his body shaking all around her. He was trying to hold back, and although she didn't know if she could take any more, with his huge, hot cock throbbing inside her, she pushed back against him, taking him deeper.

"You feel so good," she whispered. "So hard. So thick."

"Evie." He groaned and hammered into her. Evie's hands dug into the soft grass as she tried to keep up with the frantic rhythm of his thrusts. This was nothing like the first time, when they'd been shy and uncertain, their hands shaking, bodies trembling. This was wild, free, born of unrequited passion and burning need. Their bodies slammed together, the sound of flesh slapping against flesh as erotic as soft music and candlelight. Zane unleashed. Just as she'd wanted him. And he was everything she'd expected, and more.

Her orgasm built quickly, heating her body, coiling her muscles inside and out. Zane slipped one hand between them and brushed his thumb up and around her clit. Once. Twice. And then he pinched, sending her spiraling out of control.

He stretched over her back, twining the fingers of one hand with hers in the grass, his teeth piercing the sensitive skin of her nape, setting off another ripple of shock waves that sparked along every nerve of her body. Zane pounded into her and then stiffened and groaned, his shaft throbbing as he pumped deep inside her. With a last shudder, he collapsed over her sweat-slick back, pressing soft kisses to her shoulder until they both came down from the ride.

When Evie shivered, Zane drew her up, leaning back on his knees, one arm wrapped around her waist. They breathed together, their hearts pounding in unison. Finally, he pressed a soft kiss to the stinging bite on her neck and gently lowered her to the grass.

"Lie with me." He didn't wait for her response. Instead, he straightened his clothing and lay on the grass, beckoning to her with his outstretched arm. Evie pulled down her dress and joined him, curled into his warmth, her head on his shoulder, looking up at the stars, brilliant in the dark sky.

"We never did our stargazing anywhere normal," she said quietly. "Rooftops, treetops, forests, the roof of your car . . . Except then we talked about deep things like extraterrestrial beings, and war, and music, and how chemistry teachers always manage to accidentally blow things up. "

Zane chuckled. "That was a useful lesson. We needed a quick explosive one night and I told the brothers how Mr. Cooper cut into that stick of phosphorus and blew up the class. We broke into a school and stole some. Flattened one of the Jacks' money laundering facilities, a pool hall just outside Devil's Hills."

"I guess you didn't run in with a fire extinguisher and save the day like you did in school." She leaned up and pressed a kiss to the pulse at the base of his throat.

He curled his arm around her, tucking her into his body. "I threw more phosphorus onto the fire. Watched the building burn to the ground. Thought about you sitting at the campfire on the beach on your graduation night, how beautiful you looked in the firelight, how much I wanted you."

"All you had to do was cross the fire pit."

Zane felt yet another stab of regret. So many opportunities wasted. How different would things have been if he'd crossed the fire pit that night, or the playground the day he'd seen her with Mark and Ty? "I didn't want to get burned."

He felt her chest rise and fall with laughter. "What about all the nights we lay together under the stars and talked about the future? You wanted to be a firefighter after you put out that fire in the chemistry classroom. I was going to go to college and get my Fine Arts degree. We were going to come back to Stanton so we could see each other every day and meet up for stargazing at night."

A wave of nostalgia hit him hard, and with it the ache of longing he'd felt every time he was with her. "I got a confession to make. I was never looking at the stars. I was looking at you looking at the stars, wishing I could be inside you. Not easy being a teenager and having the woman of your dreams lying beside you, all sexy and sweet, and not being able to touch her."

"I was the woman of your dreams?" She tilted her head back, rubbing her cheek over the soft bristles on his jaw.

"Every one." He'd dreamed about her even after he left, saw her on street corners, heard her voice in restaurants and bars. For years, he couldn't be with a woman without thinking about her, wondering if another man was touching her the way he touched the strangers he took to his bed, keeping her safe and happy, loving her.

"It must have been hard . . ." Her voice hitched in sympathy. "When you came back and saw me with Mark and Ty."

Zane's body stiffened. That kind of pain wasn't meant to be dredged up, relived, wielded to torture him again. "It fucking killed me."

"I'm sorry."

"You had Ty to think about." Forgiving, but not forgetting. He would have waited for her forever. In some ways, he was still waiting now.

A heavy silence thickened the air and it took him a moment to realize she was waiting for him to say something else, to apologize. But the words wouldn't come. If he hadn't left, he would be in jail, locked away, forgotten. He wouldn't have trained as a firefighter, or saved Jagger's life; he wouldn't have joined the Sinners and found brothers who accepted him despite his darkness. And although he was sorry he had hurt her, staying would have hurt her more because he would have been forced to tell the truth he had hidden from her all these years; he would've shattered the illusion she had of her father as a good, kind, loving, honorable man.

"I thought you weren't coming back," she said. "After three years of waiting, alone with Ty, I gave up hope."

He knew the moment she gave up waiting now—gave up hope—from the way her body tightened, unmolding itself from him, separating, until a chasm formed between them all the deeper because it couldn't be seen.

"I guess we'd better go." She sat up as he knew she would, pushed herself to her feet. With her hair tangled, her dress rumpled and her feet bare, she looked like a forest creature, ethereally beautiful, wild.

Free.

Free to leave him. Free to walk away.

She took a step back when he stood, retreating. "I think you were right. There's too much between us. Too much hurt. Too much pain. Even when we're close I feel I can't touch you, like you're holding back, and I can't stop thinking that means you're going to leave. I don't think sex is enough to build a bridge high enough to get over that pain or long enough to cover the distance between who we were and who we are."

"I told you I wouldn't turn my back on my responsibilities."

She regarded him with a measure of resignation. "Yes, you did mention your responsibilities."

Zane let out a growl of frustration. What more did she want? He'd told her twice now that he wouldn't shirk his responsibility as a father. He would make sure they were safe and provided for, and tonight he'd shared with her more than he'd shared with anyone in his life. He'd let her see into his soul.

Evie turned and picked her way across the grass, her bare feet pale in the moonlight. No longer flying, laughing, as she had when he chased her, she weighed each step, as if she was afraid of getting hurt. For some reason her caution annoyed him more than her speech. Didn't she understand she had nothing to fear when he was with her?

Maybe it was because he wasn't good with words. He had never been an eloquent man.

Zane closed the distance between them in three easy strides. Without speaking, he lifted her in his arms, cradling against her body. Then he carried her back to the party under the twinkling stars.

Since guns and swearing had been banned, Zane wasn't sure what to talk about with Ty. He'd never hung out with a kid. He stayed away from the Sinner parties where kids were invited, never dated a woman with children, and didn't frequent locations where kids might be found. So when Evie left him alone with Ty in the safe house kitchen the morning after the party, he found himself disconcertingly unprepared.

"Where's mom?" Ty stared at Zane from across the white plastic table. Who the hell had done the decorating? The safe house looked like something out of a catalogue, all white and shiny with blue accents. Cold. Austere. Certainly not welcoming. Not that he usually cared about such things, but he wanted Evie and Ty to be comfortable.

"In the shower." He pushed the eggs and bacon Evie had cooked around his plate. Whether it was the alcohol or the fact he had to sleep alone on the couch with his guilt and frustration, he'd had the worst night of his life. Why the heck had he taken her so roughly in the forest, let her see that side of him? This was Evie, soft and sweet, not one of the women who came to his apartment wanting exactly what he needed to dish out to soothe the darkness in his soul. No wonder she'd tried to push him away. Or maybe it was like Dax said. She could sense he wasn't fully committed, that he was still half in and half out the door.

"What are we doing today?" Ty's voice pulled Zane out of yet another round of self-flagellation. "Mom says we can't go outside."

"We're all gonna go to the clubhouse. I got some work to do and the brothers are gonna be too busy to keep watch over here."

"Are there other kids there?" Ty stirred his cereal. He hadn't eaten anything since they sat down. What was up with that?

"No. It's not a place for kids except once a year when they have a summer barbeqcue, or there's a special reason for a get-together, and kids can come."

"Am I a biker kid?" He put down the spoon and pushed the cereal bowl away.

"I guess you are." Zane pointed to the bowl. "You gonna eat something? Boys need food."

"You didn't eat anything."

Fuck. Zane stared at his plate, unable to even contemplate putting anything in his mouth. Except for the conversation about coming to the clubhouse, Evie had barely spoken a word to him this morning and the idea that he had hurt her made him ache inside. "It's different when you're a grown-up."

"Mom will be mad at us," Ty said. "She doesn't like food to be wasted, although it's better now. When we lived with Mark, we had to be very careful of our money and if I didn't eat my breakfast, she made me eat it for lunch."

Mark. The man who had raised his son. The man who had slept with Evie. Zane hated him, and not just because he had been there when Zane hadn't, but because he'd hurt his girl.

He inhaled deeply to calm himself, and the scent of bacon made his stomach turn. Maybe he shouldn't have had so much to drink last night, but the thought of coming back to the apartment last night after he'd scared Evie away was almost too much to bear. Alcohol had numbed the pain, but when the buzz wore off, he felt worse than before. "Musta been tough."

Ty shrugged. "It was okay until he started yelling all the time. They thought I couldn't hear, but I could. It was always about money and where they were going to sleep. Sometimes Mark slept in another lady's house and Mom didn't like that. Once Mom said she was going to sleep somewhere else, too, but she never did. Big Bill wanted her to come and work in Conundrum because he liked how she painted people's motorcycles and she wanted to go. That's when Mark pushed her down the stairs. I saw him do it." He looked up, his eyes haunted. "Are you going to do that, too?"

Zane let out the breath he hadn't realized he was holding. That bastard, Mark, wouldn't be able to walk after Zane got through with him. "No."

Ty's gaze flicked to the kitchen door and then back to Zane. "I cried when Mom fell down the stairs. I thought she was going to be dead and there would be no one to look after me except Mark, and he didn't like me. I wished I was strong enough to fight him, but I wasn't."

Zane thought he'd fucking cry, too at what Evie and his son had to go through. "I cried when my dad died."

Ty looked up, his eyes wide. "Really?"

"Really. It doesn't make you less of a man."

"Will you teach me how to fight? Just in case I need to help Mom when you're gone."

Christ. Even his kid thought he was going to abandon them. Well, that made three of them. "Who says I won't be around?"

"Mom says you're busy with the club and maybe you'll see me on weekends, or you might go away and not come back for a long time. My friend Mason only sees his dad on weekends 'cause his parents are divorced. They get to go to restaurants all the time and football games, and he gets to sleep on his dad's couch, like you do."

"Yeah, I'll teach you to fight. But you gotta eat something. Can't fight if you have no energy."

Ty slid off his seat and reached into one of the grocery bags Arianne had brought to the safe house this morning. He pulled out a box of cookies and carefully pulled it open, his eyes never leaving Zane's face. Now there was a challenge if he ever saw one—and that he understood.

"Your mom usually let you eat cookies for breakfast?"

"Yeah. All the time." Ty bit into a cookie, watching, his body tense.

Zane bit back a smile and stretched out on his chair. "You know . . . even outlaw bikers got rules. We live by a code: honesty, integrity, brotherhood and loyalty. You want to be a biker, you gotta live by the code. You got to be able to trust your brothers just as they got to trust you, because the world we live in is not forgiving of mistakes. We had one brother, Axle, he did lotsa bad shit and betrayed his brothers. He lied, stole. . . In short, he was dishonest. In the end, he died alone."

Ty's eyes widened and he stopped chewing. "He died?"

"Yeah. You get involved in bad shit, it always comes back on you." He leaned across the table, made his son a promise. "What Mark did to your mom . . . that's gonna come back on him. Big time."

Ty placed the box and the unfinished cookie on the table. "I'm not hungry anymore."

"Didn't think you would be." Zane gave himself a mental high five. Maybe parenting wasn't so hard after all.

They cleaned up the breakfast dishes together and put the groceries away. Ty talked about his friends, the games he played, and movies he had seen with his mother. Except for that one outburst about Mark, he never talked about Stanton, and Zane wondered if he didn't remember much, or he didn't want to remember. He was an easy kid to be around, curious about Zane's life as a biker, enthusiastic about his friends, and passionate about superheroes.

"Batman. He's the only true superhero," Zane said as they put the last of the food away. "He'd win a fight against any of the others hands down 'cause he's got that streak of dark in him, makes him able to cross the line that pansies like Captain America can't cross. He doesn't take shit from anyone."

"Duh." Ty rolled his eyes and pointed to his Batman pajamas. "I know that."

Nobody had ever said "duh" to Zane since . . . well, ever. The kids at school had been afraid of him and the junior patch and prospects knew to stay out of his way. "You allowed to say 'duh' to a grown-up?"

Ty shot him a sideways look. "You allowed to say shit to a kid?"

Damn. The kid was smart. He would have to watch his mouth. He stuck his hand in his pocket and pulled out a roll of bills. "How about I pay a couple of months in advance since I seem to have used up my last advance payment?"

Ty took the money and put it in his swear jar. "Can I use some of it in case I need to swear sometimes like you?"

"Definitely not. Bikers swear. Boys don't."

Ty's smile faded and his face grew solemn. "I'm going to be a fucking biker when I grow up. I'm going to swear and shoot guns and be in car chases. I'm going to be a Sinner's Tribe motorcycle man like you. But first you have to teach me how to ride a motorcycle."

"When you're older." He let the swear slide. Boys needed to learn how to cuss so they could express themselves when they became men.

Ty deflated. "I want to learn now. Trevor's dad plays baseball with him and takes him to football games. And Jason's dad is building a clubhouse with him. I want you to do things with me. Riding a motorcycle would be epic."

"And dangerous."

"I thought that was the point. Or maybe you're not cool like I thought." Ty's bottom lip quivered and Zane's pulse kicked up a notch. What would he do if Ty cried? Evie would think he was a failure as a dad. Fifteen minutes and he couldn't keep his son happy.

"I am cool," Zane protested.

"Prove it."

Zane narrowed his eyes. What the hell was he supposed to do? What did a eight-year-old kid find cool? "You play vids?"

Ty's eyes lit up. "Yeah. What games do you play?"

"None. But we got lots of games at the clubhouse and a couple the junior patch play all the time. There's one guy, Hacker, he . . ." Zane trailed off when Ty's face fell. "What's the matter?"

"I want to play with you."

"I haven't played for a long time." Not since he'd left Stanton. Video games were something he played with Evie and Jagger. He'd thought it almost a sacrilege to play with anyone else.

"Good. Then I'll win." Ty raced to the bedroom. "I'll go grab my stuff. I brought my game console and a couple of games."

Ten minutes later, awed by his son's skill with hooking up the complicated system of wires and navigating all the Internet shit that now comprised a modern gaming system, Zane joined Ty on the couch.

"Here." Ty handed him a controller with so many buttons it resembled an airplane console. He ran through the different commands and started the game before Zane had a chance to assimilate all the information.

Ten seconds later, Ty sighed. "You're dead. Even mom plays better than you."

"*Even* mom?" Evie walked into the living room, her hair damp and curled slightly at the edges. She wore a green dress that hugged every curve and highlighted the emerald of her eyes. So damn beautiful. And last night had gone so damn wrong, although he was still trying to figure out why.

"Gimme a minute to figure it out." Zane frowned at the character on the screen. How many guns was that guy packing? No way could anyone walk with that much gear, much less leap off a ten-story building. And the magazine for the automatic Ty's character carried didn't hold unlimited rounds. Damn unrealistic.

"Move over and I'll show you how it's done." Evie sat beside him on the couch and he inhaled the floral scent of her shampoo mixed with the familiar hint of her jasmine perfume. His groin tightened when her body pressed up against him, despite the few extra inches of space between her and the armrest, and he was immediately transported back to all the afternoons he spent trying to focus on their games while trying to quell the throb of teenage arousal. But the party in his pants really got started when she reached over him to take the extra controller from Ty, her breasts brushing across his chest.

Damn. He had to get a grip. He wasn't a teenager anymore, and Ty was sitting beside him. He closed his eyes and took a few deep, calming breaths. When he opened them and saw her smirk, he knew she was teasing him on purpose, and a weight lifted from his shoulders. Okay. Maybe he hadn't screwed it up too bad.

And he wasn't messing up the damn game either. Yeah, she'd been a good player when they were kids, but he was a man now. He knew how to shoot for real and those pussies on the screen were his for the taking. He put his thumbs on the keypad and started firing.

"You're dead."

"What?" He glared at Ty and Evie, both laughing now.

"Mom killed you. She's a tenth level Feline. You need to stay away from her claws."

"Roawr." Evie made a mock swipe at him with her

fingers and he caught her hand and brought it to his mouth, brushing his lips over her knuckles until her eyes darkened with arousal.

"Just wait, Feline," he murmured. "And I'll show you how I deal with those little claws."

"You're dead, too, Mom. You got distracted." Ty bounced on the couch. "I win. I'll reset."

Evie glanced over at the screen. "I've got three power bars left. I'm very much alive, my feeble human friend." With one hand still in Zane's grasp, she leaned over and tickled Ty and they both fell back on the couch laughing.

Alive.

He'd never felt as alive as he did right now, with his Evie beside him doing what they'd always loved to do, and his son—*his son*—laughing on the couch. Yeah, he loved the Sinners, and he would never leave them. But he'd been living in the shadows since he left Stanton, and now it was time to come into the light.

Only one thing stood in his way.

He dropped Evie's hand and picked up the controller. "Where's the bad guy? It's time he got a taste of Sinner's steel."

And when he was done with that bad guy, Viper would be next.

★ SEVENTEEN ★

*Don't sweat it if you don't have formal motorcycle
repair training. Experience and the desire to do
a good job win out every time.*
—SINNER'S TRIBE MOTORCYCLE REPAIR MANUAL

"Seriously?"

Zane looked over his shoulder long enough to raise his
eyebrow, then resumed his guard position at the window
in the coffee shop. "Whipped cream on black coffee?"

"Seriously." Evie squirted an extra inch of whipped cream
on her large Americano. Her coffee headache had hit her
hard after they finished their video game—no wonder since
she hadn't had any coffee since yesterday morning, and she
hadn't slept last night after the most thrilling sexual experience of her life—and Zane had made a reluctant stop at the
coffee shop on their way to the clubhouse.

She shivered, remembering their encounter in the forest: the rasp of Zane's breath behind her; the potent mix
of fear and excitement; and the feel of his hand around her
neck when he finally caught her.

But more than that, she had been moved by his tender-
ness. Despite her emotional retreat, he carried her back to
the clubhouse, washed and bandaged her feet, and then left
her in the apartment without saying a word, as if he knew
she needed to be alone.

And he was right. The intensity of their encounter had

scared her, just as Zane scared her. And for all that she kept telling herself he was going to leave, no matter how hard she pushed, he wouldn't go away.

"You should try it." She offered him the cream-laden cup.

"Thanks, but I like my coffee black." Zane sipped his filter coffee. "Pure. And I can think of better uses for a can of whipped cream."

Desire flared white-hot inside her and her cheeks heated. She dipped her head and handed the canister to Ty, then glanced up again through the curtain of her lashes.

Zane caught her gaze, his sensuous lips parting in an erotically charged smile. Yes, she could imagine what he'd do with a bottle of whipped cream. And despite all her protests last night, she would be fully on board.

While Ty smothered his hot chocolate with cream, Evie took the first sip of her coffee, letting the mixture of bitter liquid and thick sweetness slide over her tongue. Ah. So good. She needed the kick. Hopefully one would be enough.

"Should we go?" She took the canister from Ty and placed it on the counter.

"Fuck." Zane stiffened, pulled out his phone. "Drop the drinks. Take Ty out the back. Buncha Jacks outside. Don't know if they were tailing us or if it's just a coincidence, but they're not supposed to be in Conundrum. I'll be right behind you. I'm gonna call Jagger and clear everyone outta the shop in case things go bad."

"Zane . . . don't . . ."

"Go, Evie."

She dumped the drinks and grabbed Ty's hand, pulling him into the back hallway. Behind her she could hear Zane yelling for everyone to leave.

Her heart pounded in warning, and her walk turned into a run. But just as she neared the exit door, she heard gunshots, a muffled explosion, and then the building shook around them. Evie pulled Ty close and curled around his small body until the shaking subsided. She turned back to the door but the hall had filled with smoke.

"Zane!" She didn't try to hide the panic in her voice as she peered through the haze.

"Mom. Let's go." Ty pushed the door open, but Evie hesitated. Did Zane get out in time? What if he was still inside, injured and unable to move?

"Mom. The store's on fire." Ty yanked on her hand just as fire licked the walls of the hallway, curling around the paintings of Italian landscapes and giant hills of coffee beans.

"Zane!" She shrieked his name, her pulse thudding so loud in her ears she could barely hear. With one last look behind her, she grabbed Ty's hand and pulled him outside.

Low, dark clouds hung in the sky, and the air was heavy with an impending storm. With Ty in tow, she raced down the alley to the front of the building. Sirens wailed in the distance and a crowd had gathered outside as smoke billowed through the front door.

"Zane!" She pushed her way through the crowd, searching every face, every black jacket, every head of brown hair.

With a roar, flames engulfed the building sending a thick cloud of dust and smoke across the street. Evie covered Ty's mouth and nose, turning him away from the building, startling when she saw a familiar face.

Viper.

Leaning casually in the shadows of the alley no more than ten feet away, a cigarette hanging from his thin, cruel lips, Viper nodded a greeting. His gaze swept over her body, lingering on her face, and then he lifted his weapon, and gestured her forward with a crooked finger.

"Mom? Who is that biker?" Ty turned fully in her arms drawing Viper's gaze. "Why is he pointing his gun at us?"

"Run, Ty." She turned, shoved him behind her. The last thing she wanted was for Viper to know Zane had a son. "Go into the crowd. Then find a policeman. Ask them to take you to Connie."

"No. I'm not leaving you." He wrapped his arms around her, held on tight.

"Go. Run." She tried to pry his hands away, but his fingers dug in hard. Stubborn. Just like his father.

Annoyance flickered across Viper's features and he lowered the gun.

"Fucking kids," he muttered. "Always in the fucking way. Bring him."

He beckoned her forward again, but Evie planted her feet in the pavement and shook her head, calling his bluff. They were safe out on the street. Viper wasn't going to shoot her with a crowd at her back and the police coming around the corner.

"You're not going to kill me," she said with a bravado she didn't feel in the least. "And I'm not going anywhere with you."

"Even if your man is dead? Who's going to protect you, Evangeline? Not the Sinners. You're not one of them."

Shadows moved behind him. His bodyguards. Of course, he wouldn't come here alone. "I'm not a Black Jack either. And he's not dead. He made it out."

"Such faith." Viper laughed. "But here's the thing, kitten. Even if he did make it out, it's over between you. There's a warrant for his arrest. And since the Sinners have been fucking with my business, I'm in need of some quick cash. I think the police in Stanton would be interested to know where to find him." He inhaled, then blew out a puff of smoke. "Or would that be ATF jurisdiction? I'm not sure who would tear apart the Sinner clubhouse looking for a fugitive from justice."

"Leave him out of this." Evie shuddered under a wave of anger. She wanted to ask how he had found out about

Zane, but the question would just confirm what he said was true, and she couldn't take the risk he was fishing for information. "This is between you and me."

"It was between you and me." He took another drag of his cigarette, leaned against the wall, all casual as if he hadn't just blown up a building and was now trying to blackmail her into his bed. "But then the Sinners got involved. Now the game has changed, kitten. I have to address the disrespect done to me and my club, and then I gotta get back what's mine. We were already at war with the Sinners. This just made it personal."

"So you're going to blackmail Zane?"

"If you come nicely, I'll let him off for your good behavior."

Ty shivered behind her and she prayed he didn't understand what was going on. She couldn't imagine what it would be like to finally meet the father he had dreamed about all his life, only to find out the world thought he was a murderer.

"What's to stop you from making that call even if I come with you?"

A smile tugged at the corners of his cruel lips. "Nothing. It's a risk you have to take. You have to trust me."

"I don't trust you."

"But you trust him?" Viper took a step forward, into the light. He looked older, tired, but no less formidable in his worn, leather cut, tight black T-shirt and jeans, his muscular arms colorful with tats. "The man who killed your father? The man who shot one of my junior patch in the back in cold blood? Ask him about Wheels. Or the three men he shot in a gunfight up in Whitefish. He kidnapped my old lady, threw her in the Sinner dungeon, probably tortured her for information. She's there now if you don't believe me. We aren't so different, kitten. We're both one percenters. Think about what that means."

"I know at heart he's a good man." She took a step back,

pushing Ty along the sidewalk, putting some distance between them. His offer was no offer at all. He was going to make that call regardless of what she did. Her best option was to find Zane and warn him before the police came to call.

"Are you sure about that? Do you know the truth about what happened to your father?"

Taking a deep breath, Evie spun around, grabbed Ty's hand and ran into the crowd.

"Wrong choice," Viper shouted after her. "Wrong fucking choice."

Zane shoved people out of his way as he searched the crowd. He'd managed to chase away all the staff and customers before the Jacks started shooting, and had barely made it out himself when one of the bullets triggered the explosion. Evie and Ty should have gotten out before him.

So where the fuck were they?

Fear gripped his belly as he scanned the sea of faces, a gut-wrenching sickness like nothing he'd ever felt before. He wasn't going to lose them now. Not after he'd only just found her again; not after he'd only just met his son.

He whipped out his phone and punched Jagger's number. "Jag." He drew in a shuddering breath. He'd never asked for help before. Never needed it. "The Jacks shot up the Kaufman Kafe on Stock Street. Evie and Ty were inside. I can't find them."

"I'm there, brother. Hold on."

Zane's tension eased the tiniest bit and he continued the search. But, when one wall of the building caved in with an earsplitting crash, his heart thundered so loud he thought he would break a rib.

The police arrived and cordoned off the area. Fire trucks screeched to a halt, sirens blaring, lights flashing. Ambulance attendants wheeled a gurney to an old lady lying on the sidewalk. Zane vaguely remembered pushing her outside moments before the deafening explosion. He searched the back alley, the SUV, the side streets, and then returned to the crowd out front, now ten people deep. Where were they?

Smoke filled his lungs, singed his nostrils, the scent bringing back the memory of his utter despair outside Evie's shop when he thought she was gone. Fuck. He couldn't go through this again. It was going to fucking kill him.

His heart lifted when he heard the rumble of motor-cycles. Moments later, Jagger stalked down the street, six Sinners behind him, drawing the attention of the cops who had little to do but hold the crowd back as the firefight-ers fought the blaze. Once, that had been him. He'd al-ways been the first one into a building, taking the biggest risks, simply because he had nothing to live for.

Zane met them curbside, briefed them on the layout of the block and then the Sinners dispersed.

"I called Benson. Told him to get his lazy ass down here." Jagger cut a path through the gawking onlookers with a mighty sweep of his hand. "He's going to get me copies of the witness reports so we can ID the Jacks in-volved. Crossing our border, shooting up a café filled with civilians, targeting a brother and his family . . . They've broken every damn code we have. This will bring the ATF down on all of us. National will be involved in this one. But I'm not waiting for the nod from the higher-ups. We'll find Evie and Ty, and then we'll hit them hard."

His family.

Zane had never had a real family. But he didn't correct Jagger. Evie and Ty were his to protect. He would fight for them. He would die for them. And if that meant they were family, then he'd found something he'd been looking for all his life. But goddammit the MC was no place for them. Not if they were constantly in danger.

"Zane! I got 'em." Gunner bulldozed his way toward them, Ty on his shoulders, Evie under one arm. "They were looking for you in the ambulances."

Zane had no words, no thoughts, no ability even to

move. He'd been through a lot of shit in his life, seen things no man should ever see, experienced the full range of emotions, but nothing compared to the sight of Evie—his Evie—running toward him, her face streaked with tears and soot, the most beautiful goddamn sight he had ever seen.

With a cry that dispelled the last of his doubt about how she truly felt about him, she threw herself into his arms, and buried her face in his chest. Zane wrapped his arms around her, held her to him, grounded in her warmth. Never in his life had he felt such a complete and utter conviction that he was exactly where he was meant to be.

"Me, too," Ty said.

With Gunner's help, Ty slid off his shoulders and pushed his way between Evie and Zane, hugging them both. Zane could think of no more perfect moment.

"Zane?"

"Yeah, bud."

"Mom's going to need her coffee now."

"This is your clubhouse?" Evie stared at the grand country house nestled at the foot of the Bridger Mountains. "It looks like something out of the movies where rich people go for the weekend to get away from it all."

Zane reached over and unfastened her seat belt, a small but courteous gesture, and one she hadn't expected of an outlaw biker. But then, so far Zane had defied pretty much every expectation she had of who he had become.

Except one. When faced with overwhelming emotion, he still shut down. And the scene at the café definitely fell into the overwhelming category. For both of them.

"We had another clubhouse but the Jacks burned it down," Tank said from the backseat of the SUV where he'd taken up guard duty and spent the ride cursing about Zane's driving, to Ty's utter delight.

"We got this place from a drug dealer who tried to cheat us," he continued. "It's isolated and big enough to accommodate the club, so we decided to fix it up. It's not so pretty inside. Get a buncha brothers together, and you're not gonna get any fancy decorating."

After helping Ty out of the vehicle, Zane put an arm around Evie's waist and led her up the steps. He hadn't said a word since they'd found each other outside the café, and she was glad for the chance to collect her thoughts. She couldn't get Viper's words out of her head. She'd sensed Zane was holding something back when he told her about her father's death, but had he lied? And what about the other men he allegedly killed? And the woman in the dungeon? Had she been naive about the Sinners and what they did? And what about the Jacks? Who were the monsters and who were the men?

"Stop." She paused on the threshold. "Is it . . . kid friendly inside?"

Tank laughed. "I called ahead. Made sure Sherry, our house mama, understood we needed a PG environment. She sent all the girls home, cleaned up the booze, disposed of the . . . wrappers. We're good."

Evie supposed that should make her feel better, but the thought of Zane hanging out here where girls, booze and "wrappers" made it a constant non-PG environment, sent a strange flutter through her belly. How many women had he been with? How many biker parties had he attended where he'd taken women into the shadowy corners and—

"None," he whispered, his voice a sensual rumble in her ear.

"How do you know what I'm thinking?" She didn't even pretend she didn't know what he was talking about because she wanted the answer.

"Because I know you." His arm tightened around her, and his words spilled out. "I spent a lifetime learning everything about you, the way you tense when you're stressed, the way your brow crinkles when you're confused, and how your lips tighten when you're jealous.

Good thing we don't have any pink soda in the kitchen, or any girls named Melissa."

Shocked that he remembered the isolated incident, surprised he was talking at all, she pulled up short. "That was an accident." But his smirk told her he knew she was lying. Melissa Parker, destined to be prom queen from the moment she set foot in Stanton High School, had been after Zane from day one. And when he took her to the school spring dance, the year Evie turned sixteen, and put his arms around her slim athletic body, Evie knew it was time to leave.

But of course, she didn't listen to the tiny voice of warning. Although she and Zane had an unspoken agreement not to acknowledge their feelings, there was something between them that went beyond friendship. And that night it was Melissa. At least it was until Evie "accidentally" spilled pink soda on Melissa's almost-see-through white dress. Who knew it would stain? She hadn't been able to read Zane's expression as he watched a shrieking Melissa run for the restroom. But she didn't need to. Melissa was gone, and that was all she cared about.

"I waited for you to come back that night," he said softly. "I couldn't understand why you went to so much trouble, and then left the dance."

"I was scared." She leaned her forehead against his shoulder, unable to meet his gaze. "I thought if you touched me like that, we could never be friends again."

Zane gripped her chin between his thumb and forefinger and tilted her head back, then gave her a long, lingering kiss. "You were right."

"Ewwwww. That's gross." Ty broke away and ran down the hallway, pulling up short when a biker with a thick, matted gray beard stepped out of a side room, filling the hallway with his bulk.

"Hey kid."

"Mom." Ty took one step back, and then another. Evie

broke away from Zane, and put a hand on his head. "It's okay."

"This is Shaggy," Tank said, coming to the rescue. "He's the oldest member of the club and he hasn't washed his beard in twenty years."

Ty gave him an appraising look. "Cool."

"Kid thinks I'm cool." Shaggy snorted a laugh. "Now I'm not gonna wash it for another twenty years."

"You're not gonna live another fucking twenty years, old-timer." Tank ushered Ty into the living area. "That's why T-Rex and I both got seats on the executive board. We're waiting for you to kick the shit bucket."

"I'll kick your ass, junior patch, how about that for some damn kicking?"

"Mom, can I go get the swear jar?" Ty turned to Evie, his eyes wide. "We're going to be rich!"

Zane left Evie and Ty with Tank and headed for the kitchen. Jagger had called an emergency board meeting for tomorrow morning, but Zane couldn't wait that long. He wanted Viper dead. And he wanted it done tonight.

"We were waiting for you." Cade waved him in and held up a beer. Zane shook his head. He had only just started coming down from the adrenaline rush of the afternoon, and a beer would knock him out.

Gunner, Sparky and Jagger had already cracked open a couple of cold ones and lounged on the wooden chairs in the country-style kitchen, the only room in the clubhouse that hadn't undergone a significant renovation.

"I put twenty on you showing up in fifteen minutes." Sparky twisted the top off his beer. "Jagger had his money on five. Cade on ten. Gunner didn't buy in because he spent all his money at Peelers."

"Pay up." Jagger waved his arm vaguely around the room. "I need all the cash I can get. Arianne runs through ammo like civilian ladies run through shoes."

Zane leaned against the wall as money was exchanged, too wound up to sit. Hell, he couldn't even handle a beer. He wanted Evie upstairs, in his bed, safe and in his arms. Maybe then his rage would subside.

"Viper dies tonight," he blurted out. "I'm heading out. With or without the club."

Jagger raised an eyebrow and took a long, slow drink. "I'll let that one slide because I know you've just been through fucking hell. Going after Viper alone is a suicide mission. We've got Mario undercover in the Black Jack clubhouse now and he says Viper's doing a meet at the Riverside Bar tomorrow night. We'll do a double strike. Half the brothers will go for T-Rex because security will be light with Viper gone. The other half will go to Riverside. Benson's gonna keep the cops off our back until it's done." He placed the beer carefully on the table. "I expect you to be there. If you go off tonight and get yourself killed, I will chase you down in the afterlife and hell will seem like fucking heaven when I'm done with you."

"You always were a goddamn bastard."

"You saved my life more times than I can count," Jaggers said. "I'm just returning the favor." He lifted his beer again, tipped the bottle in salute. "Now go see your woman and your son. They need you more than I need to look at your ugly face."

"He's not that ugly," Gunner mused. "Actually with those fine cheekbones and that long hair, he's kinda pretty. And ever since he met Evie, his eyes have that special glow." He batted his eyelashes and Sparky spluttered out his beer.

"You're the one who's glowing. How many times did you get your knob polished last night?"

"You're just jealous." Gunner smirked. "When's the last time you had a woman in your bed that you didn't have to pay?"

Sparky folded his arms and glared. "Look who's fucking talking. You couldn't even buy into the pool right now 'cause you blew all your cash at Peelers."

"At least I got a blow, brother. You got dick all."

Usually Zane enjoyed their banter, but right now he had no patience for jokes or laughter. He needed Evie like he needed air to breathe. She calmed him, soothed him, helped fight the darkness that threatened his control.

He didn't know what he would do if he lost her again. Probably die.

After leaving Ty to play basketball at the side of the club-house with Shooter and a jaw-droppingly handsome young biker named Hacker, Evie followed Tank back inside for a tour of the clubhouse.

As she trailed behind him, Evie was reminded of the frat parties she'd snuck into as a teen. A huge crystal chandelier dominated the massive front hall, leading to a grand, slightly curved staircase, with an ornate carved bal-ustrade. The oak floors were bare, and scuffed, although the walls clearly had been refinished and painted judging from their cleanliness relative to the rest of the clubhouse. Here and there she caught glimpses of antique furniture, covered in beer cans and riding gloves, pizza boxes and papers. Framed pictures of motorcycles and women on bikes adorned the walls, and the pungent, yeasty odor of stale beer permeated every room.

Tank led her into the kitchen just as Zane was walking out. Jagger, Cade, Sparky and Gunner were drinking beer and laughing, but Zane's face had smoothed to an expres-sionless mask as it always did when he fought against strong emotion.

"Wait." She placed a hand on Zane's chest and he froze mid-step. "There's something I need to tell you and you might want to share it with Jagger." She glanced over at her now-rapt audience and lowered her voice. "Maybe we should talk outside. Viper was there. He said something to me about Stanton."

Pain flickered across Zane's face so fast she wasn't sure if she'd seen it. "It's okay. They know about Stanton.

Everyone on the executive board and Arianne. You can say anything in front of them. I trust my brothers."

Evie wound one hand around his arm, and gave the group a nervous smile. "Viper was outside the café today. He must have been part of the shooting. He held Ty and me at gunpoint and—"

"Son of a bitch." Zane ripped her hand away. "Jag. Now."

"Let her finish." Jagger held up his hand and nodded for Evie to continue.

"He knows about the warrant for Zane's arrest. He threatened to give the information to the police unless I . . . er . . . went with him. I didn't." She shrugged. "Obviously."

Silence.

When they continued to stare at her, she swallowed and looked away. "I thought there was a better chance that you could protect Zane than taking the risk of going with Viper only to have him make the call anyway. I'm not sure how he got that information."

"T-Rex." Jagger's voice shook with rage. "He's getting intel from T-Rex."

A wave of dizziness hit her and she gripped Zane's arm. There was only one way to get information from an unwilling prisoner and she couldn't bear to think of T-Rex in pain.

"Do you believe me now?" Jagger met the gaze of every man in the room save Zane. "I told you she would never betray us. Evie's no Black Jack spy. She just didn't understand who Viper was. Now she does and she's on our side."

Shock took her breath away. She had never even considered that they would think she was a spy. And yet, Zane had never asked the question. He trusted her implicitly. He had faith in her.

So how could she ask him the questions Viper had raised? How could she ask if they had a dungeon, and if they did if they had imprisoned Viper's old lady? How could she ask about the man called Wheels or the Black Jacks Zane had supposedly shot in Whitefish? How could she make him think she didn't trust him? And, if her loyalty was in doubt, asking those questions might raise suspicions all over again. But more than that, did she really want to know? Because if Viper was right about those things, maybe he was right about her father's death, and then, what would she do?

"Let's go." Zane tugged her arm, drawing her away from the kitchen.

"They thought I was a spy," she said as they walked down the hall. "I didn't ask to be associated with the club. I didn't ask for any of this."

"We had a Black Jack rat in the house a while back." He looked straight ahead as he spoke, his body rigid, barely touching hers. "He joined the club as a prospect, and he had us fooled. His background and his papers all checked out. He hid his skills so well, he had us wondering if he was good enough to patch in, which is what they wanted. In and out. Minimize the chances of being caught. By the time we figured it out, it was almost too late. I almost lost Jagger that day. Second worst fucking day of my life."

"What was the first?"

"The day I lost you."

★ EIGHTEEN ★

*The quality of your repair will depend on your desire
to do a good job and your willingness to spend
the time to make it right.*
—SINNER'S TRIBE MOTORCYCLE REPAIR MANUAL

She should never have come here.

Evie followed Zane up the huge staircase and down a spacious hallway lined with doors and dotted with pictures of motorcycles. She traced her finger along the frame of a vintage print as Zane unlocked his door. This club, this war, these bikers, their way of life . . . everything was so far removed from what she knew.

Biker wars, guns, threats, kidnapping, drugs, politics, and death. She didn't understand the rules of this world, nor did she want to be part of it. So how would Zane fit into her life? And how could she protect Ty from being sucked into a world that was a mother's worst nightmare?

Evie followed him in to a large room containing a low-rise bed covered in rumpled sheets, a dresser and a night table. And nothing else.

"Is this your room?"

"Yeah."

"You live here?" Evie stared at the blank walls and empty surfaces. Where were the books, magazines, fast food containers, or pictures that made a room personal?

Why were there no clothes on the floor, trophies of biker outings, or any of the detritus that she had expected to see in the room of an outlaw biker? What about music? Even a dock for his phone? Or a laptop? "It looks like you just moved out."

He closed the door behind him with a firm click. "I just sleep here, and not that often."

Maybe that was it. He had a girlfriend and he stayed with her, which was why everyone had been so surprised when he'd brought her to the clubhouse. But then why did he sleep with her?

Why not? Outlaws didn't follow civilian law. Maybe they didn't follow civilian codes either. Monogamy probably wasn't part of the outlaw equation, and he probably had women falling at his feet. He'd been good-looking as a teenager, but now, all filled out, his muscles hard with use, face slightly weathered, chest tatted, he was devastatingly handsome. Breathtaking, really.

"Sure. I get it." So why did she feel so . . . angry? She kept pushing him away, and yet the thought of him with another woman made her stomach knot the way it had when he'd shown up at the high school dance with Melissa.

"What do you get?"

"Just . . . why you've got nothing personal in here. I understand." Evie twisted her hair around her finger.

"I don't think you do." Zane held out his arms. "Come to me, Evie."

She walked over to the window, took in the vast expanse of lawn, the barbed wire fence, the guards and patrol dogs. "I slept with other guys after Mark. I didn't bring them home, either." Not that this was a home. It was a fortress. And the fact they had to live this way said it all.

He gave a frustrated growl. "I don't want to hear about other guys."

She turned, folded her arms across her chest. "Did you sleep with lots of women? All those women at the party?

The ones who live at the clubhouse? That's part of the biker way of life isn't it? Along with kidnapping and torture and . . . death."

"Evie." His voice rose to a shout, startling her. "Jesus Fuck. I'm losing it here. I thought I lost you and Ty. I was fucking paralyzed. I had to call Jagger for help. I don't call people for help, Evie. I don't need people. And then I have to fucking hear that while I was trying to find you, Viper was holding a gun to your head. You were so damn brave and strong."

"I had Ty with me," she said. "Going with Viper wasn't really an option."

"There aren't many people who would have said no, sweetheart. I can guarantee it." He raked his hand through his hair, the dark strands brushing over his shoulders. "You had faith in my brothers and they didn't have faith in you. You put them to shame down there."

"I didn't mean . . ." Her voice trailed off as pain etched his face.

"I don't want to need you, but I do." His voice rose, wavered. "I need you like the air I breathe, the water I drink, the food I eat. I need you because you are the only thing that keeps the darkness away. You are my light, Evie, my hope, my salvation. When I thought I'd lost you, I lost myself. And if you don't let me hold you right now, so I know I'm not dreaming, I'm gonna lose my fucking mind."

She went to him, slid into that space in the circle of his arms that was meant for her. "I'm here, baby."

"Ah, God." He let out a relieved breath and dropped his lips to her hair. "Just needed so bad to be alone with you, to hold you. Nothing feels as good as having you in my arms."

She gave him the time he needed, tried to slow the thoughts tumbling through her mind, focused on the man and not the biker, the heart beating beneath the cut.

When his muscles relaxed and his heart slowed to a

steady rhythm, she tilted her head back and looked up at him. "I told Viper you had a good heart."

"That probably didn't go down too well."

She stroked her fingers along his jaw, remembering all the nights she lay in bed imagining how his skin would feel beneath her touch. "He said you two were the same."

"We're not." Zane brushed her hair back over her shoulder, then tangled his fingers through the long strands and gave her head a gentle tug. "We might have the same tools, but we make different choices." Then his face tightened. "Don't want to talk about Viper."

"What do you want to talk about?" She brushed her fingers over his sensual lips, his cheekbones, his strong brow, searching for the boy he used to be.

His eyes glittered with masculine pride. "Wanna talk about how you didn't like thinking of me with the other women in the club. You were jealous."

"I wasn't jealous. I just . . . it's your way of life, I guess. If that's what makes you happy . . ."

"Like you were happy when Jagger's cousin came to visit and sat beside me on the couch?" he teased.

Her face heated, but she couldn't turn away with his hand in her hair. "It wasn't like that. She was sitting in my place, and she was touching you."

He rubbed his thumb over her bottom lip, tugging it from between her teeth. "I watched you all afternoon while we were playing that video game." His voice was low, deceptively soft. "You never stopped glaring at her. When she sat on the floor between my legs, I thought you were gonna attack her."

"Well, you shouldn't have put your hand on her head," she snapped, suddenly back in the moment when she wondered if she had it in her to actually physically attack the beautiful girl with the large breasts and curvy figure who had picked up on Evie's secret crush on Zane right away and decided to rub it in her face.

"You were jealous. Say it."

She gave an exasperated laugh. "Like you need an ego boost. But okay. Ten years ago I might have been jealous. Now, if you're sleeping with me and sleeping with other women, then jealous isn't the word I'd use. More like pissed off. The kind where weapons are involved."

A grin spread across his face. "You want me."

"I always wanted you. It's just this life I'm not so sure about. You live in a world that scares me. What you've become scares me. I feel like I don't know you anymore."

"You know me better than anyone else." He cupped her head in his hand, pulling her forward to meet the heated press of his lips. His kiss was hard and fierce, bruising her mouth with passion.

"I left you once," he murmured. "But this time, I won't let you go. I'm gonna do everything I can to make you see we are meant to be together. I'll fight anyone and everyone for you, sweetheart, until you're mine again."

Acutely aware of the rise and fall of Evie's breasts against his chest, and the heat of her body, Zane almost didn't register her touch—gentle hands on his shoulders, arms twining around his neck. His groin tightened in response.

"I missed you." She tilted her head back until she met his gaze. "We saw each other almost every single day for nine years, and then suddenly you were gone. I felt like my heart had been ripped out of my chest."

"Never again."

She stepped back and pulled off her T-shirt. Zane's eyes dropped to her creamy breasts encased in . . . *oh fuck* . . . red satin, and rational thought flew out the window. But when he took a step forward, she held up her hand.

"I gave up on relationships after Mark. I figured if I didn't get involved with anyone, then I didn't have to worry about having my heart broken yet again." She reached around to unfasten her bra, letting the straps slide down her arms.

My beautiful girl.

No, not a girl. Not anymore. She'd filled out in a way that made his cock hard and his will soft. His Evie was all woman.

Zane swallowed when she sat in the center of his bed, leaned back on the pillows, folding her arms behind her head and giving him a perfect, groin-tightening view of her tight rosy nipples and lush breasts. Every instinct screamed for him to take her. His woman. Half naked. On his bed. Wanting him. But still he held back, confused by the words that belied her state of undress.

"Viper was different." She undid the top button on her jeans and Zane drew in a ragged breath.

Viper? He didn't want to talk about Viper when his cock was so hard he was ready to explode. Viper had no place in his bedroom, and even less place on Evie's lips.

"Being with him reminded me of what it felt like to be with you and Jagger." She slid her hands into the waistband of her jeans, drawing his attention to what lay beneath. "When I was with him, no one bothered me. In fact, no one dared to look at me. I never realized how much I missed feeling safe . . . craved it. But I thought I could be in control. I could go out with him but still walk away because I didn't need anyone to make me feel safe anymore." She shoved her jeans over her hips, baring red silk panties that matched her bra. But where the hell was she going with this? Did she want to be with Viper? Was this supposed to be a good-bye fuck?

"And then I saw you again."

Ah. He was part of this story. His chest swelled with pride, as he guessed the ending. She thought him more worthy than Viper, and finally they got to have sex on the bed and lived happily ever after. Zane reached for his fly and she held up her hand to stop him again.

"I didn't feel the same way about you as I did when you left," she said softly, wiggling out of her jeans, her hips undulating in such a suggestive manner, that it was all he could do not the launch himself across the room, pin her down and take her right then.

"I still don't," she continued. "No one ever hurt me as much as you did, and now you scare me. I'm afraid I don't know you anymore and I'll find out things about you I can't handle. I'm afraid of wanting you to make me feel safe. I'm afraid of loving you in case you walk away."

"What do you need, Evie? Tell me. I'll do anything."

She kicked off her jeans and stretched out on his blue cotton duvet, her stomach making an inviting concave dip, just perfect for his lips. His hand dropped to his fly as she eased her panties down, just to the top of her mound. Mouth watering in anticipation, pulse pounding in his ears, he almost missed her answer.

"The truth. What really happened the night you left?"

Zane's head jerked up. How the hell had they wound up back where they started? Except now his brain was fuzzed with lust, his cock throbbed, and he couldn't remember why he had been so hesitant to tell her in the first place. But maybe it was a good thing. Didn't they say, the truth will set you free?

"I don't want to hurt you."

"You just told me I was brave and strong. It was beautiful to hear. Now show me you mean it. Have faith in me." She stretched out on his bed, all creamy skin and soft curves. So beautiful he ached.

Anything. He would give her anything. Everything. She had only to ask. And if his words hurt her, he would be there for her, comfort her, and soothe away her pain.

"Your dad . . ." He sucked in his lips and focused on a knot in the wooden floor. "He beat me pretty bad that night he found us together. He told me I wasn't good enough for you."

"Zane, baby." Her voice caught in her throat. "Come here and tell me. Let me hold you."

He shook his head and stuffed his hands in his pockets. "He was right but it hurt to hear it and I wanted to hurt him back. So I told him I knew about him. I knew all the things he did."

Evie's voice dropped to a whisper. "What things?"

Zane clenched his hands in his pockets, forced himself to go on. "He was a dirty cop, Evie. He came to my dad's trailer to buy drugs and he transported them over the state line. But he also dealt in arms, and stolen goods. He did dirty work for some of the dealers. Basically, he was on the take. For years." He opened his mouth and closed it again. He couldn't tell her about the hookers and how her dad spent his time and dirty money while she waited for him at home, looking after her mother, thinking he was out saving the world.

"You knew all that time?"

"I knew but I couldn't tell you. I couldn't hurt you that way. You loved him so much. He made you happy. I couldn't take that from you. And he loved you. I knew that when he said I wasn't good enough for you, when he warned me away."

Her face paled, eyes growing wide, darkening in a way he'd never seen before. And before he was even aware he'd taken a step, he was sitting on the bed with Evie in his arms. "You want me to keep going?"

"There's more?"

"Yeah, sweetheart. There's more."

Evie shuddered against his chest. "Keep going."

He pulled her onto his lap and wrapped his arms around her. "I got away and ran to the trailer. My old man was there. He saw my face and figured I'd got into a fight. Told me I was good for nothing. Twice in one night. I'd been sticking around because of you but I'd had enough. I figured I'd convince you to run away with me. I'd find us a place in Missoula while you were going to college, take odd jobs to support us . . . I packed my bag and told the old man I wouldn't be back. But when I stepped outside, your dad was there."

She fisted his shirt like she needed to hold on, so he

stroked his hand down her back, over and over again as he fell back into that night. "I knew why he was there when I saw the gun."

Silence. But he'd expected that, dredging up memories he was sure she had buried forever. So he held her like he should have held her that night, instead of running off and leaving her to deal with her dad's death alone. "He said he couldn't take the risk that I'd tell you what was going on. He was afraid you'd go to the cops because you were such a fucking good person. He loved you but he didn't understand love. He needed you to think he was a hero because he knew he was a piece of shit."

"Oh, God," she whispered. "I think my mother knew. Some of the things she said . . . I think that's why she started drinking."

"He was acting crazy that night, Evie." Zane held her tight, as much for him as for her. "I think he was so afraid of losing you he wasn't thinking straight. He said he had to protect you from scum like me. My dad heard what was going on and came out of the trailer with a gun. Told your dad to leave me alone. I was so shocked my old man was standing up for me, I didn't see your dad pull the trigger. But my dad did. He threw himself in front of me and took the bullet." He drew in a shuddering breath. "Then everything was a blur. I ran at your dad, pounded on him 'till he was down. Then I ran back to check on my old man. Your dad came at us with the gun. His fucking eyes were wild. I reached for my dad's weapon . . ."

"No, Zane." Tears streaked Evie's cheeks. "No, don't tell me. I changed my mind."

"I'm gonna tell you sweetheart 'cause I don't want to keep any more secrets from you. I should have told you before, but I didn't want to hurt you. But now I know how strong you are. Stronger than me."

Evie leaned up, brushed a kiss over her lips. "We're strong together."

Damn, what a woman. But she was wrong about being strong together. He'd never met anyone like Evie. She'd gone through hell and come out of it unscathed, made a life for herself and his son, and still saw joy in the world. "My old man grabbed his gun off me." He spoke quickly now, desperate to get it done. "He told me once I killed someone there was no going back. He said he'd been no dad to me but he knew he wasn't going to make it and he wanted to do one thing for me before he died. He wanted just one time to be a good dad. Then he pulled the trigger."

A shudder ran through his body, ripping him apart. That was the night he'd been consumed by darkness. The night he lost the light.

They hugged each other. Held each other. Her hand on his back. His hand in her hair.

"A coupla neighbors came out of their trailers and started shouting that I killed the sheriff," he said, once he could breathe again. "My prints were on the gun. My tracks were everywhere. I had your dad's words in my head that I was nothing. I panicked. I figured they'd want to put someone in jail and since my old man was dead it was gonna be me. I was an easy target and once they had a scapegoat they wouldn't look for the truth. I had no faith in the system. I didn't think anyone would believe a trailer kid. So I ran. And the further I got, the more it made sense to leave you alone, let you have a good life. Then the darkness took over, Evie, and I was lost until Jagger found me." He tilted her head back and met her gaze. "That's the truth of it."

"I believe you."

He felt those words deep in his chest, filling a void in his soul, assuaging a fear that he had carried since the day he left Stanton. "I'm sorry about your dad, sweetheart."

She straddled his lap, sliding her knees on either side of his hips, the curve of her sex pressed tight against his cock that was hardening again despite the bitter past he'd dragged into the light.

"Make it go away, Zane. For both of us. I don't want to think. I just want to feel. I want you inside me. I want to drown in you until I don't know anything else."

Sweeter words he'd never heard, but it was what they meant that beat the last of the darkness away.

Forgiveness.

But could he forgive himself? Every mile he'd driven away that night had made it harder to contemplate going back. Each day had made him more certain it was best he stayed away until he was worthy and had something to offer other than just his love. Every time he looked at Ty, he was reminded of the mistake he'd made, everything he'd missed, and how he'd left his girl unprotected and she'd be taken by another man.

Never again.

He eased her down on the bed and stretched out beside her, propping his head up with his hand as he caressed her beautiful body. His hand dipped into her narrow waist and then out again over the curve of her hip, and then over the soft skin of her thigh.

"Are you trying to drive me crazy?" She slid a hand over his shoulder, cupping the back of his neck to draw him down to her lips. And then all thoughts of being slow and gentle faded away beneath the primal need to take her.

He rolled until he lay on top of her, one leg tucked between her thighs, pressed against the moist heat of her pussy. With his forearms on either side of her head, he devoured her mouth, drinking her down as if dying of thirst. Evie rocked her hips against his shaft, each small motion a sweet, painful pleasure.

"Shirt," she panted, reaching beneath the press of his body. "Off."

"Panties. Now. Or I'll tear them from you." He sat up

and tore his shirt over his head, then helped her slide her panties over her hips. For a moment, he couldn't move, drinking in her beauty, from her soft curves, to the red-gold curls at the juncture of her thighs, to her lush breasts tipped with dusky rose nipples, to the face that had haunted his dreams.

Evie blushed and turned away, her hands coming up and over her breasts. "Zane . . ."

Gently, he tugged her hands away. "You're beautiful, sweetheart. Let me look."

Her blush spread down her neck, teasing the crescents of her breasts. On impulse, he leaned forward and drew a nipple into his mouth, licking and sucking the hard peak, his hand caressing her softness until her blush had gone and she writhed on the bed beside him. Her fingers tangled in his hair and she pulled him down, sliding under his body until he had to drop his weight to his arms for fear of crushing her.

"I never really got to look at you before." He pressed a kiss to each of her breasts and then feathered his lips down her body, tasting the salt on her skin, inhaling the light floral fragrance of her perfume. Her hands clutched his hair as he followed the dip in her stomach, and when he circled her belly button with his tongue, she trembled.

His cock protested its confinement when he reached her mound, but this was about Evie, her pleasure, her need. He slid down the bed and Evie widened her legs to accommodate his shoulders, her heels digging firmly into the mattress, her hips rocking up to the heat of his mouth. But he wanted to draw it out, savor her. So he pressed a kiss to the soft skin of her inner thigh and continued his descent, kissing his way down her long lean legs until he reached her feet.

"Don't you dare." Evie pushed herself up on her elbows, her beautiful face flushed with desire. "You know how ticklish my feet are."

Yes, he knew. He remembered everything about her.

"Zane!" She shrieked and twisted when he ran his nails along the sole of her foot, and then she laughed—really laughed. It was a sound he'd never thought he'd hear again, and he pushed himself up to kiss her.

"You're different." Evie stroked her hands over the bunched muscles in his shoulders and down his back. "Aside from being bigger and stronger and likely able to leap tall buildings in a single bound, you seem more . . . self-assured."

"I know what I want."

"What do you want?" She licked her lips and all thoughts of taking her slowly flew out the window.

"You." He claimed her mouth in a kiss that served only to heighten his need. She tasted like peppermint, fresh and clean, a contrast to the thoughts he had about what he wanted to do to her while he had her in his bed.

Her fingers stroked over his chest and around to his back. She was glorious beneath him, her lips pink and swollen from his kisses, her fiery hair spread over the pillow, her nipples rosy and peaked, rising toward him with her panting breaths. She dropped her hands to the fly of his jeans and he hissed in a breath when she ripped it open.

Fuck. He needed her bad. He rolled, bringing her with him, until she was lying on top, her soft, sweet body wedged between his thighs. "Touch me."

She sat up and eased his jeans over his hips, following them down his legs until he kicked them off, then kissing her way back up. With a grin, she wrapped her hand around the base of his cock. "How do you want to be touched?"

"Suck me, sweetheart." He smoothed his hand through the silken strands of her hair. "Take me in that hot, wet mouth. Suck me deep. Make me come."

And that was pretty much the end of slow, soft, and gentle. But she didn't seem to mind.

"I always wanted to taste you," she said, dropping her head to take him in her mouth. His girl didn't tease. She tongued his length, hard and fast, then she followed her taste with a lick over his crown before she taking him in deep. Zane bucked his hips, tightened his grip on her hair, holding her still as he jerked and plundered her mouth.

Undaunted by his control, she sucked with a steady rhythm, her mouth moving up and down his shaft, her tongue swirling over tip and base, while one hand cupped and squeezed his balls. When she slid her tongue over his opening, he clutched the duvet and groaned. Christ. If she kept that up, he would lose it before they even started.

"Need to be inside you."

"Need to finish what I started."

He felt the vibration of her voice through his cock and he almost spilled into her hot, wet mouth.

"No." Gently, he tugged her head back and she released him with a soft sigh. He grabbed a condom from his night table and sheathed himself, then settled her on top as he stretched out on the bed, knees on either side of his hips, the head of his cock at her entrance.

"Zane." She rocked against his grip until he slowly lowered her down, inch by inch over his throbbing shaft. She felt so good. So right. So hot and wet he could barely hold on. He pulled her down for a hard kiss, his lips demanding all she had and more.

"More." She ground against him, and Zane thrust his hips up, driving deep until a groan ripped from her throat. He liked that she told him what she wanted, but even more that she did what he asked.

"Touch yourself. Your nipples. I want to see your pleasure."

Evie sat back and cupped her breasts as she rode him, pinching her nipples until they were tight, hard peaks. How many nights had he fantasized about her as he stroked himself to release, never imagining she would be even more beautiful than the memory, or that it would feel so right? When he felt her pussy clench around him, he feathered his fingers over her clit and teased her until she moaned.

"Harder. Don't stop."

"Come for me, Evie." He pinched her clit and she sucked in a sharp breath, her inner walls gripping him hard, and then she came with a low, guttural groan, shuddering around him. Too much. He couldn't wait. Still buried inside her, he flipped them over and slid one hand under her thigh, lifting her right leg over his shoulder, spreading her wide.

"Oh, God . . . I can't . . . not again."

"Yes, again. Come with me." He hammered into her, his muscles taut to the point of breaking, sweat beading on his brow. And when he felt her ripple around him, heard her moan of pleasure, he gave in to his need. The climax tore through him, arching his back as he pumped deep inside her, his senses filled with her beautiful face, the scent of her sex, the slickness of her skin.

When the last ripples of her orgasm had faded away, he released her and rolled off, then pulled her to his chest, skin to skin as they heaved their breaths together.

"My beautiful Evie," he murmured in her ear. "Mine before. Mine now. Mine always."

"Say it again," she whispered.

"Which part?"

"The part where I get to be yours."

He kissed her softly. "Always, sweetheart. No matter what happens, you will always be mine."

He waited until she fell asleep, her body soft and warm against him, her breathing deep and regular. Then he eased himself off the bed, pulled on his clothes, and shrugged his cut over his shoulders. From the dresser drawer he pulled out his holsters and strapped them over his body. From the closet he carefully lifted his duffel bag and drew out his weapons—knives, guns, throwing stars, and chains. When he was fully armed, he took one last look over his shoulder.

She was beautiful in sleep, long lashes resting on creamy cheeks, red hair spread across the pillow in a silken wave. His heart ached and for a moment he was tempted to wake her.

But had never been one for good-byes.

★ NINETEEN ★

*Be prepared for everything to go wrong with
your repair. Tools will break, parts will go missing,
and wires will get crossed.*
—SINNER'S TRIBE MOTORCYCLE REPAIR MANUAL

"So, this is our new digs." Connie trailed a finger over the dusty workbench at the far end of Sparky's garage. "Needs a bit of cleaning."

"Connie . . . be nice. Sparky is very kindly letting us use his shop until we sort out a new building." Evie cleared a space on one of the tables and set up her new rack of paints. Zane had left in the middle of the night after their intimate encounter two days ago and aside from a curt assurance from Jagger that he was fine, she knew nothing about where he'd gone or how long he would be away.

However, standing up to Viper, facing the truth about her father, and finally letting down her guard with Zane, had left her feeling strong and determined to take back her life. After some heavy negotiations with Sparky, she had arranged to rent out the back of Sparky's shop until she sorted out what to do with what was now her business, albeit the only things left were the land, employees, and the goodwill Bill had built up in his name.

Sparky looked up from the bike he was working on, and

mocked an affronted stare. "It's a garage, love. And I dare you to find one cleaner than this. Plus you should be thanking me for my generosity. This is a fucking palace compared to what you had."

Connie gave him an exaggerated curtsy, all the more amusing for the fact she'd dressed head to toe in black leather—pants, corset and boots—so she could "fit in" with the bikers they would be working with for the foreseeable future. "Thank you, my lord."

Sparky's eyes widened and he gave a low hum of approval. "Say it again."

"Thank you."

"No." His voice deepened to a husky growl. "The other part."

Connie's voice dropped to a throaty whisper. "My lord."

Evie cleared her throat, reminding them they weren't alone. Ty and Hacker leaned over a tool bench, heads bent together over a new tablet Jagger had brought this morning, along with a new laptop for Evie. She'd thought his gifts touching, but odd, especially since he wouldn't meet her gaze or stay and chat. It was almost like he was feeling guilty, although she had no idea what he could be feeling guilty about.

Her head jerked up when Connie giggled. She and Sparky had been flirting ever since she'd arrived with the supplies this morning. Although they had never met, the heat between them had risen steadily as Sparky helped Connie and Evie clear a space to work, and now Evie worried they might combust.

She would have been happy for Connie save for the fact she was worried about Tank. Hacker had not-so-casually mentioned, as he helped her carry her boxes of new supplies into the shop, that brothers didn't mess with other brothers' "chicks." Not only was it a club rule, it was part of the creed, for the simple reason that Sinners were by nature fiercely protective and possessive of their women.

Brothers had died in fights over women until Jagger laid down the law.

"Connie. Can you come give me a hand?" She waved her friend over, then lowered her voice.

"I don't think you should be flirting with him. What about Tank? He's really into you."

"Tank scares me." Connie sat on the worn couch and put her feet up on the coffee table. "He's too hot, too goddamn cool and loyal to a fault. He's got that quiet confidence going on, like if someone pisses him off he doesn't get visibly angry but you know the minute he puts his hand under his cut the dude is going to be dead. And in bed . . ." She fanned herself with her hand. "I travelled the world with my folks, had a multi-cultural sex education, but no one comes close to what he can do in the sack, and that's without a whole lot of talking."

"That sounds good," Evie said. "So what are you doing with Sparky?"

"Connie shrugged. "I don't actually know. Maybe I wanna see that outlaw biker edge or find out if it's all for show. I mean, Tank doesn't have a single blood patch on his cut. Not like Sparky over there. Or Jagger. Or your Zane."

"Blood patch?"

"I'm up on all the biker lingo." Connie grinned. "They get a blood patch every time they kill someone. They wear them around the bottom of their cuts. I guess so it's not staring you in the face. Tank says some of the guys don't like wearing them, but they don't have a choice. The patches are handed out by the mother ship and they gotta do what they're told."

Evie stared at Connie aghast. "And you think that's okay?"

Connie's smile faded. "C'mon. You watch TV. Don't look so surprised. And it's not like they go around killing innocent people, or looking for people to kill. It's just . . .

you know . . . the way it is. They live in a violent world. They deal with people who are always armed—drug dealers, criminals, underworld characters, and other bikers. Someone tries to kill them, they gotta defend themselves."

"Oh, God." Evie scrubbed her hands over her face. "After Zane told me what really happened in the trailer park, I was so happy to know he hadn't pulled the trigger, that he wasn't a killer. Now you're telling me he is."

"Honey." Connie put a sympathetic hand on her shoulder. "It's about bad guys killing bad guys who are doing bad things or hurting the people they care about. Tank says they don't involve civilians unless it's biker business. You know all this. You saw what happened to Bill."

Evie gripped the table so hard her knuckles whitened. "TV isn't real. The Black Jacks are bad. I just figured . . . the Sinners . . . God, I think part of me knew but I didn't want to accept it. I can't think of Zane and Jagger that way."

"Tank says because of the war that's going on between the clubs, most of the brothers have a coupla blood patches."

Evie's shoulders sagged. "Viper told me. He said he and Zane weren't so different. He made me wonder if maybe Zane did kill my dad, but after Zane told me what happened, I figured everything else Viper said was a lie. He told me Zane shot one of his men in the back, killed three of his men in Whitefish and that he kidnapped Viper's old lady and put her in the dungeon in the clubhouse."

"No shit. There's a woman imprisoned in the clubhouse?" Connie looked over her shoulder at Sparky and whispered. "Maybe we should call the police."

"We don't know if it's true, Connie. But we need to find out."

Not just to rescue the woman, if she did exist, but because she needed to know just what kind of man Zane had become. And whether she could accept him as he truly was.

They were waiting for him when he pulled up to the clubhouse three days after he'd disappeared.

Zane gritted his teeth and parked his bike. He had expected nothing less than the full executive board, but it was going to take a hell of a lot of willpower to cross the driveway and follow them out back, especially since he had returned empty-handed.

Well, not totally empty-handed. He pulled the phone from his pocket and checked the picture file one last time. At least the punishment would be worth it. He had filled the whole damn memory card with pictures of the Black Jack clubhouse, including the door to the dungeon where T-Rex was being held prisoner.

Zane took one last look at the midnight sky, clear save for a sprinkling of stars. He'd have plenty of time to look at the stars when Jagger was done with him. The last time he'd disobeyed a direct order he'd been flat on his back for three days and pissed blood for an entire week.

Yet, despite that beating, he'd left the club three days ago to go hunting. After his night with Evie, unburdening himself of the secret he'd carried for so long, he'd decided three things: first, T-Rex had to be rescued; second, Viper had to die; and third, he couldn't wait even a day if it meant Viper was out there and Evie was in danger. Simply put, he couldn't go through the hell of thinking he'd lost her again, and with Viper on the loose that was a very real possibility.

He'd spent the first day of his hunt watching the Black Jack compound from a hill, well hidden with trees. Security was tight, just as Doreen said, and he was glad Jagger had held off the raid until they pulled in some support clubs. But Viper wasn't inside. Nor had he been seen in any of the bars, restaurants, clubs, strip joints, or whorehouses around Devil's Hills where the Black Jacks were based. He knew this because he'd checked them all. The second and third days, he'd called in every favor, paid informants, and talked to every low-life scumbag he could find. Viper was off the grid. No doubt in hiding, the snake that he was. The hunt was a bust and he would pay a heavy price.

Zane took a deep breath and walked slowly up the drive. He had texted ahead to make sure Evie was out of the clubhouse and safe at Sparky's shop when he arrived. He would need a couple of days to heal up and he didn't want her to see him until he had recovered enough to stand.

"Brothers." He nodded at the group and tossed the phone to Tank. "Give that to Hacker. I got pictures and videos of the Black Jack clubhouse, roads, grounds, vehicles, terrain . . . everything you need for the raid. I tried everything I could to get to T-Rex, but they got tighter security than the White House."

Tank gave him a pained smile. As the second youngest member of the executive board, he'd only sat in on a few disciplinary sessions, and none involving a senior board member. "Will do."

Zane met Jagger's gaze full-on, felt the need to exert the small measure of control he had left. "Let's get this over with."

Jagger grimaced, his lips thinning into a tight line and he nodded for Gunner, responsible for disciplinary matters, to proceed.

"You disobeyed a direct order to stand down until we could all go after Viper together. Penalty is a kick out or an ass kicking." Gunner folded his arms across his massive chest. If Zane hadn't been so sure Jagger would take over the disciplinary session, he might have been more concerned. Gunner's ass kickings usually involved ambulances, hospital stays, and weeks in bed being attended by the club doctor. Jagger was no lightweight, but he wasn't Gun.

"You left the clubhouse on club business without letting anyone know where you were going," Gunner continued. "Penalty is an ass kicking. You put a member of the executive board, namely you, in a fucking shitload of danger. Penalty is a kick out or an ass kicking. Since you brought some useful intel and you got a good history with the club, the board has decided on an ass kicking delivered by Jagger out back at the shooting range."

"Agreed." Zane shrugged off his cut, folded it, and handed it to Tank. Then he followed the rest of the board, who had come as witnesses, to the back of the clubhouse.

"I fucking hate you for this," Jagger murmured as they walked through the long grass. "Last fucking thing I want to do. You couldn't have waited one damn fucking day?"

"If I'd waited, we would have been slaughtered. They had at least fifty men on the grounds and I think I saw some heavy artillery. They would have blown us up before we even left the main road."

Jagger exhaled a long breath. "I'll have to call National about it. Where the hell did they get that kind of weaponry? Once word gets out, the ATF will be breathing down all our necks something fierce. No one will be able to do anything around here."

Their movement tripped the motion detectors, lighting the vast grass-covered space they used as a shooting range, and for the monthly fights they set up with the local support clubs.

His brothers formed a circle and Zane grabbed Jagger's arm before stepping inside. "Just so you know. We're tight." He didn't want Jagger to worry that this would affect their friendship. He had gone on the hunt, knowing what waited for him when he returned.

"Thank fuck. Last time you didn't talk to me for two months."

Zane walked into a center of the circle, and held his hands behind his back, wrists crossed. "Tie my hands." He'd learned the hard way that it was impossible not to raise his hands to defend himself, and all that would lead to was a bunch of broken fingers, maybe a broken arm. He wanted his hands working and unbruised so that he could hold Evie again, touch her soft skin and stroke her curves, soothe away the pain.

Gunner tied a rope around his wrists binding them together. "Is she really worth it?"

Zane braced himself when Jagger hauled back, ready for the first punch. "Yeah, brother. She is."

Zane fired a second shot at the target at the end of the grassy lawn behind the clubhouse, missing the center by a good few centimeters. Four days after the beating and he still wasn't back on his game. Beside him, Arianne laughed. Then she pumped three bullets into the bull's-eye with a casual flick of her wrist. Damn, Jagger's old lady was always showing off. Just because Viper had given her a gun at the age of three, didn't mean she had to rub a guy's nose in it.

"I still have a few rounds left," Arianne said. "You want to go again?"

"Better not. Evie's coming over with Ty and Connie. Ty's gonna humiliate Hacker again in that game with tanks and Evie and Connie want to shoot some stick downstairs." He also wasn't up for another round of humiliation. Yeah, she was Viper's daughter, but she was a girl. He was a guy. Guys were supposed to shoot better so they could protect their women. Not that Arianne needed protecting, but she usually kept her skills under the radar when Jagger was around. Showing up the VP was one thing, but no one showed up the president.

He lowered his weapon, wincing as his arm brushed over his bruised ribs.

Arianne lifted an eyebrow. "Does Evie know?"

"No. And I'm not gonna tell her."

She holstered her gun and laughed. "I think I'd better hang around Jagger just in case. She might be a small-town girl but she's got old lady steel. You should have heard her bossing everyone around in Sparky's shop. Just over a week and she has her business up and running again. And if she finds out Jagger's the one who turned you black and blue, I have no doubt she'll go after him. Even if he was her friend. Even if you've been back for four days and didn't get in touch with her. And even if you deserve what you got."

Christ. Most of the women in the club had been sympathetic and caring over the last couple of days he'd stayed upstairs in his room to recover. They'd tended his wounds, fed him, and found brothers to help him up when he wanted to shower. Jagger had been up to see him every day, helped change his bandages, brought him pizza. But not Arianne. He had no doubt she'd have thrown the first punch if Jagger let her, and she would have used brass knuckles, too.

"I'd like to see you *try* to protect Jagger. You know if there's even a hint of danger, he'll be shoving you away."

"We'll shove each other." Arianne laughed and her face softened. "That's what we do best."

"Zane!" Evie came around the corner and waved.

His breath left him in a rush. How long had it been since he'd seen her? Seven days? Eight? Fuck she was even more beautiful than he remembered. The sun caught her hair as she ran toward him, catching those gold highlights and making them sparkle. Good thing. Otherwise those barely there shorts and tiny tank top stretched tight over her luscious breasts might just have distracted him entirely, instead of leaving him just enough sense to hold out a gun when she approached, blocking his body. He couldn't let her touch him without giving himself away. Even after four days he couldn't bear anything more than the clothes touching his skin.

"You wanna learn to shoot today?"

Evie pulled up short, her brow creased in a frown. "I know how to shoot. Bill taught me. And I beat you every time we played Undercover Ops."

"Shooting a TV screen isn't the same as shooting in real life, sweetheart. And you never beat me. I let you win." He handed her the gun, and her arms dropped to her sides.

"Where have you been for the last week? Is something wrong?"

"Biker business so I can't talk about it." He spun her around to face the target and put his arms around her to help her steady the gun, trying to keep a space between their bodies.

"Why do you want me to shoot so bad?" She looked up over her shoulder, her cheek soft against his jaw. "Is it not safe here? Should I take Ty away?"

"You're safe here, sweetheart." He buried his lips in the softness of her hair. She smelled of honey and jasmine, thick and sweet, and he longed for a little taste. "Pull the trigger. Let's see what you got."

She aimed the weapon, pulled the trigger and the bullet glanced off the top of the target and hit a tree.

"Like this." He repositioned her hands and bent her elbows, then gently tilted the gun barrel down an inch. Evie stepped back, pressed herself into his body. Zane hissed and jerked away at the potent mix of pleasure and pain.

"What's wrong?" Evie spun around. "Why don't you want to touch me?"

"I do." He cupped her face between his hands and bent down to kiss her, his lips moving over hers, drinking her down like he was dying of thirst. She opened for him, ran her tongue over the seam of his lips, and he stroked inside her, tangling his tongue with her own. She tasted of coffee and cream—regular, not whipped.

Evie moaned and slid her arms around his waist. Zane flinched, and she backed away.

"You're hurt."

"It's nothing." He gestured to her gun. "Let's do more shooting."

"I'll shoot if you show me what's under your shirt." She

slid her hand along the V of her shirt to the crescents of her breasts and gave him a sensual smile. "In fact, I'll forgive you for leaving and show you mine if you show me yours."

All Zane's blood rushed to his groin and his cock hardened in an instant. Too much. It had been too long. Jagger had been careful this time, taking care not to hit his face too much so Evie wouldn't get alarmed. He'd also avoided Zane's kidneys and his groin, for which Zane was particularly grateful, especially now when he wanted her so damn bad he was seconds away from taking her on the grass.

"You show me what's under your shirt and if you hit the target on two out of three tries, I'll show you what's under mine," he countered.

Evie twisted her lips to the side, considering, and then she lifted the gun. "Done. Bill spent a long time showing me how to shoot in case there was trouble at the shop." She edged the gun up, fired, and completely missed the target.

"Not that I like to speak ill of the dead," Zane said, "but if that's what he taught you, I'm glad you never had trouble at the shop. You woulda shot out a coupla nice bikes, maybe a window, but no bad guys."

Evie looked back over shoulder. "And here I thought you were the bad guy."

Oh he was bad, all right. The things he wanted to do to her right now were illegal in several states, maybe a few countries, too.

Zane growled deep in his throat. "Don't tease a man with a weapon."

"I can't help it when his weapon is so big." She wiggled her ass against him and grinned. Playful Evie. Fuck. He loved making her smile as much as he loved making her wet.

"Behave."

"I want to see you shoot with the big gun." She turned and patted the holster under his cut, her hand sliding down to his belt.

Too late he realized the danger. Evie yanked up his shirt and gasped.

"Oh. My. God. What happened to you?"

"Got in a fight."

"A fight?" She shoved his shirt higher, walked around his back. "Oh, baby. You're hurt so bad."

This was good. Her compassion had overridden her curiosity.

Ask me no questions and I'll tell you no lies.

"Not hurt everywhere, sweetheart." He turned quickly, bent down and nipped the exposed skin at the base of her neck. Christ, he loved to mark her, to see those bruises on her neck and know she belonged to him, to keep the predators at bay.

Evie shuddered as he licked the tiny wound. "Here?"

"Upstairs. You still have to make good your deal and I can promise it will make me feel a whole lot better."

He led her around the side of the clubhouse and up the front steps. Shaggy was on guard duty and waved them inside.

"Hey Zane. Nice to see you up and about. Jagger worked you over pretty good the other night. I thought you'd be laid up for at least a week. But four days! You're one tough bastard."

Evie froze on the step beside him. "Jagger did this to you?"

"Biker business." Zane put his arm on her lower back and steered her inside. "I'll explain what I can upstairs."

"Upstairs where you've been suffering for four days and no one called me?" Her voice rose in pitch. "I was only a ten-minute drive away. I could have looked after you." Eyes flashing, she spun out of his grasp.

"Jagger!" She shouted his name and stormed into the living room.

"Shit. Did I say something wrong?" Shaggy came up beside him, stroking his thick gray beard. "I thought everyone knew. Isn't that the point?"

"Yeah. But it wasn't a lesson Evie needed to learn."

He knew the exact moment Evie spotted Jagger talking to Gunner and Arianne in the vast room the MC used for church, the monthly mandatory meetings for all full-patch brothers. Save for a few couches and chairs, a long table where the board sat, and a computer table where Dax recorded minutes, the room was bare. No pictures on the walls, no curtains on the windows. Nothing to distract the brothers during the meetings.

Her feet thudded on the wooden floor, her hair fanning out behind her. She was glorious in her anger and he was glad for the small mercy Jagger hadn't been in the living room because what was about to go down wasn't something a small boy like Ty should see.

"Jagger!"

Jagger looked up, but before he could move to greet her, Arianne stepped into Evie's path.

"That's as far as you go."

"Get out of my way." Evie's voice shook with anger.

Zane crossed the floor toward her. "Let it go, sweetheart."

"Let it go? Look what he did to you." She tried to step around Arianne. "Get out here, Jagger, or are you afraid to look me in the eye and tell me what you did?"

"Zane made him do it." Arianne folded her arms, and scowled. "Jagger's hurting as much as Zane. He spent the last four days at the clubhouse looking after him. Zane broke the rules. He had to be punished. That's our way."

"Your way?" Evie's hands clenched into fists. "Your way is to beat a man half to death? What could he possibly have done to deserve that?"

"She's magnificent," Sparky murmured, coming up behind Zane. "Between her and Arianne, my shop has never run as efficiently. The brothers are afraid to step out of line."

"Definitely old lady material." Gunner sidestepped the fray to join them. "You keeping her?"

"Yeah," Zane said, his chest swelling with pride. "She's mine."

Evie's chest heaved and she glared at Arianne. Why wouldn't she get out of the way? This had nothing to do with her, and everything to do with Evie needing to know exactly what being part of this world meant.

"He went against my orders." Jagger stepped out from behind Arianne. "He broke the rules. He had a choice. Punishment or a kick out. He agreed to the punishment."

"That's barbaric." Her voice rose in pitch and she tried to bring it down, but seeing Zane so badly injured, and knowing Jagger had done it . . . Her gaze dropped to the bottom of Jagger's cut, lined with small red diamond patches.

Blood patches.

"Don't judge us," Arianne warned. "This is a different world. We play by different rules. Enforcing order in the club is a matter of survival—for both the MC and civilians."

"What's going on?" Connie ran into the room. "Evangeline? Everything okay?"

"Get Ty packed up. We're leaving." She couldn't stay here, couldn't expose Ty to this, couldn't accept that Zane was part of this world.

"But . . ." Connie's eyes widened and she jerked her head toward the door to the basement where they figured a dungeon might be. "I thought we were going to . . . play pool."

Evie's stomach twisted. Did she really want to know if there was a woman in the dungeon? Her gaze flicked down to the bottom of Zane's cut. Blood patches. Just like Viper said. How ironic that everyone thought of Viper as the bad guy, and yet he had told her the truth.

"Come upstairs with me," Zane murmured in her ear, his arm sliding around her waist. "I'll explain it to you. Answer any questions you have."

Her shoulders slumped as the fight drained out of her. It was all Viper said and more. The Sinners were no different from the Jacks. Zane no different from Viper. This wasn't a TV show, it was worse. It was real and as bad as she could have imagined.

★ TWENTY ★

*A bad repair decision may end up costing you time
and money, but that's OK. Everything can be fixed.*
        —SINNER'S TRIBE MOTORCYCLE REPAIR MANUAL

"Take off your clothes." Evie leaned against Zane's bedroom door, more for support than a means of escape.

"Evie . . ."

A growl curled in her throat, her anger growing as she
realized this was the beginning of the end. Once she saw
what was under his shirt, there would be no going back.
"Take them off. I want to see what he did to you."

He pulled his shirt over his head and tossed it on the
bed, then he stripped down to his boxers. Her legs trembled as her gaze swept over his body, starting at his feet,
her strength leaving her as she took in the discolored skin
on his shins and thighs, the cuts on his wrists, and then
gave out when she saw the full extent of his bruised and
lacerated torso.

Her beautiful Zane.

She sank down to the floor, wrapped her arms around
her legs, buried her head and sobbed, the grief ripping her
apart inside. Tears spilled down her cheeks dripping on
the floor with each ragged inhale. She cried not just for
him, but for them, and the knowledge they could never be
together.

"Fuck." Zane's voice was harsh, raw as he crossed the

room to kneel beside her. "Sweetheart, it's not as bad as it looks."

She shook her head, held herself tighter, unable to speak for the images spinning around in her mind. Jagger had no bruises on his body. That guilty look on his face when he'd come into the shop . . . the marks on Zane's wrists.

Zane hadn't fought back. His hands were tied and he hadn't fought back.

"Let me explain." He cradled her in his arms, as if she was the one hurting. She supposed, in a way, she was.

"There's nothing to say that could make this acceptable to me." Evie sniffed back her tears. "I can't do this, Zane. Seeing you like this is tearing me apart. I'll never be able to forgive Jagger, never forget what he did to you. I won't even pretend to understand how you agreed to it. The fact that you live in a world where this kind of thing goes on is bad enough, but on top of it . . . your patches . . . blood . . ."

"I'll leave the MC." Simple words and yet they weighed heavy on her heart.

"I don't want you to leave." She held herself stiff, afraid to touch his battered body. "This club means everything to you. That you would take a beating from your best friend tells me how much you love this life. You would hate me every day for taking you away from it."

"I love you more," he said. "I have always loved you. I've lived my life in the shadows because I couldn't let you go." He drew in a ragged breath, brushed his lips over her hair. "I can't lose you now. I went looking for Viper because I couldn't bear to lose you."

She struggled to sit, pushed herself to standing. "I can't bear the thought of losing you either, but I don't even know who I am anymore. All I know is that I've been stupidly naive, and this life you lead isn't for me. I want to be with you, but I don't see how this can work."

His face smoothed, eyes darkened. Even now she knew him so well, she could see his emotional retreat.

She closed her fist and hit it to her breast, her eyes

stinging with tears all over again. "It hurts me to see you in pain. It hurts me to think of you suffering. It hurts me to think of you in such danger that you have to take a life. I've spent my whole life hurting because I wanted you and couldn't have you. I just can't take the hurting anymore. I love you, Zane, but it hurts just too damn bad, and now you're taking risks for me that could get you killed. I don't want that. Even if we can't be together, I need to know you're alive and happy and doing what you love to do."

His voice, when he spoke, was thick with pain. "You want to walk away? What about Ty?"

"I don't know." God, why couldn't she stop crying? "I need some time to think about it. He adores you. He's so happy to have you in his life, I can't take that away from him."

She turned, reached for the door, but it felt too wrong. Unfinished. There was something she needed to do.

"Will you let me do something for you before I go?"

"Anything."

She gestured to his bruised, battered body. "You did this for me. I want to give something back. I want to take care of you so when I leave I'll know you're going to be okay."

Pain.

His life was all about pain.

And yet the pain in his body was nothing compared to the pain in his heart. Zane's hand clenched on his breast. If he could rip his damn heart out of his chest he would. Go back to the darkness that had sustained him for the last nine years, back to the shadows. Out of the damn light.

He heard the rush of water in the shower from the en suite bathroom, a luxury afforded only the senior patch brothers who kept rooms at the clubhouse, but he couldn't go in. He was too wound up, too out of control, too damn emotional.

What else could he do? He had meant every word when

he told her he would fight to be with her. He just hadn't realized she would be the one standing in his way.

With a roar, he thudded his fist against the wall. His hands were about the only place on his body that wasn't bruised. Might as well remedy that problem because he had saved them for nothing.

When he felt no release from his assault on the wall, he ripped a drawer from the dresser and smashed it on the ground. Clothes flew across the room and the wood cracked and splintered. Like his heart.

"Zane!"

But now that the floodgates had opened, he couldn't stop. He lifted the drawer and smashed it down again, his aching muscles protesting the impact. "Do you want Viper, Evie? Is that it? Is that what this is all about?" He knew it was ludicrous. She had seen who Viper was, but he needed a reason, something he could change.

"No, baby. You know that's not true. Now come let me wash you and look after those cuts and bruises."

Smash. Smash. Smash. He tore the drawer apart. He loved her compassion and yet he hated it if it meant the last time he touched her he would be in pain.

"I'll shower with you so I can look after you properly." She clasped the bottom of her T-shirt and tugged it over her head. Zane froze mid-strike, his primal instincts sharpening at the sight of her skin and her beautiful breasts encased in blue satin.

"I don't want your help." He threw the remnants of the drawer across the room.

"Too bad. And if you can't do it for you, then do it for me." Evie undid her bra and tossed it on the bed with her shirt. "It will make me . . . feel better." She slid her jeans and panties over her hips and then kicked them off. Gloriously naked, quietly confident, undaunted by his rage, she turned into the bathroom. "Come on."

Zane's body shook, torn between going after his woman and unleashing his frustrations on the rest of the furniture.

Don't go in. He knew what would happen if he followed her, and it wouldn't involve standing still while she treated his wounds. And with his heart raw and exposed, he didn't think he could handle that level of intimacy without totally losing control. With a growl, he ripped out another drawer, and hammered it against the wall until it shattered, pieces flying in all directions. Exhausted, he sank down on the bed, the ruins of the drawers scattered at his feet, his muscles quivering at the exertion. He could hear the shower behind him, feel the breath of steam, smell the floral fragrance of shampoo.

Evie.

Loves me.

Leaving me.

Overwhelmed with the need to touch her, he stripped off his clothes, all thoughts of staying away forgotten beneath the desire to hold her in his arms one last time.

Evie turned when he stepped into the shower, rivulets of water streaming over her beautiful body. "Took you long enough. Did you break all the drawers?"

Words deserted him. He took her in his arms and held her against him, his cock, painfully erect, pressed against her soft belly.

"It's okay," she murmured against his chest, her arms tightening around him.

He didn't know how long they stood under the warm water, but his heart finally slowed its frenetic beat and the tension eased from his body.

"You're mine."

"And you're mine. That won't change." She slid her hands up his chest ever so gently to circle his neck.

She was right about that. Nothing would change. He would find a way. He would fight for her until he couldn't fight anymore.

"Let me take care of you now." She soaked the washcloth and then gently rubbed it over his body, washing away the dried blood, cleaning carefully over his bruises.

She kept her bottom lip tight between her teeth, and when she looked up he couldn't tell if the drops on her cheeks were water or tears. Her hands were soft on his skin, gentle, and the warm water eased muscles that had been taut for days.

"I love your body." Her hands smoothed soap down his back, over his ass. His cock was stiff and hard despite his emotional turmoil, aching for her touch, the slick heat of her pussy, the need to reassert his claim to her body. "So strong. So hard. Perfect. When I touch you, I feel safe."

Not safe enough, or she wouldn't be running away.

When her breast brushed against his chest, he couldn't take anymore. Turning, he pulled her into his arms. "You are safe. I will always keep you safe, always take care of you."

He started with her lips, gently tracing over them with his finger, then licking them clean. He slid soapy hands over her cheeks and her neck, and then he moved to her breasts, cupping and squeezing them beneath the running water until she arched beneath his touch.

"I think I'm clean there now," she panted.

He knelt in front of her, kissing his way over her stomach, lapping water droplets from her skin, and the soft redgold down over her mound. Her hands tightened in his hair when he gently parted her legs and eased her back against the wall. Then he lifted her knee, opening her to him. "Over my shoulder."

"I don't want to hurt you."

"Only hurting that will happen is if you don't let me love you."

She did as he asked, locking her heel against his back, and he leaned forward and licked the sweet petals of her folds.

"Oh, God." Her leg tightened, drawing him closer and he licked again, tasting her honey as water slid over his cheeks. His cock throbbed under the pounding spray as he sucked and teased up and around her clit. She rocked her hips against his mouth, but he wanted more from her. He wanted everything.

She was his. And he wanted her body and soul.

"Hold on to the showerhead. Don't let go."

Evie's breath hitched. No hands meant no control. And this was supposed to be her show, her way of giving back to him. But she sensed he needed her like this, needed to take back some control. She reached up and his warm smile sent a wave of arousal through her slick, wet body.

Still, she wasn't prepared when he pushed a thick finger inside her. Her breath left in a rush, her back bowing as she rocked to meet his thrusts. Water jets teased her sensitive nipples, before splashing against his forehead, but he was relentless, his finger sliding in and out as his tongue circled her clit, sensation building on sensation, until there was nothing but the incessant demand of her body for more.

Zane added a second finger, stretching her, his fingertips pulsing against her sensitive inner tissue. Pressure built within her, not the usual rush to the peak, but a slow, steady roll, deep in her core. Her back arched away from the cold wall. Her leg locked on his shoulder. Her hands gripped the showerhead so hard she feared it would tear away from the wall. And when he flicked his tongue over her clit then nipped it gently, timing it to the deepest thrust of his fingers, she let go, her climax tearing a low, guttural groan from her throat, her body shuddering over and over as he drew out her orgasm with slow, shallow pulses of his fingers.

"So beautiful," he said softly. "I've wanted to see you restrained since the moment we met again, even if you were doing it yourself."

Yeah, she'd always figured her Zane had a kinky side. But she never thought she did, too.

His gaze dropped to the curls at the juncture of her thighs and her body trembled with need. Just that look, the heat of his gaze, was enough to send a tremor of excitement through her. And when he stood, curved his hands under her breasts, the rough calluses scraping over her sensitive skin, she thought she might come again just from the erotic burn.

He pushed her breasts together and sucked one nipple, then the other, his tongue unrelenting as it lashed back and forth. Her head fell back, and she went up on her toes, pain and pleasure mixing until she couldn't tell where one finished and the other began.

"I could spend all day worshiping your beautiful breasts," he murmured. "I could spend a lifetime worshiping you."

Overwhelmed by sensation and the loss of control, she strained toward him until his erection pressed against her stomach.

"I need you."

"Then spread your legs for me, sweetheart. Let me in." He moved one hand down her body and teased around her folds, circling her entrance. A tremor ran through her and she angled her hips trying to urge him inside her. The constant stream of water over her clit sent a buzz through her head and she moaned her desperate need for release.

"Gotta get a condom." He moved to leave and she grabbed his hand.

"It's okay. I'm on the pill." She looked away, not wanting to see his expression. She trusted him that much, and yet she was still walking away. God, what was she doing?

Zane's hands slid down her slick body and he cupped her ass, lifting her easily to his hips. And then he slid inside her with one hard thrust, startling her with the fullness and the sense of complete possession.

He let out a low groan. "Ah, Evie. So good to be with you this way. Like the first time we were together."

No, it was better. More. She had never felt this close to him before. Not in the forest when they'd made love, nor in the bedroom when she'd locked away that part of her that might get too involved. But now, with the water washing away all her barriers, his body hot and hard against hers, his cock throbbing inside her, with nothing between them, she felt the last of her control slip away.

"Zane." His name on her lips was more a plea than a request, but he was already moving, lifting her hips in time to his thrusts. She tightened her arms around his neck and held on for the ride, her back slick and wet against the cold tile wall.

Her inner walls tightened around his cock as he hammered into her, sliding her up and down his hard, wet body, giving her the friction she needed to hit her peak. He stroked his finger over her clit and her climax came in a rush, pleasure flooding through her veins in a molten wave. Zane grunted and pounded into her, coming hard and fast just as her pleasure began to fade.

He held her against him as the water beat down, washing away their sweat and tears. Then they washed each other all over again, and rubbed each other dry.

Evie slipped out from under Zane's arm and texted Connie to meet her downstairs. She had applied salve to all his wounds and bandaged the worst cuts. Exhausted and clearly in pain, Zane had fallen asleep holding her cradled against him. She didn't want to leave, but she needed time to think. How could she be with a man who led a life that scared her?

Connie met her downstairs with Ty, still wired after hours of gaming.

"Sparky's bringing the SUV. He'll be here in a couple of minutes." Connie gave a quick glance down the hallway, then lowered her voice. "I got downstairs and played some pool, checked the place out. It's a game room. Pool table, dartboard, foosball table, bar in the corner, but there were three steel locked doors with cameras above them, and they wouldn't let Ty come down, so I figure there's something there. I asked but no one would tell me."

"I don't think I want to know what's down there."

"You looked wrecked," Connie said softly.

"I am wrecked." Evie's shoulders slumped. "I told Zane I couldn't do this, that I needed some time. I couldn't handle seeing him hurt like that. It made me angry and ill at the same time. If Arianne hadn't been in the way I might have done some serious damage to Jagger, and yet I've never hit anyone in my life. It's how I would feel if someone hurt Ty. I wanted to protect him and care for him, but I also wanted to get him out of here. But he's a man, not a boy. And this is the life he loves. I love him, Connie, but not this world—not for me, and not for Ty. I don't know what to do."

Connie's face crumpled. "Oh honey, I'm so sorry. I guess you probably don't want to go back to the safe house."

"I'll get a hotel until I figure things out. And we'll have to find somewhere else to set up shop."

"You can stay with me." Connie picked up Ty's electronics bag and put an arm around him. "I've been trying to rent out my spare room forever. And before you start worrying about putting me in danger, Jagger already arranged to have two guys watching you wherever you go. He says it won't be for long. They're already waiting outside."

Sparky honked the horn and Evie reached for the door.

"We're leaving?" Ty shook himself, his eyes wide. "What about Zane? I didn't see him yet. I haven't seen him for a long time!"

"He's sleeping," Evie said gently. "And he's not feeling well so we don't want to disturb him."

"But he didn't say hello. And he was going to show me all the bikes." His bottom lip quivered. "And I was supposed to teach him how to play World of Tanks."

Guilt curdled her stomach. "You can do those things

with him another time. Maybe Connie can bring you back here tomorrow."

A tear rolled down Ty's cheek. "Doesn't he want to see me?"

"Hey, bud." Wincing, Zane eased himself down on the stairs leading to the second floor. He wore a long-sleeved shirt under his cut that hid all the bruises, save for the one on his cheek and the fresh cuts on his hands.

Ty ran into his arms. "Mom said you were sleeping and you weren't feeling well."

"Yeah, well, we can't be Batman all the time." He ruffled Ty's hair and his eyes flicked to Evie. "We got time to check out the bikes?"

"Of course."

Zane clasped Ty's hand and led him outside. Eyes tearing, Connie watched them go and shook her head.

"They're so good together. You can't . . ."

"I won't." A sad smile tugged the corner of her lips as she watched them go, walking with the same gait, Ty's small hand clasped tight in Zane's palm. "I don't think I could even if I tried. I was so worried that Zane wouldn't want to be involved in his life, but I have a feeling he would follow Ty no matter where we went. He said he would hand in his cut to be with us . . . leave the life . . ."

"Speaking of which . . ." Connie pointed to the floor. "Do you still want to find out about the mysterious woman in the dungeon? There's nobody downstairs right now."

Evie clenched her hands by her side. Did she want to go down there? Did she really want to know? She could just ask Zane, but it would bring up all the issues and emotions again. And yet woman's life could be at stake. After confronting Jagger, feeling the power of her anger, she wasn't as afraid of the Sinners as she had been before. She wasn't a victim. If she was even going to consider being part of this world, she needed to understand it. And if they were doing something that was morally wrong, if they were hurting innocent people, she needed to know that, too.

She reached out, gave Connie's hand a squeeze. "I need you to run interference. I'll just be five minutes."

Connie raced outside and Evie headed into the kitchen and then down the stairs to the basement. The lights were still on, illuminating the open space. She skirted around the pool table, taking care not to knock over the beer bottles lining the edges and the ashtrays full of butts. Smoke lingered in the air, and the floor was awash with hoodies, pizza boxes and crumpled newspapers.

Heart thudding, she made her way to the far end of the game room and knocked on a metal door beside a long, dark hallway. "Hello?" She waited and knocked again.

No answer.

She moved down to the second door and knocked, speaking louder this time. "Hello? Is anyone in there?"

"Who's that?"

Evie startled at the sound of a woman's voice and fought back a wave of nausea.

"Evie. My name is Evie. Are you okay?"

She heard the scrape of iron on concrete, the thud of feet, and then the woman's voice, louder now.

"Evie? You a sweet butt? House mama?" She had a harsh voice, grating and hard. "Did they send you to look after me in case I'm on the rag or PMSing or some other woman thing that'll scare the shit out of them?"

"No. I'm just . . . visiting."

The woman barked a laugh. "Visiting? This ain't no tourist attraction. You coming in?"

"No. I can't." She drew in a ragged breath. "What's your name? Did they hurt you?"

Silence. And then the woman's voice softened. "I'm Doreen. What is this? Why are you here?"

"I just . . ." Why was she here? "I heard they had a woman in the dungeon and I wanted to know if it was true, and maybe, I thought I could get you out."

"Ah." Doreen gave a heavy sigh. "You're not part of the MC, are you?"

"No."

"Didn't think so. You sound like a good person. You got a nice voice, sweet and soft. Kinda innocent like. You got kids Evie?"

"Yes. I have boy. He's eight years old."

Doreen gave a little sob. "Me too. I got a little boy. He's just learning to walk. I miss him something fierce."

Evie's heart squeezed in her chest. "Who's looking after him?"

"He lives with my mom. Viper killed his dad. I came to the morgue in Conundrum to see my Axle one last time. That's when the Sinners took me."

"Which Sinner?" Her voice dropped to a whisper, but the woman heard her.

"The dark one with the long hair is the one who caught me. I think his name is Zane."

Evie covered her mouth to stifle her moan.

"They thought Viper would pay to get me back 'cause I was wearing his old lady cut," Doreen continued. "But I told 'em, Viper doesn't care about me. He told me that the first time he threw me on his bed. Told me I was nothing but a place for his dick."

"Oh, God." She sucked in a sharp breath. "I'll do everything I can to get you out of here. I'll call the police . . ."

"No." Doreen barked the word so loud Evie stepped back from the door. "This is biker business. You don't involve the cops or everyone goes down. You gotta find another way."

Evie heard footsteps on the stairs, but there was nowhere to run, nowhere to hide. And dammit someone had to answer for this. She stiffened her spine, folded her arms, and glared when Arianne walked into the room.

"What are you doing down here?"

She opened her mouth to lie, but what was the point?

She was standing right outside the door and Arianne would have heard her talking. "There's a woman in that room."

"Yeah, I know."

Evie took a step toward Arianne. "We have to get her out of there."

"You just don't get it, do you?" Arianne gestured her away from door, keeping her voice low. "Doreen knew the risks involved if she crossed the border into Conundrum. Just like Zane knew the risks of disobeying Jagger. They both got punished the biker way, although Doreen wasn't hurt because Jagger doesn't allow violence toward women, and women usually. aren't involved in biker business. This was an exception."

"She's imprisoned. And away from her son. That's hurting her."

Arianne rolled her eyes. "She's a Black Jack old lady so it's hard to know how much she says is lies and how much is the truth. But one thing I know for sure, Viper didn't force that cut on her. The only way to get Viper's old lady cut is to get rid of the woman wearing it and be stronger than the next woman who wants it. Viper thinks it's amusing to watch them fight over him. Doreen is a hard woman. She's ruthless, conniving, and vicious. She injured two of the junior patch who were sent down to bring her food, and that's with her hands tied." Her lips curled into a grin, and she lowered her voice to a whisper. "You want a little taste? Walk up the stairs really loud then come down again real quiet."

Evie did as she asked and returned to Arianne's side. Arianne put a finger to her lips. "Yo, Doreen." She bashed her fist on the door. "She's gone, so don't waste your breath with the sob stories. We both know what goes on in the clubhouse. And guess what? Your ass is mine next time Jagger wants some intel, and I'm no softie like the boys. I know where to stick it so it hurts."

"Fuck off you fucking bitch." Doreen shrieked. "The minute I get outta here, I'm coming for you. It's your face

I'm gonna cut up first. I'm gonna make it so Jagger gets fucking sick every time he looks at you. Then I'm going after the dark one who snatched me. It'll be a slice and dice. This fucking clubhouse is gonna run red with Sinner blood. I'm saving Jagger for last. He'll be a present for Viper. I'll deliver him all wrapped up in a bow made of your sweet little girl's hair."

"Our world," Arianne said quietly. She gestured Evie toward the stairs. "You have to be strong to survive. But we do have rules and a code. And we have our own rough brand of justice."

Still shaken by Doreen's outburst, Evie paused on the stairs. "But how do people with kids handle this kind of life?"

"You should talk to Dawn, or Dax's old lady, Sandy," she said. "Or any of the other old ladies. Most of them choose to keep their family life separate from the club. And that's fine. There are no rules for old ladies. It's whatever works for them. And yeah, sometimes their men come home battered, bruised, and broken, but that happens to civilians, too. Boxers, fighters, stuntmen . . . they all put themselves in danger. The old ladies patch them up, give them heck, and then love them until they do it again. It's the risk we take to live this life. It's what we do to survive. But it's a life of freedom, honor, loyalty, and brotherhood; a life where you make the rules."

"You love this life."

Arianne's face softened. "Yes, I do. Although I almost gave it up to get away from Viper. But then I met Jagger, and I found a way to make it work for me. That's the thing about love. It makes the impossible possible. And it won't be denied."

★ TWENTY-ONE ★

If you take it apart, and you can't put it back together, don't panic. Walk away, clear your head, then start again.
—SINNER'S TRIBE MOTORCYCLE REPAIR MANUAL

Evie drove up to the Sinner clubhouse and parked outside. She hadn't been back for over a week, and she hoped the impromptu visit didn't ruffle any feathers. Although Zane had come by Connie's place several times to visit Ty, her son wanted to spend more time with his dad. Since they were passing by the clubhouse on their way home from a day in the mountains, she'd agreed to a brief stop to see if he was around when she couldn't get in touch by phone.

She waved to Shooter and Tank, tinkering with their bikes out front, and turned off the Sinner SUV Zane had insisted she keep as a matter of safety. The raid on the Black Jack clubhouse had been delayed because of the increased presence of the ATF in Conundrum, drawn by the spate of fires and the explosion at the coffee shop. For now, everyone had to lay low, although Zane had gone scouting around the Black Jack clubhouse, this time with executive board approval, to try and figure out if they could try to get T-Rex out with a two- or three-man operation.

"Can I get out, mom?" Ty didn't wait for her answer, but pushed open the door. Connie jumped out after him and they headed over to talk to Tank who they hadn't seen since returning to the safe house.

Shortly after moving in with Connie and trying to get back to her regular life, Evie received her first lesson about keeping the police out of biker business. The morning after contacting the police to report her car stolen, she'd awoken to find her vehicle burned out and wrapped around a street light beside Connie's driveway with the Black Jack initials spray painted on the remains. The Sinners had arrived with a flatbed truck to take it away and Connie, Ty, and Evie were moved back to the safe house above Sparky's shop.

Concerned about Evie's biker clients ratting her out to the Jacks, Jagger had convinced her to hold back on reopening her business in a new location. As a result, she'd kept herself busy painting Sinner bikes, talking to insurance adjusters, and trying to find a new home for her business from inside Sparky's shop. With too much time on her hands, and after hitting her quota of video games with Ty, she'd gone through her scrapbooks and reminisced about the time she and Zane had spent together.

They didn't talk now, except about Ty, and she missed him so much she ached. Although she was still wary about the life he led, now that she'd had some time to think, she was beginning to warm to the idea that the Sinners weren't all bad. But she'd hurt Zane by walking away and she didn't know how to mend the rift between them.

"He's not here." Ty ran toward her as she rounded the vehicle, Tank in tow. "Tank says he's gone away."

Usually the first with a smile, Tank shifted his feet and looked away. "Club business. Doesn't get shared with old ladies or civilians." He held out his hand to Ty and raised an inquiring eyebrow. "You wanna shoot some hoops before you head out? I gotta escort a lady to a car, then I can meet you out back."

Evie nodded at Ty's silent query and watched him race across the lawn.

"How do the old ladies do it?" she asked Connie. "If club business isn't shared with old ladies, then they never know what's going to happen when the brothers go out. Maybe they're just going for a drink, or maybe it's a shootout, or a suicidal raid on the Black Jack clubhouse. I couldn't deal with that uncertainty. I'd be an emotional wreck. And what if someone came after me or Ty when we were alone? I'm not like Arianne. I couldn't stab or shoot anyone."

"Um . . . hello." Connie waved a hand in front of Evie's face. "You stabbed Vipe when he was . . ." She choked on her words. "Hurting Bill. And if you'd had a knife when you found out Jagger was the one who beat the shit out of Zane, I have no doubt you would have used it. You didn't faint or collapse on the floor weeping like some kinda drama queen."

Connie brushed back her hair. She'd worn a tank top and a cute pair of very short shorts to go hiking in the unseasonably warm weather and Tank hadn't given her a second look. Evie wondered if he'd bowed out because of Sparky.

"I've never been the drama queen type."

Connie laughed. "It sounds like you're not worried anymore about the red patches on his cut."

"I don't think he does that part of it for kicks. At heart, he's still the same Zane."

"I don't think any of them like that part." Connie tugged at her top when Tank waved from the porch. "Far as I can tell, they're pretty decent guys, except for Shaggy, Shooter, and a couple of the others who are certifiably wacko."

Tank and Hacker emerged from the clubhouse holding a blond woman between them.

"Who's that?" Connie gave her a nudge. "She looks spitting mad."

"Get your fucking paws off me," the woman snarled as they drew near. "Your damn pathetic clubhouse is in the middle of fucking nowhere. It's not like I can run away."

Evie sucked in a sharp breath. "That's Doreen, the woman from the dungeon. They must be letting her go."

Doreen's hair was a disheveled mess of blond curls, and

her long, angular face was pale and wan. Although taller than both Evie and Connie, her thin frame gave her an almost skeletal appearance save for her generous, perfectly-shaped breasts, which Evie doubted were real.

"I'd let her go, too with a mouth like that," Connie said. "She puts the Sinners to shame, and since I've been hanging around with them, I have to say that's no easy feat."

They stood aside as Shooter drove up in a black Chrysler 300C. He left it running and raced around to open the passenger door for Doreen.

"What the fuck is this?" Doreen sneered at Connie and Evie. "A good-bye party from the girl scouts?"

"I'm Evie. I talked to you downstairs."

Doreen stared at her for a long moment, and then she tilted her head to the side. "You got red hair. And your name . . . Evie. Is that short for something?"

"Evangeline."

Doreen's eyes widened and the look she gave Evie was cold, calculating. "You're the one Viper wants. No one could figure it out but now I get it. He wants a taste of the other side. Innocence. Soft and sweet. Tell me, little kitten, when he pets your widdle pussy do you purr?"

Evie recoiled, her nose wrinkling in disgust. Doreen laughed and moved toward Shooter, standing by the open door.

"Aren't you the looker?" She leaned up, her breasts brushing against his chest. "Lucky me. Jagger sent the young blood to take me home. A couple of junior patch and you just gotta be a prospect. Even if it wasn't written on your cut, I can smell the newness on you."

Shooter narrowed his eyes. "Back off, bitch."

Evie had never seen anyone move as fast, but before Shooter could push her away, Doreen yanked one of his weapons from its holster, spun, and held it to Evie's head.

"Evie!" Connie took a step forward as Hacker and Tank drew their weapons. Doreen pushed Evie in front of her, using her as a shield.

"Don't come any closer or I'll off the little kitten right here, right now. Serves Jagger right for sending a buncha boys to do a man's job." She gestured to Connie and tipped her chin at the 300C. "Open the passenger door."

"She has a little boy," Connie said. "Why don't you take me?"

"I got a little boy, too, and the Sinners threw me in the fucking dungeon. Kids aren't part of this." Doreen ushered Evie into the vehicle, making her climb over the center console to the driver's seat, seemingly oblivious to the guns trained on her back.

"You're the one Viper wants," she said, sliding into the passenger seat beside Evie. "And I'm gonna give you to him all wrapped up with a pretty little bow."

Zane had always wanted to destroy a police car. However, the crunch of glass under his bat, although supremely satisfying, didn't solve the bigger problem. T-Rex wasn't free.

"What. The. Fuck?" He slammed the bat on the hood of Benson's vehicle over and over again until Jagger pulled him away and walked him a few feet down the dirt road near the Black Jack clubhouse.

He was losing it. Big time. But a week of seeing Evie and not being able to touch her, brief conversations about Ty and nothing else, and the possibility of a future limited by the damn warrant over his head, which meant a civilian life with her wasn't an option, had finally taken their toll. Deputy Benson was damn lucky it was only the car bearing the brunt of Zane's frustration. After all, he'd just screwed up big-time.

"I told you where the dungeon was." Zane hefted the bat, and scowled at Benson. "You were supposed to tip off the ATF then go in with our ATF mole."

Benson had the good grace to look uncomfortable. "I was there. And I still can't believe Jagger pulled in that favor. Having someone in the ATF in your pocket could have saved you from some real deep shit more than once."

Wrenching himself out of Jagger's grasp, Zane stalked across the road where he and a handful of brothers had been hiding, expecting Benson to return with T-Rex. He grabbed Benson by the collar. "You saying T-Rex isn't worth a favor?"

"Of course not." Benson struggled to free himself from Zane's grip. "But it was a waste of a favor because Viper was ready for them. Someone must have tipped him off. The place was virtually empty. There were only a handful of bikes in the parking lot, and I'm pretty sure if the Black Jacks' attorney hadn't made mincemeat out of the warrant, they wouldn't have found any guns or drugs."

"They woulda found fucking T-Rex," Zane spat out. "You should have done something. Fucking waste of a mark."

"Easy, brother." Jagger loosened Zane's grip on Benson's neck. "We'll find another way."

Zane flung the bat across the grass bordering the road. "I should've just gone on my own. Snuck in while everyone was distracted. I coulda been in and outta there with T-Rex by now."

"Not a chance." Benson loosened the collar of his blue police shirt. "Even though it's pretty much deserted, that place is like a fortress, and they've left all their guards. We passed through an electric fence, dogs, a metal detector, and a slab of muscle at the door just to get into the clubhouse. They have cameras everywhere."

"I don't need to get *into* the clubhouse." Zane wiped the sweat from his temple. "The door is on the outside."

"We can try another day," Benson said.

Jagger and Zane shared a glance and Zane's tension eased. They were on the same page. They'd waited too long already. Today was the day and if Plan A didn't work, then they would move to Plan B.

"I think we need to take advantage of the opportunity we bought ourselves." Jagger mused, rubbing his brow. "The club is running on a skeleton staff and they'll have moved their weapons. We need a distraction. Something to keep them busy while we cut the fence and go inside. I was thinking—"

"Runaway truck filled with explosives?" Cade joined them beside the wrecked police car.

"That's getting old." Jagger chuckled. "I was thinking of a full-on assault."

Cade raised his brows. "Suicide."

"Not if we're in the hills with sniper rifles." Zane took the plan, rolled with it. "We can set up a roadblock by the bridge. Sparky's still got a truck in his shop from the last transport job. We'll park it sideways and toss the keys."

"What about the electric fence?" Cade had offered to be Zane's second when they'd first talked about breaching the perimeter. "It's twenty-five feet high and has 10,000 volts running through it. They're not gonna turn it off once we start shooting. Only way it goes off is if the gate is open."

"Ram the gate," Benson said. "That can be part of the distraction. Get me a truck and I'll do it. I'm a dead man anyway once the sheriff or the ATF figure out the tip came from me. They're already suspicious because of some of the work I've been doing for you. T-Rex is a good kid, and if this helps end the war between the clubs and saves lives, it's worth the risk." He held up a hand when Zane opened his mouth. "And before you try to talk me out of it, I'm not going in there actually thinking I'm gonna die. I'll go in armed and in a vest, and I'll bail at the earliest opportunity. But, yeah, there's a risk, and if I come out of it alive, I want something from you."

Jagger lifted an eyebrow in silent query.

"I wanna join your MC."

"It's not an open door policy," Zane said, no small bit impressed by the cop's audacity. "Everyone goes through the process."

"We'll need a new prospect after Shooter's patched in."

Jagger's lips twitched at the corners. "You know how to polish a bike, Benson?"

"Until it shines."

Jagger's phone vibrated in his hand and he checked the screen. "Got a message from Shooter. I'll text him, and tell him to get the brothers together and bring out the trucks. Then we'll go get T-Rex."

Zane shook Benson's hand. "Welcome to the club."

Not happening. Not happening. Not happening.

Evie turned onto the highway heading south out of Conundrum. They'd stopped at four traffic lights and two stop signs and so far she hadn't managed to draw anyone's attention to the woman holding her at gunpoint in the vehicle. Where were the police who always seemed to catch her when she drove a measly five miles per hour over the speed limit? They hadn't passed one single cruiser during their ride through the town.

The Sinners would be behind them. Somewhere. She had no doubt about that. But what were they going to do if she was in the Black Jack clubhouse? From what she'd heard around the club, the Jacks lacked even the semblance of humanity she'd been surprised to see in Zane's biker brothers.

"I'm not with them," she said as they passed the last of the residential areas.

"Yeah. I got that when I saw you standing there all innocent and pretty." Doreen snorted her derision. "You gotta be hard to be a one-percenter biker chick, and that goes for lays, sweet butts, house mamas, and old ladies."

"So let me go." Evie clutched the steering wheel so tight her knuckles turned white. She'd briefly considered crashing the car, but she didn't have the courage to do it. What if she died in the crash, or was so badly injured she couldn't care for Ty? Alive she could maybe talk her way out, or find a way to escape. Doreen's decision to kidnap her had to be opportunistic at best. Maybe Viper wouldn't be interested now that he knew she was with Zane.

"This world is about survival." Doreen lowered the gun when a minivan overtook them. "And if there's one thing I know how to do it's survive. Being Viper's old lady has got its perks but Viper is one sadistic bastard and I need a fucking break. You're no threat to me and you'll keep him busy so I don't gotta be bustin' my voice box screaming every night so he can get off. Viper will let me take a little vaycay 'cause I brought him a present, and I can go to Ennis to see my boy, JC. Turn here."

Evie drove down a narrow road that led into the foothills. Dry grass and scrub brush gave the area a desolate feel. "You don't care if he sleeps with other women?"

"It's gonna happen so why kick up a fuss? It's worth it for the old lady status and it means I don't gotta share the love with anyone else, if you know what I mean. Viper might fuck other women, but he's crazy possessive about the ones that belong to him. He killed his first old lady when he thought she was having an affair."

Evie felt a flicker of anger at the thought of Zane sleeping with other women while she wore his cut. No way would she allow it. And she was damn sure Arianne wouldn't allow it with Jagger either. Arianne was one of the strongest women she had ever met. She was pretty sure Arianne wouldn't have allowed anyone to kidnap her at gunpoint. And she'd bet anything Arianne would have crashed the car rather than drive like a good little girl to the big bad wolf's lair.

So what was she doing? She might not be good with a gun, but Zane thought she was strong and brave. Was she really any less of a woman than Arianne? She just needed time and more information to come up with a plan.

"Arianne said you were lying about having a son."

"I lied about pretty much everything else, but not that, and not Axle." Doreen raised the gun again. "Needed something to tug on the heartstrings that had a ring of truth to it. Except JC isn't really Axle's son." Her voice tightened. "I'm telling you this 'cause I feel sorry for you since you won't be leaving that clubhouse until you're too broken to talk. Axle and I were together before he joined the Jacks. Not the best of guys, but not the worst 'cause he had ambition. He wanted to lead his own club. And since it couldn't be the Sinners, he set his sights on the Jacks. He kissed up to them something fierce until finally Viper agreed to patch him in."

"He wanted to take over from Viper?" Evie's gaze flicked to Doreen. "Was he crazy?"

"Go big or go home, that was Axle's motto." Doreen sighed. "First night Axle brought me to a Black Jack party, Viper called me to his room. He told Axle women in the club were shared and if he had a problem with that he'd take back the patch. I did what old ladies do, which is what their old men tell them to do. Not that I was complaining. Everyone wants Viper's attention. If you're wearing his cut, you get a shitload of respect. So I went with Viper. He wouldn't join the "no glove no love" party, so nine months later . . ."

"Viper's son?"

"I told Axle the boy was his and I put Axle's name on the birth certificate. I fucked up my life but I didn't want to fuck up his. Viper wouldn't have given a damn about his son, but Axle did. He wanted kids. He was good with JC. He would have been a good dad. But the minute I found out Axle was dead, I took JC to my mom's place, and I did what I had to do."

"You became Viper's old lady."

Doreen didn't miss a beat. "You gotta look out for yourself in this life. You gotta be strong. You get caught, you figure your own way out. That's the biker way. It's all about self-reliance. It's all about doing what it takes to survive. It's a fucking rush, I gotta tell you. Now I got power, respect, and soon I'll have enough money to get him away from my mom and give him a good life."

Evie studied the road ahead. All signs of civilization slowly disappeared until they were deep into the low rolling foothills of the Bridger Mountains. She had no doubt if she drove into the Black Jack clubhouse she wouldn't survive—at least, not emotionally. So why was she looking in her rearview mirror every five minutes hoping to see the Sinners? Why couldn't she handle this on her own? Was she that afraid to take a risk?

She caught a glint of metal on the road ahead, and slowed the vehicle. Doreen stabbed her in the side with the gun. "Keep driving. Whatever it is, go right through it."

"Get that thing out of my side." She'd had enough of Doreen and her rough voice and her harsh words. She'd had enough of driving and worrying about what would happen to Ty. She'd had enough of wondering if she had what it took to cut it in this world. Because dammit, despite her best efforts, she was in this world. She would do what it took to survive, and that meant there was no fucking way she was going to let Doreen take her to Viper.

Closer now, she could see motorcycles parked across the road, blocking the way. But she didn't give a damn who they were. All she knew was that she was finished with this bullshit. Doreen might think she was a kitten, but she had claws.

Evie pulled the vehicle over to the side of the road, and turned off the ignition.

"What the fuck?" Doreen poked her again. "Start that vehicle up and get going."

Evie's heart pounded in her chest and she dropped her left hand to the driving console and felt for the window button. "Shoot me."

Damn, it felt good to take a risk, just like she'd done when she was young. Except Zane had always been there to catch her if she fell.

"Stop playing games," Doreen snarled.

Evie pressed the button and the window rolled down.

She reached for the key. "Okay. Okay. I'll get going. The heat is getting to me. I needed some air."

"Now."

Swallowing hard, Evie yanked out the key and threw it into the bush. "You aren't going to shoot me because Viper wants me, and I'll bet he won't be happy if you bring me back dead."

"You fucking bitch." Doreen slammed the butt of the gun into Evie's head. "Yeah, he wants you, all soft and pretty. But you pull this kinda shit and he won't want you anymore I promise you won't be wanting what he dishes out to women at the club who he doesn't want to pet."

Dazed, her head throbbing, Evie gripped the steering wheel and tried to regain her focus, but Doreen was already pushing open the door.

"Climb over the console toward me. Nice and slow. We're gonna go get that key." She stepped out of the vehicle and gestured Evie toward her.

Still stunned from the blow to her head, Evie climbed over the console toward Doreen. In the distance she heard the rumble of an engine, the thud of feet, and then . . .

"Evie."

She knew that voice. She had heard it in her dreams since she was eight years old.

Taking advantage of the distraction, she brought up her knees and slammed Doreen in the chest, knocking her to the ground. Doreen stumbled back, falling to the ground. Evie dove after her and grabbed the gun. She pointed it at Doreen, lying sprawled in the dirt and smiled at Zane and Jagger as they jogged to a stop.

"I want to deliver her to Viper. All wrapped up in a pretty bow."

"No."

Zane hugged Evie to him and glared at Doreen, now securely trussed in the back of the 300C and out of earshot.

After what Doreen had pulled, he could think of a dozen other things to do with her rather than drive her back to the Black Jack clubhouse, and none of them involved leaving her unharmed.

He tightened his arms, pulling Evie into his chest. He couldn't think about what would have happened if they hadn't been on the road, planning the raid on the Black Jacks clubhouse. Of course if they hadn't been on the road, they would have been at the clubhouse, and Doreen wouldn't have had the opportunity to take his Evie captive.

"It's our best chance." Evie looked up at him from the circle of his arms. Zane hadn't let her go since he'd rescued her from Doreen. Okay. Maybe not rescued. Evie had been doing fine on her own. More than fine. In fact, she'd reminded him of Arianne when she delivered a couple of kicks to Doreen's stomach, stomped on her hand and threatened to blow off her head before Jagger had taken away her gun. Maybe she'd been hanging around the club too much.

But at least she was talking to him now, holding him, letting him hold her . . . He startled when he caught the tail end of Evie's sentence and realized she'd been laying out a plan.

"I'll put on your bandanna and sunglasses and drive up to the gate with Doreen," she continued. "They aren't going to feel threatened by a woman. They'll have to open the gates to let her in, which means the electric current will go off. I'll stall them as long as I can. You can cut through the wires at the back and go with Cade to get T-Rex, since you know the layout best. No need for sniper guns or people getting hurt."

"I like it," said Jagger, leaning against the vehicle beside them. "Except for the part about not getting to shoot any Jacks."

Betrayer. Zane weighed the likelihood of another disciplinary session against the pleasure he would get from punching Jagger in the face to stop him from moving forward with Evie's ridiculous plan.

"I don't like it," Zane said. "So it's not happening."

"Baby, relax." Evie nuzzled his neck. "I'm okay. Better than okay. I nailed that bitch and it felt so damn good. I want to do this."

He growled low in his throat, feathered kisses along her jaw. "Wouldn't have happened if I was there. Won't happen again."

"But if it does, I can take care of myself." She leaned up and nipped his earlobe. "And you know what?" She dropped her voice to a whisper. "It makes me hot."

"How hot?"

Evie pressed her lips to his ear and murmured. "So hot I want you to strip off my clothes, spread me out on the hood of the 300C, and then lick me until I scream. Then I want you to flip me over and fuck me hard, one hand in my hair pulling me back, one hand on my hip, holding me tight, as my nails scratch the paint and my hips smack against the grill, and the whole car shakes from the force of your thrusts as you hammer in to me with all the brothers watching." Then she ground her hips against his hardened length. "That hot."

He slid his hands down her back, cupped her ass and lifted her against him. "You talk dirty like that to me, sweetheart, prepare to have your wish come true." He carried her away from the brothers to the front of the vehicle and settled her on the hood. Then he eased himself between her parted legs, held her face between his hands and kissed her hard. "You're on the vehicle. What comes next?"

Evie's eyes sparkled with the challenge, and she licked her lips. "You strip me."

He slid his hands under her shirt. Although he had no intention of letting his brothers see what was for his eyes alone, he wanted to know just how far she would take this. Pretty far, he guessed, because in this moment she reminded him of the Evie he had left behind—the risk taker—confident, wild, fun and free.

"I do this, that mean we're good again?" He smoothed his hands over her warm skin. "Can you deal with Jagger occasionally taking out his frustrations on me when I bend the rules?"

Evie mocked a frown. "If you put yourself in that position again, you'll get no loving for all the nights you're hurting. So before you make any stupid decisions, like putting your life at risk, just think about that." She covered his hands with hers and pushed her shirt up to the bottom of her bra, baring her midriff.

A dark possessive growl left his lips and he tugged her shirt down. "Not here. Otherwise, I'll have to kill all the brothers for looking at you and then we'll never save T-Rex."

"Too bad." She slid closer until the curve of her sex pressed up against his cock, now straining beneath his fly. "I always wanted to be fucked on a car."

"Behave." He gave her a mock slap on the ass. Her eyes widened and her lips parted forming a silent *oh*. Zane filed that reaction away for later.

Jagger rounded the vehicle and cleared his throat, intruding on their moment. "All ready to drop off the parcel? Hacker and Tank will be here soon with the trucks."

"Actually, I'd rather wrap her around a street light," Evie said. "Just like Viper did to my car."

Jagger handed her Sparky's red bandanna. "You'll have to settle for this. It's as close as we'll get to a bow."

Evie laughed and twisted it between her hands. She seemed to have forgiven Jagger, which was a relief since Zane harbored no ill will toward him. He'd put Jagger in that position knowing the consequences, and in the end the sacrifice was worth it for the knowledge they'd gained about the Black Jack compound.

Sweat trickled down Zane's back and it wasn't just from

the heat. How could he stop this? He'd almost lost Evie again. His heart couldn't handle anymore.

"It'll be fine." Evie gave Zane's arm a squeeze. "I know that look on your face and I know what you're thinking. But I'm not going into the clubhouse. I'll drop Doreen off and once they open the gate I'll drive away."

"We'll be covering her from the hill," Jagger said. "Even if Doreen tells them who she is, they won't be able to catch her, and you and Cade should have just enough time to get through the fence."

Why did Jagger keep pretending he was on board with this plan? No way would he have agreed to allow Arianne to drive a vehicle right up to Viper's door. Not that he could have stopped her . . . just as it seemed he wouldn't be able to stop Evie unless he wanted to throw her over his shoulder, caveman style. The thought held some appeal.

He heard the rumble of trucks in the distance. Jagger looked up and smiled. "Trucks are here. Let's roll."

Let's roll? Zane released Evie and cut Jagger off from his bike, making one last effort to head off imminent disaster. "When did we start involving women and kids in club business?"

"Evie wants to do this, brother." Jagger put a sympathetic hand on his shoulder. "And since she's not your old lady, I gotta respect her wishes."

Evie's eyes sparkled and she flashed Zane a grin. "I know you'll be there to catch me. You always are."

Christ. How could he refuse her when she looked at him like that? The answer came in a heartbeat: he never could.

★ TWENTY-TWO ★

Sometimes, no matter what you do, no matter how hard you try, things just won't go according to plan.
—SINNER'S TRIBE MOTORCYCLE REPAIR MANUAL

"I got a text from Hacker. The electric current is off." Zane grabbed a pair of wire cutters and joined Cade at the fence.

"How long you figure we got?" Cade worked efficiently cutting from the bottom, while Zane worked from the top.

"Depends how long Evie can keep them talking."

Cade stopped to wipe his brow. "She's one hell of a woman. I can see why you couldn't forget her all those years. She's got the kind of inner strength that makes for a good old lady."

"Yeah." But did he want her as an old lady if it meant she was at risk of being kidnapped, hurt or even killed? She had a nice normal civilian life in her little white house with the white picket fence on the shady street with kids playing outside, people walking their dogs . . .

Something niggled at the back of Zane's mind. "Where are the dogs? They've got four dogs. Big ones. They were here every time I came to do surveillance."

"Maybe they took them when they got the tip about the ATF."

Zane stood and scanned the clubhouse grounds. "And

the guards? Usually they had at least five guards patrolling the fence. Benson said they'd left the guards behind." The skin on the back of his neck prickled and he looked over at the shed where he'd seen the Jacks' heavy artillery. "Gimme your binoculars."

"We're running out of time." Cade pushed back the wire. "If we're gonna save T-Rex, we have to go. We still have to get through the door."

Zane ran his hand through his hair. "Something's wrong. It's all too convenient. The Jacks disappearing, the botched ATF raid . . . Do you think they know we've got someone inside the sheriff's office? Are they playing us?"

Cade stepped through the fence. "Zane. C'mon man. We got one chance to get . . ."

Cade's voice trailed off when a whistling sound filled the air. And then the world exploded in front of them, grass and dirt flying up on the other side of the fence.

Ambush. Where the fuck were the scouts?

Zane flew back, landing hard. He scrambled to his feet and spotted Cade, semiconscious, on the other side of the fence. In the distance, he heard the sound of gunfire.

Evie! He was supposed to be there to keep her safe. Catch her if she fell.

But he couldn't leave Cade.

Small explosions peppered the ground around the club-house. Sons of bitches knew what they were after, and Cade was exposed. Zane pushed himself up and stepped through the fence, then squatted beside Cade.

"Can you walk, brother?"

"Must have hit my head." Cade staggered to his feet. "Everything's kinda blurry."

"We need to get you out of here." He angled up under Cade's shoulder and helped him through the fence, then half-walked, half-dragged him away from the range of fire and into a small copse of trees. He settled Cade against a rock and called the clubhouse. After explaining the situation to Shaggy, he gave their location and arranged a pickup for Cade, as well as reinforcements and vans to retrieve damaged bikes.

Gunshots rang through the forest and adrenaline coursed through his body. "We gotta get moving. You okay?"

"Just stunned." Cade put his hand to his head and it came away covered in blood. "Maybe a scrape or two." He dug his phone from his pocket. "Call Dawn."

"Don't need to call her." He brushed Cade's hand away. "We'll get you to the road for a pickup. You can call her then."

"Zane . . ." Cade's voice tightened and he keened to the side. "Call her."

Zane gritted his teeth and fought back a wave of panic. Cade needed him to be strong, just as he'd been strong for Jagger, and for Evie every time she took a risk. "I don't have time to be calling old ladies. I gotta get you to the road and go back for . . ."

"Evie." Cade waved him away. "I know it's killing you to be here. You go. Leave me."

"Christ. Get the fuck up. We're less than a quarter mile from the road. We can make it. If I left you behind, Jagger would make that beating I took the other day feel like a hug after he got through with me." Fear and anger gave him the strength to take Cade's weight as they made the slow, agonizing walk through the bush to the road.

"She'll be alright," Cade said. "She was in the vehicle, and she stays cool under pressure. The first shot and she would have been out of there."

Zane grunted his response. He couldn't talk. Couldn't think. His body was wired, primed to find Evie as soon as Cade was safe.

He could only hope someone had been there to catch her.

* * *

Evie startled awake, blinking to clear her vision. She jerked but couldn't move with the seat belt tight around her. What had happened? One minute she was driving away from the gate after dropping off Doreen, then she heard gunfire, lost control of her vehicle, spun around, and then . . .

Ah. The air bag had deployed. No wonder she felt like someone had just punched her in the face.

Hands shaking, she unclipped the seatbelt and pushed open the door. Her vehicle rested sideways on the road, the passenger door up against a tree. She slid past the air bag and stepped out to check the damage. With the front tire was in pieces—shot out, she guessed—it was no wonder she'd lost control.

Smoke billowed around her, giving the scene an almost dreamlike quality. She felt light, almost weightless as she wandered down the road, not sure where she should go. Ahead, the club house burned bright, a white truck embedded in one wall, engulfed in flames. The thick, acrid smoke burned her lungs and she coughed, tried to breathe into her sleeve.

Where was everyone? Her foot hit something and she stumbled, fell. She bent down, recognized the long blond hair.

"Doreen?" She shook Doreen gently, felt for a pulse. But when she patted her down, blood seeped through Doreen's clothes.

She fell back with a gasp.

"Evie!" Zane's voice rang out in the stillness.

"Zane. Over here. I need help."

Zane emerged from the smoke, ran towards her. Then he froze, his face contorting in horror.

"Help me. She's not breathing."

Still, he didn't move.

"What?" She looked back over her shoulder, pushed herself to her feet. "What's wrong? Is someone behind me?"

"You."

Evie put her hand to her face. It came away sticky and red. She touched her nose, winced in pain.

"The air bag went off." Her vision blurred and a wave of nausea gripped her stomach. "I must have a nosebleed."

Zane frowned, shook his head. His mouth opened but she couldn't make out his words. Evie took a step forward, and then she lost her footing and fell into the smoke.

"She gonna be okay?"

Zane nodded from the chair beside his bed as Jagger closed the door behind him. Evie had been asleep most of the day, and save for checking in on Ty and putting him to bed in a spare room in the clubhouse, Zane hadn't left her side.

"Yeah. She's bruised up from the air bag hitting her face, and she had a nosebleed and a minor concussion. Took her to the hospital and they said she'd be okay. Doc suggested we stay at the clubhouse since he'll be here all night fixing up the brothers and he could check in on her. How's everyone doing?"

Jagger settled on the edge of dresser. His face was lined and worn, and he still hadn't changed out of his blood-soaked clothes after helping treat all the brothers who had been injured in the raid. "Lots of casualties, but everyone made it out alive."

"Thank fuck. What happened?"

Jagger scrubbed his hands over his face. "They were hiding out in the hills around the clubhouse. Not sure if they were still hiding from the ATF, or if they knew we were coming, but our scouts missed them. They started shooting just after Evie dropped off Doreen. Looks like they hit her tire and she lost control of her vehicle. Benson thought that was the signal to go so he started the truck, drew their attention. They got him through the window, hit his arm, and he couldn't get it out of gear. The truck crashed through the gate and they kept shooting at it, triggered an explosion. Damaged the building pretty bad. Took out three Jacks. Benson made it out in time. But T-Rex . . ."

"He didn't make it?"

"Sparky and Gunner had gone around to help you with T-Rex. When they didn't see you, they went through the hole you'd cut in the fence while the Jacks were distracted by the truck. Gun broke the lock on the door to the dungeon. They found . . ." Jagger choked on his words. "A body. Not breathing. No pulse. They were pretty sure it was T-Rex although his face was so beaten it was unrecognizable, and it was dark. Same color hair though, same size, and Mario said he was in there. They couldn't find his cut, but they found this." He held up the medallion T-Rex had always worn around his neck—gift from Tank when T-Rex been patched into the club, along with a special blade.

Zane's heart squeezed in his chest. "Fuck."

"They couldn't get him out." Jagger's voice tightened and he looked away. "They tried . . . but we'd spotted more Jacks on the way. I couldn't lose them, too. When they called me, I told them to get out of there. He was dead. There wasn't anything we could do for him."

Zane felt the news like a fist in his gut. T-Rex had died to save his Evie. It was a debt he could never repay.

"I don't want this life for her, Jag." He reached over, threaded his fingers through hers. "I want her to have the kind of life she had before. Safe. Peaceful. I can't give her that when I'm wearing this cut, and I can't give it to her as a civilian with a damn warrant hanging over my head."

"You'd give up the life?" Jagger rubbed his thumb absently over the Sinner's skull ring on his finger—the president's mark.

"I'd give up anything for her."

Jagger let out a long, ragged breath. "She wouldn't want that. I don't want it. Before you do anything drastic, you need to talk to her about it first."

Jagger was right. Evie wouldn't want him to give up his cut. But he was wrong about the talking. Zane had a plan.

He'd already talked to Richard, the club attorney, and worked out the details. If he stayed, Evie might talk him out of it. If he left, it would be done and they could move on.

"I want to give her the option." He scraped a hand through his hair, and it came away black with soot from the fire. "As long as I'm a wanted man, I can't give them a normal life. And I'll always be looking over my shoulder, waiting for the day Viper or someone like him goes to the cops. But it's not just that. I've lived my whole life in hiding. I've lived in the shadows. Evie brought me to the light. I don't want to hide anymore. I want the truth to come out. The truth about what happened the night I left Stanton. The truth about how I feel."

He shrugged off his cut, folded it carefully, and handed it to Jagger. "I talked to Richard. He says if I go up to Stanton and turn myself in they'll process me and stick me in the slammer for a coupla days, maybe a week. He'll be there for the interview and to arrange bail."

"Fuck." Jagger scrubbed his hands over his face. "Don't do this. You know we'll protect you."

"I gotta do it, Jag. It's the only way."

"The club will bail you out then," Jagger said. "Whatever the cost."

Zane nodded his appreciation. "Richard said the bail conditions usually include not associating with known felons or criminal organizations. I'm guessing he means the club. I'll be there for T-Rex's funeral unless something goes wrong, but I'll stay away from the brothers. He says our big chance is the preliminary hearing where we try to show the judge there's not enough evidence to go to trial. Best-case scenario, I walk. Worst-case scenario, I spend the next twenty years in jail for something I didn't do."

"That won't happen. If it gets to that we'll break you out."

Zane laughed. "I thought you were gonna say you'd hire a better lawyer. But, yeah, break me out. I'd go fucking crazy if I had to spend twenty years staring at the same four walls. Grand gestures are only good if there's someone to appreciate them."

"She might not take you back if you leave her again," Jagger warned.

Emotion welled up in Zane's throat. "This time I'm not leaving her alone or unprotected. And this time I'm not running away. I'm trying to come home. Make sure she understands that."

He brushed his lips over Evie's cheek and then he and Jagger clasped shoulders. "Look after her and Ty until I get back."

"Like they were my very own."

Zane stood in the doorway and drank in the sight of Evie, her hair fanned over the pillow, her face restful in sleep.

After all he'd been through, he had come full circle. He loved her. And yet he had to leave her again.

★ TWENTY-THREE ★

*If your repair doesn't work, don't give up, Go back
to the beginning and start again.*
—SINNER'S TRIBE MOTORCYCLE REPAIR MANUAL

Evie squeezed Connie's hand as the biker procession entered the cemetery. Although there was no body to bury, the Sinners had erected a tombstone in their dedicated plot at the Conundrum Cemetery and invited support clubs and local friendlies to honor T-Rex's memory. T-Rex's parents had declined the invitation to attend the ceremony, saying that T-Rex had been dead to them for many years and they had already mourned his passing. Jagger had smashed the phone after that conversation and added T-Rex's family to his blacklist, to be punished at a later date.

Almost two hundred bikers converged on the cemetery, a testament to T-Rex's popularity, not just in the club, but in the biker community. Of course, politics factored into who showed and who didn't, which clubs sent presidents or VPs and which sent junior patch. All duly noted, of course, by Tank who had been assigned secretarial duty for the day and stood with Evie and Connie translating biker funeral customs into civilian terms so they could understand what was going on.

"Support clubs gotta send at least two board members and two junior patch," he said, as he snapped pictures with his phone. "I'll be making a list to give to Jagger and if anyone didn't show, he'll send Gunner out with a team to put them in their place."

"I like that idea." Connie pulled a collapsible umbrella from her purse and shook it out under the tree where they'd been standing for the last ten minutes. They had chosen a position on a small rise near the edge of the cemetery—close enough to hear, but far enough away that their civilian presence would not offend the biker gathering. "If I die, I want you and Evie to go beat up any of my friends who don't show for the funeral. Especially Gene. So he regrets never making a move before he had the chance."

Tank lowered his camera. "Are you fucking kidding me? You're mine. Gene doesn't touch you. And after I had words with Sparky, he won't be touching you either. No one touches you. Except me." He cupped his hand behind her head and pulled her in for a hard, possessive kiss.

"This is why I like bikers," Connie said in a breathy voice after he released her. "The whole possessive caveman thing is very hot. You should see what he does if I show any interest in the guys at the bar."

Evie tried, but failed to smile. T-Rex's funeral had reopened the black hole in her chest that she hadn't managed to heal since he'd sacrificed himself to save her. She felt guilty moving on with her life, guilty for every laugh, because T-Rex would never laugh again. And she had no one to share her grief. She'd awoken the morning after the big raid with a splitting headache, and no Zane.

That had been two weeks ago.

Despite her best efforts and the worst of her threats, she had been unable to convince Jagger to tell her where Zane had gone or how long he would be away. However, he had helped her find a small warehouse south of town big enough for a new shop and garage, and a small rental house only a ten-minute drive from Ty's school. Evie hadn't seen any Jacks lurking around, and she hadn't heard anything from Viper. She figured he had better things to do with his time now that he had a clubhouse to rebuild and, no doubt, revenge to plan.

A biker minister said a few words after the crowd had assembled. Evie wondered how the minister reconciled his duties with the ethos of an outlaw biker gang, or what his superiors thought about him wearing a cut. She didn't recognize his patch, but he was darkly handsome, almost exotic in appearance, with deeply tanned skin and long blond hair, tied back in a ponytail.

Jagger's speech about T-Rex moved her to tears. Powerful, moving, quietly eloquent, he mentioned the little things that had made T-Rex the most well-regarded member of the club: small kindnesses, thoughtfulness, and a selflessness that put them all to shame. And in the end, he had died true to his nature, sacrificing himself to keep another safe.

Gunner followed with a story about T-Rex as a prospect, bursting into a board meeting to tell them Jagger had been kidnapped and then almost falling over when he saw Jagger alive. After Sparky and Dax gave their speeches, and the service had come to a close, Evie stayed behind so she could spend a few minutes alone at the grave.

She had only a few minutes of reflection before she sensed another presence near the grave. Her head jerked up and she saw Zane on the other side of the headstone, thumbs looped in the belt hooks of his worn, black jeans. The dark shadow of a beard covered his jaw and his hair looked like it hadn't been combed in weeks. He had lost weight—his T-shirt hung loose under his cut, and although he still cut an imposing figure he looked . . . diminished, not just physically, but emotionally, too.

Her first instinct was to run, and maybe weeks ago that's what she would have done. But she'd changed since Zane walked back into her life, and in the last few weeks she'd moved on. She had always known he would leave her again. This time she wasn't prepared to take him back.

"You missed it," she said.

Pain flickered across Zane's face as stared at the tombstone. "I watched from the rise," he pointed to a hill behind him. "I have to keep a low profile. The brothers knew I was there."

Evie swallowed past the lump in her throat. It was all too much. T-Rex. The funeral. Zane's sudden appearance, and now this. "But not me."

"I can explain it all to you." He took a step toward her. "You want to talk here or at your place?"

"I moved." She lifted her chin, met his gaze. "And I'm not interested in anything you have to say. I knew you'd leave me again. I just didn't expect it to be so soon." Caught in a maelstrom of emotion, Evie turned and walked away.

"Evie."

She heard his voice and kept walking, past small benches and tombstones, neatly clipped bushes and vases of flowers. Only when she reached her vehicle did she let go.

With a growl of frustration, she kicked the tire over and over until her foot went numb. When she raised her fist to pound on the hood, Zane grabbed her from behind, pinning her arms by her sides.

"Stop."

"Let me go." She twisted and struggled in his grasp as all her pain came out in a rush. "You left me again. No note. No call. Not even a goodbye. T-Rex is dead because of me. And Bill . . . I couldn't save him either."

Zane tightened his grip and pressed his mouth to her ear. "I've got you. Use me. Take it out on me."

I've got you. Those three words tipped her over the edge. He'd had her since she was eight years old. He had her when no one else cared. He had her and he left her. Again and again.

She turned in his arms and pounded on his chest, huge guttural sobs ripping from her throat as she let out her sorrow for T-Rex, for Bill, for the past she and Zane had lost to fear, for the future they might never have. Zane didn't move, didn't blink; he simply absorbed her blows as if he wanted her pain.

When she was worn out, he held her in his arms and kissed her, a soft brush of his mouth over hers, lips drinking her tears. "I left for us," he said. "I left so we could have the chance of a future together."

"Where did you go?"

"Stanton. I turned myself in. I'm out on bail until the preliminary hearing."

A groan ripped from her throat. "Oh, God, Zane. Why? Why would you do that?"

"I want to be free," he said simply. "I'm not a good man, Evie. Not in civilian terms. I've broken laws, committed crimes. But I can sleep at night because I've never hurt anyone who didn't deserve it. After I met you again, I realized I've been living my life under the shadow of a lie. I loved you, but I denied it. I pretended those false charges meant nothing to me, but they do because they mean I can't give you and Ty what I want to give—a choice."

She felt a prickle at the back of her neck. "What choice?"

"Whether we live or leave the life is up to you."

Evie fisted his shirt, pulled him close. "And what if it all goes wrong? What if they put you in jail for the next twenty years? What then?"

"I've loved you for almost twenty years, Evie; I'll love you for twenty more. And I would wait a lifetime to hold you again."

His utter and absolute faith, his conviction, his heartfelt words turned the tide and washed away the last of her reservations. "I need you," she whispered. "I want to feel. I want to live so T-Rex didn't die for nothing."

"Over there." He pointed to the caretaker's potting shed just over the rise. They made their way through the soft grass to the door and Zane used his knife to snap the lock.

Rich and fragrant, the mingled scents of flowers and potting soil surrounded them when they stepped inside. Rows of freshly potted flowers lined the wall, and the small table under the sole window in the shed heaved under an array of potting equipment, bags of soil, fertilizer, watering cans and gloves. A large wooden table took up the center space and worn shelves lined the dark, wood walls.

Frantic to touch him, she shoved up his shirt as soon as he turned from bolting the door. She ran her hands over the hard planes of his chest, then she trailed kisses over his newly grown beard. "I'm not sure if I like all these prickles."

Zane grabbed her ass and ground his erection against her belly. "You'll love it when I'm between your thighs, licking your sweet pussy."

"Arrogant."

"You love that, too."

He took control, spinning her around and then pushing her over the workbench in the center of the shed. "It's not the hood of a 300C, but since I haven't been able to get that image out of my mind, this will have to do."

The rich scent of earth rose up from the wooden surface, raw and primal. "It's perfect. Don't make me wait."

Zane leaned over her, pressing her body against the table with his weight, then he clasped her neck and pushed her cheek against the rough, wood surface. "You want it dirty, sweetheart?"

"Yes."

"You want it rough?"

"Yes."

"You want me to fuck you so damn hard you can't think of anything but the orgasm I won't give you till you beg?"

"God, yes. Make me pay for letting T-Rex give his life for me."

"No." He released her, backing away, leaving her bereft.

Evie cried out in frustration. "Please, Zane. Make it all go away."

Zane grabbed her hair and yanked, forcing her back to arch, and her ass to ride high against him. "I'll give you what you want, sweetheart, the way you want it, but you don't pay for T-Rex's sacrifice. He was a Sinner and the debt is a Sinner debt—my debt. The only thing you can do for T-Rex is live and enjoy your life so his sacrifice means something. I want you to feel—pleasure, pain, and desire. I want you to know the love I have for you. I want you to understand that I will always be there for you. You are my life, Evie. You have my heart."

He tugged her up by the hair and unzipped the sleeveless black dress she had worn for the funeral, shoving it down over her hips until it pooled on the floor in a black puddle. Then he unclasped her black bra and tossed it on the tool shelf beneath a small window covered with torn plastic curtains. Although the day was gray and misty, a sliver of light speared the darkness, falling on the workbench on which she lay.

"Another time I might play with these." He traced his finger along the inside edge of her matching black lace thong, then traced the string between her buttocks to her wet center. "But today . . ." He kicked her legs apart. "They need to come off." With a vicious jerk, her tore her panties away and tossed them on the shelf.

"Boots?" She looked back over her shoulder, licked her lips. Her long black leather boots, sleek and supple and crisscrossed with laces, had been an extravagance at a two-for-one sale. She and Connie had split the cost when Connie found a pair of fringed suede boots she just had to have.

"I like this look." Zane slicked his fingers along her wet pussy, holding her tight against his shoulder with his fist in her hair. "Naked in boots. Wet and wanting. Under my control and at my mercy." He cupped her sex, then splayed his fingers, forcing her legs to part. "Open wider for me, sweetheart. Got a lot of playing to do down here and I don't want to bruise those pretty thighs."

Evie eased her legs further apart, leaving her totally open to him, vulnerable and exposed.

"Beautiful." He stroked her ass gently even as he pressed her against the table. Her nipples brushed over the cold, damp, gritty surface. Sinfully erotic.

"Up on your elbows. Hands apart. Hold the corners of the table. If you let go, I'll tie them in place." His low, sensual command turned her blood to molten lava and she spread her arms and gripped the rough, hewn wood. The edge of the table dug into her belly, just above her mound, the painful pressure only inflaming her need as her body stretched to accommodate his demands.

She heard the snap of his cut, the soft rustle of clothing, and the rattle of a chain. But when she tried to look over her shoulder, Zane pressed her head down, cheek to the table.

"This is my show." He leaned over, his bare chest hot against her cool skin, his hard, cock wedged firmly between her open thighs. "And I want to spend some time playing dirty with you."

Before Evie could ask how much dirtier he could get, he pulled her hips back from the table, then crouched in front of her and feathered kisses along the inside of her thigh, his beard an erotic prickle over her skin. "I wanna taste you, Evie. I spent a week in jail in Stanton imagining every sweet inch of your body, trying to remember your honey."

"Yes." Unable to see or touch him, she gripped the edges of the table and focused on the rasp of his breathing as he worked his way toward her center, and the brush of his lips over her heated skin. She wiggled, angled her hips to get him where she wanted him to go. She needed him, craved his touch and the release only he could give her.

"Stay still." His finger slicked through her folds in a slow, gentle caress that made her jerk against him.

"More."

Zane chuckled, a low deep rumble that vibrated in her core. "This?" He slicked his finger through her pussy, spreading her moisture up and around her clit. "Or this?"

He flicked his tongue over the throbbing bundle of nerves, as his bristles scraped over her sensitive skin. Evie shuddered in response.

"Lick me again."

He teased her clit with the tip of his hot, wet tongue, the touch so light she wanted to scream, and then he thrust a finger inside her. Evie groaned at the intimate intrusion. Zane added a second finger, thrusting with firm, relentless pressure as he teased her clit, licking up and around, but never where she wanted him to go. With his expert touch, he held her on the edge, letting her peak and bringing her down before she could sail into oblivion.

"Zane. I can't take anymore. Please."

He thrust again, curling his fingers against her sensitive inner walls, and then his mouth clamped over her clit. Her climax came in a rush of wet heat, flooding her pussy and sending her spiraling in a wave of sensation.

"I'm gonna fuck you, sweetheart. Dirty and rough like you want." He pulled away as she heaved in her breaths, and then he was behind her, one hand in her hair forcing her to arch back against him, her ass in the air, the other hand on her hip, holding her steady as he thrust into her wetness.

"Keep those legs open for me." He tightened his grip on her hair and then he drew out and thrust deep. "Fuck, Evie. I missed you. I couldn't stop thinking about you. I want you so bad."

He slapped her ass, sending heat racing over her skin and straight to her aching pussy. Her desire spiraled again and she tightened her inner muscles against the steel of his shaft as he pounded into her.

"Oh, sweet heart." He groaned. "Just like that."

Her body burned with sensation, from the rich scent of earth mixed with pine from the table, to the musky smell of sex, and the damp fragrant air brushing over her skin. Every nerve ending in her body flared as she jerked against the table, rough wood over tender nipples, sharp edges against her palms and stomach, her pussy wet and throbbing.

"Who can give you what you want?"

Zane grunted and changed his rhythm, his thrusts coming hard and fast, his fingers digging into her hip, holding her steady.

"You."

"Only me." He reached around to flick her oversensitive clit. "Come with me, Evie. Together."

Her muscles tensed and her back arched as the climax ripped through her, her pussy clenching around his hardened length. With a deep, guttural growl, Zane joined her, his cock driving deep and hard, sending her over the edge again.

He collapsed on top of her and for a few moments there was nothing but the combined rasp of their breaths and the warmth of his chest on her sweat-slicked back.

"My Evie." He brushed her hair over her shoulder and pressed a kiss to her neck. "My dirty girl likes it rough."

Finally he pulled away and she shivered as cool air rushed over her skin. When he helped her up, she looked down and grimaced at the sight of her soil-covered breasts.

"When I agreed to dirty sex, I didn't mean it literally."

Zane chuckled and gently brushed her clean with a damp cloth from the sink in the corner. "I like all ways of dirty if they involve you."

"I have a feeling I've just seen the tip of the iceberg." She fastened her bra and then her arms dropped as a wave of sadness crashed over her.

"I didn't know T-Rex that well, but from what I saw, he was a special person."

Zane pulled her into his chest, wrapping his strong arms around her. "I'll miss him," he said softly. "But I'll be grateful to him every day of my life for keeping you safe and giving me another chance. There hasn't been a single day in the last nine years that I haven't regretted leaving you the way I did. Every year, I spent the last week of summer riding in the mountains, thinking about you, and what I could have done differently. After I saw you and Mark together, I just imagined a different life where I made different choices."

"Then you wouldn't be you." She reached up to stroke his bristly chin. You wouldn't have found the Sinners. You wouldn't be a biker. You wouldn't be the man I love. And I have to admit, the whole badass biker thing is kinda hot. Every time I see you in that cut, or on your bike, I just want to jump your bones."

"Anytime. Anywhere. Any way you want."

"I'll wait for you, Zane." She pressed a kiss to his cheek. "As long as it takes. Five years. Ten. Twenty. I'll be here for you. And when you're free, I want to see you in that cut. I can make it work because I know in my heart you're a good person, and I know I have the strength to survive in your world. Arianne showed me there is more than one way to live the life. I can still be me. I can run my shop, be a soccer mom, and give you heck when you put yourself in danger. It will be you and me and Ty and your MC. Together." And then, because she could feel the tears welling in her eyes, she smiled. "Of course it won't be that long. I believed you when you told me the truth about what happened that night. The judge will believe you, too."

"Your faith means everything to me." He rested his forehead against hers, closed his eyes. "Now that I've seen you and put T-Rex to rest, I'm gonna deal with Viper. Then I'm gonna take that faith back with me to Stanton, knowing that if it does go wrong, you'll be safe until I see you again."

Viper.

She had almost forgotten about him. But she was dead certain he hadn't forgotten about her.

★ TWENTY-FOUR ★

Don't get too cocky after your first successful repair.
There are always hidden problems.
—SINNER'S TRIBE MOTORCYCLE REPAIR MANUAL

Evie awoke from a dream of being seduced by a man with dark hair and darker eyes, only to discover it was no dream at all; her seducer had one hand between her legs and the other on her breast.

"What the . . ."

"Shhhh," Zane whispered. "You fell asleep at the party. Had to bring you home in a cage."

Evie grimaced. Ah, yes. The party after the funeral. Part Irish, T-Rex had asked that his brothers throw an Irish wake if he died and the Sinners had gone all out to honor his wishes, renting out Banks Bar, where Arianne and Dawn worked part-time, and inviting as many Sinners as it could hold.

After standing outside for a full five minutes, Zane had decided there weren't any felons in Banks Bar that he personally knew, and the Sinners weren't really a criminal organization; they were just a bunch of guys who liked to ride bikes. Plus, he'd seen someone's hand on Evie's ass, and that was the end of his good behavior.

"Knees up, sweetheart. Curl up and bring them to your chest." Zane's deep voice slid over her like a warm blanket. The morning light was already streaming through the crack in the curtains, filling the master bedroom of her new rental with the soft rays of dawn.

Half asleep, her body languid and relaxed, she complied, curling up in front of him, half wondering what he was up to now.

His hand slid over her ass to cup her sex, now fully exposed to his questing fingers. "You're so wet. That's my fault. I couldn't keep my hands off you all night." He slicked a finger through her folds and brushed her wetness along her inner thigh. "I never saw you drunk before. You were very affectionate. Shooter should be out of the hospital this afternoon. I only hit him a coupla times. And Patches is . . . well, we can go visit him tomorrow."

Evie groaned and turned her face into the pillow. "Don't tell me anything else."

"So you don't want to hear the part where you tried to rip off my clothes?" His hand stroked down her body to caress her breast, then over her curves to touch her intimately once more. Evie gasped as pleasure surged through her. She released her knees, and Zane growled softly.

"Don't move. Back in position."

Evie bit back a smile. She liked this side of him, confident, dominant, unyielding. It was a side she hadn't seen when they were young, but she had always suspected was there.

He kissed her neck, then bit her gently as his finger pressed against her wet entrance. "All ready for me. But then you were ready for me hours ago, weren't you, sweetheart?" He licked the bite, wrapped one arm around her knees, and before she realized what he intended, he drove his cock into her hard and deep.

"Oh, God." No teasing. No more foreplay. But she was more than ready for him.

Her body tensed at the intimate intrusion, but in the tight position she couldn't move to relieve the pressure, or shift to accommodate him in any other way. The world narrowed to the slide of his cock into her pussy, the press of flesh on flesh, and the deep sensations as he pushed inside inch by inch, so slowly she wanted to scream, to rock her hips . . .

Zane ground against her until he was buried to the hilt. "Take me, Evie. Take all of me and let me take care of you."

Her senses heightened: his scent of sex with a hint of cologne; his body warm around her and hard inside her; the taste of his last kiss before she fell asleep; and the sight of him moving gently behind her in the mirror across from the bed. So erotic.

He always wanted to take care of her. And yet, although she loved his protectiveness, she didn't need it. Not anymore. Maybe, for once, she could take care of him in the bedroom; she could drive him crazy, the way he did to her. She could be in control.

Evie twisted away then quickly turned and gently pushed Zane to his back. She straddled him, his shaft nestled between her folds, grinning as his face registered surprise, then curiosity.

"How about I take care of you?" She rocked over him, and Zane's corded throat tightened when he swallowed.

"How about you do that when I'm inside you?"

"Not yet." Evie licked her lips. "I want to play." She leaned up to kiss him, easing herself up until his swollen head brushed her entrance. Zane groaned, clamped his hands on her hips and tried to pull her down.

"If you're naughty, you don't get to be inside me at all." She feathered kisses over the soft bristles on his jaw, down his neck, over his pecs, then licked her way along the ridges of his abdomen. Zane threaded his hands through her hair, his finger gripping her scalp.

"If I'd known you were planning to torture me, I would never have come back."

"It's a good kind of torture," she said as she slid down between his legs. "The kind where you get to beg."

She flicked her tongue over his crown and Zane

growled. "You do that again, and I won't be responsible for my actions."

She licked.

He grabbed her shoulders, hauled her up, and settled her on top of his rock hard shaft. "You got two choices, sweetheart. We do this your way, with you on top, or my way, with you beneath me. But both of them involve me inside you by the time I finish talking."

With a laugh, Evie lifted her hips and took him deep. His cock slid easily into her wet center, and she gasped with pleasure.

"My, what a big cock you have," she teased.

"All the better to fuck you with." He gripped her hips and filled her with slow, easy thrusts.

"Ah. Ah." Evie gritted her teeth, trying to resist the urge to grind against him. "I'm doing the fucking. You're doing the watching." She cupped her breasts, rolled each nipple between her thumb and forefinger, the sensation all the more intense for Zane's rapt attention, his taut muscles, and the jerk of his hips as he tried to entice her to give in to the passion burning between them.

She slid one hand down to her clit, and stroked gently around the sensitive bundle of nerves. Sweat beaded on her forehead and her heart pounded, as everything inside her clenched tight, making her tremble with pent-up desire.

"Evie." Zane groaned. "Sweetheart. You're too fucking sexy. Too hot. Too wet. I can't take any more."

"You want me to take care of you?"

"Fuck, yeah." He shuddered as she rocked over his shaft.

"You want me to take care of you the way you take care of me?"

"Yes. God, Evie. Yes. Please."

Falling forward, hands on his shoulders, she lifted her hips and took him inside as far as he could go. "Okay, baby." She pulled up, slow and easy, then drove down hard and fast, grinding her clit against him in a steady rhythm until soft ragged whimpers escaped his lips, and her muscles ached. Zane cupped her ass and took over, driving her down as he thrust inside her, driving her to the edge, her muscles taut and trembling, her breaths coming in pants. She reached between them, brushed a finger over her clit. Her climax came without warning—a sharp burst of pleasure that ripped the breath from her lungs.

"Christ." He came with a grunt and one last hard thrust, his arms tightening around her, his cock jerking with his release.

Evie collapsed over his chest, buried her face in his neck, felt the steady throb of his pulse against her cheek.

"Fuck, sweetheart," he said. "It just gets better and better."

Evie laughed. "I aim to please."

"Actually, I think you aim to drive me crazy in all senses of the word." He caressed her back, his hand gliding from her nape to her ass and back again. "If it goes wrong in Stanton, Jagger's gonna bust me outta jail. I'll have to go on the run . . ."

"We'll deal with that problem if it comes up," she murmured. "And whatever happens, we'll find a way to be together. I don't want to lose you again. All those years I woke up so lonely it hurt, so empty I didn't think I could get out of bed . . . it was because I missed you. I've been looking for you ever since."

"We'll make it through this." He pressed a kiss to her forehead. "You're all I ever thought about, Evie, from the moment I left until I saw you again. And now I have you and Ty . . ."

She Evie heard footsteps in the hall outside the door and threw herself to the side, yanking the covers over them.

The door creaked open and Evie pushed herself up on one elbow. She could feel Zane tense behind her.

"Fuck. The door. I forgot."

"Mom? How come you're . . ." Ty froze in the doorway, stared at Zane. Then his face tightened.

"How come he's here?"

"Zane brought me home late from the party." Evie pulled the sheet up over her shoulder. "So he decided to sleep over."

"But he's on my side of the bed." Ty's voice wavered. "And he's sleeping on my pillow."

Damn. She fished around on the floor for her nightdress and then remembered Zane had put her to bed. Naked. "It was just for tonight, darling."

"No. That's where I sleep when I'm scared. That's where I cuddle with you in the morning." Tears glistened in Ty's eyes and his shoulders trembled visibly beneath his superhero pajamas.

Evie's stomach tightened. She'd never brought a man home after Mark, keeping her liaisons as discreet as possible. And Ty was already off balance after Zane's recent disappearance. He needed a hug but she had nothing on and her nightdress was in the dresser. "You can climb in with us. Just give me a second to get dressed and I'll find another pillow."

But Ty had never dealt well with change and she hadn't even thought about discussing the possibility about Zane sleeping over.

"That's my place," he shouted, the tears spilling down his cheeks. "And it's Saturday. We're supposed to cuddle and tell stories and then you're supposed to make pancakes. That's what we do. I don't want it to be like how it was when Mark was here. I want it to just be you and me in the house and Zane stays at the clubhouse and we can visit him."

"Hey, bud." Zane pushed himself up. "Nothing's gonna change."

"It's all changed. You changed it. Mom didn't used to go out all the time. She didn't leave me alone. No one slept in my place. We were happy and you ruined it all. You came back and then you went away. I want you to go home."

"Ty." Evie raised her voice. "We don't talk to guests like that."

"I thought he was my dad, not a guest," he said bitterly.

"You're right. And dads sometimes stay over so we can try and be a family."

He hugged his stuffie to his chest, a blue bear her mother had given him when he was born, the only gift she had given him before she died. "No." His little body shook. "I want it to be how it was. I want Zane gone. I don't want a family. You're mine. I don't want to share." He turned and ran from the room, his gut-wrenching sobs tearing through Evie's heart.

"I'll go talk to him." Zane pushed aside the sheet, but Evie stopped him.

"Let me. This is my fault. I didn't prepare him. I've never brought anyone home before, and it was hard with Mark. That's all he knows about my relationships." She slid out of bed and grabbed her jeans and underwear from the dresser.

"You want me to leave till he's feeling better?"

"No." She pulled on her clothes. "If we want to try to be a family, then we need to deal with this as a family."

The front door opened and slammed shut and her pulse kicked up a notch. "I'd better go before he gets out of sight."

Zane's face creased with consternation. "I'll be right behind you. It's still not safe."

Evie finished dressing and raced out the door. Ty was nowhere in sight, and the street was empty save for a white panel van just turning the corner toward the main road. Evie raced in the direction of the van. Ty had a new friend at the end of the block. He must have gone that way.

She made it half a block, before she saw the bear.

* * *

Zane heard her scream as he reached for the front door. And then he ran like he'd never run before, flying down the steps and along the sidewalk, his feet barely hitting the pavement until she slammed into him, Ty's toy bear clutched in her hand.

"They have him. I found his bear. I saw the van." She gasped for breath. "I have to call the police."

Zane's blood chilled and he scanned the street. "Are you sure he didn't go to a friend's house? Maybe he dropped the bear because he was upset? Did you check with the neighbors? How about out back? Did you look for him there?"

"I know him." Her voice rose as she struggled in his grasp. "He would NEVER leave the bear behind, no matter how angry or upset he was. NEVER."

"Has he been this upset before?"

"Zane!" She shrieked and pushed him away. "Viper has him. I KNOW it."

"The police won't be able to help you." He grabbed her shoulders to hold her still. "Viper pays them off to look the other way, and the ones who aren't on the take are too afraid to get involved. If he has Ty, then the Sinners will get him back. But Viper's been quiet for weeks so I'm not sure if that's what has happened. We need to make sure he's not in the area before we set something in motion that could escalate the war. Does he have any friends on the street?"

"The blue house at the end of the road."

"You check with them and I'll ride around the area, and check the backyards, the park and the school. If we don't find him in ten minutes, I'll call the MC. I had Hacker put a GPS tracker in Ty's watch the last time he was at the clubhouse."

"You what?"

He cupped her face between his hands. "We'll find him, Evie. I promise."

Returning to Evie's house ten minutes later, with still

no sight of Ty, he began to suspect that Evie was right. And if Viper was prepared to victimize children to win the war, the MC would have some difficult decisions to make.

He called Jagger first. Then he called Benson and told him to get his damn deputy ass out to Evie's house and issue a police alert, although it would do no good. Hacker claimed to be out of town, but said could be at the clubhouse in an hour. He gave Zane detailed instructions about how to work the computer and the tracking system. Zane asked what language he was speaking. He suggested if Hacker wasn't at the clubhouse in twenty minutes, he could say good-bye to his face.

Unable to sit still, Zane went outside to meet Benson and the brothers who were coming to help with the search. Had the Jacks found Evie's new house? Had they seen his bike parked outside? Was this about Viper's obsession with Evie or was it directed at the MC? Not wanting to leave Evie alone, he headed back inside, and then he froze.

"What the hell?" He knew exactly what she was planning to do the moment he saw her dressed in that slinky black dress, her breasts barely covered by the plunging neckline, all legs in her black stilettoes. Her hair was loose and spread across her bare shoulders, and her face was barely recognizable beneath the thick layer of makeup.

"I'm going to see Viper. He had one of his minions call me on my landline. Stupid of me not to change the number when we moved. I'm supposed to go to a certain location, and after they make sure I'm alone, they'll text me the address." She pulled the contents from her bag and dropped the items one by one into a shiny black purse.

"No. Absolutely not." Zane folded his arms and stood in front of the door, all his past fears coming to a head in an instant. She was distraught and emotionally unstable if she thought for a moment he would let her go to meet Viper.

"You can't stop me. I'm not your wife, or your girl-friend, or your old lady. Not that it would make any difference." She snapped her purse closed and he had to admit she appeared calm and rational despite the crazy words coming out of her mouth.

"I won't let you go," Zane said. "I won't let you do this. You're mine, Evie."

"Yes. I am yours," she whispered. "No matter what happens, in my heart I will always be yours. But this isn't about you and me. It's about Ty. And I will do anything to get him back."

"Then wait. Trust me. The Sinners will handle this."

"Trust *me*, Zane. Believe in me this time and how I feel about you. I love you. Nothing will ever change that. Even if I don't see you again, I will never stop loving you."

Even if I don't see you again. Did she really think it would go that far?

He had no hesitation about what he had to do. Evie was his to love, his to protect, and he would keep her and Ty safe until he drew his last breath. "If that's what you want."

"That's what I want." Her eyes glistened, her emotions belying her words, and it was that, more than anything, that gave him the strength to act.

"Gimme one minute before you leave." He didn't wait for an answer, but jogged down the street until he found Benson coming up the sidewalk toward him.

"Need your cuffs."

Benson handed them over without question. "I probably won't need them again. This is my last week on the job. I gave in my notice after escaping the fire."

"You did a good job with that truck."

"Yeah about that," Benson said. "Maybe next time you want to blow up a building with a truck you should drive."

Zane made his way back to the house where Evie was waiting and shrugged at her questioning glance. "Had to talk to Benson before he started his search." He stepped to the side, giving her a clear path to the door, but as she reached for the handle, he yanked the cuffs from his pocket and snapped one around her wrist.

"What the . . . ?" She stared at him aghast. Before she could react, he dragged her over to the radiator and snapped the second cuff to the metal frame. Thank fuck for old houses and old-fashioned heating systems.

"No!" She yanked against the radiator and her face contorted in fury. "You can't do this. Let me go."

Nausea roiled in his belly and he took a step back. "I can't let you sacrifice yourself for Ty. I can't let you give yourself to Viper. He will never let you go, Evie. You must know that."

"It's my choice," she shouted. "You can't take that from me."

"I can. And I will." He reached for the door. "I made a mistake, Evie. We don't choose the biker life. It chooses us. I thought I could give it up, but it won't let me go. This is my world, and I need to deal with it my way. It's the only way to keep you and Ty safe. I'll bring him back to you. I swear."

"You bastard." She yanked on the cuffs so hard blood welled up on her skin. "Take these off."

Zane pulled open the door and looked back over his shoulder. "I lost you once. It won't happen again. I love you, Evie, and I will never let you go."

★ TWENTY-FIVE ★

*Repair and repair again. That's the nature
of the beast. So learn your skills well.*

—SINNER'S TRIBE MOTORCYCLE REPAIR MANUAL

She was going to kill him. No doubt about it. The second
she got these damn cuffs off she would hunt him down and
then . . .

No. Death would be too good for him. She would make
him suffer instead. Then she would kill him. Metaphor-
ically speaking, of course.

But first, she needed to get to Ty.

A wave of nausea crashed over Evie at the thought of
Ty running down the street, so distressed he'd left in his
pajamas, only to be grabbed by strangers. He would have
been so frightened and he didn't even have his bear.
Despair gripped her throat and she forced herself to
take a breath. And then another. She couldn't help Ty if
she broke down now.

The handcuffs rattled as she pulled against the chain.
Damn radiator refused to move and her wrist was raw and
bleeding from trying to work her hand free; it looked so
easy in the movies.

"Help!" She kneeled beside the window and shouted
through the glass. But, of course, so early on a Saturday
morning, no one was around.

She slumped against the wall and cursed Zane under

her breath using every single bad word she'd ever learned. Damn him. Damn him for being protective and loving, and then railroading over her wishes when it mattered the most.

Her phone buzzed in her purse and Evie groaned. She'd already tried to reach her bag, but it was near the door and there was nothing close she could use to pull it toward her. But what about a push?

Her gaze fell on the toy box she'd emptied in her first attempt to reach her purse. Lego bricks, superhero figures, trucks and spaceships, and a remote-control car Zane had bought for Ty yesterday after the funeral. Evie picked up the remote and turned the car on. Ty had been impressed with her ability to maneuver the car around the furniture, but was it strong enough to push her purse? She cleared a path around her and steered it toward the door, the tiny tail-lights flashing as she drove it under the coffee table and into the tiled entrance way. So far so good. She turned it the vehicle around and aimed it at her purse. Go, car, go.

At first, the car drove over her purse sailing over the edge like a dune buggy in the desert. She reduced the speed and the back wheels whined as they spun against the carpet. Evie backed the car up and tried again, this time hitting the purse at just the right angle, and with enough speed to make it move. Sweat trickled between her breasts as the purse inched closer and closer until, finally, it was close enough to touch.

Score! Ty would have been proud. All those years hanging around with Zane and Jagger had come in useful, and not just for video game skills.

She called Connie first, telling her to come with something strong enough to break handcuffs. Although Deputy Benson was outside, she suspected he wouldn't give her the key for fear of what Zane might do to him if he found out Benson let her go.

Connie arrived twenty minutes later with a pair of bolt cutters, borrowed from a neighbor, and twenty dollars for the swear jar so she could fully express her disdain for

Zane without restraint or inhibition. The moment the cuffs slipped off her wrist, Evie raced to the bathroom, a minor detail Zane seemed to have forgotten in his haste to keep her away from Viper.

"Glad you were able to hold it," Connie shouted through the bathroom door. "I wouldn't have come over here as fast if I thought you'd pissed yourself, too."

"Nice. Very nice." Evie glared as she walked out of the bathroom a few minutes later. "I'm glad to know the limits of our friendship."

"Piss is definitely one of them." Connie looked Evie up and down and her smile faded. "So you're still going through with it? You're gonna go see Viper?"

"I don't have a choice. The police aren't going to be able to get to Ty, and I'm not leaving his life in the hands of a gang of outlaw bikers who live by a code that puts their club first, or a man who asked me to trust him, then showed his love by handcuffing me to the radiator. Ty needs someone who is there for him and only him, and the only person who can do that is me."

"You can't go in alone." Connie reached into her purse and pulled out a .22. "I'll go with you. I've even got a gun. Tank made me buy it. He said if I was hanging out with bikers, then I needed to be armed. He even taught me a few things about shooting."

And get herself shot in the meantime. Evie placed a gentle hand on Connie's arm. "I can't let you come with me. Viper took Ty to get to me and not, as Zane seems to think, to get back at the club. I have to deal with him on my own."

"Babe, you gotta have backup. We've watched enough movies together so you know what happens when someone decides to face the bad guy alone." Connie shook Evie gently by the shoulders. "They never come out alive. And then you're left wondering who the new main character's gonna be."

"He's not going to kill me."

"You don't know that," Connie said. "You think you know Viper. You think maybe he can be tamed. But really, he's still a wild animal—the elephant who runs off into the jungle with tourists on his back, or the lion who bites off his trainer's head after they've been together for twenty years. It's like that story I read to Ty the other night . . . the one about the frog who carried the scorpion across the water because the scorpion promised not to sting him, and then they both died because the scorpion stung him anyway because it was in his nature."

"I never knew about that morbid streak of yours," Evie said, but Connie's words gave her pause. Viper had seemed like a normal guy when he first came into her shop. They'd talked, laughed, discussed her art . . . Even when they'd gone for dinner he'd behaved like a regular guy. And then he'd killed Bill and burned down her shop and acted like nothing had happened. Like Connie said, violence was in his nature. *Okay.* She couldn't go in without backup, or at least some kind of leverage. And she had to do it the biker way.

But who should she call?

Of course. Arianne.

"I can't fucking believe it." Cade handed the binoculars to Zane. "Is Viper that fucking arrogant? He's only got six guards down there."

Zane flattened himself on the rise above Viper's cabin hideaway, still struggling to believe he wasn't here alone. But as he'd strapped on his weapons at the clubhouse, ready to do battle with Viper and rescue his son, he thought about T-Rex's funeral and how the brothers were all there for each other, and how together they had made it through the most difficult times. He had steeled himself to ask for help, but when he went down the stairs, they were all armed and waiting. His brothers. His friends.

"He probably thinks no one will find him," Jagger said. "My place is pretty isolated. Unless someone ratted me out, I'd be surprised if a bunch of Jacks showed up."

"How did we find him?" Sparky unzipped his pack and pulled out a box of ammo.

Zane focused his binoculars on the house. "I had Hacker put a GPS tracker in Ty's Batman watch last time he was at the clubhouse playing vids. It worked so well tracking down Cade after Benson locked him in the slammer, I figured it was good idea. I also had Hacker put trackers in Evie's new vehicle and a bug in her phone."

Sparky let out a long low whistle. "I'm guessing she doesn't know."

"We all do it," Cade said. "And none of the old ladies know. But we gotta keep them safe. Make sure we know where they are at all times . . ."

"Cade's still worried Dawn's got a thing for Benson," Jagger said, smirking. "After all, she almost went into witness protection with him."

Cade slammed a magazine into his gun. "Benson knows if he even looks at Dawn I'll rip off his fucking arms."

"I don't think those are the guards." Dax handed the binoculars to Sparky. "They're busy like little ants. I think they're doing some kind of construction. The guards are the ones standing around looking bored."

Zane lay down and looked over the rise. "What the fuck do you know about ants? Did you torture them for fun when you were a kid?"

"Yeah, I did. Burned them with a magnifying glass. Just got an ant farm for my oldest. But I told him not to do what I did 'cause it's cruel."

Cade snorted. "Says the club torturer."

Dax gave an indignant sniff. "I don't hurt indiscriminately. Only the bastards you bring me. And only until they give me the information I want." He hesitated and then shrugged. "Okay. And afterward, maybe a bit for fun."

Sparky snapped open the tripod on his Barnett M98B

sniper rifle. "So what's the plan? I take them all out by my-self while you losers yap like a bunch of old ladies?"

"I prefer the stealth approach." Zane rolled over and pulled out his knife. "No noise. No gunshots to warn everyone we're coming."

"Ah. Ah. Ah . . . I think slicing a Black Jack's throat might be a breach of your bail conditions." Cade chuck-led. "And I think some of us are felons. Someone call the fucking cops and haul this fucker's ass back to jail."

"Anyone need a weapon?" Tank came up behind them with the duffel bag he and Gunner had hauled up the hill. "Evie and Connie dug up the weapons Big Bill stole from the Jacks last week. He had them stashed in his father's grave. Gun and I bought them for the club, although I think we might have overpaid. They drove a pretty hard bargain."

Jesus Fucking Christ. What the hell was going on? Why was Evie selling stolen weapons, and why the fuck hadn't she told him about them? How could they trust each other if she was going to go behind his back and put herself in danger? Of course, he had handcuffed her to the radiator, but still . . . that was a trust issue. Dealing in stolen weap-ons had to do with safety.

"You wanna call Evie?" Jagger gave Zane a nudge. "Tell her we've found him and we're going in so she doesn't worry?"

"She won't be able to get to the phone." He felt a stab of remorse, but then he thought about what she'd intended to do and his resolve hardened. Damn woman had no idea of the danger she was in, or the risk to Ty if she followed the course of action she intended to take.

Jagger lifted an eyebrow. "Do I want to know?"

"You may want to send a coupla brothers over there with this key." He pulled the key out of his pocket and handed it to Jagger. "She was gonna go to Viper and bar-gain herself for Ty so I handcuffed her to the radiator. Whoever goes to get her should be armed and wearing a padded safety suit, maybe a helmet and a face mask. I got Benson checking on her through the window every half hour or so.

"You've got to be fucking kidding me." Jagger tucked the key into the pocket of his cut. "Well, that's the end of that relationship."

"Nah." Dax laughed. "That's called having a family. Anything to do with the kids and the old ladies go fucking ballistic and start thinkin' they're gonna handle things themselves. A man's gotta know how to deal with them. I always keep a set of cuffs in the house."

"Listen to the big talker shootin' off his mouth like Sandy doesn't have him by the balls." Cade snorted. "You got those cuffs 'cause you're a kinky bastard."

"Guess we're all kinky bastards 'cause I heard you cuffed Dawn to the bathroom sink when she found out some bully hit one of your little twin girls."

"My girls. My responsibility." Cade puffed out his chest. "That nine-year-old bully's not gonna be saying dick to anyone on that playground ever again. And after I got home and uncuffed Dawn I made sure she understand how things were gonna be with me and the girls."

"Wasn't that the day you showed up with a black eye?" Gunner pushed himself to his feet and grabbed a branch for balance. His old injury from the night the Jacks burned down the Sinner clubhouse still bothered him, but he would never admit to suffering any pain.

"You want a fucking black eye now?"

"Like I said." Jagger looked over at Zane and grinned. "That's the end of that relationship."

"No, like I said." Dax laughed. "It's called having a family. Sinner style."

★ TWENTY-SIX ★

*If you use the right tools, take your time, and follow
the manual, the risk of disaster is quite low.*
—SINNER'S TRIBE MOTORCYCLE REPAIR MANUAL

Viper's bodyguard gestured for Evie to follow him through
the spacious, chalet-style cabin, set into the side of the
mountain and surrounded by dense forest. Evie breathed
in the fresh scent of pine and cedar as they emerged into
an open-plan living room with vaulted ceilings and giant
picture windows boasting views over the valley below.
Across the room she could see a honey oak kitchen,
separated from the living space with a granite-topped
counter and four tall stools. Bright rugs covered the polished teak floors, and large, comfortable sofas and chairs
surrounded an open Victorian fireplace.

"Not what you expected?" Sprawled on the couch, his
arms across the burnt amber cushions, legs parted wide,
Viper gestured for her to sit. "Doreen did the decorating.
Or maybe it was Shelly. I go through old ladies so fast,
it's hard to keep track."

Evie wasn't interested in pleasantries. Or sitting.
"Where's Ty?"

Viper cocked his head to the side. "Is that anyway to
greet your man?"

"You're not my man. I thought I made that clear." Her

heart drummed in her chest when he leaned forward, resting his elbows on his knees.

"And I thought I made it clear that you are mine. Apparently you didn't get the memo. I hear you've been spreading your legs for the Sinners. If I'd known you were such a little slut, I'd have taken you that first day I saw you in your shop. I would have tied you to the bench and fucked you till you screamed."

"Who I fuck is none of your business." Unable to stay still, she walked over to the window. Construction materials littered the lawn. Four workers were busy erecting, of all things, a white picket fence, while a few bored Black Jacks looked on.

"It is if the man you're fucking is supposed to be me." His voice was soft and all the more threatening for it. Evie shivered and her hand strayed to the phone hidden in her jacket, a backup in case Viper or his bodyguards took her purse. Arianne had also given her a gun, but Evie couldn't even think about using it.

She turned and sat on the windowsill, the position giving her some courage because the workers could see in, and she could easily escape to the balcony if necessary. "I don't understand how you think. Yes, I enjoyed your company. You are interesting, well read, articulate, and very savvy about the world. But you also killed Bill and T-Rex, threatened me, burned down my shop, and kidnapped my child. Pick one, and it's a deal killer. Put them together and there isn't a chance in hell I would ever want to spend another minute with you."

His lips quirked, amused. "And yet you want to be with the Sinner VP, who I can assure you has committed crimes no less heinous than the list you just spat out?"

"The difference is in the choices you make." Her fingers tightened on her purse. "You liked me. You wanted me. And when it didn't work out, you chose violence to get me. Zane wanted me, too. So he chose to sacrifice himself, to give up the life to keep me safe. He protected me. I don't think there is anything in this world that I would ask that he wouldn't do for me. And I would do the same for him. I'm not about to judge him when he does what he does to protect the people he cares about."

Viper's face tightened. "As do I."

"I want to see Ty," she snapped, her patience at an end.

"And I want the pleasure of your company, Evangeline. I'll let you see Ty and then we'll have dinner together. That *is* why you got all dressed up, isn't it?"

"I dressed up because you made it a condition for seeing Ty," she said. "I didn't dress up for you."

"Shame." Viper turned on the television and she saw Ty in a bedroom sitting on a red race-car bed playing a video game. The shelves around him were filled with toys. Her heart ached when she saw his tear-streaked face, but at least he didn't appear to be harmed.

"I want to see him in person."

"You will, but not yet," Viper said. "But just to ease your anxiety, he's upstairs. When I moved here I had them bring Jeff's old things from my house. My son, Jeff, was spoiled so Ty will be well entertained."

Hope flared in her chest. She had made a big assumption that Viper wanted her because she wasn't part of the biker world, and that he wouldn't be violent unless she forced his hand. But the main premise of her rescue attempt was that Viper would care about his now mother-less son, and that he would fear for his safety if he knew the Sinners had him. The hostage trade hadn't worked before because he clearly had no feelings for Doreen. But if he'd brought Jeff's old toys to his new house, maybe there was hope for her plan after all.

Arianne had told her that although Viper had been a hard and cruel father, deep down he had feelings for Jeff and he had been devastated when his son died. From the conversations she'd had with Viper, Evie thought he also cared deeply about Arianne, even admired her for defying him and becoming Jagger's old lady. Arianne didn't believe Evie, however; she had been more than happy to go to Ennis to visit her new stepbrother.

Since meeting Zane, Evie had realized that people weren't black and white, monsters or men. Everyone had a little bit of both inside them; it was their choices that made the difference.

Viper turned off the television and stood, holding out his hand. "Come. My chef has dinner waiting. And since you're here because you want to be here, I'm looking forward to our meal together."

She accepted his outstretched hand, grimacing when he squeezed it just a little too hard, and followed him to the kitchen where Viper introduced her to Mario, a short, nervous, slightly balding man wearing a white apron.

"Mario came to me looking for work after the Sinners burned down his restaurant." Viper pulled out Evie's chair and she took her seat. "Saved me from hunting him down. He was paying off his debt to us by keeping my boys fed. Now he cooks just for me, and we're gonna rebuild his restaurant after we repair the clubhouse. The Sinners broke an unspoken rule when they took out a civilian building."

"There seems to be a lot of that going around."

"Don't get nasty, kitten, he snapped. "It doesn't become you."

Mario placed a dish of antipasto in front of them: cured meats, olives, mushrooms, anchovies, artichoke hearts, various cheeses, and vegetables in oil. He removed the napkin from beside Evie's fork and placed it over her lap, then did the same for Viper. Bizarre didn't even begin to describe the absurdity of eating a fancy meal, prepared by a chef in a well-appointed kitchen, across the table from a rough, grizzled outlaw biker, while her son was a prisoner somewhere upstairs. And if Arianne didn't hurry up and call to let Evie know she had Doreen's son in a secure location, she'd actually have to try to choke the food down.

"I thought you were smart enough to know I would never give up." Viper tasted the wine and nodded for Mario to fill his glass. The rich, red liquid reminded Evie of blood and her stomach curdled.

"You've been around bikers long enough to understand what it means when we make a claim," he continued.

Evie covered her glass when Mario approached with the wine. "No, thank you."

"I insist." Viper gently knocked her hand away. "It's an Amarone and goes perfectly with the pasta. And it will help you relax. You seem a bit tense."

Tense? Was he crazy? Maybe that was it. He *was* crazy. How else could he possibly think she would want to be with him after what he'd done? Or was he so far gone that he was unable to see that what he was doing was wrong? If Arianne hadn't texted earlier to say that Doreen's mother was even less fit to be a parent than Viper—and that was saying something—Evie might have reconsidered her plan to let Viper know he had a son.

Evie scrunched the napkin in her fist under the table as Mario poured the wine. Goddamn it. Why hadn't Arianne called? She couldn't pull off this charade for much longer, and it was all she could do not to grab her knife, stab Viper and race upstairs to . . .

"You wouldn't even make it across the kitchen." Viper pried her fingers off the knife she hadn't even realized she was holding. "I know what you want. And you know what I want. I'm sure we can come to some arrangement that satisfies us both." He laced his fingers through hers, and brought her hand to his lips, seemingly oblivious to Mario standing in the doorway. "And if not, I'll just take you, although I would much prefer things to be the way they were when you wanted to be with me."

"You severed that connection when you murdered Bill, and everything you have done since then has ensured it will never come back." Her voice rose in pitch, and she wrenched her hand away.

"You don't fucking get it." Viper pounded his fist on the table, upsetting the plate of antipasto, and rattling the glasses. "The things you hold in such contempt I do for my club. I have to keep order. I have to keep control. Bill stole from us. If I didn't send out a message, then every gang, every criminal, every MC would start circling. This is a world where only the strongest survive. And if you think the Sinners are not exactly the same, then you are totally and utterly naive." He barked the last words and Evie stood so quickly, her chair crashed to the floor.

"They aren't the same as the Jacks," she countered. "They have honor and integrity. They have a creed and a code, and despite what they do, they have a sense of moral decency. Everyone in the club volunteered to help rescue T-Rex, despite the risks. Nothing was more important to them. They refused to leave a man behind. And yet, when your old lady was in the Sinner dungeon, you didn't give a damn."

"She knew better than to let herself get caught," he spat out.

"And that's where you're different. No one said that about T-Rex. They honored him for his sacrifice. They admired him. And they mourn him."

"Jagger killed my son." Viper's voice rose to a shout. "He turned my daughter against me. The Sinners kidnapped Doreen, burnt down Mario's restaurant, and blew up my clubhouse without even considering that someone might be inside." He stood and rounded the table, coming at her so fast she was forced to back away. "Where is the honor in that?"

"*You* killed your son." She hit the wall and put out a hand to stop him. "Arianne told me what happened. You kidnapped her. You were trying to kill her and Jeff intervened. And *you* alienated her. *You* beat her and gave her to your VP when she was sixteen."

"I would never have killed her," he growled. "She was bait for Jagger. And when he showed up, I tried to kill him, but she was in the way." He grabbed Evie's wrists and pinned them to the wall on either side of her shoulders.

"Don't tell me there is any difference between the Jacks and the Sinners. And don't use that as a justification for your decision to fuck a Sinner when you belong to me. What I do as president of the club has nothing to do with who I am as a man, and that's who you wanted. Marcus. Not Viper. And that's who wants you." He bent down to kiss her and Evie turned her head so his lips landed on her cheek.

"You can't have me. Not the way you want. Even when you want to be Marcus, Viper comes through. You want to kiss me and yet you're hurting me. You want me to come to you willingly, and yet you kidnap my son to bring me here. Violence is in your nature. Violence is who you are. Violence for the sake of violence. Violence is your choice for achieving your ends. That's the difference between you and Zane. He can be violent, but at heart he is not a violent man."

Despite his outlaw life, the Zane she'd fallen in love with as a child was still there. Always trying to protect her, save her, keep her from getting hurt. She had no doubt, if he had known about Ty, he would never have left Stanton. Just as she had no doubt that he was on his way now.

"Jesus Christ." Viper tightened his grip on her wrists. "Don't you understand? I gave you Marcus. I have never asked a woman out. I have never gone on a date, nor have I ever walked away when I could have had a woman in my bed. I could have taken you the first time we met. I could have stripped off your clothes and fucked you over a table in your shop and no one—not Bill, or the mechanics, or any of my men—would have stopped me. I pretended to be a goddamn civilian for you, and I got nothing for it except to find out you're fucking the enemy. I even spared T-Rex for you because despite his Sinner cut, he was trying to save your life."

Her brain fuzzed with pain. Was T-Rex still alive? What about the body they'd found in the Black Jacks' dungeon? "You're hurting me."

"And you hurt me. But no more. I will have you,

Evangeline. Whether you are willing or not." He thrust his knee between her thighs and kicked her legs apart.

"Don't do this." She struggled in his ironclad grasp. "Marcus . . . you're just showing me I was right about you. Show me I'm wrong. Show me the humanity that I know you have inside you. Show me man who mourns his son and misses his daughter."

"Viper to you," he growled. "You had your chance with the man. Now you get the beast." He fisted her hair, yanked her head to the side, and bit her neck, not a gentle love bite, but a skin-piercing dig into her flesh.

Evie screamed. Out of the corner of her eye, she caught a blur of motion, the faintest disturbance in the air, and then Viper stiffened and arched back, losing his grip. He spun around and her eyes widened at the sight of the knife in his back, and Mario, his hand still in the air.

The back door exploded open and Viper's bodyguards raced into the kitchen, heading straight for Viper. "Fucking Mario did this," he roared. "He's gotta be a Sinner rat. Get him and get the fucking knife out of my back."

Seizing her chance, Evie ran through the house and up the stairs, opening doors in the immaculate hallway until she found one locked.

"Ty!" She thumped on the door. "Are you in there?"

"Mom. Mom. Get me out of here."

She found the key on the cabinet down the hall and unlocked the door. Ty flew out and into her arms.

"I'm sorry, Mom. I'm sorry I ran away. I don't hate Zane. Really. I don't." He hugged her so tight she could barely breathe, his body shaking with sobs. She wanted to hold him and never let go, but they didn't have time to linger.

"Shhh, baby. It's not your fault. But we have to get out of here quickly."

"There's a bat inside. I'll get it. Just in case." He grabbed a baseball bat and they ran down the stairs only to find

Viper and one of his bodyguards blocking their way. Evie stopped short and pushed Ty behind her.

"You had a knife in your back. How can you be walking around?"

"I always wear a vest, kitten. Even to dinner. Never know who's going to stab you in the back."

Her phone buzzed in her pocket, and she pulled it out and saw the picture of Arianne with a little boy who looked to be just over a year old.

Finally.

"I'm leaving with Ty." She held up the phone so Viper could see the picture of his son with Arianne. "Once we're safe I'll let Arianne know she can end her visit with her stepbrother . . . your son."

"I don't have a son."

"You do. Doreen's boy. He's your son; not Axel's. And now he doesn't have a mother."

A multitude of emotions crossed his face, from disbelief to anger, but not fear. Evie's heart sank. If he didn't fear for his son, then he had no reason to let her or Ty go.

"Arianne won't hurt him." Viper snorted a laugh. "She suffers from compassion, which is why she didn't kill me when she had the chance."

Evie pushed Ty backward, step by step. There was a door leading out from the living room. If they ran fast enough, they could get outside. "You're right," she said. "Arianne won't hurt him. But the Sinners can arrange for him to disappear. You lost one son. Do you want to lose another?"

"I could say the same to you. One of my brothers is behind the door, waiting for me to tell him what to do. Stalemate, kitten."

"I think the word is checkmate." Zane stepped into the room, a semiautomatic weapon in each hand, and wearing more guns than the soldiers from Ty's video games.

Evie heard shouts outside. Gunfire.

"You both okay?" Zane's gaze slid from her to Ty and back to her.

"I knew you'd come."

"Sorry about the delay," Jagger said, walking into the room behind Zane. "We were up on the mountain when you drove in. Took us longer than we thought to get down. Then we had to clean up the yard." He looked over at Ty. "You can put down the bat, Ty. Looks like your dad has got things in hand."

"I'm his backup," Ty said. "Just in case."

Zane's jaw tightened and pride shone in his eyes. "Good man. You get your mom out of here. There are Sinners outside waiting with a cage. Jagger and I got this one."

Evie clasped Ty's hand and tugged him toward the door. "Don't kill him."

"Evie . . ." The square set of Zane's shoulders told her that was exactly what he planned to do.

"He would have let us go." She met Viper's implacable gaze, trying to read his face. "He has a son, too. One he hasn't met. Arianne is with him. She's waiting for me to call to tell her what to do. What if Ty never got to meet you?"

"This isn't the time for compassion," Zane snapped. "This is our chance to win the war. If our roles were reversed, I'd already be dead. People don't change, Evie. He is who he is, and if we don't deal with him now, he'll come after you."

"I changed. So did you." She crossed the room toward Jagger and the exit, leading Ty by the hand. As they passed Viper she looked back over her shoulder mentally urging him to say something to save himself. But he remained silent. No assurance that he would leave Evie alone. No begging for his life. No refuting the fact he would have killed Zane if he had him under his gun. And yet she saw pain flicker across his face, so fleeting she wondered if she'd missed it.

"Jesus Christ," Jagger spluttered. "I knew Arianne was up to something. Damn old ladies sticking their noses into club business. But this is my call, Evie. I heard what you had to say. You take Ty out and Zane and I will—"

Viper moved in a blur, darting around the counter as he pulled a gun from the holster beneath his vest and aimed it at Jagger. But Ty was in the way.

"No!" Zane dove in front of Ty as the shot echoed in the room. He hit the floor hard as momentum carried him down. Viper barreled through the back door and Jagger took off in pursuit.

"Dad!" Ty raced to Zane's side. "Mom! Call 911."

"I'm okay." Zane wrapped his arms around his son. "The bullet went over my head, and Viper won't get far. We've got men all over the yard."

"Lean on me, Dad. I'll help you up."

Zane put a hand on Ty's shoulder, although he didn't need the help. He looked over at Evie and smiled.

"He called me Dad."

★ TWENTY-SEVEN ★

Once you figure it out, try to return the favor.
Spread your repair knowledge around.
—SINNER'S TRIBE MOTORCYCLE REPAIR MANUAL

While waiting for the preliminary hearing, Zane rented the house across the street from Evie and Ty. Although Evie said she understood why he handcuffed her to the radiator, she wasn't quick to forgive. The stunt cost him, but as long as he could be near her and Ty, he was willing to pay the price. And it was just a matter of time. He knew this because she let him sleep at her place at least five times a week. Not that he was counting, but he'd managed to push it up from one night, undoubtedly because of his skill in bed. Yes, he could make his Evie scream.

Of course he'd had a bit of a setback when he erected a giant fence around her property. He'd also installed a security system in her house and changed the locks, all with the landlord's consent, of course. Evie hadn't been pleased he'd gone over her head, yet again, and his weekly nocturnal visits were reduced to two. But now he was back up to five, so that was an improvement.

The car had been another setback. Evie wanted her own transportation so she went out and bought an old junker from a used-car dealer without consulting Zane. He checked out her purchase while she slept and decided it was a piece of crap. The next day, while she was at work, he and Gunner hot-wired her car and drove it back to the dealer. After a brief discussion, and only two broken fingers, the dealer switched it out for a brand-new, safe, red Volvo. Evie liked the Volvo, but not the subterfuge. She also didn't like it when he said vehicle selection was a man's job because women didn't know shit about vehicles.

Arianne showed up at his house the next day with her new SIG Sauer P226.

Zane spent the night at the clubhouse with his door locked.

He hadn't been invited to spend the night at Evie's place for an entire week after that, so he'd spent his evenings sitting on his porch watching her house, wondering if she was wearing that silky nightgown she'd bought to celebrate the one-month anniversary of the opening of her new shop. Damn, he loved the feel of that silk, the way it covered her, hinting at what was underneath—which was nothing, just the way he liked it.

Today was going to be another one of the days where his sex quota would likely be reduced, but he was ready to do what had to be done, and if he was cut back to two nightly visits, he'd just have to work his way back up.

His closest brothers and their old ladies had arrived at his place earlier in the afternoon to get ready for the party. Tank had the barbecue going in the backyard, and Connie was helping him marinate the meat. Zane had asked Tank to bring her along, just in case things didn't go as expected, but Connie hadn't shared his sense of doom.

"It's not gonna be as bad as you think," she said to Zane, as she brushed Tank's secret sauce over the tray of steak. "I mean, the Ty part will be bad. But the Evie part . . . I don't think you've got to worry. Of course you will have to worry 'cause she'll be pissed about Ty, but I think you'll get her to come round. I hear you can be very persuasive once you get her out of her clothes."

Zane didn't want to think about what she and Connie discussed regarding his intimate time with Evie, so he stared at his watch. "Did she say what time she's leaving the shop today?"

"She was just waiting for a shipment of new bikes and then she was gonna pick Ty up from his friend's house. She should be here soon. You want me to text her?"

"Jagger's not here yet, so no rush."

Where the fuck was Jagger? He was supposed to be at the party an hour ago and he didn't have the Jacks as an excuse to keep him busy. Viper had managed to slither away yet again, disappearing down some kind of rabbit hole that none of the Sinners could find. They'd heard from National that Viper's decision to kidnap Ty had earned him a stern rebuke from the Black Jack national president, and a forced cessation of hostilities between the two clubs for six months. Arianne had also come under fire for her trip up to Ennis. Jagger had managed to get her off with just a warning, and the only real rebuke she'd received had been from him. In private. Zane would have loved to have been there that night.

He joined Arianne on the back steps, and she broke off her conversation with Dawn to greet him. "You're look-ing for Jagger; I can tell from your scowl.

He made the mistake of sending Shooter down to the shop to pick up the order and Shooter got a little riled when it wasn't ready. Jagger had to go make good with the owner and pay to have the bullet holes removed from the walls."

Dawn ruffled the hair of one of her twin girls. Zane couldn't tell them apart, but they were around the same age as Ty and they all enjoyed playing together. Although when one of them chased Ty and tried to kiss him, Zane had to put his foot down. He knew better than anyone the dangers of eight-year-old girls and how easily they could capture a boy's heart. "You think he's gonna change his mind about Shooter?"

Shooter was due to receive his cut tonight. The board had decided that despite being trigger-happy, Shooter was more an asset than a liability and, except for the occasional mess Jagger had to clean up, he had made a significant contribution to the club.

Arianne laughed. "You know Jagger. He'll rant, shout, and scowl, but in the end, Shooter is good for the club and he'll get his cut. Plus, the club now has Benson as a prospect and that's just going to be all kinds of fun. A cop as a prospect. Jagger's got all sorts of humiliation planned for him."

"You hear what he's planned for Shooter's patch-in?" Zane gestured to a big painted target near his back fence. "He had Evie paint the Sinner's Tribe logo on that target. I folded up an old cut to fit in the middle and pinned it there. He's gonna tell Shooter that's his real cut and he only gets it if he can shoot through each one of the skull's eyes without hitting it."

"Bastard." Dawn pressed her lips together. "Sometimes his sense of humor borders on cruel."

"He has gone a bit overboard since he tricked T-Rex with that package to get his cut." Arianne's smile faded. "I miss T-Rex. The party won't be the same without him."

"The MC isn't the same without him," Zane said. Once the truce was over, Viper would face Sinner justice. Despite Evie's plea for mercy, Zane and Jagger would have finished him off if he hadn't escaped. Viper had been responsible for too many Sinner deaths, and kidnapping Ty wasn't something he could ever forgive.

Evie joined them, dressed in her favorite skintight jeans, leather boots, and a black leather jacket. She gave him a hug, and Ty ran off to play with Dax's and Cade's kids on the play structure Zane had built after he rented the house.

"You look too damn sexy." He wrapped his arms around her and leaned down to nuzzle her neck. "Might be I'll have to drag you away from the party for a bit."

"Beast. This is Shooter's patch-in party. You're not supposed to be thinking about sex."

"I wouldn't have to think about it if I had you in my bed every night." He nipped her ear. "Man sees his woman looking so hot, he has needs."

"And women don't?"

He cupped her face between his hands. "You asking me for something, sweetheart? Because I am more than happy to blow off the party after Shooter's got his cut."

"Maybe I am." She pressed a key into his hand. "And we have a new house to try it out."

"What's this?"

"The start of our new life together, I hope." Her smile wavered when he scowled.

"You bought a house without me? What happened to the idea of making big purchases together?"

Evie slid her arms around his waist. "You seemed to have trouble with the concept so I just followed your lead."

How could he complain when he'd just been handed the key to his dream—a life with Evie and Ty, a family and a home, and her acceptance of his brothers and his life with the MC? Only the impending court hearing loomed over his head. But if Evie wasn't worried, then he'd put his concerns aside and deal with it when the day came.

"Well then . . ." He brushed a kiss over her forehead. "I guess you won't have a problem with the gift I got Ty." He called Ty over and they walked toward the garage, reaching the front door just as Jagger stepped out. He gave Zane a nod to let him know everything was set and made a quick exit.

"Now I'm really worried," Evie said as she entered the garage. "You and Jagger together equals trouble."

Zane flicked on the lights, although there was enough light streaming through the open door to illuminate the space. He wanted to be sure Ty got a good view.

"Ready, Ty?" His heart thrummed in anticipation. He couldn't remember being this excited about giving a gift since he'd given Evie the picture frame so long ago. With one last glance over at Evie, he tugged away the sheet in the corner.

"No way!" Ty's eyes widened." You got me a dirt bike? Mom's going to kill you!"

"Yes she is," Evie said from the doorway, her lips pressed into a thin line.

Zane bit back a laugh. "I got him a kick-ass helmet and safety suit so damn thick, he's gonna bounce when he falls."

"When? Not if he falls?"

"I won't fall," Ty said.

"We all fall. The trick is to get back on the bike and keep riding. That lesson took me a lifetime to learn." He gave Evie a questioning look and she sighed.

"I guess I can't really say no since I did buy us a house in Oak Village right next door to Ty's best friend."

"This is the best day ever." Ty raced over to hug them both, before returning to inspect his bike.

"I got something for you, too." Zane reached for the bag Jagger had left on the workbench in the corner, but as he pulled the zipper, memories assailed him: the frame he had worked so hard to perfect, the picture that had been so hard to part with, Evie and Jagger in the kitchen, and the pain that had sent him running into the forest. He pushed back the memories and focused on what came after: Evie's tears when she saw the picture, their night together, and Ty. They had been through hell, but now they were back together. Loved and forgiven. A family.

With only one thing missing.

He pulled the cut from the bag and handed it to her, his mouth going dry when she opened it and spun it around so she could read the back.

"Property of Zane." A smile spread across her face. "I've waited eighteen years to be yours."

"You were always mine. Ever since that day on the playground."

He reached into the bag again and pulled out a second cut, then called Ty over. "We don't usually give prospect cuts to kids, but what you did at Viper's place—protecting your mom, and helping out your old man—Ty, you made me damn proud. The executive board agreed that showing courage like that deserves a reward." He held out the small prospect vest with the Sinner's Tribe logo emblazoned across the back, and slid it over Ty's shoulders.

A grin spread across Ty's face and he posed in front of his new bike. "How do I look, Dad?"

"Like my son." He put his arm around his Evie and pulled her close. "Our son."

★ EPILOGUE ★

Three Months Later

"Zane. Stop. Please."

Evie's voice rang out in the forest, and Zane slowed his pace. He'd never felt such joy as he did today, save for the last time he had been to Stanton Creek.

He stopped under the willow tree and sucked the warm Montana summer air into his lungs. He would do anything for her, even if it meant his heart bursting all over again.

Evie heaved in a breath as she came up behind him, her steps barely audible in the soft grass. "What's wrong? Why did you leave? Jagger said you bolted out of the courthouse and didn't even tell him what happened. I was so worried. I didn't know where you were. And then I figured you might come here. What did the judge say? I won't lose you, Zane. If we have to, we'll go on the run."

For a moment, he couldn't speak. How could he explain the emotions he'd kept bottled up inside for the last few months, the hopes and dreams that had come true when the judge dismissed the case?

"I'm free." He braced himself, and turned to face her. "All the charges have been dropped."

"Oh." She gasped and her hand flew to her mouth. "Oh Zane. I'm so happy." She threw herself into his arms, her new riding leathers creaking. He'd bought her a full set of leathers for the trip to Stanton. And after she'd tried them on in their bedroom, he stripped them right off her. He had a wild streak when it came to his old lady, and the sight of her in leather had given him all sorts of ideas.

He was having those ideas right now. His Evie was beautiful in the twilight, her hair shining to gold, almost the same color as the late summer leaves of the willow tree.

"Come sit with me." She pulled away. "Here by the creek like we used to do. Tell me all about it."

Zane shook his head. "I promised if this day came, I would give you a choice. I need to know, Evie. Do we live or leave the life? It's up to you."

Her beautiful face softened. "I made my choice a long time ago. Wherever you go, whatever you do, however you live your life, I want to be with you "

Zane's heart squeezed in his chest. He was nothing and came from nothing. And yet, he had made something of his life. He had a family now, and enough money that assured they would want for nothing. He had his brothers, a home, a kick-ass bike, and an embarrassing, but safe, Volvo. And he had dared to hope. Twenty-eight years old and he still wanted the girl he'd met when he was ten.

"It's always been you," she said. "Ever since the day we first met. I've loved you since I was eight years old and I'll love you always."

His world shifted, darkness becoming light, despair turning to desire. Although he had dreamed of this moment, wanted her with an intensity that took his breath away, he reigned it all in and kissed her with a gentleness that belied the torrent of emotions flooding through his body.

She sighed into his mouth and he crushed her against him as he had last night when they thought it might be their last time together. Sensation overwhelmed him: the coffee and cream taste on her lips, her scent of jasmine and the open road, the warm summer breeze, the softness of her body beneath her leathers.

"I have a present for you." She handed him a package wrapped in pink tissue paper. "It's nothing big. I'm sure what Jagger got you . . ."

"Jagger got me a custom set of pipes that he was planning to take back if I wound up in jail." He gave her a wry smile. "So unless you got the same thing, I'll love it. And even if it is, I'll love it, because it came from you."

He tore off the paper and stared at the photograph in the handmade frame, painted with Evie's signature style. Jagger had taken the picture of him, Evie, and Ty on the couch one afternoon while they were playing a new video game. Zane had managed to survive for the first ten levels before Evie ripped off his head with her feline claws.

Emotion welled up in his throat. "It's good."

"Good?" Her eyes narrowed. "Do you know how long it took me to make that frame?"

Yeah, he knew. Because he had made one nine years ago, never imagining that one day it would be sitting on the mantle in the home he shared with Evie and their son.

Gently, he drew her down to the forest floor. He had hoped for this moment, dreamed of this moment. His heart made whole again.

And he made love to his beautiful Evie under the setting sun on the last day of summer in Stanton.

Also By

SARAH CASTILLE

★ **ROUGH JUSTICE** ★
(SINNER'S TRIBE MOTORCYCLE CLUB #1)

★ **BEYOND THE CUT** ★
(SINNER'S TRIBE MOTORCYCLE CLUB #2)